A bewitching, scandalous saga of love, dreams, power and corruption—the stuff best sellers are made of.

BONNIE BLISS, who, at age 14, gave birth to the sweetest little baby in the world's largest red-light district, Storyville.

AMELIA BLISS HARLOW, her daughter—and matriarch of the Harlows. She never forgave fate—and vowed revenge.

ELEANOR HARLOW, one of Amelia's twins, who discovered that it was a long way from Earth, Texas, to Bryn Mawr, Pennsylvania— thank God!

BLISS HARLOW, the other twin, whose meteoric life was joined to that of a beautiful, sad woman—briefly.

CAROLINE FORSYTH HARRINGTON, widow of a young American pilot—could she guess what she was getting into with Bliss?

WILL HARLOW, Amelia's young country-doctor husband, who had a secret that would shatter both of them.

KATE HARLOW, Amelia's granddaughter, the family hope, but a young woman with confused loyalties and an uncertain destiny.

Morning Glory

Julia Cleaver Smith

PUBLISHED BY POCKET BOOKS NEW YORK

Another *Original* publication of POCKET BOOKS

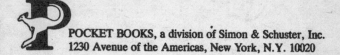

POCKET BOOKS, a division of Simon & Schuster, Inc.
1230 Avenue of the Americas, New York, N.Y. 10020

ISBN: 0-671-42603-6

First Pocket Books printing February, 1984

10 9 8 7 6 5 4 3 2 1

POCKET and colophon are registered trademarks of Simon & Schuster, Inc.

Printed in the U.S.A.

*To Deborah and Sabrina
and Texas friends*

Contents

Prologue   1

PART ONE
     The Louisiana-Texas Border
         January 1917   9
     Dallas, Texas   October 1918   70
     Earth, Texas   January 1924   96

PART TWO
         New York   April 1945   127
         Havana, Cuba   May 1945   169

PART THREE
     Earth, Texas   April 1958   191
     Earth, Texas   June 1959   228
     Earth, Texas   September 1960   266

PART FOUR
     New York   The First Monday
         in August 1975   287
     Earth, Texas   The Second Monday
         in August 1975   321

Morning Glory

Prologue

The August sun rises fast and hot in Texas, scraping the air dry while the sky is still washed with red. In the northeast quarter of the state, the dust from the pine hills kicks up by seven and then hangs suspended over the valleys, a pale, fine-grained dust that locks the heat in, sealing the day shut like an oven door.

It was almost eight when she left the big white house at the edge of town that first Sunday in August. The screen door swung shut behind her and she stood for a moment in the deep shade of the porch. It was so blue and bright out there that the hills on the far horizon seemed to dance in the glare.

A slender, honey-tanned hand reached to the dark glasses perched on her blond head and lowered them over her eyes. She was glad to be taking the drive out to the cemetery early in the day this year. By noon it would be 100 degrees in the shade.

The Lincoln had been left waiting with the door ajar, the engine running long enough for the air conditioner to cool the leather seats. An armful of summer flowers

1

gathered from the back gardens this morning—wild lilies and mountain pinks, bluebonnets and white daisies, their yellow centers bright and sharp—filled the passenger side. She shifted into gear and felt the gravel beneath the wheels crunch and spin away as the sleek white Lincoln swung into the soft rise in the hill toward the thick grove of cottonwoods. The driveway took her through massive iron-grill gates, across the old railroad tracks, and onto Main Street. The sign on the right-hand side declared this town Earth, population 2,523.

An old man in weary overalls emerged from the gas station on her left, tipped his battered wide-brimmed straw hat, and then melted back into the shade. Except for the two ancient Ford pickups, parked solid as the ground they stood on, the streets ahead were deserted, the citizens of Earth still at home preparing for church at eleven and huge family dinners at one. The wooden steps leading to the covered sidewalks were empty, the stores were shuttered and still—stores whose names were as familiar to her as her own. Irma's Beauty Shoppe, Trixie's Gifts, Carr's Dry Goods and Drug Store, all stood blank and silent now in the early morning heat.

The white Lincoln swept on, past the stone Methodist church and the white clapboard Baptist church, like twin portals of salvation waiting patiently for their congregations. Past the bank, bright and new and raw-looking between old frame houses with their run-around porches. Past the eight-story red-brick newspaper building, its broad windows dark beneath white canvas awnings. Dead ahead stood the county courthouse, broad granite steps leading to granite Gothic arches that climbed to a single Gothic bell tower. High above her, the bell was sounding out the last strokes of the hour, sweet and clear.

She slowed at the intersection and glanced into the rearview mirror. The white-walled compound she'd left moments before telescoped in the reflection, its iron gates like miniature filigree. From here, the walls with their ruffle of cottonwoods dominated the town.

She settled back into the soft leather of the contoured seat and stepped on the accelerator. To the right a hundred-foot-tall radio tower rose high into the sky, its red lights blinking pale in the sun. Beyond lay the expressway into Dallas, fifty miles southwest. She swung left, into the hills.

She'd driven this two-lane strip all her life, knew its shape, knew where she was by the feel of the road under her. Once, a long time ago, on a dare from her brother, she'd raced him home along this strip. She'd won, and even now the memory of it pleased her. She smiled, then switched on the radio, already tuned to station KLIP. A church choir was singing, deep tenor voices praising the day.

She didn't see the truck.

It lumbered down the slow wooded curve as she sped up along the same arc, her foot hard on the accelerator now, pushing toward eighty miles an hour and the long stretch ahead. Her last thought as she hit the truck was that she had to keep her hands on the wheel, had to stay in control.

Bright sky and green pines swam in frantic reflection across the hard white surface of the Lincoln. The windshield split open, the air exploding in a spray of glass and shattered flowers. The Lincoln shrieked off the road, bounced into the culvert running alongside, and cartwheeled into the field of summer wheat waiting to be harvested. Then there was only the faint hum of wheels spinning free in the bright, hot morning air.

Night came to Earth, thick and sultry with the promise of a summer storm. It was nearly midnight when it finally began to rain, and by then the iron gates to the compound at the edge of town had swung shut.

Toward three in the morning, Amelia Harlow woke from a restless sleep. She lay in the dark for a moment listening to the rain and then heard the softer, almost imperceptible sound of a piano. She rose and drew a silk wrap around her and wandered down the long hallway toward the curved staircase. A yellow night light lit the steps, and a brighter light spilled across the high-polished surface of the floor below. The music was louder now and she moved down the steps and on to the cavernous room at the back of the house.

A young woman sat at the piano, dark head bent to the keys, slender fingers working out a soft tune. She glanced up when Amelia came into the room, and the music stopped. "Did I wake you?" she asked.

"Not you. The rain, I suppose. Don't stop."

Her granddaughter bent her head to the keys again, a different tune now as Amelia wandered across to the terrace windows.

High above Earth the red lights of the radio tower were blinking through the dark and the drizzle, running red down the windowpanes. She was an old woman, but Amelia Harlow wished on them like a child wishing on stars, wished with anger and pain and rage that the death on this day had been hers and that tomorrow would never come.

But the news that her daughter was dead was already hitting the newspapers, from Dallas to San Francisco, from New York to London and beyond. The red lights blinked on, pressing her toward morning, when it would begin again.

"Tell me," asked the reporter of the Texan, "is it true that in Texas . . ."

"It's true, son," said the Texan. "Whatever it is, it's true. Somewhere in Texas, it happened. Somewhere. Sometime."

PART ONE

The Louisiana-Texas Border

January 1917

1

It was early morning when they drove across the state line in Will Harlow's new green roadster. She would always remember the moment, precise and separate from all others. There was no sign, only Will calling out, "We're here."

She looked up—and would, she felt sure, have known already that she'd left the South and moved into the West. The sky suddenly seemed bigger, bluer, a Texas sky now, huge and hollow and brassy blue. She reached up to hold her traveling bonnet in place and turned to look back one last time. Tendrils of hair whipped across her face, and a hairpin slid down her neck.

Louisiana, frail and lush, glowing like a mirage in the early morning light, was fading away behind her. Ahead, at the end of the long, dusty road dipping into a pine-strewn valley, lay her new home. She and the sun were moving west together.

She took Will's arm, smiled up at him.

"Excited, Amelia?"

"I can't wait. Tell me more, Will, just so I remember it all. Tell me about your mother again, about the house and the town. And the boys and the newspaper and . . ."

He laughed, a big, deep laugh. "I love you, Amelia Harlow," he shouted above the wind and the roar of the motor. "I love you," and he grinned down at her, his eyes shining.

"Don't laugh," she said. "I want to know everything —I do. The name of your father's newspaper . . ."

"The Earth, Texas, *Bugle-Times.*"

"And your little brothers are . . ."

"Are Rob and . . ."

"No—wait. I remember that part. They're Rob and Joey, ages twelve and ten, and your mother is Evangeline. She gardens and makes rhubarb and apple pie, and your father smokes cigars."

"He does," Will laughed. "And he'll blow wonderful smoke rings if you ask." He shifted gears, then stepped harder on the accelerator and sped on, a young man marveling at the young bride beside him. Her eyes were gray, her face small and oval, framed by pale hair and a wide straw bonnet. The hand resting on his arm was small and slender, the nails so delicate they sometimes made him catch his breath in wonder.

He'd warned her that Earth wasn't an exciting, sophisticated city like New Orleans, but she'd smiled and said, "Now tell me, Dr. Harlow. What do you suppose is so exciting about living in a convent?" Her eyes had turned grave then, her face serious. "I think I will like it. I think I'll like your little town very much."

"I want you to like it, Amelia," he'd said. "I want to make you happy."

"I'm going to be," she'd said that day in the convent garden. "I'll make you proud of me too, you'll see," and she'd slipped her hand into his.

He shifted down now and the green Chevrolet roadster topped another hill, speeding on through that quiet

Texas morning. Three hundred miles to the south the worst drought anyone could remember had taken over the center of the state. The early crops were already failing and the sheep and cattle were beginning to drop in the sun. In Austin the politicians were impeaching the governor, a Democrat caught with his hand in the till, and out in the bigger world, war raged in Europe.

But all of that was very distant and very remote. Up here in the northeast quarter of Texas, drought was nonexistent this year and it was almost spring. The pines were flushed with new growth, the rolling hills soft with promise, and Dr. Will Harlow was going home, to the family and the town that had raised him, bringing with him the girl he'd taken as his bride, a young girl he'd found in New Orleans.

It was the end of November then, one of those days when the sky hangs so low that it seems as if no other world exists. Will Harlow dug his hands into his pockets and walked south down the Esplanade. He was exhausted and lonely, oblivious to the soft sway of the moss-hung oaks and the distant cry of the riverboats on the big brown Mississippi ahead.

At twenty-six he was a tall, smooth-skinned Texan who'd plunged through the Princeton undergraduate course in three years, then onto the Tulane Medical School and an internship at the New Orleans city hospital. He was eager to see it all—gunshot wounds, maimings and slashings, pox and flu, typhoid and yellow fever, endless cases of yellow fever. It flourished in that rat-infested port as violence flourished on the docks and syphilis flourished in the ghetto they called Storyville, where the prostitutes plied their trade. He thought he'd learned to protect himself from the human misery that filled the hospital wards, but he'd been stunned by the screams of the little Creole girl in the emergency ward that morning. They'd delivered her of a dead male child, then watched her, already weak from the fever, suddenly hemorrhage to death. Will got someone to cover for him and left for a walk, glad to be going home to Texas soon, to sprained ankles and sore tonsils and Texas women like his mother who scrubbed their houses with lye and gave birth to healthy, bawling children.

He turned and went west on Lafayette Street, his pace quickening as he crossed the square and entered the French Quarter. The air seemed to throb with the smells of chickory and anisette and roasting coffee, the rattle of streetcars, and the deep, throaty cry of peddlers. The streets were narrow and the crowd was dotted with the bright colors of the Greek sailors' uniforms and the black cassocks of priests. The walks were lined with water-stained stucco walls and dappled with the deep shadows of the wrought-iron balconies. Just to the north, a tenor saxophone played a faintly disturbing tune from the music they called jazz. He wandered east, then south again, and was nearly at Canal Street when he saw her face in the window.

A small, fragile face that seemed to float in the milky reflections of the shop window. "Madame Boniface," the sign on the door read. "Chapeaux de Paris."

A streetcar conductor cursed as Will Harlow dodged across the street. The shop bell tinkled frantically; the girl in the window glanced up. He pulled his tall, lanky body through the narrow doorway into a tiny room filled with feathers and lace and row upon row of hats.

A thin, middle-aged woman he assumed to be Madame Boniface herself emerged abruptly from a cubicle in the back, her dark, sleek hair pulled into a severe bun.

"May I be of assistance, Monsieur?" she asked, her white hands fluttering in proprietary dismay over the hats his presence seemed to have disrupted.

"Yes, ma'am." He smoothed back his sun-colored hair, straightened his cravat. "I want a hat." He heard the girl in the window giggle. "For my mother," he said firmly.

Madame discussed many hats as the girl, silent and shy, displayed them one by one. But Will hardly noticed the hats; his attention was held by the girl. He chose a gray felt toque with a short veil of fine black lace. "The newest thing from Paris," Madame assured him. "A transitional piece, Monsieur. A perfect choice." He was uncertain what "transitional" meant and doubted his mother would ever wear it, but she would, he knew, adore owning it.

He left a moment later with a big rose-colored hatbox banging at his long legs and crossed the street to a small cafe where he could sit, drink *café noir* and wait. It was six o'clock when Madame Boniface left the shop and disappeared into the crowds. The girl left fifteen minutes later.

Will stood and spilled some change on the table, watching her as she glanced at the cafe. She turned, pulled a wooden blind across the window, and locked it with a large iron key. She placed the key ring in a bag, smoothed her high-necked white shirt, and then began walking down the sidewalk toward Royale Street.

He was almost sure now that she'd seen him. She moved as if she were waiting for him, just as he'd waited for her. He grabbed his hatbox and ran.

"Mademoiselle! Excuse me, Mademoiselle."

She stopped at the sound of his voice and he stood looking down into deep, dark-lashed eyes, suddenly too shy to speak.

"The hat, sir?" she finally asked. "Is it something about the hat?"

"No, no. Not at all," he said. He liked the sound of her voice. It wasn't French after all, simply soft and Southern and filled with a rush, an eagerness, that caught at him. "I waited to ask if I may walk you home," he said. "It would give me great pleasure."

She nodded, her face flooding with color, and they continued together down Royale and on into St. Charles Avenue. It was a long walk that took them to the edge of the Garden District and the walls of the convent of the Sisters of Charity. She had been raised here as an orphan, she told him, and this was where she'd lived all her life.

"Then who do I ask if I can call on you?" he said.

She would speak to Mother Superior, she promised, and make sure he was expected.

Her blood was tingling when she stepped inside the convent. She leaned back against the heavy door, heard it click shut, and then felt the excitement sweeping through her body. She hung her jacket on the big oak coatrack and walked down the marble halls, the long years of reprimands and practice keeping her pace measured and even.

She found Sister Mary Theresa in her study reading by the light of a gas lamp and a small fire in the hearth. She sat in a chair by the hearth, her feet on a hassock, her prayer book on her lap, a cup of tea to her lips. She put the cup down as Amelia entered, her broad, round face impassive. "You're late, child. We worried."

"I know. I'm sorry, Sister. I didn't take the streetcar. I walked—with a young man, Sister. He wants to call on me. A very tall young man, from Texas. A doctor."

Sister Mary Theresa smiled at the excited face and the rush of words. "And do you want him to call on you, child?"

"Oh yes, Sister. He's coming to see you tomorrow. I said he should. Is that all right? Was that the right thing to do?"

"Of course it was. If he's a fine young man, and I expect he is, there's every reason he should call," and Sister Mary Theresa smiled again at the girl standing in the soft light of the study. She should live a larger life, should be able to give to a man the love that Sister

Mary Theresa had placed with her God. She removed her feet from the hassock and patted it. "Come and sit down for a minute, Amelia."

The girl tucked her skirts around her and sat at her feet. Sister Mary Theresa stretched her hand toward the flames of the fire.

"There is only the question of your mother, my dear. Shall I tell him? Shall you?"

The small oval face went blank. "Not now, Sister. Another time perhaps. Besides, he hasn't even called yet." But she smiled, confident that he would.

2

At seventeen Amelia was an expert at forgetting the past. She'd come to the convent on the edge of the Garden District from a house in Storyville where she was born, a "trick baby" whose father was unknown, so they said, a mistake on the part of the young woman who had been her mother.

Bonnie Bliss had been born in the same house in Storyville. Her birth had killed her own mother within the hour, and Bonnie had been raised by the black kitchen staff, the girls, and the madame herself. They supposed their gurgling, flaxen-haired house pet would grow to be an Amazon one day, tall and statuesque as her ten-pound birth weight promised. But Bonnie stopped growing when she was twelve. She was five feet two inches tall by then, with a freckled nose and little pink buds for breasts. But between her legs the yellow curls flourished so thick and soft that Miss Lucy, fifty years old and a highly successful madame for nearly thirty of them, decided that what she saw through her emerald-studded monocle was all she was ever likely to get: the child's time had come.

Miss Lucy had been in the business all her life, and she knew New Orleans, knew her girls, and knew her

clients. She ran a quiet house on Bienville Street for the
local carriage trade and the amusement of the police
commissioner, a gentleman whose tastes ran to two-
somes and threesomes. He was a big man, beefy, tall,
and almost bald, with a deep, thick New Orleans drawl.
He'd hinted at boredom recently—threatened it, Miss
Lucy feared. He no longer danced or sang to the tunes
that flowed from the player piano that had come, at
great expense plus delivery charges, from the W. B.
Ringrose Furniture Emporium downtown. Gone was
the happy gusto with which he used to attack the food,
the champagne, and Miss Lucy's seven young ladies.

It was on a soft summer New Orleans evening heavy
with the scent of oleander and magnolia when, with the
promise of something special, the commissioner was
led to the Turkish room on the second story of the
house in Bienville Street. Miss Lucy was next door,
stationed by the peephole. A host of candles cast their
glow over the reproduction oriental rugs and glinted off
the commissioner's bald pate. There was the sound of a
door opening, closing, and Bonnie Bliss made her
entrance.

She wore, after hours of indecision on Miss Lucy's
part, no makeup, not even a dusting of powder to
obscure her freckles, and she was dressed in a child's
white camisole tied with pastel ribbons that tumbled to
her round little belly. Miss Lucy had devised the
costume herself, and it belied the vast knowledge
Bonnie had acquired over the years and the even vaster
curiosity Miss Lucy knew was tingling up and down the
girl's spine. She watched Bonnie move to the center of
the room. And now, now was the moment Miss Lucy
had rehearsed with the girl a dozen, two dozen times:
the tremble, the step back, the sudden dash for the
door—and, if she could manage them, the tears, the
final stylish note of virginal terror in the little playlet of
rape Miss Lucy had devised.

But Bonnie did not tremble, or turn. Instead, she

grinned, gave a little wave at the commissioner, and then skipped a few remaining steps to the bed. More surprising to Miss Lucy, the commissioner did not immediately proceed to deflower the youngest member of her house. In fact, when Miss Lucy finally left the peephole, the commissioner was still fully clothed and still making extraordinarily imaginative love to the hungry little body sprawled, whimpering, across his lap.

Miss Lucy finally concluded it was one of those rare cases of mutual sexual addiction—and certainly the biggest stroke of luck in her own generally lucky life. The commissioner's now weekly calls not only guaranteed her survival on Bienville Street; they threw a yoke of stability around her house, and she began attracting an ever wealthier, ever wider clientele, one which allowed her to contemplate replacing the imitation orientals in the Turkish room with the real thing.

And then, eighteen months later, the commissioner dropped dead of coronary arrest as he was ascending the staircase for a visit to the second floor. Bonnie, age fourteen, grieved for weeks. Miss Lucy's recovery was almost instantaneous.

It was Sidney Story, an obscure New Orleans alderman, who replaced the commissioner in Miss Lucy's regard. The city law he drafted and had passed was a simple, sensible law. It became effective on January 1, 1898, and it made prostitution if not quite legal in New Orleans, then not illegal either. It segregated "any woman, notoriously abandoned to lewdness," to an area just north of the French Quarter, an area that included Bienville Street. On New Year's Eve, while Bonnie sulked in her tiny room up on the fourth floor, Miss Lucy was downstairs, decked out in her diamond choker and emerald monocle, playing hostess to a celebratory gathering of favored madames, prostitutes, pimps, and musicians. Someone sat down at the player piano and was swinging into the opening bars of "Auld

Lang Syne" when a gilded whore called from the crowd, "No! Not to the past, honey! To the future! To the future!"

"To Alderman Story," laughed a pinstriped pimp.

"To Storyville," said Miss Lucy, thus christening, amid flying champagne corks, catcalls, and stomping feet, what was about to become the most notorious red-light district in all America.

The ghetto where Bonnie Bliss's daughter was born was bounded on the east by St. Louis Street and on the west by Canal. Clairborne marked the northern border, and Basin Street marked the southern. The thirty-eight blocks in between those boundaries were a world unto themselves. The streets were unpaved, the gutters ran with the refuse of chamber pots and with dead rats, but the leading "parlor houses," forty in all, flourished. For the first time in her career, Miss Lucy hired an accountant, a dwarf who cruised the house each evening in white tie and tails to supervise the heady flow of cash. His miniature suits and rows of carefully polished shoes lined the closet in a small room off the servants' wing, and on Sunday afternoons, "Captain Jack" stumped up the stairs to the second-floor office to review the books with Miss Lucy.

A dozen cases of champagne, a dozen cases of Raleigh Rye: weekly purchase price $500, resale at 400 percent markup, and a net profit of $1,500.

The efforts of the girls themselves, eight in all if you included Bonnie, sharing the client fees with the house on an 80/20 split in favor of the house: $8,400 a week to Miss Lucy.

Gambling—blackjack and poker; a little cocaine: net take $5,000.

That was $14,900, less an estimated weekly overhead of $3,500 to cover furniture and fixtures, telephone and gas bills, staff salaries, medical expenses, miscellaneous bribes, and food—New Orleans' best for the best table in the District. That still left Miss Lucy in the money, clearing $11,400 a week. She sent to New York for two oriental rugs and allowed herself to be talked into a real piano player for the piano. There was only one nagging little worry to mar Miss Lucy's success, and that was Bonnie.

When she fully recovered from her baby's birth, Bonnie dressed in a fresh gown each evening, drew on her red-and-white-striped dancing hose, and followed the rest of the girls downstairs to the first floor receiving parlors. The other girls laughed and sang and wound their arms around the gentlemen who came to call. But Bonnie sat on a silk settee in the corner, mourning the future that might have been.

She could barely recall the big beefy commissioner's face by now, but he would have married her. She was sure of it. He would have divorced his wife, made her a lady, and taken her away to a big white house in the Delta, with pickaninnies to run and fetch chocolates just for her. Instead he'd died, all red and gasping for breath and sprawled over the stairs in that embarrassing way. Now here she was, stuck with a baby she wasn't sure was his and nothing to look forward to at all—nothing but men flopping on and off her, not even bothering to take off their shoes. She sipped her champagne, a tear of frustration and outrage trickling down her small freckled face.

Her baby thrived without her. Miss Lucy named her Amelia, put her to breast with a black washerwoman, and watched her grow from a tiny infant into a remarkably beautiful, rather small child with a mop of corn-colored hair that was a shade or two darker than Bonnie's. She was transferred to the care of the house staff when she was weaned, and her day began at noon when theirs did. Smells of chickory coffee and hot fat sausages floated into her room beyond the kitchen, and she woke to the sounds of the people she thought of as the daytime people. They were the iceman and the rag peddler, and Zozo the voodoo woman, who came to scrub the stoops with brick dust to keep the evil spirits away. Each day ended just after midnight when the cook snared her into the kitchen, lifted her to the counter, and coaxed her to take tidbits of ham and chicken and cold shrimp from the banquet that would close the house down at three A.M. And a sip of warm red wine to make her sleep.

Her first love was Eulalie, a black housemaid who ground gris-gris and cat bones together and hung them around Amelia's neck in a little silk sack to keep her safe. On Saturdays she let Amelia tear long strips from the newspaper and dip the strips in white vinegar one by one while Eulalie, perched on the ladder above, washed the crystal hearts on the big chandelier hanging in the central hall. "Picture show," Amelia nagged on Sunday afternoons, and they took the streetcar to the black district uptown, sat together in the nickelodeons, and wept over sad stories in the dark while the music played on.

She loved Eulalie and she loved Captain Jack. He was little, like her, and he gave her nickels when Buglin' Sam the Waffle Man came winding through the streets of Storyville in his big red van. When she heard the high, clear, mournful notes of his old army bugle sounding far off down Bienville Street and then the soft plop of horse's hooves on the mud, Amelia would run to find Captain Jack. "Nickel," she would beg, and clatter down the steps to stuff her mouth with waffles.

Sometimes Captain Jack took her on his business tours of the District. They set out hand in hand, the dwarf in his striped suit and spats, and Amelia in her cleanest dress. Their route through the steamy city ran up Bienville, across to the liquor store on Conti, and north to the drugstore on Villere where Captain Jack negotiated the cocaine purchase. Amelia wandered the drugstore aisles, mesmerized by the colored bottles and the bright letters on the signs that lined the shelves:

GOOFER DUST

GET TOGETHER DUST

BEND OVER OIL

From the drugstore they headed south to the bank where she waited at the green-tinted windows, watching the trains pull into the Basin Street station. The big, snarling trains from far away disgorged clouds of steam and carloads of people she learned to look at with Captain Jack's discerning eye.

There were people with style—delicate ladies with handsome men to take care of them. They moved through the station, barking sharp orders to the porters to hurry with the piles of trunks and valises as if the crowds pressing around them didn't exist. They stepped out into hot streets and then up into waiting carriages that took them away. Amelia watched those women with style, and noticed the softer colors of their clothes, the richer fabrics, and the creamy skin of their faces under the protective shadow of their hats. She imagined herself coming through a train station in a long dress one day, stepping into a carriage, and being swept away.

She could pick out the riffraff too. "People," Captain Jack said with a sniff, "whose pasts you would not like to inquire into, Amelia." Those were the gamblers and the women who came from nowhere with their flashy clothes and made-up names like Cherry Red, Scratch, Flamin' Mamie, or Bang Zang. They set up business in the Basin Street cribs, rows of tiny shacks with no space for anything but a bed and washbasin. They threw kisses at people on the street and had no style at all.

Fridays there were tourists on the trains and they, according to Miss Lucy, were worst of all. "I do *not*,"

Amelia heard Miss Lucy say in her grandest voice, "I do *not* and never will run a fleabitten tourist trap for out-of-town pikers."

But there were tourists in Miss Lucy's house. When they came out of the Basin Street station with red guide books in their hands, they were sure to come to Bienville Street. The Red Book, Captain Jack told her, called Miss Lucy's "the most refined house in the Tenderloin, where good wine and sweet music reign supreme."

Amelia was glad she lived in the most refined house in the District. The Professor said he wouldn't work anyplace but a nice house where they kept the piano tuned, and of all the people in the world Amelia loved the Professor best.

He was Miss Lucy's piano player and every night at seven he came whistling up the steps, into the front hall, and on into the main parlor where the piano waited. His suits were gray, his boater was straw, and his shoes were black patent leather with bright white spats. Diamonds twinkled on his fingers and in his teeth, and he was black. "Black as sin, baby," he laughed. "Black as *sin!* Now climb on up here and punch that piano key!"

While the girls were upstairs taking their baths, while Captain Jack was in his room slipping into his white tie and tails, Amelia sat in the parlor plucking out a dizzy ragtime beat on the high C while the Professor's big black hands went tearing up and down the keyboard. They sang "Alexander's Ragtime Band" and "Baby, Won't You Please Come Home." They sang fast songs and slow songs, and in between they talked. The Professor allowed Amelia to choose the subject of the evening from the three conversational categories he said were worth their time: Life, Liberty, or the Pursuit of Happiness. They talked and talked, the sunny-haired trick baby chattering away at the big black jazzman in his soft gray suit.

At eight the front doorbell began ringing and the girls came down the central staircase in their pretty dresses and striped stockings. The house filled with hearty male voices, the clinking of glasses, and the laughter of the girls. Amelia kept the Professor's own glass stocked with ice and Raleigh Rye through the evening, and later, when cook put her to bed, she lay on her cot listening to the soft sounds of the streets and the last lines of the lullaby he played for her. "Basin Street, Basin Street," it went. The distant notes, unbearably sweet, came whispering through the dark, tender and haunting, cradling her in the Storyville night. "Basin Street . . . Land of dreams."

Amelia was nearly six when she realized that Bonnie Bliss was in fact her mother, and she was seven when Bonnie sent her away from the house on Bienville Street.

Bonnie had undergone a major transformation in the years after Amelia was born. She buckled down and worked very successfully under Miss Lucy's guidance, saving almost all the considerable sum it would take to school her daughter and get them both out of New Orleans and "the life" altogether.

"See, sweetie?" she said to Amelia. "You'll go to school just for a little, learn all your sums and things, and I'll come every Saturday. Promise. And then a year from now or so, I'll come for you permanent and we'll go away—to Chicago maybe, or New York. See?"

"No," said Amelia.

Her answer was always no, a no that grew bigger and louder and more hysterical as the days wore on. She sat on the piano bench beside the Professor in the evenings with tears running down her face, sobbing about her liberty. But the day came when her mother pried her away from the teary-eyed crowd gathered in the house on Bienville Street and took her by streetcar to the convent of the Sisters of Charity. Bonnie walked away,

back to the lights and music of Storyville, leaving
Amelia standing alone in the dark, quiet hall of the
convent school.

At first Bonnie visited her daughter every Saturday
morning, but giggles echoed down the marble halls
when she arrived. Once a convent girl peered around
the waiting-room door, peeking to see if Amelia Bliss's
mother really did look like a Storyville whore. The
visits became less regular after that, and when Bonnie
failed to stop by two, finally three, Saturdays in a row,
Amelia only shrugged and was relieved. And then that
Sunday night, the Professor and Captain Jack arrived to
tell her that Bonnie was dead. The doctor had said it
was the fever, but the Professor said it was the life.

"Gets us all, one way or the other," said Captain
Jack, nodding.

Amelia sat on the hard wooden bench in the convent's musty, high-ceilinged visiting room, nodding
back at the big black Professor with the mournful eyes
and the dwarf in his striped suit and spats. Her hair had
been pulled into a single braid that traveled down her
back, like a yellow exclamation mark against the black
gabardine of her uniform. Pale and big-eyed, she
looked from the jazzman to the accountant, from one
face to the other. Those two faces were more familiar
and real to her than Bonnie's had ever been. She felt
nothing. Nothing at all.

"It's all right," she said. "I'll just get my bag now and
come on home."

"No, baby." The voice was soft, but it came like a
shot, nailing her in place.

"What the Professor means to say . . ." It was the
higher voice of Captain Jack now, precise and clipped
and clear. "What the Professor means to say is this is
your home now. Bonnie's money goes to the school
here. So they can make you a lady like she wanted you
to be." And though Bonnie hadn't left quite enough
money to accomplish all that, Captain Jack had seen to

it that Miss Lucy made up the difference herself, finally depositing a single sum with Mother Superior to guarantee Amelia's board and room and education through her sixteenth year.

The full implication of what he was saying came slowly to Amelia, but when it did her small body twitched in panic and she slid down from the bench and gripped the jazzman's hand in her own.

"Please don't make me stay," she said, her voice almost a moan. "Please? Please let me come home? I'll be good, I promise."

But the jazzman shook his head and she turned to Captain Jack. "Please?" she begged. "They hate me here, the sisters, the girls. The girls laugh. I'm all alone. Please let me come home."

"You can't," the dwarf sighed, smiling gently at a child who was even now nearly as tall as he. "The little girls will forget, and so will you. Your mother did right by you, bringing you here, so you forget about all the rest now, Amelia. Forget about me and the Professor and Bienville Street. Forget about the District and the life."

"That's right, baby," and the jazzman squeezed her hand and let it drop. "What Captain Jack says is right."

"But you'll come back," she said. "You'll come back to visit. Won't you?"

They exchanged a single furtive glance that made the silence in the room large and hollow. It was the Professor who finally spoke.

"I want you to remember that we loved you, baby. I do want you to remember that. Remember that for us you were the sweetest little thing in all Storyville. When nighttime comes and I play my music, when I'm sitting there at the piano hitting that big old high C, I want you to know that I'll be thinking of you, wherever I might be. But you forget about me, baby. Me and Captain Jack and all the others. We're no good for you now. No good at all."

The dwarf in his spats leaned forward to kiss her cheek. His small smile was crooked and his voice was choked and strangled and far away.

"Forget us, Amelia. We've got no style, Amelia. No style."

The tall black man and the dwarf crossed the hard, bare floors of the waiting room, opened the door, and were gone. She heard their footsteps echoing unevenly down the marble hall, and then the soft distant rush of New Orleans' city sounds melting into the convent.

She slept hard that night, and all the childhood nights to come. She slept long and hard, rolled into a sweaty, silent little ball. At first that was the only visible mark of her grief, for she had found it difficult, almost impossible in her first months at the convent, to sleep at night at all. When the pain finally receded, she emerged as before: angry and undisciplined, nearly illiterate, and possessed of a restlessness, an intense, almost electric energy that upset the very space around her. Though no one had sensed that in her in the nighttime world of Storyville, it unnerved the nuns when she arrived, and it unnerved them now. But now that she was theirs, not for a year but for the duration, they set out to civilize her, promptly and completely.

They rapped her knuckles when she retreated into eating with her fingers and forced her to sit up straight with a ruler strapped to her back. They polished her grammar and her speech to Southern perfection and dealt with fits and tantrums expeditiously with an hour alone in an empty room. They weren't unkind, but they were unrelenting. They indulged no fault and no mistake and rewarded her, not for progress with her manners and her lessons, but for attainment. The rewards were spare—a pillow for her dormitory bed, a black grosgrain ribbon for her long yellow braid, a place in the choir that sang matins in the chapel each morning at dawn.

They didn't try to coax her out of her isolation from

the convent's day students or the few girls who boarded as she did. They recognized her loneliness, but they were lonely in their own way too, and loneliness was not, after all, a sin. Sin was sloth and unruliness, and indisputably, sin was what she had come from, her unmentionable past.

Mother Superior spoke of it forcefully and often in her study, reminding Amelia that they must all say she was an orphan left to the care of the convent as an infant. Amelia must not say differently, must never say differently, must forget completely. Amelia always nodded and was dismissed.

But Amelia did remember. At night, when the dormitory was dark and quiet, filled only with the soft, rhythmic breathing of small bodies, she remembered the lights and colors and sounds of Storyville, the cry of the Waffle Man, the laughter of pretty girls in pretty clothes. She struggled to hang on to the tunes the jazzman played and to her hatred of Bonnie. And then gradually it all began to fade. The girls who had sneered at her went away and other girls came. The anger dissolved. Memories of the piano grew dim. The day came when the past was as Mother Superior said it was—unspeakable. The wild child seemed to disappear, and the unnerving energy was channeled into geography and algebra and the creation of a neat blind stitch for her hems. She spoke too quickly for a Southern child, but that was all.

By the time Sister Mary Theresa journeyed from the East to assume her new position as Mother Superior of the New Orleans convent school, Amelia Bliss was, at sixteen, a credit to the sisters who had devoted their time and effort to her training. Perhaps they had been firmer than Mary Theresa would have been on the question of the mother and Eternal Sin, but Mary Theresa was a member of the order of the Sisters of Charity, and, with charity in her heart, she let it lie.

When Madame Boniface called at the convent to

offer an apprenticeship in her hat shop, Sister Mary
Theresa said that Amelia Bliss was their most appropriate candidate, quick and willing, hard-working and well
mannered. Eighteen months later, she said something
of the same thing to Dr. Will Harlow when he came to
her study, filling her room with his long, lanky Texas
presence.

"A great credit to my colleagues," she said. "And
lovely of course. Quite lovely." She smiled at the young
man sitting across from her. "But then that's why
you're here, I gather."

"I want to take care of her," he said. "She's so
vulnerable, so alone." And then, embarrassed that
Sister Mary Theresa might think him unappreciative of
their care, he said, "I mean, no family, no people of her
own."

"She's young, Dr. Harlow, and, as you say, alone.
But don't confuse youth and inexperience with vulnera-
bility. Amelia Bliss has strengths. She is, you will see,
quite special."

She went on to question him closely and liked the
frank, open way he discussed his position and his
prospects. She gave permission for him to call, and said
nothing more. The past was the past, best left behind.
It was the future that glowed in Amelia Bliss's face
now.

In December, Sister Mary Theresa gave her consent
to a January wedding and she herself supervised the
preparations for the chapel ceremony. Her gift to
Amelia was a small wicker valise with ribbon handles
that she helped her pack, and after the ceremony, she
kissed her goodbye. She wished her happiness and
sincerely hoped she would have it—the girl who, three
days later, crossed the Louisiana state border in the
bright green roadster and, toward dusk, came down
out of the pine hills into the valley where Earth, Texas,
lay.

* * *

"There it is, Amelia. There's Earth," Will called out, and for the first time Amelia Harlow saw the small, dusty Texas town sitting on the cusp of the South and the West. The county courthouse stood at the western edge, its bell tower rising in Gothic splendor to the evening sky. Down at the other edge of town, on the hill overlooking the railroad tracks, sat the Harlow house, just visible against the cottonwood trees. Main Street stretched between; a row of shops under the shadows of a covered walk lined one side, and a Baptist church and the small squat shapes of frame buildings were scattered along the other.

A moment later they were there, Amelia laughing out loud as Will Harlow sent the bright green roadster zigzagging down Main Street, kicking dust into the lavender shadows of a setting sun.

3

The Conquistadors had come first, five hundred strong, marching north up out of the City of Mexico and across the Rio Grande. They broke out of the timberline in 1540, and an expeditionary force of thirty set out with a Pawnee guide to search for the fabled Cities of Cibola. Seven cities, the Pawnee promised, lay somewhere in the endless waves of grass. Each one was larger than the City of Mexico, and all of them were glazed with gold and studded with turquoise and pearl. Months later, those who weren't lost forever returned to garrote the Pawnee guide. A secretary, Castañeda, chronicled the expedition. The Pawnee lied, he wrote his king. There was no gold, no water. There was nothing. He led us out to die.

Castañeda was wrong. The High Plains of Texas floated on water, but the Conquistadors turned back, marred in some indelible, indefinable way by the desolation that lay beyond the timberline. Three hundred and twenty-five years later, in the summer of 1865, three men in a small wagon caravan out of Atlanta pulled their mules to a halt at the edge of the High Plains and then, like the Conquistadors, they too turned back.

The men had fought together in the War Between the States and came home to Atlanta the spring the war was over. Noah Carr and his cousin Perryman returned to the brides they'd left four years before, and Colonel Justiss Harlow came home to his wife and the son she'd borne while he was away. A week later, the three defeated soldiers, their women, and the boy left Atlanta in ashes and the South in ruins and headed west. They passed old plantations where the burnt-out mansions still smoldered and the cotton fields rotted in the sun; plodded through the towns of Alabama and Mississippi and Arkansas where children stood at the gateposts as the caravan moved on by.

Their destination was Dallas. Nothing much to speak of, they'd heard, just a big muddy Texas town out there on the banks of the Trinity. But war hadn't touched Dallas, and there was a future for a man there—land to be had and money to be made in that big, wide-open, get-rich Texas town.

The caravan pushed on, cutting south through the pine hills of the northeast quarter of Texas by the middle of July 1865. And there, at the edge of the timberline, they stopped dead.

Sky. Scrub grass.

More scrub grass, and more sky.

An endless, mindless, numbing ocean of scrub grass baking under a summer sky.

Of all of them, it was Justiss Harlow's wife who was the most relieved when they turned back and retraced their route to the pine hills. They founded their town in a valley there and called it, at her suggestion, Earth. Justiss Harlow's wife was a witty woman and the name pleased her. It was a small celebration, not so much of what the land was but of what it wasn't. It wasn't scrub grass.

The town grew and became a service town for the ranchers scattered in the hills. Main Street stretched out, east to west, straight as a stick. Colonel Harlow and Noah Carr founded a bank, and Perryman Carr built his dry goods and drug store next door. A black family wandered through and settled to the west on what came to be called Sugar Hill. Alabama people drifted in, followed by a family from Virginia and another from South Carolina. They felt at home there, something in the place reminding them of the South that had been. They stayed to raise cows, chop cotton, seed corn, and build houses in town and ranches in the hills.

Justiss Harlow got out of banking in the 1870s and went into politics. He saw to it that the railroad came through his town and that they made his town the county seat, and then he went on to raise the money to build the courthouse on Main Street. It wasn't complete until Justiss Harlow was dead, but there it sat, with its back turned against the West, that spring evening of 1917 when his grandson drove his new bride down Main Street.

She saw just the house at first, isolated on its hill at the eastern edge of town. It was a two-story frame house with a hipped roof and ivy-covered chimneys at either end. A wide porch extended across the back, and an alley of sorts ran through the middle, dividing the first story in half. That was the dogtrot porch Will had described to her, to catch the summer breezes.

Then she saw a man, a woman, and two little boys standing on the porch. The man was broad-shouldered and thickset with a square proud head. The smoke from his cigar curled out over the yard. The woman, tall and lanky like Will, wore a gingham dress, and her arms were around the shoulders of her two towheaded, fresh-scrubbed boys.

Suddenly the panic that had gnawed at the margin of Amelia's thoughts for weeks was at the center. Please, she wished, please let them like me. Even a little. Please let me be all right.

Will honked the horn—once, twice. The boys erupted in shrieks, tumbling down the steps and across the yard. Will bumped to a halt and ran to meet them, catching them up in his arms at the gate, and then he was surrounded by Harlows, all laughing and hugging, and complete.

Amelia watched from a pool of loneliness that spread through the green roadster. Will turned, opened the car door and led her to the gate. At his urging, she stepped through, to be looked at, admired, and then embraced in his mother's arms. "Such a long journey," Evangeline Harlow said. "We're so glad you're here at last."

"Mama," Will called, "a present for you."

The hatbox dangled from Will's hand, bright and pink against a landscape that was a mosaic of dusty browns.

"Open it." Will grinned. "It came from the same shop in New Orleans where I found my bride."

Evangeline's eyes darted to Amelia and then back to the box. Amelia wished he hadn't said that, and wished, seeing Evangeline, that he'd chosen a different hat. "Go ahead," he said. "Open it."

Evangeline opened the pink box and settled the hat on her head. "Is that right?" she laughed. "Is that the way it's supposed to be?" and she stepped to catch her reflection in the roadster window. It looked odd perched on the braids that already circled her head, its black veil askew and too fine against the square lines of her face.

"Perfect," said Will, "isn't it, Amelia?" and he reached his hand out to her. "I know you'll never wear it, but . . ."

"Wear it! My dear, I won't be able to take it off. This whole town is beside itself with your new bride. Such a string of parties and teas to go to. And you'll see—I'll have to wear it to every single one." She linked her arm through Amelia's. "I'm so glad to have her—to have them both," and her square brown hand patted the black lace as she led Amelia up the path to the house beyond.

Inside, wide, dark pine floorboards stretched through cool rooms that smelled of fresh linen and lemon wax. Heavy pine doors closed with satisfying clicks when the latches fell into place. Every surface was covered with Evangeline Harlow's crochet work, the brilliant, subtle colors of the delicate doilies and antimacassars curving around the arms and backs of solid Victorian chairs and sofas. Floral prints lined the walls of the front parlor, and in the back parlor there was a massive stone fireplace with the Confederate flag and a musket in the place of honor above.

The last of the sunlight flooded the kitchen that lay on the other side of the dogtrot porch, and Evangeline moved briskly to the enormous oak table that filled one end of the room, lifting white linen cloths to reveal the supper feast she had prepared. There were cold fried chickens and spiced hams, bowls of bean salad, beet salad, potato salad, and platters heaped high with fresh corn bread. Willow pattern plates shone from six place settings, one of them for Amelia.

"To welcome you," Evangeline Harlow smiled as she lowered the cloth. "To welcome you home."

"Thank you," Amelia said, her voice small. "More than I can ever say."

Evangeline Harlow glanced at her, then let the cloth drop. She came to Amelia, tipped her chin up and kissed her quickly on the cheek. "Why don't you come upstairs with me? I've made over Will's room for you and I think you should see it now."

A small room on the second floor had been transformed and the boyhood treasures exiled to a trunk in the attic.

"It's lovely," Amelia said when she saw it. It was fresh and clean and new-smelling. The wallpaper was new, a field of eggshell blue sprinkled with a yellow flower. The bedstead was new, all the way from Dallas, Evangeline said. Its rosewood posters reached nearly to the ceiling, and soft folds of white netting fell around the patchwork quilt Evangeline had made. The stripes of the Mexican rugs scattered on the floor contrasted brightly with the paler colors of the patchwork and the linens.

"I know you won't be here long," Evangeline said. "You'll build your own house, you and Will, and have your own place. But I was a bride once too. I remember that it felt very foreign at first—they all feel a little foreign, the families we join. It feels at first like you'll never belong, and I wanted you to know . . . well, how should I say, that this is your room, and your home. I do welcome you home, my dear. You do belong and I hope you'll feel that one day soon."

The chill Amelia had felt in the car had long melted away. She smiled up at Evangeline. "Thank you," she said. "I think I'm going to cry."

A soft smile curled at the corner of Evangeline's mouth. "Well, that's all right. You go right ahead and cry."

The latch clicked into place and from down the hall came the sound of boots and Evangeline's voice. "Leave those bags right there at the head of the stairs, boys, then run wash up for supper." The boots clattered back down, and Amelia's tears began to fall, making the colors in the room run.

Even years later, Amelia would look back on her first weeks as the young Mrs. Harlow and feel a suffusion of gratitude for Evangeline Harlow and the sting of tears. The feeling was never diluted by time, never altered, never became only a remembered sensation. Whenever she turned back to that part of her past and came to Evangeline, she would see once again the hat from New Orleans set firmly on the crown of old-fashioned braids, the soft eyes, and the gently lined face, strong and good and open. She would see herself at eighteen with a new wedding ring on her hand, and hear Evangeline's voice playing across time, "Welcome home. You'll belong. Welcome home, welcome home." Like a ribbon that bound together all the early days of her marriage.

Half an hour later, freshly washed and dressed in the pale blue middy that was her second-best daytime dress, Amelia slipped downstairs to supper.

"There you are," Evangeline smiled. "Suppertime, everyone." With a bang of screen doors, the Harlow males descended on the evening feast. The little boys bounced and scraped their chairs into place and began to swamp her with the chorus of their names.

"He's Joey. I'm Rob."

"I can talk for myself. I'm Joey and *he*'s Rob, Miss Bliss, and . . ."

" 'Miss Bliss!' " howled Will. "She's Mrs. Harlow now, Joe."

"Yes, ma'am. Sorry, ma'am," and the little boy blushed.

"You mustn't call me ma'am, Joey, or I'll have to call you sir—and then where will we be? Try Amelia—just once."

"Amelia," Joey whispered. "That's pretty."

Carter Harlow stubbed out his cigar and nodded at her from his chair at the head of the oak table. He was handsome and dark from years in the sun, and the lines around his bright blue eyes were deep and hard. He was a shorter man than Will, but seemed bigger somehow, his head massive, his well-cut leather jacket adding width to his wide, thick shoulders.

He nodded again, then cleared his throat. "Will's told us, Amelia, about the convent. No family of your own?"

Amelia glanced down, her cheeks flushing as she stared at the willow pattern plate before her.

"Can't have been easy for you growing up like that. Just want you to know that you have a place now. Here with us."

Somewhere beyond his deep bass voice she could feel the truth hanging at the edge of space, and the words forming somewhere inside her: "I'm not who you think I am. My mother—" But she couldn't imagine those words at this table. She'd tell Will. She'd wanted to tell him all along. It was just that it had all happened so fast. But she would tell him and then perhaps they could talk to his parents together. But not yet.

Carter Harlow's voice went on. "Well, we welcome you, Amelia. Hope you're prepared for us to make a Texan out of you."

She looked up then and smiled. "Yes, sir. As soon as you can."

Napkins were unfolded in laps and willow plates were heaped high with ham and chicken and corn bread. Carter Harlow's drawl went on rolling around the room.

Ample office space, he was saying. Will would want ample space. The nearest doctor was in Daingerfield, fifteen miles away, and that was still fifteen miles too far. There were cotton dust problems down Mount Pleasant way, and a couple of men with mangled hands on Sugar Hill just waiting for Will to come home.

The talk went on in a buzz of unfamiliar names and places as food was passed from hand to hand and the two little boys darted bright expectant looks in Amelia's direction, blushing and staring at the ceiling when she smiled back. The talk turned to Texas politics and town gossip, then back again to Will.

"Excuse me," she finally said, shy at first, but with

more conviction when Will urged her on. "I can help out. It'll be awfully expensive to hire someone, especially in the beginning when we're just starting out. And I can help."

Carter Harlow smiled. "Little thing like you? Wading through all that blood?"

"I wasn't thinking of nursing," she rushed on. "I was thinking of the appointment book. Of keeping medical records, sending bills and letters and . . ."

"You're going to have a house of your own to look after soon and plenty to do, but I'll tell you what. You fix Will's office up once he's found it, curtains and such. And then maybe I'll give you a typewriter to play with and you can peck out some bills. How'll that be?"

Her eyes were shining. "I'd like that very much."

"Well, that's fine. But you let Will take care of his wife then, just like he planned. Like Harlow men always have. Right, Will?"

They moved out to the porch then for coffee, and Amelia stood in the evening cool beside Will, warming her hands on the hot coffee cup. The little boys' voices called through the dusk, and the creak of the swing sounded from the far corner of the porch. She pressed closer to Will.

"Was I all right, Will? Do you think it went well?"

"You were wonderful. And I'm glad you want to help. I think that's sweet."

Later, in Will's old boyhood room, they made love. It was easier for her now and Will had promised it would go on getting better. The shame she'd felt the first time he'd undressed her, the agony of fear that he would find her unsuitable in some way, all that was past. The light of the Texas moon came spilling through the white net canopy and she opened her arms to him and brought him close. His mouth moved across hers and she felt him growing hard, then harder. She smiled, secure in his need of her, winding her arms around him as he entered. It still felt odd, another body pressing into hers, but he would cradle and croon to her when it was over and she would murmur back.

She fell asleep that night in Texas, sure that all she ever wanted, she had. This family, this man.

4

She woke in the mornings astonished that she wasn't still a shopgirl. But she wasn't. She was the young Mrs. Harlow now, of Earth, Texas. At odd moments during her day, in the midst of snapping beans, running into town to buy liniment for scraped knees, or learning to bake bread with Evangeline, her concentration would suddenly break and she would fill with smiles.

And Carter Harlow was right. There was enough to do. There was a house to plan on the lot out back, Evangeline's house to clean and shine, her garden to discover. It was an old-fashioned English garden and in the mornings, Evangeline, trowel in hand, wearing an old straw bonnet and a brown cotton apron with huge pockets, worked in it diligently.

Evangeline's father had been a Massachusetts sea captain who'd met her mother in the British town of Portsmouth and brought her back to America. They'd settled in Ohio, where Evangeline's mother wrought a garden to remind her of home. "And then we moved to Mount Pleasant and that's where I grew up and met Will's daddy." She had two sisters, Emily and Ellen, married now and still living in Titus County.

"And do they have English gardens too?" Amelia wanted to know.

Evangeline shook her head. "No, they don't. Oh, they like to look, but they don't find the peace I do making things grow."

Amelia wanted a garden when she had her house, and she watched as Evangeline turned the soil where the yellow roses grew and fertilized the rock garden in

the far corner that would tumble with bougainvillea.
Together they cleaned the small pond under the willow
tree and decided to stock it with lilies and let them laze
in the sun.

There were the little boys to learn about. At ten Joey
was solemn and quiet, immersed in books and rocks
and leaves and a vast collection of butterflies. Twelve-
year-old Rob was bigger and sturdier, banging through
screen doors, then back out again to play games of
kick-the-can down by the railroad tracks. There were
meals to cook, dishes to wash, and a whole town to
learn about.

Earth wasn't much of anything at first look that
spring of 1917, just a small town, population 3,020,
with a main street that was dusty and sleepy in the
afternoons. It was just like thousands of other small
towns strung all across the West, but for Amelia, the
people behind shop doors made it, more and more, her
home.

Old Perryman Carr at the dry goods and drug store
turned out the best homemade ice cream she'd ever
had. Young Noah Carr ran the bank and waved at her
through the deep green glass windows and there was
still another Carr who smiled at her from the ticket
office at the moving-picture show. The sheriff tipped his
hat when he passed her under the shade of the covered
sidewalks, and the principal of the Colonel Justiss
Harlow Public School tipped his. The postmaster collected stamps for her to sort through with Joey, and
Mary Cherry from the telephone and telegraph office
next door would call out to her as she passed, "My,
isn't it nice? Just the nicest day?"

Carter Harlow's newspaper office sat in the middle of
it all under a black gum tree, and when he called to say
he couldn't make it home for lunch one day, she boxed
cold chicken and apple pie and took it downtown
herself. She was still a little in awe of him, but she
wanted the excuse to look.

A white sign hung from the red brick façade, and Earth *Bugle-Times* was blazoned across it in black letters. Narrow steps led up to a pressroom that smelled of ink and dust, and the men and boys working there wore green eye shades and paper cuffs to protect their white shirt sleeves. A big fat man seemed to be in charge, his voice escaping the chewing tobacco he shifted from cheek to cheek to boom out over the roar of the machinery. And at the back, big brass letters were nailed to a thick door. "Carter Harlow: Publisher."

He'd spent four not unpleasant years at Princeton doing not much of anything and graduated respectably enough in the study of English literature. When he came back home Colonel Harlow asked him what he wanted to do next, and he replied, "Looks like we could use a newspaper around town. Think I'll just start one." Now, nearly thirty years later, he sat in his office with his Stetson pushed back on his head and his boots propped up on a scarred desk piled high with almanacs and sheets of newsprint. He was on the phone, but he nodded at Amelia and she stepped forward to set the boxed lunch on his desk. He pointed at a chair and she sat.

He was listening to someone on the other end of the line and she smiled uneasily, more aware than ever of her discomfort with the way he always looked at her. There was a question in his eyes that he never asked. But then, before she'd met Will the only men she'd known were priests. And that was hardly the same. Carter Harlow was an important man in the world and she supposed she'd get used to him in time.

He began to drum his fingers on the arm of his chair and then his voice cut through the quiet. "Tell you what, Mary Cherry. You give 'em five minutes and then pull the line. Just cut 'em off. We got a paper to get out today. Not tomorrow. Today." The receiver smacked into place as his feet hit the floor.

"Like it, Amelia?" He took her by the arm and led her back to the pressroom. "When I began this paper we used pigeons to get the news around, from here to Tyler, to Daingerfield, all the way to Dallas. Now we got the best machinery the good ol' American dollar can buy." He waved his hat. "Boys," his voice cracked over the huge room. "Want you all to say hello to my Will's bride here, the newest Mrs. Harlow." Heads bobbed up, grinning welcome. She smiled back and followed her father-in-law down the aisles.

"Fred Billings here, my managing editor." The fat man with the chewing tobacco nodded. "And this is Eb Graves on the Mergenthaler." An old man with a toothless grin glanced up at her while his bony fingers continued to flash over a vast keyboard. Metal molds clattered into channels below, and molten lead appeared at the push of a control button. She stared at the speed of it all, at the magic of type forming the mirror image of words and sentences.

"Sets five lines a minute," Carter Harlow yelled above the noise. "Used to take old Eb two days to set two pages by hand." He grinned and led her on, his hands caressing massive units of steel and lead as they passed. "Joined the Associated Press a year back and all the national news comes over this teletype here. Costs a fortune, let me tell you. Best money I ever spent. Sheet-fed Harris here, best they make; little ol' Cincinnati over there for job work, hand-cranked. Got a Dexter folder, and a loading dock downstairs. You print, you fold, you tie 'em up, and down the chute they go, smartest-looking weekly in Texas."

"Phone, Mr. Harlow!" an ink-stained boy was hollering from down the aisle. "Austin on the line, Mr. Harlow." Carter Harlow pecked her on the cheek, waved her in the direction of the door, and disappeared.

She wandered alone through the pressroom, then down the dim stairs and out onto Main Street—a girl, flushed and exhilarated, stepping into what seemed for a moment a pool of brilliantly lit, stunning silence.

But it was all exciting—the new town, new people, and the sudden sense she had sometimes that she'd stumbled into a foreign land. Texas wasn't just a state. It was a state of mind, a particular vision of space, of sky.

It was hugeness itself, and the reckless driving urgency of wildcatters drilling for oil to the south. It was the Texas pines, shimmering against the horizon, and the Texas talk, seductive and sweet. People didn't say "Come in." They said "Light and set, honey. Light and set." They didn't say "Goodbye." They said "Hurry on back now, hear?" It was the stretch of the land, and the food—the chili, the chicken-fried steak you dipped in eggs and milk and flour and then slung into a skillet sizzling with fat. And barbecue.

"Now, down in the Big Bend Country, where my mama came from?" It was a Sunday afternoon and the Reverend Mrs. Claude Pack and Amelia were laying red-and-white-checked tablecloths over the long tables that lined the Packs' sun porch.

"Well," Mrs. Pack went on, her old dimpled hands smoothing out an imaginary wrinkle in the checks, "down in the Big Bend Country where my mama came from, we always gave a barbecue to welcome the brides. We haven't had a bride in this town for so long," and she squeezed Amelia's hand.

Perfectly normal people, she discovered, were perfectly capable of being silly about Texas. They were giddy about the sheer size of it all. "Bigger than all of France itself," she learned to say when the subject came up, as it always did. And they were proud of its mythic terrors. Hailstones the size of doorknobs. Torrential rains that filled Sugar Creek. Blue northers smashing down out of the Central Plains, bringing snow in July. Tornados spinning up out of nowhere.

"Tornado of eighty-nine?" the postmaster said.

"Picked my mama up right along with the milk cow, put 'em down twenty yards away. Cow keeled over dead, but not my mama. Didn't turn a hair on her head. Went right back to shelling peas.

"Now, young lady," and he handed Amelia the stamps she'd come for. "You believe a single word out of all that?"

"Yes, sir, Mr. Farrier," she said. "I think I do."

"Well, good. Glad to hear it." His old eyes were gay, enormous behind his wire-rim glasses. "It's not true of course, but I like to believe it. Glad you do too."

By the end of January, Will found his offices, three rooms at the back of Reverend Pack's church that would be ready, freshly painted floor to ceiling, by mid-February. They celebrated that day with a picnic out back where their house would sit and with a tour of the county in the green roadster, just the two of them. They sped down the dusty roads and up into the pine hills. They'd circled around, stopping underneath the pines by the cemetery for a view of Earth far below when the idea popped into Amelia's head.

"Teach me to drive, Will. Please! I think it must be *wonderful.*"

He did, howling with laughter as she jerked the roadster around and around the tree-lined dirt road that circled the neat rows of stones. "The clutch," he yelled. "The clutch! You can't shift without the clutch. And slow down. You're driving like a maniac!"

And then she got the hang of it and they drove on, Will grinning and waving at a farmer who stared as they passed.

Will's office opened on schedule and they drove to town every morning at nine. Will had an increasing flow of patients, and Amelia kept the appointment book and typed the patients' records on file cards, using the black Remington Carter Harlow had sent down. Every evening after supper they pulled out paper and pencils and planned their house—how it should look, how it should sit on the land.

"Maybe Amelia would like a house to remind her of New Orleans," Evangeline suggested one evening. "With some of those wrought-iron balconies along the second floor? Wouldn't that look pretty out beyond the cottonwoods."

"No," said Amelia.

She hadn't thought of New Orleans, not once in all these weeks, but the memories flooded her now, making her hands go clammy. She'd meant to tell Will, but she'd been so busy, and it didn't matter. Not really. Her life was here now, not New Orleans.

"No," she said again. Her voice was sharper than she'd intended and she softened it with a rush of chatter.

New Orleans was just a dirty old city full of strangers. Dank in the summer, dank in the winter, and so run over with rats it was a miracle anyone survived at all—wasn't it, Will? "Besides," she said, "I'm a Texan now. I want a Texas house, Evangeline—like yours. With a dogtrot porch and a pond out back." She squeezed her pencil and buried herself in the sketches and the questions. How many rooms, how big, how to catch the sun, how to keep it cool. They'd begin building soon. Come April, they'd break ground.

And then it was the first day of March, a Thursday that year, bright and warm and clear.

Carter Harlow was at the door of the *Bugle* office, pulling on his jacket to go home for lunch, when the teletype machine suddenly came alive, chattering through the noon-hour quiet of the pressroom.

He looked back, saw Fred Billings amble toward the machine, and watched his managing editor's hand suddenly jerk toward the roll of paper spitting out.

"Carter! You there? Better come and read this." And then, "Jesus, Carter!"

Evangeline Harlow was in her kitchen stringing beans when the phone call came through from her husband. She put down the sharp knife, wiped her hands on a towel. She passed the oven, and the warm smell of the ham filled her nostrils, sending pleasurable pains of hunger through her body.

Will was washing his hands before examining the Reverend's aching back when he heard the sudden commotion in his reception room.

Amelia had just typed "Yours sincerely" at the foot of a letter to a New York drug company when Dotty Pack came bursting into the office, her arms piled with bundles, her face white.

Rob and Joey were scuffling over a ball in the schoolyard. They didn't see the boy from the newspaper office running down the street and were too far away to hear.

But old Perryman Carr wasn't. He glanced up from the new window display of hoes and trowels and flower seeds he was arranging, peered through the watery glass at the figure of the boy racing down the street outside. Then, for no good reason at all, Perryman Carr was nineteen again, a boy dressed in gray. The Georgia woods were exploding around him and there was the sharp, acrid smell of muskets, the agonized screams of men and a dying horse somewhere, and Justiss Harlow's voice, choked and afraid. "This way, Carr, this way!" And then he was running, sobbing, through the underbrush.

Slowly, Perryman Carr made his way to the front door of his dry goods and drug store. The bell tinkled and he stepped out onto the dusty wooden walk. The boy was halfway up the block by now, stumbling up the steps to the sheriff's office.

"War!" he was screaming, his voice young and thin and sweet.

"War!"

5

The news spread, from house to house, farm to farm. By midafternoon half the 3,000 people within the boundaries of Earth had drifted into Main Street. It was a somber crowd of husbands holding wives close, wives holding the children who'd flooded out of the school yard, neighbors speaking in hushed tones. They arrived on foot and on horseback, in horse-drawn carts and half a dozen automobiles that came clattering and wheezing through the streets. They gathered in front of the *Bugle* offices, waiting patiently for the one-sheet special edition Carter Harlow was putting together. At three the slow slap, slap, slap of the Harris press began sounding above them, then dissolved into a rhythmic hum. Half an hour later Carter Harlow came down the stairs with the first hundred sheets still damp in his arms.

The crowd knotted and surged forward, calling for copies. Amelia, her hand through Will's arm, bent her head to read.

"SHOCKING PLOT REVEALED" marched, blood-red, across the page, headlining the full eight columns of type. Amelia read on, fighting to understand the meaning of the lines tombstoning down the page.

GERMANY AT WAR SEEKS ALLIANCE WITH MEXICO
TEXAS OFFERED AS BOOTY FOR
SURPRISE ATTACK ON U.S.A.
LONE-STAR STATE TO BOW TO MEXICAN FLAG
JAPAN ASKED TO JOIN: CALIFORNIA THEIRS

March 1, 1917: The Associated Press is now able to reveal that President Woodrow Wilson holds in his possession irrefutable evidence that German Foreign Secretary Arthur Zimmermann has issued formal instructions to offer Mexico the Sovereign States of Texas, New Mexico, and Arizona as reward for their joint conduct of successful war. The issue now shifts, from Germany against Britain to Germany against the United States.

It went on and on, a grim, hysteria-provoking warning of war in Europe suddenly leaping the Atlantic, throwing the United States under siege. It was a warning of carnage at the hands of a German-Mexican army, of the Yellow Peril storming the Pacific Gate. The story ran in thousands of newspapers across America, but none of them matched the defiant promise that Carter Harlow wrote and printed that day. "With quiet modesty and simple truth," the publisher of the *Bugle-Times* concluded, "we can now declare that if the Mexicans seek to enslave this great state of ours, not a Texan will be left alive unless he's across the Rio Grande, fighting his way back." And then Carter Harlow joined the Congress of the United States "in a salute to Commander in Chief Woodrow Wilson, whose declaration of War on Germany is expected within the hour."

In that, Carter Harlow was wrong. It would in fact take the President of the United States, the man he began to refer to in his editorials as "yellow-belly Granny Wilson," a month and a half to declare war on the Central Powers. But nothing, not even time, would dull the thrill of anger that rolled through the crowd gathered at the steps of the *Bugle* that first day of March 1917.

"Nobody here gonna fly the goddamned wetback flag," the sheriff spat as he pushed through the crowd. "Not man, woman, child." The crowd's anger erupted into outrage as he fought his way up the *Bugle* steps.

"Nobody here gonna let the wetbacks snatch the land we won fair and square! Gonna give 'em a run for their money!"

The crowd swarmed in hysteria, and an old man's voice rose, shrill and clear, "Remember the Alamo!" and then the air was suddenly lighter with laughter and contempt.

Amelia, the newspaper still tight in her fist, listened, flushed with excitement and pride as the voices rolled on, shrieking out a call to duty and to arms. "Gonna let the huns know Texas is coming their way," someone bellowed. "Gonna wipe the Kaiser off the face of the map!" There was a cry of approval, then others clamoring for a turn, and finally the Reverend Pack was giving his benediction, his long, thin arm raised in prayer, snuffing out the sounds of the crowd. It was over then. The women drifted home, to calm wide-eyed children, to gather at picket fences and wait for their men.

Will shifted down into third gear and the green roadster ground on through the dusk, up the road that led to Sugar Hill. One of the boys in the back had brought a flask along and by the time they pulled into the hollow where the Sugar Hill bar lay, Carter Harlow was leading all eight of them through the last chorus of "Dixie." The roadster jerked to a halt and arm in arm, bourbon-inspired voices working in perfect harmony, they crossed the clearing to the bar door and piled in.

It was a long, open room. The bar, with its elaborate beveled mirrors and a glittering stock of bottles, ran for fifty feet and was tended that night by three cheerful girls and Jake Matthews, the owner. The bar had belonged to Jake's mother before him, a woman who'd been left at a boardinghouse in Tyler with her newborn son and a husband's promise that when he'd made his fortune in California he'd come back and take them West. Jake's mother didn't wait.

She worked as a bar girl in a local saloon and saved

her money. Then she built her own saloon on a tract of
no-man's land in Sugar Hill and taught her boy Jake all
about liquor and men. Jake hired a bouncer to keep
things pleasant, a couple of girls to hustle drinks and
whatever else they liked, and never touched a drop. On
March 1, 1917, the Sugar Hill bar had been in continual
operation for twenty-seven years.

By the time Carter Harlow and the boys rolled in that
night, the air was full of smoke and war talk, and the
long brass rail thick with men. Carter pushed his way
forward, shaking hands, calling out to friends.

"Gonna get 'em, Carter," someone called. "Gonna
get 'em good."

"Mr. Harlow, sir?" A boy of no more than sixteen
was tugging at his sleeve. "When do you think we'll get
our orders, Mr. Harlow?" his eyes wide with expectation.

"Hell, it'll take 'em weeks, maybe months to call
everybody." He put his arm around the boy's shoulders. "Now if I was a young fella like you, I'd probably
volunteer right away."

"Damn right," a rancher said, and slugged back his
shot of whiskey. "Gotta move fast or it might be over
before we get there."

A large, thick-bodied man, his face lined by the sun,
shoved forward and pulled his young son to his side.
"This boy's not going anywhere. 'Cept home. War's for
men, not children." He pushed his son ahead of him,
through the crowd and out the bar door, Carter Harlow
roaring after them, "Well shit! How the hell do boys
become men if you don't let 'em fight!" He looked at
Will, leaning quietly against the bar. "My boy's going,
aren't you, boy?"

Will glanced up, confusion and uncertainty on his
face. Carter Harlow beamed, raising his glass in salute
to his son, to the lean, blond young man with the soft
blue eyes whose shot glass finally came up to meet his
own.

And Jake Matthews, who knew how to work a drinking crowd when he had one, called for a round on the house.

The train that took Will Harlow to war one morning in May was festooned with red, white and blue bunting. So were the shops lining Main Street and the drums of the high school marching band. It was a perfect day. The crops in northeast Texas had never been richer, the land never greener, the sky never bigger or wider, the hill the Harlow house sat on never massed with blue-bonnets bluer than they were that day.

Amelia drove Will to the station just after daybreak. She turned off the engine and they sat alone in the green roadster, the silence of the town not yet awake settling around them.

"You'll write every day."

Will nodded. "You too?"

She leaned her head against his shoulder. "Every day. And I'll look in on the office once a week. You'll see," and she smiled up at him. "When you come back it'll be clean and white. As if you'd never been away."

"It won't be long. A couple of months. Six at the outside."

She nodded and they took each other's hands, lovers with nothing more to say.

It was nearly eight when they heard the cranking of the train hauling in from Texarkana. They watched the lights grow brighter and the streamers celebrating the glory of the day grow redder as the train edged down the tracks toward town. The train stopped, the doors opened, and from behind them they heard the umpah-umpah of the high school band.

The band came marching up the center of Main Street, the red, white and blue streamers snapping smartly in time with the ruffles of the drums. Behind, in ragged formation, came the dozen volunteers who would take the train with Will that day. At twenty and

twenty-one, they were tall and broad, their bodies built
big on the Texas land. They smiled and waved, the dust
from their marching feet melting into the faces of the
families and friends who lined the streets. They came
swinging down the railroad tracks and then they were
there, crowding past the roadster, a shower of hugs and
kisses and "Give 'em hell!" sweeping them aboard.

Will stepped out of the roadster into Evangeline's
arms. He freed himself after a moment and shook his
father's hand a last time. With the little boys still
wrapped around his long legs, he buried his face in
Amelia's hair. "I'll come back. You'll see," he whispered. "I love you, Amelia."

She wanted to say something. She wanted to say no.
And yes. Don't go. And be safe. She wanted to say
remember me, but there were only the silent, sickening
waves of pride and fear, and she couldn't speak.

He stepped free then and boarded the train. It jerked
once, twice, began pulling away.

"I love you, Will," she suddenly cried. "I love you."

But her voice was lost in the clanging of the wheels
and the hiss of the steam as the train picked up speed,
taking Will farther and farther away until all she could
see was the red, white and blue bunting and the empty
train tracks.

6

Amelia waited.

She read the *Bugle* for the war news, read every daily
paper that found its way to the house at the edge of
town—the Dallas *Morning News* and the Galveston
News, the Hearst papers from Chicago, and once an
edition of the *New York Times*. It was three weeks old,
but she read it anyway. She pored over maps to locate
the battlefields in the war reports and developed a kind
of sixth sense for the distant hum in the sky above the

hills of Earth. She would stop and listen to the breeze
running through the pine trees, to the sudden silence of
the birds as the hum became a drone. The air would
suddenly chill, the dark spot in the sky would come
closer, and what in the distance looked like a tiny
dragonfly dancing on the wind would emerge as a
single-engine war plane dragging its dark shadow south
to the landing strips at Love Field.

Will's letters came, first from Galveston, then from
the battleship *Texas* when it sailed out of Galveston
harbor in June, and finally from some unidentified
place "over there." These last were thick square blue
envelopes addressed to Mrs. Will Harlow, Earth,
Texas, and their lower left-hand corners bled with the
ink from the censor's stamp: a purple eagle, eight tiny
stars in a circle, and "B. W. Kiley 2nd Lt. U.S. Inf." in
tiny block letters.

She stored Will's letters in a willow basket that sat by
the bedside table in their room and wrote long letters in
return. Polly Carr was having a baby. Joey got an A in
arithmetic, and she and Evangeline had joined Dotty
Pack's Liberty Circle. They knitted socks and scarves
every Wednesday now, wrapped bandages for the
medical supply units. Louise Huff and Jack Pickford
were playing at the picture house in *Great Expectations*. It was wonderful and were there any cities left in
Europe; did he ever have leave? Could he see *Great
Expectations* too? But the blue envelopes were rare and
criss-crossed with hers in the mail, and there were no
answers to her questions.

She wrote every day, a one-way conversation in a
void that seemed deeper and deeper. She wrote that
she and Robby were practicing for his county spelling
bee in September and she was organizing a food-supply
service for military transport trains coming through
Earth. The bluebonnets were gone now and tiger lilies
were coming up. Fall would be cooler. Everyone said
so.

She didn't write that Polly Carr lost her baby and died two days later when the doctor couldn't make it in from Daingerfield. She didn't say July was like an oven, that August was so insufferably hot she carried smelling salts with her in terror of fainting, and she didn't write that the whole county was caught up in anti-German fever that began to seem as hot and ugly as August itself.

She didn't write about the itinerant printer who'd wandered into town in search of work at the *Bugle*. He'd come in response to word that Carter Harlow was losing a pressman to the draft, but he never made it to the *Bugle* offices.

Carter Harlow told them about it over supper that night. His name was Ernst Liepman and his accent was German. He stepped down off the train, went to ask directions at the railroad ticket office, and was mobbed at the window.

"He'd have been murdered too. Ripped to pieces right there on the spot if the sheriff hadn't come along and heaved him back on the San Antonio train."

"You mean he's *gone?*" The chicken leg Robby had reached for hit his plate and rolled across the oak table.

"Robert!"

"Daddy!" he yelled. "He was *German*. We could've hung him at the courthouse and all us kids could've watched! Or maybe a real shooting squad and I could've plugged his stinking old kraut body with my BB gun. Except now he's *gone?*"

"No, Robby."

Evangeline's hand snaked out, leaving a bright red circle on Robby's cheek. She stood, rigid and grim in the silence. When she finally spoke her voice was hard and bitter. "This war will ruin us all," and then she knelt by her young son, took him in her arms and began to cry.

Amelia wrote Will about none of that. It seemed unfair to burden him with the problems back home, and there seemed no way to describe her growing sense that the world hadn't just come to a halt. It was changing, and she was changing. She tried to write more about the military food-supply service she had running smoothly in mid-September, but the subject was a painful one in the Harlow house and the odd page or two she did write sounded defensive and hysterical. She ripped them up. She would tell him about it privately, when he came home.

Soldiers flooded the town of Earth that fall. They came in on military transport trains from the north, the whistles sounding day and night as the trains pulled into the sea of army tents three miles out of town.

The letters to the editor that Carter Harlow printed on his editorial page, cautiously optimistic at first, became increasingly sour about the lack of organization and the threat of a frontier-style camp on the edge of town. Finally, they brought a Major Fitzsimmons to the *Bugle* offices and then home to dinner one August evening. Over iced tea and coffee on the porch, the Harlows listened to the major relate his problems. It was almost impossible to deal efficiently with thousands of men passing through his hands, almost impossible to feed them all. By the time food got there in the heat, most of it was going bad. "But that's war for you," he said, shrugging. "No way out of it until winter cools things down a little."

Amelia folded her paper fan in her lap and gazed up at the major.

"Why do you have it shipped in?" she asked.

"Have what shipped in, ma'am?"

"Your food," said Amelia. "Why don't you get your food from the farmers here?"

"Can't do that, young lady," the major said. "We're talking about thousands of men arriving over the course of the next few months. Have to bring the food in. It's the only way."

"But you're in the middle of good farmland. If the

army's prepared to pay the farmers the going rate, they could sell to you directly."

"Maybe," he said. "Maybe. But I don't have the time or the manpower to organize something like that."

"Well, let me." Her voice fell into a sudden silence, but she didn't notice. She was on her feet, the words coming in a rush. "I need to do something. I need to help. Let me organize it, Major. We have a women's group, don't we, Evangeline, just full of good cooks. They make wonderful barbecue and chicken and ham and . . ."

Carter Harlow began to laugh. "Amelia, honey, the major has to deal with thousands of men, and he needs thousands of pounds of food. It's not like throwing a church social."

She turned again to Fitzsimmons.

"Explain what you need and when, then let me try. If it doesn't work, you won't lose anything. Will you?" And she smiled.

Carter Harlow was angry. "Amelia . . ." But Fitzsimmons held up his hand. "That's quite all right, Mr. Harlow. You come and see my supply officer tomorrow, young lady. Nine sharp."

Amelia was up at six. By eleven she knew approximately how much food it took to feed an army, and by one she was turning south out of Mount Pleasant, pushing the green roadster down the bumpy dirt road that led to Eustice Jarvis' thousand-acre spread. Short and squat, with a thick head of long, curly white hair, he was known universally as "Pappy" and he was the biggest rancher around. His main crop was wheat, his livestock were cattle and pigs and turkeys, and his voice a deep, rolling roar of welcome as Amelia pulled up to the back door.

"Prettiest piece of goods in East Texas!" Pappy bellowed. "Just in time for a steak or two. Light and set, honey. Light and set."

She was home by six. The Jarvis hands would butcher

a hundred head of cattle and fifty hogs, and Pappy Jarvis would hold ninety turkeys for Thanksgiving.

"Plucked?" she'd asked.

"Ready to cook," he'd promised.

"It's going to work," she announced over the dinner table that evening. "I think it's really going to work."

Carter Harlow's napkin slapped to the table; his chair scraped hard across the floor. "Busybody work, that's all it is—messin' with people, stirring things up. I don't like busybody women, Amelia. Never have."

"We're at war," Amelia said, her voice shaking. "I want to help. It's not just Will's war. It's my war too." But Carter Harlow had stalked from the room.

She never spoke to Carter Harlow of her work again and he never asked. Evangeline stayed away from the food service out of deference to her husband, but she was proud of Amelia, and the Reverend Mrs. Claude Pack was thrilled. Dotty's dimpled little hands reached for Amelia's across the Packs' kitchen table the next morning and squeezed them tight. "Honey," she said, "that's about the best idea yet. Just the other day I was thinking that if I had to look one more sock in the eye I was going to be downright *sick.*"

So the Liberty Circle went into the volunteer food business. The food came in—sides of beef and pork from Pappy Jarvis, hundred-pound sacks of flour from the Mount Pleasant mill, fifty-pound sacks of potatoes and carrots and corn and peas from the farms that circled Earth. Through September and October and into November the food went out. The military bureaucracy was mind-boggling, the paperwork almost overwhelming, but the food went out—in vats of stews and soups and troughs of barbecued ribs, in sheets of bread and twenty-quart kettles of greens.

Thanksgiving was a triumph of Jarvis turkey and local potatoes, buttered carrots and corn pudding. Christmas was beef and beans and two hundred sweet-potato pies. The Easter of 1918 was ham and applesauce, collard greens and Dotty Pack's own black-eyed peas. And Amelia Harlow, twenty years old that spring, her feet aching, her body sore and sticky with sweat, leaned against a post in the mess tent by the railroad tracks at the edge of town, lusting for a cup of coffee she was too bone-tired to go and get. She was amazed by it all sometimes, how far she'd traveled and how much she'd changed. She felt like a woman now, not a wide-eyed bride, and she liked the change. There was a new assurance inside her, and the sense somehow that she was real.

She reached up to rub an aching shoulder and then watched as the fifteen members of the Liberty Circle's Easter shift came from the kitchen, their faces breaking into smiles at the chorus of "Thank you, ma'ams" welling up from the recruits filing by. The line of soldiers stretched all the way around the tent, and waiting out in the spring evening there were more. They looked young to Amelia, far younger than the men who'd gone marching out of town nearly a year ago. They looked like boys, five hundred boys with empty stomachs and clumsy boots and doughboy caps tucked neatly under their young arms. Five hundred boys ripe for their graves in the fields of Europe.

She shook her head and cleared the thought away. You couldn't think like that. If you did, you'd never be able to go on. And you had to go on. Everybody knew that.

Major Fitzsimmons was waving at her from two aisles away and raising his coffee cup in a congratulatory toast. She smiled and waved back, then cocked her head. A spring drizzle drummed softly on the roof of the tent. The cropped heads of the boys filing in now were damp and somewhere out in the dusk some of them began to sing:

> Oh, we'll hang the Kaiser
> On a sour apple tree . . .

It was May when Mary Cherry from the telephone and telegraph office brought Amelia the yellow envelope. She brought it to the house herself, but no one at the Harlow breakfast table would touch it, so she put it down among the willow plates and went away. It lay there on the shining oak surface until Carter Harlow finally sliced it open. He looked at it for a long time and then passed it to Amelia. The War Department regretted to inform her that Captain Will Harlow, M.D., Forty-Second Division Medical Corps, was missing in action and presumed dead.

Amelia didn't cry then. The tears came later, alone in the room that belonged to her and Will. She pulled his pillow into her arms and sobbed dry, wracking sobs. Then, tearing herself away from its mocking comfort, she flung the pillow across the room. It hit the vase of flowers sitting on the table by the window, smashing the china to bits.

In the fall the rest of her world disappeared.

The influenza epidemic started at Fort Riley, Kansas, four hundred miles to the north. It rolled from army base to army base on the wheels of military transport trains and snaked around the globe on troop ships and barges. It came to Texas at Galveston on the *Hiram Walker,* a steamship out of Tampico Bay, arriving in Earth on a night train in September of 1918. They quarantined the army camp on the edge of town, but it didn't matter.

Two days later Evangeline spoke vaguely of a headache. The next morning Amelia found her kneeling over the chrysanthemums in her rock garden, her eyes glazed, her trowel poised in her hand. Amelia took the trowel and helped her stand, and together they walked toward the house.

More than any of them, the war had changed Evangeline. She'd gone on, preparing meals and taking care of her garden and her boys, politely inquiring of her husband if he'd had a good day. She never laughed, rarely smiled, and her face, once so open, had hardened and closed. She never spoke of Will after the telegram came but she did that morning as she lay against a pillow on the long Victorian sofa in the front parlor, her hand in Amelia's. "He was such a happy little boy," she said softly. "That's what I remember most about Will."

The parlor was dark, the curtains pulled against the bright, hot day, the floral prints on the wall almost lost in the shadows. A screen door banged, bare feet sounded across a bare floor. Another door banged and then it was still.

"I remember he'd get up in the morning singing songs," she went on, a small smile in the corner of her mouth. "'Old Black Joe' was his favorite the year he was three, and I thought I'd go crazy before he learned something else." Her hand tightened around Amelia's. "Such a happy little boy. And you made my son a happy man. Thank you for that."

Amelia felt a sob clutch her throat, choking her voice. "He'll come back," she whispered. "You'll see."

Evangeline's head turned, her eyes glazed in tears. "No he won't," she said. "I thought you knew that, child."

They stared at each other for a moment, and then Evangeline smiled, her face glistening with sweat.

Amelia didn't wait for the doctor to come. She drove to Daingerfield herself and pounded on his door with her fists. He followed her home and helped her move Evangeline upstairs that afternoon.

Amelia and Carter Harlow worked over her in shifts for the next two days. At midnight of the third day Carter knocked on Amelia's door, his face lined and gray, the collar of his shirt hanging open on one stud.

"She's dead."

Amelia stared up at him. The floor seemed to open under her, sucking her into a long tunnel of nothingness. "She's dead, Amelia." She tried to focus on her father-in-law and finally saw him, a big man suddenly helpless, the heart of him gone. The heart of all of them was gone.

Numb with loss, she followed Carter Harlow down the hallway toward the light spilling from the open door at the other end of the narrow passage.

They buried Evangeline in the cemetery in the pine hills above town. More than six hundred of their neighbors were sick with the flu now and Carter Harlow, his two young sons, and his daughter-in-law stood alone at the side of the grave they'd dug by themselves.

The town opened the courthouse to the sick and dying the next day. Whole families moved in, and the doctor came again, but he didn't know where it came from or when it would go away. No one knew anything, he told Amelia Harlow, except that it was deadly for old people and children, pregnant women and people with kidney and heart disease. He shook his head, his useless medical bag in his hands.

"I called Dallas," he told her when she followed him out to the steps of the courthouse to demand something, anything more. "I called twice. I called San Francisco. But the big cities are worse off then we are. They can't even find people willing to bury the dead."

"But there are specialists," she insisted. "Did you . . ."

"I know there are specialists, Mrs. Harlow. I know that." He looked into her eyes and saw they had grown small and hard with hurt and anger. "Somebody said a man from the East has a theory that it's carried at night. Maybe sunlight will help, if you want to believe that." He shrugged and went to his car and drove away.

She did want to believe. It was the only hope anyone offered, and every morning she was up at the first sign of daybreak to dress and drive to the courthouse, to pull back the shutters and capture the sun.

She drove down through a deserted town, drove back home through a deserted town. The press was shut and the stores and the bank had closed down. Sunday services were discontinued. The school didn't open at all. Earth, Texas—its men, its women, its children—lay in the courthouse. They lay in the wide front hall, in every office, in the judge's chambers, and on the benches lining the gallery.

Dotty Pack died, her hands reaching for Amelia's, her eyes round with surprise. The Reverend went the next day. Jake Matthews came in from his Sugar Hill bar, but he didn't make it through the night. Samuel Farrier from the post office died and so did Eb Graves from the press, crying for the sons who brought him into the front hall of the courthouse and then quietly left town.

Dozens left, then dozens more, but there was no place to go. Perryman Carr went to a cabin he kept for hunting in the hills and came back a day later, afraid to die alone. He was the last of the people Amelia had grown to know well and she nursed him through the nights, trying to hold on in some way to a saner, older world. She sat by him as he wheezed and coughed and cried out in panic. She wiped the spittle from his lips, cleaned his aging, fever-ridden body time and time again, and held his head when he threw up the green bile. She was repulsed by his frailty and drawn to his agony, comforted in some obscure way by the nightmares that plagued his few hours of sleep. Those nightmares were normal and somehow made the other one, the one that had taken over all the days and nights, feel less insane.

He was calmer on the third night and talked coherently for the first time in days. "I think it's over, Amelia," he said. "I think I've beaten it." An hour later he was dead.

Carter Harlow brought the boys in toward dawn of that day. They didn't recognize her by then and they died within a few hours of each other. Amelia was curled on the floor between them, smiling wistfully as the sun came bursting through the tall windows, splashing down the hall.

There were no more coffins, so she and her father-in-law swaddled the small bodies in fresh sheets, then walked beside the wagon that took them down to the railroad tracks. They lifted the bodies out themselves and then gently placed them on the stacks waiting for the new supply of coffins due in from Dallas next week.

It began the next day. Amelia saw it first in his eyes and the staggering twist of his body over hers in the house she now shared only with her father-in-law. He was disintegrating and it frightened her, but she let him mourn alone in the back parlor with his bourbon and his cigars and the fresh memories of his dead.

But Carter Harlow, his chair pulled close to the fireplace with its Confederate flag and its Confederate musket above—Carter Harlow wasn't thinking of the fresh dead. He was thinking of a past that had never died.

He was almost four when he saw his father for the first time. He'd been playing on the back porch when he heard his mother cry out. "It's your father. Your father's home." And they'd run down the hill toward the horse and rider that even now he could still see before him.

Part of him knew that the man must have been tired, that the horse must have been half dead. But in his imagination it wasn't like that. The horse he saw was fresh, pounding out of the Georgia pines in a spray of rich red earth. The flag was fresh. The soldier was fresh. His uniform was gray and sharp-creased, spangled and splashed with colonel's medals. His father pulled him into his arms and there was the smell of victory and sweat and glory. Carter saw the little boy carry the musket and the bright Confederate flag back to the house—carry them all the way to Texas where they hung now, over the massive stone fireplace in the back parlor of the house at the edge of Earth.

Carter jerked at the bourbon bottle and then set it back on the floor. He rolled the bourbon around in his mouth and once again swallowed the old, old shame.

The soldier from the woods swung off the horse, pulling the woman up into his arms, then the boy. There was the smell of sweat, the sudden, overpowering smell of his own fear, and then the little-boy urine splashing down his legs. He'd squealed and sobbed and pulled away from the stranger with the strange smells. "What's the matter with that boy?" his father said. "Come on back here." He pushed the musket and the flag into his small, thin arms and made him carry them, stumbling, up the hill. Carter Harlow could still hear the damning voice in his ears. "We'll make a man of him yet, that boy."

The musket and the tattered, faded flag came West in a trunk and they hung wherever Carter Harlow lived, bright with the past.

He tried. The town his father founded needed a newspaper and it needed a doctor, and he gave both. He even tried to go to war once, but Teddy Roosevelt was halfway up San Juan Hill by the time he shipped out, and the Spanish-American War, eight weeks old that summer of 1898, died a month later. Instead, he'd loaned his own son to war, and found that the loan was a gift.

Of a son.

Two sons. Three sons.

Of a wife. And a doctor, schooled in the best medicine money could buy, who could have—no, would have saved them all, and saved the town Justiss Harlow had made on the land. Carter Harlow pulled on the bourbon again, drowning the irony and the pain and the loss and the failure.

But there was no drowning the other irony—of the

girl who had survived them all. He scratched back,
trying to remember how long he'd known about her.

He'd always been curious. A stranger like that, with
no family, no one at all, suddenly coming into his
family like that. Evangeline said it made no difference,
but it made a difference to him: blood always made a
difference. So he'd sent one of the boys from the press
that first summer Will was off at war. Fred Billings.
He'd sent Fred Billings on a news story about Louisiana and asked him to drop by the city hall in New
Orleans and pick up a copy of the girl's birth certificate.
Except there was no birth certificate. He shrugged and
told Fred to forget about it, that there was a mistake,
but then he'd hired a detective out of Dallas to go find
out why.

He'd found out all right, hadn't he, and it sure as hell
did matter—blood like that.

Carter Harlow sat in his chair before the flag and
musket in the back parlor, the cigar butts piling up, the
bourbon bottles stacking up, rolling across the rug,
clattering into the corner. The sun rose and set, rose
again, the soldier came pounding out of the Georgia
woods, and Carter Harlow kept trying to forget his final
failure—a daughter-in-law who was a whore.

It was on the morning of the third day that Amelia
knocked at the parlor door and came in. Sickened by
the smell and the mess, she began to open the windows
wide.

"Leave it."

She turned. "I've fixed breakfast for you. Eggs and
bacon. And griddle cakes." There was no response.
"You should eat, you know you should. Please come."

He shook his head, and then looked up at her from
the armchair. "Steak," he mumbled.

"Everything's ready now. Warm in the oven. Please
come."

"I want steak."

"I already made the griddle cakes, and the bacon and eggs. Could I make you a steak for supper? Would you like that?"

"Do what I say. Now." He lurched out of the chair, stumbling through the bottles and cigar stubs.

"Stop it!" she screamed. *"Stop it. You reek!"*

She screamed out of fear and rage. Then she ran, slamming the door behind her.

"Amelia!"

Carter Harlow's voice caught her on the dogtrot porch. He stood at the parlor door, his eyelids heavy, his eyes red, but his voice was a hard, clear roll. "You'll do what I say. Now. This is my house and you live on here by my grace."

She stared at him. Stood on the dogtrot porch and stared at him in the shadow of the parlor door.

He wouldn't have to push her into the kitchen. He was right. The house was his, and the acres out back, the newspaper. All of it. She had nothing, he owed her nothing. She lived on here by his grace.

She cooked the steak.

She cleared away the eggs and bacon and griddle cakes, dipped the steak in egg and milk and flour the way Evangeline did, and threw it in a hot pan. She warmed a willow plate, piled it with cold potatoes, then slipped the steak in place and set it on the oak table beside the fresh linen napkin and the fork. She added a knife, salt and pepper shakers, the red chili sauce, and then she went up to her room, locked the door, and sat very still for a very long time.

It was almost dusk before she remembered the green roadster sitting by the front gate, and finally knew that she would go. She ripped clothes from hangers and shelves and hooks, wadding them into the wicker case with the striped ribbon handles. She shut the wardrobe door and then remembered the letters. She glanced over at the bedside table. The letters sat beside it in their basket, and she gathered them up in two fistfuls, stuffed them into the suitcase, then strapped it up and headed down the hall toward the stairs.

Carter Harlow sat at the oak table in the big room at the bottom of the staircase. His bottle of bourbon was empty and the steak was untouched. He glanced up, watching her come down the stairs.

She was at the bottom of the staircase now, and even in the half light he could see those little breasts of hers pushing at him through the fabric of her dress, the thighs scissoring across the room, the little buttocks flashing past. He grabbed her at the door.

She froze. She let the suitcase drop to the floor, and then, mesmerized by a sudden sick-animal refusal to see or hear or understand, she stared at the hand gripping her arm, at the blunt, heavy fingers that went inching in and out of the buttons along the bodice of her dress.

"You're not going anywhere, young lady." His smile was certain, his voice soft. "Not going anywhere." She gazed blindly at a bare breast, at the hand with the broken, dirty fingernails that reached up to his mouth and came away wet, to cup the flesh, twist the nipple into a damp, pink knot. His head bent, and she ran.

Raced up the stairs, her dress tangling and snarling around her legs, her sobs choking her, her breath shrieking in her ears. She stumbled—heard his steps on the stairs behind her. She pushed herself up the last three steps, ran down the hall to the safety of her room, hurled through the door, and slammed it behind her. She turned to lock it—and saw Carter Harlow's foot already inside.

Cries of terror bubbled from her mouth and she pushed back on a door that slowly caved open and then suddenly swung wide. He stood in the doorway, one hand gripping the knife he'd taken from the table she'd set that morning.

The room seemed to swim for a moment in a little

pool of patchwork and blue paper shot through with yellow flowers, and then she was spread across the bed she'd shared with Will and the knife was slicing her dress away until she was naked before him. His fingers wound through her hair, holding her head back, then he slid the knife to the bedside table, unbuckled his belt, and told her about the detective. "I know what you are, honey. I know. And now you're going to know too. Gonna know what you're good for and what we do with girls like you."

He smiled, his fingers winding tighter through her hair, forcing her to watch as he reached inside his trousers and pulled himself free. He ripped her thighs wide, bent his mouth to her mouth. She seemed to come alive suddenly, bucking and jerking beneath him, and he felt himself stiffen. His hands dug into her breasts, then into her buttocks, raising them up off the quilt. He plunged into her, and didn't see her reach for the knife.

It took, it seemed, a long time for Carter Harlow to die. In some quarter of her mind she realized that that should surprise her, but it didn't. She'd unburied something of herself, a hard, nerveless energy older than the convent walls, older than memory. That surprised her, but nothing else did, not the time it took to make him die, and not the blood. It sprayed the walls, bubbled from his mouth, his throat, and finally pumped out with the urine in little geysers of flag red. It was still pumping when she left, stumbling downstairs wrapped in a blanket she found in the boys' room. She stood for a moment at the bottom of the stairs, waiting for the death sounds to quiet, and then she cleared the back parlor of his bottles and cigar butts, the kitchen table of his dishes. She slept ten hours on the porch swing, curled in a tight, sweaty ball, as still and silent as Carter Harlow above her.

The next morning she cleaned the blood from the

body and wrapped it in a shroud of patchwork and
clean linen sheets. It took an hour to drag him down the
long narrow hall to his room, and then she scrubbed
her own body with lye soap. She washed and brushed
her hair, pulled it back up on her head. She dug a fresh,
clean cotton dress out of the suitcase in the kitchen,
then rang the telephone and telegraph office to tell
them there was one more victim of the flu.

The wagon came at noon. She watched it creak up
the hill, and then down the hill, fading into the trees
lining the railroad tracks. She went upstairs again and
worked five hours to wash his blood from her mattress,
the walls, the bright Mexican carpets and the pine floor.
At dusk she gave up and doused Carter Harlow's house
with gasoline.

She doused each floor, each room, and methodically
lit match after match. She took nothing from Carter
Harlow, nothing from his house but her wicker suitcase. She set it down by the picket fence and turned to
watch.

There was only smoke at first, blackening the sky,
but somewhere inside willow plates were shattering,
and a hatbox from a shop in New Orleans was bursting
into flames. A rosewood headboard all the way from
Dallas was turning to ash. Blue wallpaper sprinkled
with yellow flowers was darkening with smoke, curling,
and Joey's butterflies were burning. Up in the attic the
treasures of Will's boyhood were dissolving in the heat
too. She'd always meant to go up one day, open the
trunk, see what Will had loved—and for a moment,
standing by the fence, it seemed possible that there
might still be time. Up the stairs, down the hall. She
would be quick; she'd take a broom to beat at the
smoke.

She was halfway up the front steps when the glass
panel on the front door exploded. Splinters of hot ice
went skidding across the porch, splashing her dress, her
hands, her face. It occurred to her that it should hurt,

that she should feel pain. And more distantly, as if she were peering at someone else from far, far away, that the girl on the burning porch must be going mad. She stumbled to the steps, felt the night air splash her face like cold water.

"It's yours."

"You belong."

"We'll make a Texan of you."

Lies. All of it. She hadn't understood until Carter Harlow made her see the truth. That she was nothing, that she'd been wrong to trust. He'd been the powerful one. Not Will, not Evangeline. They'd existed by his grace as she had. It was all his, even her. But she wasn't anybody's anymore. She would never belong to anyone again.

She wandered back to the open gate and watched through the night as the Harlow house burned, watched until there was nothing to see but the flames licking up against the dark, burning a red hole into the big Texas sky.

Dallas, Texas

October 1918

7

The epidemic raged on in the larger cities of the North, in Europe and Asia, beating its way to a final estimated death toll of twenty-one million lives. It picked up a name along the way—the "Spanish Lady"—and by the time it was over it was officially a pandemic, a devastation that killed a third as many as the Black Death that had wiped away the world of Europe's Middle Ages. People would say later that the Great War shot out all the lights that lit Europe and murdered a whole generation. The Spanish Lady was the last insult, the final ignominious blow.

It lasted only a week in East Texas, from the fourteenth through the twenty-first of September 1918, but it fell like an ax, chopping the month in half and leaving in its wake a deep hush and a change in the weather. First it occurred to people that it was almost cool, that summer was coming to an end, and then the sick began to get better and the dying stopped.

They began to pick up the pieces of their lives then, to bury their dead, to start fall harvests and open their shops, and tentatively, like skaters testing a fresh sheet

70

of winter ice, the children went back to school. Houses and farms were scrubbed and aired, and one weekday morning in the begirv ing of October a green roadster left the town of Earth with a young woman in the driver's seat, a wicker suitcase and a summer straw hat at her side. She drove west on Route 30, and then due south on a long, dusty ribbon of a road that took her to the outskirts of Dallas and then on into the center of the city.

It was almost noon when she arrived, and the storefront office she'd been looking for on Lamar Street was closed. She parked and waited across the way, watching the office for some sign of life. The sun climbed high, then higher, and the office, sandwiched between a sleepy drugstore on one side and an empty clothing emporium on the other, sank into the shadows.

Nearly two hours later, a short, stocky figure wearing a black suit, string tie, and Western boots came ambling along the empty sidewalk. His head was bare, and though his hair was thinning and his face drawn, he looked younger than she'd expected. Thirty, she guessed as she watched him pull a chain from his pocket and unlock the door.

She waited a minute, then walked quickly across the street. The sign on the door—"Benedict & Benedict, Attorneys at Law"—was small and the paint was beginning to peel. She bent to examine it, knocked and then knocked once again.

"S'open," a voice hollered through the glass door. She almost jumped. It was the loudest voice she'd heard in a week.

"It's open! Come in."

She pushed and walked in.

It was a long, narrow room. The reception area with its single desk and wooden chairs sat dusty and empty, and there was only the young man in the black suit to occupy the book-lined space beyond. He stood with a scrape of his chair and an arm raised, waving her in. She leaned back against the door and pressed it shut.

Clayton Benedict watched a girl in a pale summer dress and wide summer hat, a wicker suitcase in her hand, cross the reception area and swing through the half-gate. Her hair was pale, and the long strands curled free around her face. She looked very young, sixteen perhaps—and then suddenly far older as she approached his desk. Her eyes sat like bright stones in her head and there was a high tilt to her chin. And there was something else—an icy energy to her as she clipped across the floor. It made him aware of his own exhaustion and of the dust and clutter his secretary's death had left behind. She'd died in the epidemic, and he hoped suddenly that the young woman was job hunting, and if she wasn't, then whoever she was, he hoped she'd come back a different day.

"Mr. Benedict?"

"Yes, ma'am. Can I help you?"

"Davis Benedict?"

"Nope. Clayton. My father was Davis, but he's been dead a while now. I never bothered to change the listing on the door.

Silence. And then, "Oh."

"You counted on seeing him?"

"Your name wasn't in the files, but I suppose it doesn't matter. You do handle his business now, is that right?"

The hope of a new secretary disappeared, but he resisted the urge to send her away.

"That's right." He pulled his own chair up and sat, indicating the sounder of the two chairs opposite the desk. "And you're Miss? Mrs.?"

"Mrs." She slid into the seat, sitting ramrod straight on the edge, gazing at him with her glittery eyes. "Mrs. Will Harlow, from Earth, Texas."

The Harlow name was vaguely familiar and he

nodded, fishing for help. "What did I hear recently? That . . ."

"I suppose you heard that my husband's dead, Mr. Benedict. He went to war and now he's dead. They're all dead, all of the Harlows. Except me."

Her voice sounded hard and a little bitter.

"The flu, you mean?"

"It took them all. My father-in-law, his wife, their younger sons. Half the town of Earth is dead, Mr. Benedict."

He nodded again. "I see. If you can wait a minute, I'll try and find the files."

"Thank you. That's why I came."

They were old and dusty and he'd looked through them only once before, five years ago maybe, right after he'd come home from the University of Texas law school. He stood at the file cabinets to rifle through the papers, and found his notes—a minor matter involving the purchase of some interest in an oil field. He remembered Carter Harlow distinctly now and he returned to his desk, flipped back to the front of the file, and began to read. He scanned the pages quickly while scratching notes on a yellow legal pad. It wasn't a thick file and it didn't take long, and when he finally glanced up she was as before, ramrod straight and waiting.

"A couple of questions, Mrs. Harlow."

She nodded.

"You have a marriage certificate, I assume?"

"Yes. Yes, I do." She reached for the suitcase, opened it on her lap, and slid several neatly folded documents across the desk. "I thought you'd need them all. There's the marriage certificate and his family's burial papers." She shut the suitcase and set it back on the floor.

"And his?"

She looked up. "His?"

"I'm sorry. I mean your husband's."

"My husband's?"

"Your husband went to war. He died over there, that right? Then there's something from the government or maybe the military. A notice of death, burial . . ."

"There's only the telegram from six months ago. All it says is that he's missing in action and presumed dead. But he's dead, Mr. Benedict. We always knew that."

He explained the estate then, watching that cool, pale little face with the glittery eyes. Carter Harlow had been a client of his father's for some twenty-five years. There'd been no business after Davis Benedict's death, and not much before either. The file contained title deeds to the land and the real estate in town, long-paid mortgages on the building that housed the *Bugle-Times*. There were corporation papers for the newspaper, bank papers, insurance policies, the oil stock Clayton had remembered, and a last will two years old. Nothing complex, nothing out of the ordinary.

"But the problem, Mrs. Harlow," he went on, "is that his last surviving relative inherits, and for the moment at least, until there's official word that he's dead, that's his son Will."

"And then," she asked. "What then?"

"Then I can do something for you. Unless there's some other claimant . . ."

She shook her head.

"Then basically it looks like it'll be yours."

"And in the meantime?"

He shrugged. "In the meantime, it's your husband's. The estate has an obligation to support you, house you, feed you, but other than that . . . Well, you're sort of in limbo for a while."

"Limbo," she said. "Limbo is a state without grace, Mr. Benedict," and she smiled. "I went to school with nuns, so I know. It's practically at the very gates of hell."

He smiled too, warming to her. "It's not that bad. It just means you can't legally remarry or . . ."

She shook her head. "What I need to know, Mr. Benedict, is can I run the newspaper from your limbo?"

It was out now, why she'd come. The newspaper felt right, had always felt right, ever since she got used to the idea that it might be hers, just for the taking. There was no one to tell her now that she wasn't a Harlow. They were all dead, except her.

"Run the newspaper, Mrs. Harlow?"

He was staring at her, but she only stared back, silent as a stone. A car passed on the street outside, backfiring once, and then it was quiet again.

He pushed his chair back, swung first one boot to the desk, then the other, but Clay Benedict couldn't read that face any better than he could when she'd first walked in. Fragile, hard, too young, too old. A question occurred to him and he ran a hand through his hair.

"You even twenty-one yet, Mrs. Harlow?"

She shook her head. "Does it matter?" Her voice was suddenly very small.

He shrugged. "Maybe not. But look, I don't know what the financial situation is yet, but if things are bad, well . . ." He shrugged again and hooked his thumbs through his belt. "Maybe I could find a buyer for the *Bugle.* Dealy over at the Dallas *Morning News,* maybe he'd take it off your hands, give you fair value, more or less. Do you want me to look into that?"

She shook her head. "I'll run it, Mr. Benedict."

"Mind telling me what you want to do that for?"

He waited for an answer, but there was none and finally he went on. "Look, why not just take it easy for a while, Mrs. Harlow? Stay on in the house . . ."

"There is no house, Mr. Benedict. It burned, right down to the ground." There was a small curl to her mouth and something odd in her voice, triumph maybe, or a challenge, but he couldn't be sure.

"So where you hanging that hat of yours these days, Mrs. Harlow?"

"The *Bugle* office." Her head tilted again in that hard little way. "I like it there. And I intend to stay."

She wasn't smiling now, but he was, smiling at her with a big, wide grin. "You know what, Mrs. Harlow?" And he laughed out loud. "It sounds to me like they'll have to burn that joint down too, just to get you outta there. That right?"

"That's right, Mr. Benedict." She nodded. "That's precisely right."

"Look," he finally said, "it's fine with me." He grinned again. "Want a lawyer?"

"Will you, Mr. Benedict?" She was very earnest now, almost shy. "I know I need help. I do know that."

"Lady, do you ever. Better stick with me while I'm still cheap."

She was almost happy that afternoon in Dallas, for the first time in all those months.

Clayton Benedict checked her into the Adolphus on Commerce Street and suggested dinner later, at eight. She nodded and said goodbye. An elderly black bell-hop in a scarlet uniform took her up to her second-floor room, opened the door with a flourish, and ushered her in. Then she was alone, and every ounce of energy, all the tension wiring her together, was gone.

She'd survived Carter Harlow's attorney and his inquisitive stare. A part of her had been terrified of Mr. Clayton Benedict, that he would suspect somehow, then order the body unburied and know what she had done. But he hadn't suspected, hadn't even laughed at her plans.

She doused her face with cold water, splashed her neck, her dress. She had three, nearly four hours to herself, and she wanted to spend it all here, in the luxury of this room.

The soft, thick pastel carpet was dotted with pretty

chairs with fine, slender legs. Ornate oak moldings framed pale walls, and a telephone sat on the desk. "Room service," read the printed card alongside. "Housekeeper." There was a separate number for each, and down at the bottom a line that read: "Maid. We Kindly Request She Draw Your Bath."

She smiled and called them all. Room service for lemonade, the housekeeper to press out her best dress, the maid to draw a hot scented tub in the black-and-white tile bath. It felt rich and elegant and civilized, like a satin cushion at the end of the fifty-mile-long highway that brought her into Dallas that morning.

She had driven through towns she'd never heard of, towns called Fate and Lone Oak, small towns dotting a land that was bigger, vaster, flatter, and more over-whelming than she'd imagined from the pine hills of Earth. She'd never left the pine hills before, and the evidence of destruction startled her. The burnt-out pastures of land hadn't seen rain for more than a year; farms were abandoned by death, only dogs left to bark alone. Thin cattle bleated in the fields, and town streets lay deserted except for old men checking their watches and young women with children on their arms, their husbands still overseas or already dead.

She longed for Earth then, for the easier cup of the land and the small patchwork of streets where she had grown up and come into her own. She wanted a place for herself there, and knew now, as she luxuriated in the scented blue water of a bath at the Adolphus, that she had one.

It had been so simple, really—walking up the stairs of the *Bugle* office that first morning after the fire, on through the pressroom, all the machines lying there, silent and useless. Only the teletype chattered away, oozing yards and yards of news-service bulletins across the floor. She thought how odd it was that the world hadn't stopped or even paused in its own dying.

There was no discernible genesis to the idea that she

would put the machines to use herself. She'd gone on
back to Carter Harlow's office and rummaged through
the files until she'd found the detective's report on her
that she'd come for in the first place. She sat down
then—in Carter Harlow's chair in Carter Harlow's
office with his name on the door and his machines in the
room beyond—simply to rip the report up and take a
piece of her own life. She walked back out a moment
later realizing that she could take possession of everything that had been his.

She wanted it then, for the revenge, and simply
because it was there. She wondered later if she'd have
felt the same if he'd run a ranch or a flour mill. But she
didn't know. She'd never know and it didn't matter.
She'd done what she had done, and she would go on
doing what she had to do to keep it, hold it, and make it
her own.

It seemed to Clayton Benedict that the young woman
who joined him for dinner that evening at eight was
remarkably more relaxed than the one who'd appeared
in his office that afternoon. The glittery eyes seemed
softer now and her iciness had melted into a quick,
bright manner that had its charm. She wore a soft-
dove-gray dress that was high at the neck and scalloped
with lace at the hem. The headwaiter at the Adolphus
dining room bowed in admiration, seating them at a
table where the glow of a small rose-shaded lamp suited
her well. She looked lovely there against the deep red
silk of the walls and the hard black shine of the window
panes beyond. To his amusement she was entranced by
the other diners, her eyes dancing around the room.
The menus came, and when he asked if she would like
him to order for them both, he was amused again when
she nodded and said, "I haven't the faintest idea how to
begin. I've never been in a real restaurant before."

He ordered vichyssoise and sautéed shrimp, a bottle
of white French wine, and entertained her over dinner

with stories of his boyhood, of wanting to be a lawyer like his father, of his sister who lived in Paris.

"Paris, France?"

"No," he laughed. "Paris, Texas."

Then he told her about the other Paris and the European trip he'd taken before the war to Italy and Germany, England and France. But he stopped suddenly, remembering that Europe for her wasn't just a storybook land.

"I'm sorry," he said. "That was a little thoughtless."

"That's all right. I don't mind." But she did. Her face seemed to harden almost imperceptibly and he changed the subject, slipping the conversation around to the *Bugle-Times* and her plans for the future. He asked questions, took notes, and left two hours later with the promise that he would start first thing next morning.

He began with phone calls to the war office in Washington, the probate courts in Austin, and to the State Bank of Earth for Carter Harlow's cash assets, a reassuring hundred thousand dollars and loose change.

The next calls were more difficult, consuming three hours and requiring dozens of long-distance connections that led him in and out of the old German settlements scattered to the south of Austin.

"I got a client here," he explained over and over. "Newspaper lady from Earth, Texas. Lost a lot of men in the epidemic." Then there would be the condolences, the trading of death tolls, the Texas talk, and finally they'd get back to the point.

"She says she's set on a young German-speaking fellow. Master printer, man by the name of Liepman, Ernst Liepman."

And then, time after time, "No sir. Sorry, that's all we got. Just a name."

By the time she arrived for the lunch appointment they had set, he was convinced it wouldn't work.

"But it has to work," she said, her eyes big under the shadow of her hat. She extracted the letter of inquiry she'd found buried in Carter Harlow's files and told him once again the story of the German printer who'd been rescued from the mob by the sheriff and a south-bound train.

"A south-bound train," she said. "I'm sure it was a south-bound train and I'm sure he's still in Texas, somewhere. And see?" She read from the list at the bottom of Ernst Liepman's letter—the New York *Record*, Atlanta *Tribune*, Mergenthaler, Dexter, flatbed, perfector. "He can operate all of those machines. And I don't want anyone else. I want him. He'll be loyal. You understand."

He understood. It was shrewd of her to hire someone weaker, more vulnerable than she.

After another day of phone calls, Ernst Liepman was found working in a restaurant in the small German community of New Braunfels. He came to Dallas by train the following day, a man in his thirties with a cap pulled low over his head who stepped, tentatively, into the station where they sat waiting.

His manner was formal and his fine-boned face almost elegant. He listened in silence as the man named Benedict introduced him to Amelia Harlow and explained about the pressroom that was nearly deserted and the job as manager waiting for him.

"And the name of the paper?" he asked.

"The *Bugle-Times*, Mr. Liepman." It was Amelia Harlow who replied. "A weekly in the town of Earth, just north of here."

He frowned. "I was there." And then, "Yes, I was. You will forgive me, Mrs. Harlow. I don't think I will go back."

"Mr. Liepman, I know what happened and I'm sorry. It won't happen again. I promise."

He smiled, his small mouth curving into a bitter little grin. "You are very nice. You are also very young. You have a private army perhaps? Someone to protect your presses from the mobs?"

"Things are different now, Mr. Liepman. Almost a quarter of the people are dead. The people who are left, they're different now too. It will never be the same."

She was very earnest and she was offering him a job.

It had been a long time since he had had a job. He had lost his position at the Atlanta *Tribune* when war broke out, and moved from town to town looking for another, making his way west through town after town. When America went to war, it became so brutal that only his own disbelief that America could be anything but good pushed him on. He'd tried to understand. They were a young people of course—and like children, refusing to give up their good German frankfurters and calling them Liberty Dogs instead. Americans were very young and very personal about their wars.

He learned to play dumb, do the odd job, and get by. Once he'd written fifty letters to fifty papers all across Oklahoma and Texas—letters winging into nothingness, letters unanswered, letters convincing him that he didn't exist. And now here she was with one of those letters. And a job.

A Texas job. Texas had been the worst at first, and then, oddly enough, it became his haven. No one back home in Cologne had ever heard of the Texas villages full of Germans who spoke in the old ways, growing rich in the American way. He'd planned to stay on in the restaurant in New Braunfels, until she offered what he'd traveled all those miles to find. A newspaper. And a job.

He smiled, suddenly glad.

"I would be honored, Mrs. Harlow. When will you need me?"

"Yesterday, Mr. Liepman," she said. "I believe I needed you yesterday."

She left Dallas the following day. She had seen nothing of the city, met no one, and remembered in the

end only one other person, a nameless bellhop who
came on brisk little legs to collect her bag when she left,
his smile bright in the round black face that appeared at
her door.

"Bags ready? For sure do hope you enjoyed your
stay."

She nodded and smiled back as he shifted the old
wicker bag with its ribbon handles up under one arm.
He was already halfway down the hall when she
suddenly remembered.

"Wait!" she called as she hurried after him. "I
forgot . . ."

"Forgot a bag, did we?" and he plowed back down
the hall.

"No, it's not that. It's . . ." and she stopped, helpless
with confusion.

He peered curiously at the young woman in the wide
hallway and suddenly understood.

"You worried about the tip—that's it, isn't it, little
lady?"

She nodded.

"You don't have to bother 'bout that. It's my pleasure, sure thing, nice lady like you."

"No, please. I want to know."

"Well now." He cast a glance down both directions
of the dim hall and then put her suitcase on the floor.
"You listen up good so you get it just right." He stood
in the corridor, proud in his bright red uniform, ticking
the items off on one hand.

"Five cents a bag, now that's the rule of thumb in
Dallas town. Trains, hotels, cabs, the lot. Ever go to
New York," he twinkled, "it's a dime. Nickel for any
staff might come around, couple of pennies extra for
the maid. On the bureau, usually, that ought to do.
And don't overtip, you hear?" He wagged his finger.
"People won't think you're fine."

"Thank you," she said. "Very much," and she bent

to her bag, taking a handful of change from her coin purse to distribute her first tips.

She left Dallas that afternoon and was home just before dark, sliding the green roadster to a halt in front of the *Bugle-Times*. The streets were nearly empty and the pressroom was quiet. She found a steel ruler on Carter Harlow's desk and then set to work prying his name off her office door.

8

Her German master printer arrived in Earth two days later, swinging off the train with his valise, eager to begin work in the pressroom she had scrubbed and whitewashed and cleaned. It was a skeleton staff for the moment. Old Fred Billings, managing editor during Carter Harlow's days, was still struggling with the last of the flu, but he wished Amelia luck and said that when the going got a little easier and he could pull himself out of bed, he'd come on down, offer a little advice. Liepman shrugged off his absence and Amelia herself wasn't sorry. It seemed more exciting to start all over, all new except for the two boys, Jimmy Bob and his cousin Pete. They were fifteen and sixteen, freckle-faced and doubtful about their future under a woman, but glad for the work, glad to be back.

The problem, Liepman said, wasn't staff. The problem was that a quarter of the population of Earth itself was dead, and nearly as many ranchers and farmers in the surrounding hills. Circulation figures were going to go down and so would advertising until shops opened under new management. The figures would be disastrous unless Mrs. Harlow found new subscribers and new advertising in other shops and stores in other towns.

They sat in her newly whitewashed office by the black

gum tree, its leaves already wine red with the fall. She would have to expand, Ernst Liepman went on, and publish her newspaper for every village she could distribute to during the narrow forty-eight-hour period in which the *Bugle*'s weekly dateline would be fresh.

She had to have more newsboys, more advertisers and subscribers. She had to have paper and ink and news, and she had to have them all now.

"Now?" she whispered.

Liepman's small hands spread wide in apology. "Five days? A week at most, and then something must come off the press." He was stunningly, awesomely calm.

"I'd thought a month or two."

"No, no, Mrs. Harlow. Newspapers, you see— they're a habit, not a necessity. Like candy. A reader loses the habit, or picks up another—perhaps another newspaper from some other town. Then you have lost your subscriber, sometimes for life."

She nodded again, mute with the knowledge, too terrifying to share, that the last edition of the *Bugle* was by now nearly a month old.

The only reassurance Liepman offered was the news. There was news to print. There were lists of the dead and stacks of news-service reports, more than they could shape into a first issue. But nothing, no solution or reassurance, made the task ahead seem anything but overwhelming. She pushed back her chair and stood, galvanized with panic. "What do I do, Mr. Liepman?"

"The older boy?"

"Petey?"

"Yes. This Petey will be thrilled to get the coroner's list. It will make him a reporter for a day. I will organize for the run, the paper, the press."

"And me? What do I do, Mr. Liepman?"

He eyed the old black skirt she wore, her plain white blouse. "You have a pretty dress. Something blue, I think. And your nice hat. I would put them on, Mrs.

Harlow. I would put them on and get in your green car and go get the ads."

"Do I just . . . ask?"

"Ask. Or beg."

"Beg? I couldn't ever . . ."

"Oh yes, Mrs. Harlow. If it comes to it, I would beg."

She drove back to the frame house on Magnolia where she'd taken a room and twenty minutes later set out in her blue dress and wide straw hat to search, ask, beg for ads. First she visited the old advertisers in Earth, and then new ones, hunting them out in Mount Pleasant and Daingerfield, in Omaha, Naples, Sugar Hill.

She devoted her days to that, and in the evenings, long into the night, she sat with Petey in the office, driving him and driving herself through the completion of the lists of the dead and then on to the front-page story on the Armistice due at any time. Liepman set the front-page type, murmuring over the machine like a man going slightly mad. The first version was too long, the second three inches too short. She cursed the day Fred Billings fell sick. She cursed the glue pot that went empty as she cut a wire service insert into a galley proof. She cursed her own ignorance of politics—and blessed Jimmy Bob for typing up a list of the Allies, hammering it finally to the wall so she'd know who they were.

There was one ad hole left, and reluctantly, regretting Perryman Carr's death more sharply than the rest, she went for the first time to the drugstore on Main Street that had been his.

It had seemed sometimes like another kind of spring as she made her daily journeys through the towns of the pine hills. Shops were coming back to life with familiar faces and interesting new ones. A gentle and more vigorous young pastor from the North had arrived to take Reverend Pack's place at the church. A new postmaster filled the space next to Mary Cherry at the telephone and telegraph office, and a big bruiser of a man named Billy picked up the back taxes on the Sugar Hill bar and would open it in November as a dance hall.

"Prohibition coming in sure as you're sitting there," he'd told her. "Just sure as shootin'. But I'll tell you what. That don't mean a man don't want a good time, now does it. And look—" He grinned at her, his blue eyes dancing, his big red hands spread wide over the bar. "Somebody sneaks a little gin in a baby bottle, say. Wants to maybe swig a drop or two in his coffee cup? Well, what the hell am I supposed to do? Can't call the sheriff in on a customer, now can I?"

"Billy," she said, her face as serious as the prohibition amendment itself, "all you have to do is let people know you're here and you are going to be rich. Now, quarter-page ad sounds about right, don't you think?" And she gazed directly at Billy's baby-blue eyes, her chin cupped in her hand, her notebook open on the bar. "A nice formal size for an opening announcement, wouldn't you agree?"

"In a big fancy box, sort of? With little curlicues at the edge?"

"Billy, curlicues all around."

But it felt sad walking into Perryman Carr's dry goods and drug store. The black-and-white tile floor seemed less bright and the wrong Carr face was behind the ice cream counter. He was old Perryman's only grandson, a young man in his early twenties, and he nodded when Amelia walked in.

"Howard," she smiled. "Nice to see you," and she slipped onto a high mahogany stool. "I'd love an ice cream soda."

He rummaged through the glasses and then proceeded through the ancient ritual of soda making with a hopeless lack of expertise, finally sliding the unappetizing concoction in her direction. "So, hear a lot about you, Amelia. Starting up again and all."

His face was long and slender like his grandfather's, and completely different in tone. It was a tight face, as unappealing, she decided, as his soda.

"Everybody's trying to start up again, aren't they, Howard? I hope you'll want to do as your grandfather did and advertise in the *Bugle*."

"I don't think so, Amelia. Tell you frankly, everybody knows who we are now, what with our being around all these years."

"I know how long the Carrs have been around, Howard."

"You should, Amelia. The families founded this town, didn't they, Carrs and Harlows both. A real nice town for white folks. The right kind of white folks."

She took another sip of her soda in silence, then pushed the heavy-stemmed glass, still half full, to the far edge of the counter. "And does somebody strike you as not right, Howard?"

There was no answer, so she provided her own.

"Maybe it's Mr. Liepman who strikes you as not right? Though I do assume you know he's been an American citizen for some time."

He busied himself behind the counter, emptying her glass, dipping it into soapy water, sorting straws.

"Well, Howard?"

"I just think I'd rather not say, Amelia. You run your business. I'll run mine."

"Into the ground, Howard? Is that what you plan to do?" Her body was rigid and her voice was like ice. "Because I'll tell you right now, Howard. There's a new dry goods store opening in Daingerfield, twice the size of yours. Northerners, I believe. You know, Howard. Dirty Yankees?" She smiled, wishing suddenly to goad him into a screaming rage. "The pushy sort with an advertising schedule I'd be glad to review with you."

He turned his back. She opened her notebook with a satisfying pop.

"They plan half a page a week. Full page quarterly—that's winter, spring, summer and fall, Howard. Those will be illustrated ads for cut-rate bargain specials. We're discussing a Christmas insert and needless to say I'll be running a story on their store, a feature on the third page. Or shall I put in on the front page, Howard? Perhaps that will suit you even better?" She let her voice run sweet, deep Southern sweet, and smiled a sweet smile as he snapped around to stare at her.

"Stop advertising if you wish, Mr. Carr. As you say, you run your business and I'll run mine."

She left an unheard-of tip when she walked out, clipping smartly down the aisles in her best shoes, and felt an almost breathtaking rush of triumph when the copy for his ad came that afternoon: "Carr's Cotton Yardage. Available Now. Half Price."

They put the issue to bed that night. The four pages that rolled off press had the high, heady smell of ink and looked to her like the most beautiful thing she'd ever seen.

It always looked beautiful to her, that first edition. The *Bugle-Times* would change over the course of the next months, grow back to eight pages and then expand to twelve. It would fill with political stories and international news, stock prices and financial stories. There would be a women's page for the women who had changed with the war, as she had—a page filled with news about clothes and styles and time-saving appliances. There was a page of local announcements and notes about who was visiting in town. The ads were Amelia's private triumph, especially the full-page ads from the Yankee who owned the Daingerfield dry goods store, space she had to give away in the end at her own half-price bargain rate.

But nothing ever changed the wonder of that first edition. She had the front page framed and hung it in the area downstairs that became the lobby. Even when it was under glass, she could smell the rich smell of the ink as Ernst Liepman handed her the first pages of the final roll.

"Congratulations, Mrs. Harlow."

"Congratulations to you, Mr. Liepman."

It felt thick and substantial. It felt real, more real than she did now, even more real than the masthead line that read, "Amelia Bliss Harlow, Publisher."

And the citizens of Earth were proud—of the girl from New Orleans they took as their own, and of the town newspaper she'd raised, phoenix-like, from its grave. Most of them grew to admire her German master printer and forgot that he hadn't always been there, that Amelia Harlow hadn't always been there. They forgot the house that had been on the edge of town and the different world that had existed before the Great War. And months later, when the year turned and it was spring again and word came tap-tap into the telegraph office that Will Harlow was alive and well and whole and coming home, they gathered below the black gum tree to cheer and shout the news.

She sat alone behind closed doors at her desk, staring in disbelief at the telegram Ernst Liepman had handed her, willing the clack of the teletype to drown out the sounds from the street so she could think. Finally she went to them, through the pressroom, down the stairs to the street, crying with shock and grief at a god somewhere who was playing with her life, taking away and giving back, too late.

9

Will Harlow came home on a Saturday morning in May 1919. The high school band was there at the train station, and the notes of "The Yellow Rose of Texas" bobbed through the warm air as he stepped onto the platform. There was a welcoming committee of people who should have been familiar but weren't, and with an increasing sense of dislocation, he searched the faces for his wife and the family he had left behind. From the corner of his eye he saw two children emerge from the crowd and he turned, a smile on his mouth. But they were little girls with yellow roses in their arms. And then there was only Amelia.

She stepped forward, moving toward the man with the soft hair. He looked old, lost in the loose folds of his uniform, and she was suddenly aware that Captain Harlow, M.D., was thin, rail thin.

Their eyes locked, and for one split second they were what they had been—very young, very in love, a doctor and his bride. With the band loud in their ears, and the cries of the crowd urging them on, they moved along the platform and embraced with the knowledge that they were strangers.

They took a house on Jefferson Street and Will recuperated there. The war was rarely mentioned, never discussed, simply understood between them as an event that had changed who they were. For Will there would always be the aftereffects of the mustard gas and the memories—of boys blown to bits by hand grenades, scattered over the fields like debris; the scabrous wounds he couldn't treat; the filth; the noise; the exhaustion; the stench of death. They jerked him awake at night, shot him out of his pew at church one Sunday in a cold, stringy sweat. A child had dropped a prayer book and he was back again, in a filth-ridden medical camp tent over there.

He'd served in England and then Belgium and then France. There in a village outside Cambrai, in the massive German counterattack in November of 1917, he'd picked up a gun and joined the war. He inched, belly inch by belly inch, down a cobblestone street running with blood and loud with terror, and survived, though something in him died.

The Germans took him near the eastern border of France. Time stopped in the monotony of a prisoner-of-war camp, and then six months later, he was free.

He spent the months after Armistice in a hospital camp, one of a thousand anonymous half-lives somebody was trying to identify so he could be mustered out. He came home that spring and felt, once he arrived, like a victim of a severe amputation. He heard his little brothers' voices in the school yard, saw his mother on the streets of Earth, and watched Amelia with resentment. His energy was sapped. She flowed with it. Her visions were of the future, his were of the past.

She arrived home late in the evenings, occasionally after the woman she'd hired had served his dinner and gone. She came swinging up the sidewalk, too bright, too gay, and her talk wasn't of catalogs or the grocer or teas now. It was of the work she'd found for herself, of presses and paper and subscribers.

"Don't, Amelia," he finally said. "It's your plaything, not mine."

In his worst depressions he resented her use of the green roadster from New Orleans, and he watched it one evening from the porch of the Jefferson Street house as it came careening around the corner. She still drove like a bat out of hell, and the roadster looked like it, sputtering to a halt, its body covered with scratches, the fender bent, the running board sagging to the ground.

"Not four years old, and that car's just about had it, Amelia."

She came to sit beside him on the porch. "It's not too bad, is it?"

"Looks a bit like me, I'd say. Beat up."

"Oh, Will, that's not true." She knelt by his chair, his hand in hers. "All you need is a rest and you'll be fine." She turned to look at the roadster again, and then turned back to him, her eyes bright.

"We'll get a new car. Two new cars."

"Would you like a new husband too, Amelia?" He smiled.

She held his hand against her cheek, her eyes soft. "It's only an old car, Will. Old cars fall apart. Your body will heal. Just a little more time and you'll be fine."

"You think so, Amelia?"

He'd been home a month, sleeping beside her each night with his hand around hers, waiting to want her. And that night he wanted her again. He wanted time to go back, wanted to be young and whole again with a new medical degree and a new wife, wanted the moon to be full again in a star-filled Texas sky. He kissed her tentatively, gently, and felt her stiffen. He kissed her again savagely, and felt her jerk away. He reached for her, bearing down on her with all his hunger and all his hurt, pushing away her hands as he searched for her breasts and the dark sweetness hidden between her thighs. She was crying, begging him to stop, but he was begging too, needing her to respond. The need was suddenly huge and hard, sending him rummaging across her body, panting and pushing. She screamed as he entered, but he didn't hear, her cries drowned out by the pounding in his own head and his long, hard cry of relief. He slept, his head buried against hers in the pillow.

Amelia lay in the quiet, waiting for the dark to soothe her. She could feel his tears on her face and she reached a hand up to wipe them away. But everything ached and she let the hand drop, lay staring at the ceiling, willing the waves of pain and anger to go away.

The anger had come with Will's first kiss, demanding her response. Nothing he could have done would have made any difference. She knew that now. Not his old patience, or the half-remembered tenderness of the hands that began to teach her body its possibilities in those few nights before the war. It had been a fragile awakening, just a small beginning, and she knew now that too much had changed, that she wouldn't be able to go back. She reached out to pull the sheet up, then lay listening to the even breathing of the thin form stretched out at her side. She felt whole again now that it was over, and she had Carter Harlow's newspaper. She did have that. Her plaything now, Will had said. Hers.

Will woke again that night and made love to her again, his way into her body eased this time by the wetness he'd left inside. Amelia tried to remember the bed in his old boyhood room and all the colors in the patchwork quilt Evangeline had made for them.

Will was better by the spring of 1920. The physical pain receded and the war slipped away. He was absorbed now in the planning of a three-story clapboard house with a dozen wide steps leading up to a pillared run-around porch. He supervised the construction himself and watched it go up, plank by plank, just beyond the cottonwoods that backed the site of the old place. He saw it emerge, stark white against the raw land, and planted the first cottonwood of the grove that one day would bury the old foundations. In the fall he turned to his medical practice in the offices behind the church and began repairing the hurts and pains of the living.

Amelia devoted herself to the press. She gave it increasing energy now and saw, with her fine animal instinct for self-preservation, that radio could bring her empire tumbling down. The Dallas *Morning News* had a radio station. She wanted a radio station.

Clay Benedict applied for the license for station KLIP and Amelia met with a string of potential managers, finally settling on a red-cheeked young man from Chicago who wore big bow ties and seemed as frenetic as the decade itself.

"Interviews, that's the answer," said Richard Cooper. "On-the-street interviews. Coffee-shop interviews, right in town—that's your local interest stuff. See? National news comes from your AP, right? We just rip and read. A little church stuff on Sunday, talent shows for kids—let 'em sing 'Dixie,' see. And music. Real music from the Victrola records. Jazz. Ragtime. Ragtime's hot. Ever hear ragtime?"

"Yes," she laughed. "I know ragtime."

"That's right. Somebody said you came from New Orleans. It all started right there on Basin Street. Jazz, ragtime, blues. In the red-light district there—Storyville, you know?" He blushed and straightened his bow tie. "Well, you wouldn't know about a place like Storyville, Mrs. Harlow, but what a time that must have been. All that hot music playing right there on the streets. Am I sorry I missed that."

"Missed it, Mr. Cooper?"

"It's gone. They closed Storyville down, sometime during the war."

"Interesting," she said.

She gave away radio advertising time at first—an offer that brought them flocking in, and Pappy Jarvis was among them.

"Honey," he bellowed when he blew into her office from his Mount Pleasant ranch. "Gonna run for Congress, Amelia. Stinking Klan is coming back, people going crazy with the times. Don't like it. One bit."

He squeezed into a chair across from her desk, his

mane of hair flowing white, his black Stetson pushed back on his head,

"I want your support, you know, honey. A little time on that radio station of yours, or a nice editorial maybe. A feature story maybe, but only if you can see your way clear to it. I don't want to take advantage, you might say, or . . ."

"No, no, Pappy, that's fine. I'm glad to help."

"Well thank you, honey. Maybe between us, we'll keep East Texas clean."

The wireless tower went up, the music played, the voices talked, and the town doctor and his wife went on with their lives. The shock of rage she felt at his return was folded away when she realized that Will wouldn't take anything away from her after all. She ran her newspaper and her radio station, and at night, in their bedroom in the white house at the edge of town, she did what was required of her. When it was needed, she offered her dry young body to his, and when he was quiet again, she looked out the windows and watched the lights of station KLIP blinking through the dark, like stars she'd set in the Texas sky.

Earth, Texas

January 1924

10

They were born at seven and seven-thirty in the morning on the third day of the New Year. Hours later, Amelia woke from the stupor of labor with Will stroking her forehead, pushing back the fine hair, dark and matted with sweat.

"We have twins, Amelia. A boy and a girl." He held her cold hands and saw that the fingernails were blue. Remembering the delicate, porcelain hands once poised on the sleeve of his jacket, his heart dropped, and it seemed to him a near miracle that she had survived.

It was a miracle to Matty, plain and simple. The labor had gone on for four days, gone from one year right into the next. Then Matty took a tiny, angry baby girl from Dr. Will and half an hour later she took the boy, about four pounds, she guessed, of half-dead, silent humanity.

It was the worst labor Matty had ever seen. She'd seen bad labor before, but nothing like what that little white lady went through. Matty knew she was going to die, and she was pretty sure Dr. Will knew it too when he came back from an overnight trip to someone else's baby and sent her to his office for the morphine that didn't do much good anyway. Maybe she'd last another hour or so now that it was over, but Matty wasn't sure about that. She wasn't sure about the little boy either, but she took him up the stairs to the third-floor nursery and put him in the crib right next to the little girl, like a runt puppy you hoped might catch some life warmth from the rest of the litter.

But it didn't look good to Matty that January day, none of it. Her Duke stood flat against the nursery door, his black face as pale as it was ever going to get. Her cousin Rosie rocked and sobbed in the chair by the window, and her breasts, taut with milk, heaved with hiccups.

Matty sniffed. She'd never thought much of Rosie—a round, dimpled, stupid little thing with that high yellow color Matty never could stand. In this case it was the result of a cousin's messing with some Mexican at the border. She even named the child Rosita, a trashy name Matty made into Rosie. Nevertheless, when Mrs. Harlow's time came, Rosie was the only candidate for wet nurse Matty knew of and so she sent for her. She came, weepy-eyed over the loss of her own baby, and so hysterical by the second day of Mrs. Harlow's labor that Matty told her to go sleep in the barn. The last thing she'd need was a wet nurse slappin' around the house with her milk going sour. She and Duke would lose their jobs that way for sure, and Matty didn't want to lose this job.

Matty and Duke came from Sugar Hill where they had grown up on the hills between the creeks. Matty's family had come to Texas from Alabama after the Civil War with Reconstruction Yankees full of good intentions, and when they gave up and went on West, Matty's family stayed, finally drifting to Sugar Hill.

Duke Washington's family had been there just about forever, it seemed, and he and Matty had grown up together, third generation Texans without a future.

The water was good, sweetest water in Texas, some people said. Drink it once and you'll never let it alone. Makes no difference where you go, people said, you'll come back. The land along the creeks was good, thick with switch cane, dappled with light. But it wasn't good growing land anymore. You needed education for that now, and no place, anyplace, a black Texas man like her Duke was going to get that. So Matty stood, neat and tidy on the porch of the Sugar Hill house she and Duke had scratched together, listening silently, weighing and measuring, while Dr. Will said come to town, Matty. I'll build you a little place all your own out near mine, you and Duke both. You come take care of Mrs. Harlow and me, Matty, and you'll never be sorry.

She hadn't been sorry. They cooked and cleaned, gardened and served, and thought of going back to Sugar Hill. To the sweet, sweet water and the dappled light. And knew they never would.

And now Matty stood in the nursery on the top floor of the doctor's house in Earth, cooing softly over the twins curled in the crib. The girl was fine, no question about that, and the boy was looking a little brighter, already a little less worse for wear. Sweet little babies, with soft yellow hair just beginning to curl. They would need her, even if Mrs. Harlow wouldn't anymore. She picked them up, one in each hand, took them to Rosie. She watched them nuzzle and begin to nurse as the house settled into silence.

Later, Dr. Will slipped a little something extra into the big gingham pocket of Matty's apron and said she'd saved his boy. Matty knew how to be gracious when the white folks sweetened their gratitude with cold cash. She smiled her big smile and nodded. But as far as she could figure out, it was somebody's God saved that boy.

What Matty never figured out was how Mrs. Harlow survived. But there she was two months later, standing in church to baptize those babies, a little thin-looking in her blue pleated dress and one of those wide-brimmed hats she always wore, fashionable or not, when she stepped outside. This one was straw with long blue ribbons to match her dress, and it dipped and curved to her shoulders, almost hiding the cropped head and the short curls capping a face as sexless as the faces of the twins Matty held in her arms.

Behind the brim of her hat, Amelia Harlow's eyes were closed. She listened to the tune the minister's wife picked out on the small organ in the simple church and wished for a moment for the chant of nuns, for the incense-laden air and the lavish ceremonies that had decorated a part of her own childhood. She shook the disloyalty away and thought of her children.

The realization that her body was going to bear children surprised her at first, and her body went on surprising her. Her belly swelled and kept on swelling, her breasts grew larger and heavier, bursting with a sexuality that seemed to have a life foreign and separate from hers. When bathing she would glance down at their indiscreet ripeness, then look away, puzzled and shy and increasingly surprised that this should be happening to her.

She went into labor early and Will promised her it wouldn't take long. Texas women are good at babies, he said—fast, like cats. When she went under morphine on the second day, Amelia thought she heard a cat splitting the air with its animal scream. A few moments later, when the pain eased and the trembling stopped, she realized that her last bit of courage and self-control had dissolved under the drug. The scream had been hers.

You don't remember labor—every woman Amelia knew told her that. But Amelia remembered, not the pain but the humiliation: the reduction to a screaming, begging, sweating animal; and the hands, pushing at her knees, spreading her thighs wide, like another kind of rape. She remembered that, very clearly, even when it was long over.

Her breasts deflated. She ordered single beds from a Dallas store and called a hairdresser to come and cut the long hair Will liked to touch at night. She'd given him all the children any man could reasonably expect, a boy and a girl. They had their babies now and she was afraid of more.

"You understand," she said. "I know you understand," and she then waited, watching him in silence. He stood with his hands jammed into his white pockets and his eyes on the bed she'd told him was his.

"I liked your hair," he finally said. "It was lovely, like you. I liked it, Amelia." He shrugged with an odd smile, then turned and went upstairs to the twins.

The organ music was swelling now; the young minister from the North was beckoning them forward so the baptism could begin. She couldn't remember anymore when she'd first been told there were two children, a girl and a boy. But she had promised then and she promised now: that her daughter would have all that she had missed, a life that was only good and gentle; and, because it was different for a boy, that her son would have all that she was building, the press, the radio station. She would never leave him to the ruin of war as Will had been left. Somehow, when the time came, if the time came, she would see to it that her son would never know what his father had known. With that promise in mind, she knew the first name she'd chosen was right. And because she expected special things of both her children, she took their middle names from the map of Texas.

The sun was flooding the stained-glass windows of the Baptist church in Earth. Will was smiling gently as he took his screaming daughter from Matty's arms. She opened her own arms then, took her son, and rocked him against her as they were baptized: Bliss Houston Harlow and his sister, Eleanor Austin.

11

He was three. He lay in his crib, watching the morning sun come in through the windows, streaking the panes.

Across the nursery, Eleanor was in bed too, diving nosefirst under the covers, screaming and kicking in ecstasy as Rosie struggled to capture her. Bliss smiled. Eleanor was winning. But soon Rosie would catch her, and she would comb Eleanor's hair and wash her face, dress her in a neat, clean dress, and then she'd dress him too. After that Rosie would lead them, one in each hand, downstairs to Matty for inspection. Matty would pull and pat at a shoelace or a buckle or a hair out of place, and then they would go to the big hallway to wait for the Golden Lady to come down the long curved staircase.

She would be laughing and waving, smelling sweet and very clean. She'd kneel down on the big rug, scoop them up in her arms, and call them funny names, like Button and Monkey and Sugar Drops. That was why Bliss called her Golden Lady. It was his special name for her, like Button was her special name for him. Then she'd be very serious for a minute—half serious really because her eyes still smiled—and she'd tell them to be good and practice their best manners at breakfast, lunch too, and when she came home again they would all have tea with Daddy in the sun-room.

Tea was nice. There were little things to nibble on, puzzles to play with and books to look at. Their father presented them with their favorite toy at one of those tea times—a fat brown teddy bear that Eleanor insisted on calling Goose. Bliss thought that was very funny, but it made Daddy frown and peer at Eleanor. "It's not a goose, baby. It's a bear. Why don't you call it Bear, or Teddy?"

Eleanor giggled again and then Bliss did too. He poked her until she said, "We call it Goose because it's *not*. See?"

Daddy looked puzzled. "Maybe you need a goose. A big, fuzzy yellow one?" But Bliss poked Eleanor again and shook his head.

"No, Daddy," she said, "we *have* one now," and she buried her nose in its brown bear fuzz and burst into another avalanche of giggles.

That tea time hadn't, after all, gone very well, but mostly they were among the best times of the day. Only the mornings were better. They were the special times with the Golden Lady, who always stopped at the bottom of the staircase to fold his kiss into the palm of her hand.

"Don't lose it," he whispered.

"I won't," she whispered back.

Bliss flopped over on his belly to gaze at Eleanor through the rails of his crib and smiled at her struggles with Rosie.

She talked; he rarely bothered. She turned her head to spit out the food they didn't like and said "No." She grabbed Matty's skirts, said "Won't." She had the grown-up bed; he insisted on keeping his crib, for both of them. When life defeated her and she was miserable, she padded across the nursery floor, climbed up and over the rail, and flopped down beside him.

Daddy had tried taking the crib away, but he'd held on to the wooden bars and cried. "Don't be silly, Bliss. Don't you want a big bed too?" He knew it made Daddy angry, but Bliss didn't care; he wanted the crib. It was Matty who finally intervened. "He'll grow out of it," she said. "Don't worry yourself, Dr. Will." Daddy gave up, and Bliss turned to Eleanor and smiled.

They looked exactly alike except for Eleanor's long

hair. When they dressed as they liked, in pants and hats, they went to the mirror in the upstairs hall, spun around until they were dizzy, then stopped on cue and looked. Even they couldn't tell, just at first, which was which, who was who. They were One and would, they promised each other, always be One. He vaguely realized that his mother didn't understand. She reversed them in her head and made him brave and Eleanor gentle. But he didn't mind. He forgave her that each morning when he went to the foot of the stairs to kiss her hand.

He was four, and his mother was upset. She still came down the circular staircase every morning and still came home each evening to tea in the sun-room. But her eyes were dark and worried and sometimes she went back to the office after tea. Something called a "takeover" was happening, except Mommy said over her dead body. Nobody was taking anything of hers.

People started coming to the house in lines of cars, and lines of men in dark suits kept getting out and climbing up the front steps. He recognized Mr. Benedict and Mr. Liepman, and once the man who looked like Santa Claus in everyday clothes and always said, "Call me Pappy, son; call me Pappy." He and Eleanor watched from the nursery window, their foreheads pressed against the windowpanes, and looked again the next morning for the cars, but they were always gone. Nothing to see but the tracks they'd left in the gravel and the empty cottonwoods beyond.

Bliss picked flowers to take to his mother at tea time. Eleanor tried hard to be good. Daddy repeated all the funny phrases people were using, like "cat's pajamas" and "twenty-three skiddoo," and told the jokes he said rolled into his office as often as head colds.

"Then there's the one about Calvin Coolidge. Now he's the President, and a little like you, Bliss. The silent type." He smiled and pulled Bliss into his lap. "Seems a lady came to dinner and said he just had to talk to her. Seems she'd made a bet that she could get more than two words out of him and she was depending on him. But President Coolidge, he just shook his head. 'You lose,' he said."

Eleanor roared with laughter. "I can get Bliss to say more than two words, Mommy. Look, Mommy," and she pushed Bliss onto the floor, tickling him until he finally exploded with whoops and sputtering screams. "I'll get you, I'll get you."

"See, Mommy," Eleanor said, hiding behind her father's chair in mock fear as Bliss lunged toward her. "Three whole words!" And they ran giggling and screaming up and down the sun-room until their mother smiled a vacant smile that froze her son's heart.

When she began going to the office every Saturday, and even Sunday, Bliss and Eleanor started going too. Rosie packed a big bag with crayons and blocks, stuck Goose on top, and off they went in the car, Mommy and Eleanor and Bliss and Goose.

His mother's secretary, Miss Sarah Leslie, was there to look after them. She called his mother "ma'am," and her short brown hair was even shorter than his mother's. This Saturday she wore a short, pleated skirt and a necklace that fell way below her waist.

"My," she said when she hugged them both. "You certainly are growing fast, aren't you?" She took them by the hand. "Let's go on up to the pressroom. I know you love to look at all those machines." She tugged on Bliss's hand and smiled down at him. "Especially when they're quiet."

They'd come once before when the machines were working and the noise made Bliss cry. "I like them better on Saturdays," Miss Leslie said, pushing open the door to the pressroom. "Such a racket when they get going you can hardly hear yourself think."

Bliss didn't like them much on Saturdays either. He

had more fun playing with the phones in Mr. Liepman's office, and after that Miss Leslie gave them lemonade in her office and a pile of pencils to sharpen for Mommy.

It was late in the afternoon and not quite dark that Saturday in November of 1928. Miss Leslie was sitting at her desk with her work, reaching across to turn on the lamp. Bliss and Eleanor were stretched out on the rug with their pencil sharpeners, Goose settled quietly between them, when something stirred on the street outside and Bliss looked up. The red leaves on the black gum tree outside were just beginning to shake.

Later, the young minister from the North and his wife told Amelia Harlow that they'd seen them slide around the corner of the bank and then run down Main Street. Halloween had already come and gone, but at first they thought they were trick-or-treaters in ghost costumes, and then, a moment later, they knew they were wrong. They could see that their hoods were peaked, with gaping holes for the eyes. They melted into the dusk as quickly as they came, a single figure breaking stride to hurl an object into the branches of the black gum tree.

Amelia heard a sound, like a pop, and then the piercing scream of an explosion and the higher, even more piercing scream of a child. She didn't see the windows of her office shatter. She was at the door, and Bliss was in her arms, blood pumping from the gash on his cheek, down his face, across her hands. She was crushing him to her until it hurt and they were running through the corridors, Bliss in her arms, Eleanor in Sarah Leslie's.

They stopped finally in the pressroom. The only sounds were Bliss's leftover sobs and Sarah Leslie's panting. Her face was pink and her eyes wide. "My, wasn't *that* exciting," Sarah Leslie said. Her voice was small and cracked, but Amelia was grateful anyway.

"You'd think it was the Fourth of July around here," Sarah babbled on. "You truly would. All those fire-crackers going off like that."

Eleanor wriggled down from Sarah's grasp and shook her pinafore so that the glass tinkled to the floor. "Good," she said. "Now is it our turn to do fireworks too?"

Amelia forced herself to smile. "Yes, pet," she said. "I think it is our turn," and then she was shaking with her own fear and a sudden animal instinct to attack. It was an oddly familiar feeling, and then she remembered. She'd had that feeling with Carter Harlow, and now she had it again.

She hid her face against Bliss, feeling his little-boy body secure in her arms and his legs clutched around her waist. He smelled of lemonade and crayons and fresh-laundered cotton. And then, when she lifted her head again, she smelled the acrid aftereffects of the homemade bomb.

Later, that night, when Will was upstairs with the twins, Amelia sat alone in the sun-room with the curtains drawn against the night, formulating a plan to ruin the man who had bombed her offices that day.

His name was Strickland Dart, "Sam" to his friends in the Ku Klux Klan and to his employees. He owned the East Texas *Times,* the flagship paper of a small chain of weeklies he distributed in a half-dozen towns east of Dallas. They were just four-sheeters, but each issue was dedicated to "the whitest people living on the blackest land in Texas."

His first offer to buy a half interest in the *Bugle* and station KLIP came to Clayton Benedict's Dallas office. It was a handsome offer, considering the mortgage still outstanding on the radio station. The second offer was higher. The third was unnerving and so was the pressure from Noah Carr's bank to accept. The late-night meetings began and the long hours, but it wasn't until Pappy Jarvis rolled back in from Washington, D.C., that Amelia finally knew that Sam Dart didn't want the paper. He wanted the radio station.

He'd applied for a radio license of his own the year before, and Pappy, white hair flying, had sailed down the Hill and into the offices of the Federal Radio Commission, swearing that if anybody granted a radio license to that filthy redneck, that blight on the heart of Texas, he'd personally raise such a goddamn stink about the sanctity of the hallowed public airwaves that nobody would ever forget it. Ever. Pappy had banged on the desk and raged some more and finally the request had been tabled for further consideration by a stunned assistant to the Commission. Now Sam Dart wanted a blind share of KLIP for politicking, and he wanted it bad.

It was dawn on a Friday morning when Joe Gasparini, the *Bugle*'s distributor in Mount Pleasant, found three heavyset men lounging outside his office by the railroad ticket office. The *Bugle* was arranged in its neat, bound piles on the platform, and a dozen frightened delivery boys stood across the tracks with their bicycles at their sides.

The largest of the men stepped up to Joe Gasparini. "You're not handling the *Bugle* today," he said, shifting a toothpick around in his mouth. He was a big man, and the gray hairs on his thick chest curled above his open workshirt collar. "There's not time for it today. Hear that, wop?"

Joe Gasparini wasn't much bigger than his delivery boys, or much older. He shrugged. "I'll have to tell Mrs. Harlow what you said. She won't like it."

The man with the toothpick laughed. "What you and Mrs. Harlow gonna do about it, wop? Huh?"

He motioned his men to their feet and Joe watched them rip the rope from around the papers, then kick at the stacks with their boots. Two thousand copies of the *Bugle* scattered like debris on the railroad tracks. The head man smiled at Gasparini. "Tell Mrs. Harlow to listen next time she gets an offer. Tell her that, wop."

Joe did tell Mrs. Harlow, and so did the delivery boys in Daingerfield when they found five blank-faced thugs ripping the spokes from their bikes. A resident of Omaha, twenty miles away, told Amelia about the man who showed up on her doorstep to hand her what turned out to be a dead rat wrapped in the pages of the *Bugle-Times*. Two weeks later the bomb blew out the windows of the office in Earth.

The following Monday morning, Amelia drove to Dallas alone.

Sam Dart kept her waiting twenty-five minutes and she imagined, correctly, that he was counting the minutes, measuring them out like teaspoons of humiliation. It made her smile and when she was finally shown to his office she refused the seat he offered and stood like a contrite schoolgirl with her face bowed beneath the shadow of her hat.

He was nothing like his name. He was short and fat, with rolls of flesh overflowing his chair and sweat stains like dark half-moons on his striped shirt. "Glad you came to see it my way, little lady." He grinned. "We're gonna be real happy together, you and me."

"Yes indeed, Mr. Dart." She kept her eyes glued to the floor and invited him to contact her attorney about an exchange of stock.

"I'll do that, honey. Don't you worry your pretty little head about all the details. I'm gonna deal fair and square. Always have, always will."

She nodded. "I'm sure of that, Mr. Dart."

An hour later she was in the office of his distributor with cash in hand, carefully, methodically outlining her plan to starve Sam Dart out.

It took eleven months. From November of 1928 through September of the following year. By spring the

subscribers to Sam Dart's East Texas *Times* weren't
getting their Wednesday newspapers on time and by
April their complaints brought advertising revenues
down. Sam Dart barely noticed. The negotiations for
55 percent of the stock in KLIP were intense now and
highly complex. Subscriptions dropped disastrously in
June, but by the time Sam Dart caught on it was a
Wednesday in August, and too late. Not a single
newspaper boy showed up to deliver the East Texas
Times that day. They were on their way to the Fort
Worth Stock Show instead, their train tickets and
front-row seats to the main events compliments of an
anonymous donor.

There was only one bidder for the East Texas *Times*
when it went on the block in early October, and if Sam
Dart had any doubts that he'd sold out at five cents on
the dollar to a dummy corporation of Amelia Harlow's,
those doubts vanished on receipt of a hand-delivered
note that came to his Dallas home that evening.

Dear Mr. Dart:
It will give me great pleasure to ship the last issue
of your newspaper to the offices of the *Bugle-
Times*. There I shall have the edition stacked in
the Men's Room, trusting to the good sense of
my pressman that its sheets shall at last be used
for the sole purpose I have long felt they were
meant.

> Sincerely,
> Amelia Bliss Harlow
> Publisher

Only Noah Carr was left. It hadn't taken Clayton
Benedict long to confirm her suspicion that the State
Bank of Earth had financed Dart's operation. Three
weeks after Sam Dart went out of business she phoned
Noah Carr at the bank and cut through the pleasantries
of his jovial hellos.

"Would you be so good as to check my balance?" she asked. "I'll hold."

"What you got in mind, Amelia?" There was a sudden strain in his voice as it echoed down the line.

"I'm not sure yet, Noah. But I would like that balance."

She heard the papers rustling at the other end of the phone and the sound of Noah pulling on his cigar. "Gotta pencil handy? It's one hundred thousand, five hundred twenty-eight dollars and thirty-four cents."

"Thank you, Noah," she said, and savored for a second the very special pleasure of her next order. She didn't bother to frame it as a request. "I'll take it," she said. "In cash. Today."

She smiled at his shocked intake of breath. "But Amelia, that wipes out my reserves. You can't do this."

"I'll be there before three, Noah. Thank you." She put down the phone, vaguely aware that her hands were wet.

A week later, on Friday, October 25, unusually large sales of Kennecott Copper and General Motors stock sparked a panic in the New York Exchange. By noon, stock prices began to slip dramatically. Leading New York banking houses, J. P. Morgan among them, raised 240 million dollars to stem the tide, but that patriotic effort was ineffectual. The New York press dubbed the day Black Friday, and though prices held on Monday, on Tuesday, October 29, they dropped again, as much as sixty dollars a share.

The crash had come, and as Amelia Harlow watched the news on the endless rolls of AP reports, she took pleasure in knowing that Noah Carr had been ruined before it began.

Will was livid. His grandfather, he reminded her over dinner one night, had founded the bank.

"Noah backed a Klan man, Will. He backed a man who bombed the press. Your children were there, if you recall."

"But Noah didn't know that, Amelia. He couldn't have. You're killing a man for his politics."

"Not his politics, Will. His attempt to impose his on mine."

She was right, Will supposed, but he didn't care about Noah Carr's politics. He cared about his town and holding on to what was left of the past. He watched her sitting there across the table, cool and contained, her eyes bright with her predatory kill. He wondered if she'd ever been as he'd once imagined her—vulnerable, fragile, like a piece of china in a window-pane on a half-forgotten street. He wondered if he hated her now, and if not now, when. Tomorrow, next year, the year after?

"How did it come to this, Amelia?" He reached for his glass and sipped the last of his bourbon.

"You know what happened. Noah Carr . . ."

"No. Not Noah. You. How did you get so—clever?" He stopped on the word, making it sound ugly. He shrugged and stood, then moved to the sideboard for a fresh bottle of bourbon. He uncapped it and topped off his glass. "How'd you do it, Amelia? What happened?"

Something inside Amelia hurt. He was judging her and it hurt, and somewhere deeper inside she wanted to tell him about the years when he had been away. But the pain and the need were distant, almost out of reach, and when she spoke her voice was cool. "It wasn't sudden, Will. I learned because I had to. I had to, and I wanted to. And now I've taken the cash out of Noah Carr's bank."

The food sat untouched that night and the Harlow money stayed out of Noah Carr's bank. It went instead to revitalizing Sam Dart's chain and wedding it with the *Bugle-Times*. A year later they were both running smoothly as a single, tight system centralized in Earth. Advertising was down, but there was a depression on and she would survive. She had the sense that she could survive anything now.

12

The hammers woke him. The hammers woke him every morning now, and Bliss hated it this morning as much as he had the first.

He was seven. His first pair of long pants hung in the closet, his blond curls were cropped close to his head, and he had his own room. It was blue, with red fire engines going up and down the wall. Blue was the best color for a boy's room. It was next to the nursery and had been Rosie's room once, but Rosie had her own house now, next to Matty and Duke's at the back. She had her own boy too. He was tea-colored like Rosie and his name was George. George had come as a surprise to Bliss, and he'd brought the subject up with Matty one Saturday. "I thought you had to be married to have babies, Matty. But Rosie isn't married. Is she?"

"Well now," Matty said. "No, she isn't, but as you can tell, Rosie hasn't been entirely overlooked. Here." She gave him a cookie and told him to scoot.

He'd looked for his father to discuss it further, but it was hard to find his father these days. He was busy—busy on Saturdays, too busy to share tea in the sun-room, and once a week he wasn't home at all. That was why, though Bliss wasn't exactly sure how it fitted together—that was why the hammers sounded each morning, each day, all day. His mother was building a big new room of her own on top of the sun-room. That was why the workmen came and went with their hammers, nailing a new silence into the house with each blow.

And Bliss was right.

He hadn't heard Will drive up from town late one night, cutting the motor as he came through the cottonwoods. He hadn't seen his ghostly form in the white linen suit move through the dark house, up the stairs to the bedroom he shared with Amelia. When he bent to say goodnight, Bliss hadn't heard his mother say, "Don't. I can smell her through the bourbon."

Will and Amelia struck their bargain that night. Amelia had one condition. "Do as you must. Take your mistress, but don't humiliate the children, Will. Ever." Will nodded in the dark.

"No, Amelia. Of course not. Never."

She lived in Tyler, the "Rose City" of Texas, and her name was Anna. Anna Elizabeth Janes. She always wished, she told Dr. Harlow, that somebody had thought to call her Betsy or Liz. But there it was, Anna Janes, minor variations on the two most common names in the English-speaking world, and she laughed a soft, low, tinkling laugh that lit up her sweet, round face.

She taught reading, sums, and art to the children at the grade school three blocks away. In the afternoons and on weekends she tended her garden. Her father had been a rose grower in Tyler before he died and she grew roses too at the back of the small brick house where she lived with her mother. She weeded, pruned and fertilized them until they banked the back fence in a great rush of color, came marching up to the house, curving around a small pond where goldfish flashed in the sun.

They sat there on a little stone bench that first Saturday, the roses high around them. It hurt Will Harlow to confirm for her what her family doctor had told her, that the old woman in the larger upstairs bedroom had suffered a stroke. It hurt even more to say it looked bad, with a slow dying ahead. But she smiled and thanked him for his honesty. At least she could plan now. Life and death wouldn't be lurking in dark corners, springing out to surprise her.

He came back the next Saturday with a cutting from a rose bush in his own garden, yellow roses like his mother once had, he said. They made love in the parlor

that afternoon—Will Harlow to a soft, gentle woman
whose body welcomed his, Anna Janes to a man who
unleashed in her a kind of hunger, surprising her with
life after all.

Bliss knew none of this, but he felt it in his father's
absence, in the increased drive with which his mother
hurtled through her days, and in the sound of the
hammers that filled his own days.

Eleanor didn't mind as much. She had her own room
now too. It was suitable, he supposed, for a girl. He
was glad it wasn't so cute that it was pink, but it was
definitely a girl's room. The walls were pale yellow and
there were yellow polka-dot ruffles over everything in
sight. Even her desk was yellow and above it there was
a little place on the wall for her favorite pictures, the
place of honor in the center going to a picture of the
matched pair of bays that belonged to her and Bliss.

Eleanor's room was on the far side of the old
nursery. Sometimes in the summer they slept in their
old room, in front of a big fan Matty set beside a block
of ice in a big old bucket she brought up from the
storeroom. But most of the time it was a play room for
their common goods.

The big, cathedral-like radio was there, and they
could play "Amos 'n Andy" as loud as they liked. The
books and trucks and paints were there, and so were
the blocks nobody played with anymore. Goose, who
nobody played with much anymore either, sat like a
brown lump on the windowseat. During the months the
hammers sounded, Bliss and Eleanor met there every
night.

They crept in from opposite sides of the room after
they should have been asleep and sat in the light of the
Texas moon that came through the windowpanes. They
faced each other like two mirrors, one dark with pain,
one lit with a brittle, bright confidence.

"Maybe she just wants a nice room for herself, like I

have," Eleanor whispered one night. "I mean, I have a room and you have a room, and now they both want rooms too, to match up with us. That's all."

"Oh, Eleanor, don't be so dumb," he hissed. "You said that before, and you know nobody's parents want separate rooms. They're not even supposed to."

"Maybe she'll paint it blue, like yours, and you'll like it special."

"I'll never like it. I'll never even go in, *ever.*"

"Don't be so dumb yourself. You always say that and you will too go in. Lots."

A footstep creaked on the stairs. "Matty," they whispered, and melted into the rooms on either side of the old nursery.

When it was finished, their mother's room was white with dark wood floors that flowed on into the white dressing room and private bath. White fans hung from high white ceilings. White shutters opened off the long windows, two at each end and six more facing the back gardens. White pillows, round, square, oblong, sat on a large double bed with a white comforter. There was a white chaise longue, and four white Chinese Chippendale chairs around a glass table. A lacquered white chest, dotted with silver-framed pictures of the twins, sat by the bed.

Bliss was too surprised to speak. It looked like a room for a bride, and on the other hand it didn't. It looked like a stranger's room, and then it didn't.

"It's beautiful," Eleanor sighed. "Just like an ice palace, for a snow queen."

And then, three years later, Bliss began to understand what it really meant to be his mother's son.

He was nine the year the union movement came to Earth, Texas, and ten when she crushed it. She wasn't without sympathy, but it was a simple matter of a wage increase for them or survival for her. The pressroom emptied out when negotiations came to a halt and picket lines formed under the black gum tree. But she and her master printer and the reporters who stayed cut back the page count and ran the press themselves under armed guard—and watched the picket line break a month later, and the union movement begin to die.

It was almost spring, and Duke drove her children, as he always had, to and from school in Amelia's Packard Phaeton with the caned sides. He waited for them at eight forty-five every morning of the week, holding the door for them as they jumped down the steps from the porch with their book bags banging against their knees. They'd climb in and sprawl across the rich leather seats in the back while Duke drove on through the cotton-woods, down the half mile of gravel road to the railroad tracks, and up Main Street. He turned right on Willow, and then the Phaeton would roll to a gentle halt at the school yard two blocks down.

School was easy for Eleanor. She made the girls jump rope and play games, and if there was any hostility, Eleanor could ignore it. But it was different for Bliss.

He felt it instantly, as soon as it began. There was a coolness in the classroom and an isolation in the playground that burned deeper and deeper as the days wore on. At first he assigned it to the fact they came to school in the Phaeton. One evening, over tea in the sun-room with his mother, he put his foot down, and to his astonishment, he won.

"Fine," his mother said, her teacup settling back to its saucer. "You're certainly old enough to walk to school now and I suppose you feel a little different, don't you? It's hard sometimes to be different, I know. You won't mind, will you, Eleanor?"

Eleanor shrugged. "*Now* what time do we have to leave?" she wanted to know, groaning when her mother said she supposed eight o'clock or so. But there she was at eight sharp the next day, dressed for the sudden rain in her yellow slicker and boots, waiting for him. But it didn't help.

It was April, a school lunch hour, and he stood in silence on the edge of the playing field, waiting to be chosen. His fist was curled, hitting hard and harder into his mitt. He'd been blackballed from the lunch-hour baseball game for three days and had cried himself to sleep for two nights. He'd cried so hard that there was nothing of self-pity left. There was only the clean, white-hot anger that sent the sweat rolling down his back as he stalked up to the school-yard captain.

"My turn to pitch."

"No it ain't."

"Yes it is. I'm best and you know it. And I haven't pitched for three days."

"Tough."

"Oh yeah? How come?"

"We don't like you," Buddy Prescott said. "And we don't like the way you play ball."

A ring of boys was forming around them now. They were circling and smiling, nudging each other with glee.

"I play good ball," Bliss said. "You can't say I don't."

"Okay, smartass," Buddy snarled. "You think you're better 'cause you're rich, you and that ol' lady of yours. She cuts wages and then hands out potatoes to feed us folks that's poor. But potatoes, they ain't wages." He spit and held the bat in the air above Bliss's head. "That's what my daddy says. He don't like that, and me, I don't like you."

Bliss didn't shift his gaze, but in his head he did a quick count of the lunch-hour ball teams. Buddy's father was a pressman. Six, maybe seven more of the boys' fathers worked for his mother. Then he heard the whispers. "Company boy," somebody said. There was a giggle. "Mama's boy."

Bliss swung. He connected hard with Buddy Prescott's belly and heard him choke for breath. Bliss burst into tears, clawed for the bat, and then he was rolling on the ground and pounding Buddy until blood came running from his nose.

"Now you listen," he hissed, and then stood up with the bat gripped tight. "You listen good. My mother doesn't play baseball. I do. And don't you ever, ever forget it, hear?"

He turned to look at the silent circle of boys and lifted the bat high. "Let's play ball."

And that was how Bliss Harlow learned who he was. That was how he learned he lived in a Company town, and they were the Company. That was how he learned there was something going on called the Great Depression, and that it had come to Texas, to Earth, and even to the press itself. That was how he learned his mother was cutting wages by 10 percent to avoid cutting staff. The Santa Claus who said "Call me Pappy, call me Pappy" was, it turned out, a United States congressman from the Sovereign State of Texas, and he and his mother were throwing land open out near Mount Pleasant. Come one . . . come all . . . grow your own vegetables for Hard Times. But Buddy Prescott's father would rather have had the cash.

In the end, that was what Bliss Harlow remembered about his childhood. He didn't remember the Golden Lady. He remembered the struggle to get onto the ball field and the sudden, burning isolation that came with knowing that she had made him different.

13

But what Eleanor remembered most vividly of their childhood was a Sunday in the fall of 1937. It was the first cool afternoon in months and she and Bliss were in the back seat of Will's aging LaSalle convertible with their faces pressed into the wind.

She was almost fourteen that fall. She was tired of

the depression and tired of Franklin Roosevelt reminding them all that there was nothing to fear but fear itself. As far as she could tell, President Roosevelt was wrong. There was lots to fear.

She'd decided earlier that year that maybe she'd want to be a nurse when she grew up, and all that spring and summer, Saturdays and Sundays and school holidays, she went on rounds with her father.

Sometimes they went south, to Tyler, where they saw an old lady who was bedridden with a stroke. Afterward they had iced tea in the rose garden with the lady's daughter, Miss Janes, and once they had lunch. She helped Miss Janes fix special little cucumber sandwiches in her kitchen and she got to crank the peach ice cream herself. It was a very grown-up lunch, Eleanor thought. The talk was grown-up too, much more grown-up than at home. They talked of bread lines in the East and about the Midwest caving under and turning into a dust bowl. There were people selling apples, right on the streets of Tyler, Texas, itself, Miss Janes told Eleanor.

Times were bad for lots of people, and as often as not her father's patients paid him "in kind," in eggs and sides of salted beef or bushels of fruit. Sometimes, up on Sugar Hill or on the smaller farms beyond, people didn't pay at all. "I know you're good for it," her father would say when people came out to the car. "Times get better and we're going to look forward to some of that lemon pie of yours." They loved Dr. Will for honoring their pride, and so did Eleanor.

People kept saying it would get better, but it didn't. It stayed the same, except when you drove past the timberline it got worse. She drove out there with her father once and they had to wait almost an hour at the bridge that would take them across the Sabine River. It was hot parked under the mesquite, and the sun pounded on her Stetson as they sat there watching the dust rolling across the dry cracked bed of one of the biggest rivers in Texas. Dozens of people were shambling across the bridge on foot. Their beat-up trucks were loaded with boxes and pulled by mules. They didn't look as though they'd make it across the bridge, much less to California. That's where they were probably going, her father told her, to California. Lots of people were going to California now.

She felt peculiar when a tall, skinny man broke from the line and came over to her father's side of the car, and when he ran a finger along the butt of the gun strapped to his side, she felt her heart lurch with fear.

"Gettin' an eyeful?" he sneered.

"No sir," said her father. "Waiting for you all to pass. Nothing more. Nothing less."

"Don't have to stare, do you?"

"Didn't mean to stare."

"Sorry," the man finally said, and he pushed back his hat, wiped away the sweat running down the dust on his long, thin, lined face. He had more sweat than the river had water, he told them, and now they were finished. After nearly twenty years of trying to farm in Texas, they were finished—all of them. The whole damn town was picking up and moving on. He eyed her father and his white hat and dusty white suit. "What's your line, if you don't mind me asking."

"Medicine," replied her father. "I'm a doctor. Harlow's the name."

"Bates here," and they shook hands.

"And this is my girl, Eleanor."

Eleanor nodded. "Hello," she wanted to say, but her mouth had gone dry.

"Howdy," he said, and he tipped his hat. "Could've used your ol' man round here last week. Might have saved my youngest kid. Though you come right down to it, fact is the wife dried up, just like the old Sabine River. Couldn't feed the baby last week, couldn't feed her this. Guess it would've been just a waste of time."

A woman broke from the crowd on the bridge and

sidled up to him. "Time to go," she said. "Got to push on." He turned to put an arm around her shoulder. "The wife," he said.

Eleanor had never seen a face like hers. It was dead brown from the sun, and the bones were almost visible beneath skin that shriveled into the lines running down her neck. Her glanced slipped to the woman's breasts, and she tried to imagine the child suckling there. The breasts were flat, and in the heat and shimmering sun Eleanor could almost see a baby shriveling up like the woman, turning into an inhuman shape.

She felt her stomach lurch, and then Mr. Bates thumped the hood of the car with the flat of his hand in a hollow, tinny salute. "Well," he said, "so long."

Eleanor waited until they joined the last of the crowd filing off the bridge and watched them disappear into the clouds of dust and mesquite and heat. "I'm going to be sick, Daddy," and she lunged for the car door and threw up on the riverbank.

"Better?" asked Will. He soaked his handkerchief in the cool water of a canteen and reached over to wash his daughter's face. "Better?" He tugged gently at one of her long braids.

They bumped over the bridge and drove on as Will told his daughter again about her great-grandfather Justiss Harlow who had come out of Atlanta with the God-given good sense to settle in a part of Texas that made good sense too. By the time he finished they were pulling up to the farmhouse that was their destination. But the creek here was dry too, and the people were gone. There was only a cur dog, crawling with maggots, lying in the depression sun.

By fall, Eleanor wasn't so sure she wanted to be a nurse. There really wasn't much point, not if people were going to pick up and move to California or die of starvation in Texas instead. She thought somebody should give President Roosevelt a kick in the pants for not fixing things better or maybe they should let somebody else be president. She'd been a president, twice in fact, once of the sixth grade, and once of the secret club she and her best friend had formed until they had another fight and broke everything up again. It was easy being president. You told people what to do and they did it. She was pretty sure that once she went to Washington and saw what was what, she wouldn't have too much trouble making things all right again.

And that's what Eleanor Austin Harlow was thinking that first cool day in the fall of 1937 when she and Bliss sat in the back seat of the LaSalle with their faces pressed into the wind.

It was a Sunday and the four of them had left home late in the afternoon, driving west through the hills, then south, into vast reaches of raw space spreading out under a purple sky. Near dusk they stopped and stepped out onto a land that was cratered and cracked and dry. Eleanor scraped a tick off a tire with her boot and heard her father's sigh and her mother's soft, insistent voice.

"Take it," her mother said. "As much as you can get."

Her father scanned the scrub and brush, squinting against the light and dust.

"No, Amelia," he said. "There's nothing to be done with this. Never has been, never will be. You know that. It's a wasteland."

Eleanor raised her eyes, and then shifted her gaze to follow her mother's, straining to see what her mother saw in the miles beyond. She knew only that one of her father's patients, forced out by the depression and drought, had offered to pay in cattle or in land—this land.

"You're right. It's not land," her mother said. "It's real estate. Take it."

And then Eleanor saw. She pushed through her sense of terrible disloyalty to her father and suddenly saw what her mother saw, instinctively knew what her mother knew. It was Dallas, sitting out there like a sun chip on the long, long platter of the horizon.

She never forgot that day. "It was like Monopoly," she would say years later. "You buy cheap and sell dear, and then . . . well, then you're rich, aren't you?" And then she would laugh, her eyes bright with the exhilaration of it.

What would be almost impossible to explain was the sense, more exhilarating somehow, that she and her mother had abandoned the tradition of a family locked on the cusp of the South and the West and finally thrown their lot in with the boom-town world of Dallas, with the big, brassy-blue future of the West.

PART TWO

New York

April 1945

14

It was almost sunrise. The long stretch of Fifth Avenue sat still and silent in the early morning during the fourth spring of another war. Flags hung limp from their brass poles along the Avenue, and up at the corner of Central Park South, the fairy-tale façade of the Plaza Hotel was dark. The sun rose slowly at first, just a shimmer in the east that cast the park and the buildings across the way in a translucent glow. A taxi passed, breaking the early morning quiet. A flock of pigeons, startled into flight, scattered in the pale sky. Then the only sounds were the high giggles of a girl in a black evening dress who was scaling the sides of the fountain across from the hotel.

Her black skirts were hiked above her knees, her silver slippers were clutched in one hand, and she giggled again when she reached her goal, splashing her bare legs in the pool. She leaned back, gazed up at the statue of Minerva in the center of the fountain, and frowned. A hairpin slipped loose and another intricate twist of blond hair tumbled to her shoulders.

"Betcha don't know who posed for the statue," she

said. She was very drunk and her voice cut uncertainly through the clear morning air.

The young man at her side took off another sock and dipped another long leg into the chill of the pool. "Evelyn Nesbitt," he said. "Circa 1900."

"Right!" she announced. "*Another* torchy little tart." She smirked at him, then her face melted with guilt. "I'm sorry. I know it's not your fault. Not really. Please don't sulk, promise?"

"Promise," he sighed, and then they both—Eleanor Harlow, twenty-one now and a senior at Bryn Mawr, and Alfred Reece, her brother's Princeton roommate—went on sulking over the indisputable fact that Bliss had dumped them.

He'd slouched into Princeton at seventeen. He was tall and slender, and his thick curls were still blond, still cropped close to his head. He was charming and moody, and there was now an unpredictability about him, something dark and urgent beneath the slender, almost languid grace of his form. That urgency had deepened in the year before he came to Princeton, and there were days, even weeks, when the only person he could tolerate was his sister.

Nobody but Eleanor knew what it meant to Bliss that August afternoon of 1940 when they flicked the dials on the radio in the old nursery on the third floor and finally picked up the voice of Edward R. Murrow. "This . . . is London," clear and measured and mournful from the other side of the world.

It was eleven-thirty at night by Big Ben. An eerie wail filled Trafalgar Square and echoed through the old nursery in Earth, Texas. "The sound of the air-raid sirens," Murrow said, and Bliss Harlow felt his whole body respond as if an electric current had shot up his spine.

There was the drone of the planes overhead and a voice calling out into the silence. "Stretcher party, one ambulance, one car to 114 High Street." Bliss had never been east of the Mississippi, but he knew the London of the blackout then, the dark, fog-streaked streets, the Thames lapping quietly against its banks, the dome of St. Paul's dark against the dark sky. Murrow's microphone picked up the sound of footsteps, a quiet voice asking someone for a light, and then the sudden *ack-ack* of antiaircraft fire bursting around them as the Battle of Britain began.

The rush of excitement, the very adrenalin pumping madly through his veins, his conviction that America had to go to war now—they were all illicit and unmentionable at the Harlow dinner table where the Earth *Bugle-Times* appeared each Friday with its resolutely antiwar editorials.

The bombs went on falling on the city by the Thames, and in the sanctuary of the old nursery, Bliss finally announced, "I'm going. I'm going to Canada and joining the air force."

Eleanor rolled her eyes. Still boyish despite the long blond hair that rippled into tight ringlets in the hot Texas summers, still flat as a board, Eleanor was what she had always been—brittle and sure. And she was very sure now. "Don't be stupid," she groaned. "And *don't* ask Daddy either. He'd say yes and then Mother'd kill him for sure. You know you're going to Princeton, so forget it."

"But they're fighting for civilization in England. Without England there wouldn't be a Princeton."

"Very nice thought," Eleanor said. "Very romantic, very international. I bet you could even work it up, you know? Make it into a nice, snappy slogan. But if I were you, that's all I'd do with it. Believe me."

The bombs fell, dinner went on being served, and in the nursery Edward R. Murrow beckoned. "This . . . is London."

"Mother?"

Amelia Harlow took off the glasses she wore for

reading now and smiled as Bliss walked into her room.
"What a nice surprise."

He flung himself across the foot of the bed, and for a
moment it felt to Amelia like the old days when he was
small and serious, passionate about her, certain that
she was all he ever wanted, and certain that she was his.
He looked very unlike his small-boy self, but the mouth
was the same, soft where the smile curled at the corner.
The eyes were the same, gray and wide and very direct.

"I want to go."

"I know you do."

"Canada, I mean. To join up, you know? To learn
how to fly. I could be in Europe in six months. I want to
do that."

"I know," and she did know. She could sense his
longing to leap into the world and make it his own with
one brilliant declaration of his presence. She closed the
file she'd been poring over and let it slip aside. "It's not
what you think it is, my love. It's not. War is ruination.
And worse, far worse than you can know."

"I don't care. I want to go. I want to help," his eyes
begging her to see.

"You don't know. You don't know what it did to your
father, or how he was before he went to the other one,
the other war. There were camps and gas, mutilation."

"It won't be like that for me."

She shook her head. "You don't know."

He looked away then, focusing on the white room
with the lazy, languid turn of the white fans overhead.
She supposed he hated her and was sure he did when he
spoke again.

"It's my life, you know. You can't control it forever.
You won't."

She nodded. "I know. But I do now. I'm sorry, but
you're only seventeen and I do now." She tried to make
that an assurance, not a hurt or a humiliation or a
wound, and knew, even before she finished, that she
had failed.

He said nothing, but when he left the room he slammed the door so hard it shook the frame.

His moodiness increased and deepened into unbroken silences. He nursed his burning anger, made elaborate plans to run away, and finally decided to lose his virginity instead, making the rounds of the women who frequented Billy's dance hall on Sugar Hill.

Amelia noted the new swagger, minded the new sullen edge to him, and was relieved anyway. He wasn't dead. She sent them both off to school, Eleanor to Bryn Mawr, Bliss to Princeton, and hoped that it would give him something, some small measure of all he wanted, all he dreamed. If nothing else, she hoped that he would simply like it.

He did like the Gothic walls of Princeton, the town spread out on its perimeters, and the elegant old homes as gracious as the oaks and elms arching the streets. There was nothing of the rawness of Texas towns and he began to feel it might be all right for a while. He settled into his rooms and waited.

Four months later, on Sunday, December 7, the Japanese bombed Pearl Harbor. On January 4, 1942, the day after his eighteenth birthday, Bliss cut his midyear holiday short and flew from Dallas to Newark, New Jersey. On the fifth, he tried to enlist in the marines.

He tried Newark.

"Name?"

"Harlow, sir. Bliss."

The captain at the recruiting center glanced down at the list in front of him. "Sorry, sonny. We're into the second half of the alphabet this week. Okay?"

He tried New York.

The line in Times Square was two blocks long. He waited all afternoon, inching forward, watching the city sweep by, the lights of dozens of movie theaters blinking weakly in the daylight, and the people surging through the streets. The too-tall buildings and the ceaseless noise made him feel claustrophobic at first, but the feeling wore off in a couple of hours, and at four-thirty he stepped inside the United States Recruiting Office.

"Name?" asked the sergeant.

"Harlow."

The sergeant began to write, stopped, and then rifled through a sheaf of papers.

"Age?"

"Eighteen, sir," he said.

"Date of birth?"

"January 3, 1924."

The sergeant glanced up. "Place of birth?"

"Earth, Texas."

"Sorry, kid. Next?"

"Whaddya mean—sorry? Sir, I've been standing here for four hours!"

"Buster, I said next," and the boy behind Bliss snapped forward.

He took a night train south, and the next morning tried Washington, D.C.

"Name?"

"Griggs, sir. John."

"Age?"

"Eighteen."

"Got any ID? Driver's license? Birth certificate?"

Bliss stared at him for a moment, and then wandered out into the street.

It took a lot of phone calls, but two days later Pappy Jarvis found him in Baltimore at the Hotel Trenton.

"You in there, boy?" The door to the grimy room opened and Pappy stood on the threshold. His black suit was wrinkled, his white hair was matted under his Stetson, and his round face was red with irritation. He handed the manager a five-dollar bill and slammed the door. Bliss was slouched in a tattered chair, gazing through the grimy window. A Baltimore cockroach staggered up the wall and made for the ceiling.

"Well, ain't this a pretty sight," Pappy said, his glance taking in the roach, the empty beer bottles, Bliss's bleary eyes, and the clothes he'd obviously slept in.

"Come on, boy," he sighed. "We're gonna get you cleaned up a bit and then we'll get some food and a lot of hot, black, strong coffee in you. Up you come."

"Fuck off, Pappy. And tell my mother to fuck off too." And Bliss reached for a fresh bottle of beer.

Pappy snatched it. "Now that's no way to talk, Bliss. Your mother went to a lot of effort, called in a lot of chips, and we got you a real good spot at the Pentagon. A nice desk job in the war office."

"Jesus, Pappy. None of this is even legal."

"Maybe not, boy. Maybe not. But the fact of the matter is, not a draft board in the country is ever gonna take you. Your name got . . . well, sorta excised, you might say. So come on, son. Hike up your pants and let's move 'em out."

"Fuck it," said Bliss, and went back to Princeton. Princeton he could do on his own.

In the fall of his junior year, with his trunks and tennis rackets sprawled in the hall and a box of books in his arms, he kicked open the door of the room he'd been assigned and found someone already there.

"You got the wrong room," Bliss said. "Out."

"Sorry, fella," said the invader, and he stood up. And up.

Bliss was tall, but the young man unwinding from the sagging armchair in the corner of the room was taller. He was very tall, very thin, with a long bony face and a thick head of dark wavy hair that fell over one eye. He wore pinstriped suit pants and a vest, a blue shirt with a high white collar, and he leaned nonchalantly on the handle of a long silver-handled walking stick.

"Look. I always room alone."

"Not this year, mister."

"I'm going to do you a favor. Okay? I'm going to tell you to switch. I'm a loner. I've got a foul temper and I tend to get mean."

"I'll drink to that," said Alfred Reece, and he reached into his trunk and cracked open a bottle of scotch.

He was a New Yorker and the only son of wealthy German Jews. Two years older than Bliss, he'd seen 423 days of service in the Pacific and a single night of action. A lone Japanese bomber pilot dumped all he had across the bow of the U.S.S. *Endeavor* that night, but Alfred Reece, on his way from the bridge, didn't see a thing. He didn't feel anything either, but when he recovered consciousness he was aware of a dim ache where the shrapnel had shattered his right foot. As far as he was concerned, the war was over. No glory, no medals. He spent six months convalescing, then went back to Princeton with a bad limp as a member now of the class of forty-five. "Let's face it," Reece grinned as he and Bliss sipped scotch from paper cups that first day, "The Jap saved this boy's Jewish ass."

The anger in Bliss began to retreat and finally faded. They became, in those two years together at Princeton, a hallmark of their class—Alfred Reece with his impeccable suits and silver-handled stick, like a dandy from an earlier era, and Bliss Harlow with his jeans, the boots he planted everywhere, the languid Texas drawl.

"You'll like him," he told his sister when he went to collect her at the train station in Princeton one weekend.

"I'd better," she said as she came swinging down the platform. One hand was stuffed into the pocket of a camel-hair coat, the other was draped through Bitsy Wade's arm, and their loafers made a loud, comfortable shuffle on the worn boards.

Bitsy had shot up too late to acquire a more appropriate nickname. Born Honor Lee Disston Wade, she was the shortest girl in her freshman class at St.

Timothy's and the tallest graduating senior. She was as tall as Eleanor now, with dark hair and the prominent cheekbones of a family that encrusted Philadelphia's Main Line, the side streets of New York's Upper East Side, and the shorelines of Bar Harbor, Maine, where they'd summered for generations. Her family's history was already so thick with quiet, disciplined service to God and the Arts, Industry, Country and Flag— Confederate and Union both—that Bitsy had taken on herself the elaborate responsibilities of the black sheep. "For the chiaroscuro effect," she explained to Eleanor.

Taking courage from each other, Eleanor and Bitsy canceled the long-laid plans for their debuts in Dallas and Philadelphia respectively, declared majors in political theory, and planned to forgo marriage and travel instead. India, they decided, then Africa. Their future thus decided, they set out to have a good time.

That did not include the football game Bliss had tickets to that weekend.

"Football?" asked Bitsy. "Oh dear," and tapped her fingers nervously on the wide arm of the hotel lobby chair where she sat.

"I think," yawned Eleanor, "that I will be ill if I ever see a football game again."

Reece nudged Bliss with the silver handle of his stick. "Don't be an ass. You sister wants a gin mill. In New York."

Eleanor glanced up at him, sudden interest widening her gray eyes.

Bliss half thought she might fall in love with Reece that weekend, but she didn't. They all became friends, and throughout their junior and senior years, on long weekends and school holidays, sometimes with Bitsy, more often alone, they roamed New York. They saw Lily Pons sing *Daughter of the Regiment,* her voice soaring through the lavish, gilded tiers of the Metropolitan Opera House. They saw John Raitt in *Oklahoma!,* Laurette Taylor in *The Glass Menagerie,* and Katharine

Hepburn and Joseph Cotten in *The Philadelphia Story*.
They ate at the Chambord on Forty-ninth and Third
Avenue, went jitterbugging at the Savoy Ballroom in
Harlem, tea-dancing to the music of Cab Calloway at
the Cotton Club on Broadway, and fox-trotting to Eddy
Duchin and Carmen Cavallero at the Rainbow Room.
They gaped at King Paul of Yugoslavia at "21," drank
gin at Julius's, and more gin at Cafe Society Downtown
in the Village where Billie Holiday was singing that
night. They laughed and danced and called themselves
the Very Terrible Three. They felt wonderful. There
was nothing like the frenetic, high-wire world of Manhattan trying to forget, or remember, the war.

They stayed at Reece's family's apartment on West
End Avenue, a cavernous duplex of fourteen rooms
filled with the warmth of parents and sisters, cousins
and uncles and aunts who drifted in and out. There
were stories, dark stories, of camps in Europe, but they
were denied by the government and the press, and
there was only the bright present, and the future.
Reece knew he wanted to go on into law. Bliss, like
Reece, applied to Harvard law. And like Reece, he was
accepted for the class of forty-eight. It promised an
extension of the present and a delay of his future in the
town of Earth, Texas.

And then it was April, the tag end of their senior
year. Their final foray together was Reece's idea. They
needed something special before the crush of exams
and graduation, like rooms at the Plaza and a party if
they could find one. Reece reserved the rooms and then
he found a party.

It was on a yacht, a sleek white giant gleaming with
brass, brought home from the south of France in 1939
and docked on the Hudson.

It was going to be a very swanky party, and Eleanor
wore Bitsy's long black dress with flimsy sleeves to the
wrist and a dipping boat neck. They hemmed the dress
up two inches so that it brushed the top of Eleanor's

silver slippers, and then Bitsy called her aunt's New York stylist and Madame sent her best hairdresser and the manicurist to Eleanor's room at the Plaza. She emerged from the two-hour session at six-thirty that Saturday with pale pink nail polish and elegant coils of blond hair wrapped and twisted around her head. "Thank you," she breathed when she was allowed to turn and gaze at herself in the mirror. "Oh, thank you."

She dressed, applied a touch of rose lipstick to her mouth, and powdered her glowing cheeks. When Bliss knocked at her door at seven, she was ready. She patted her small breasts one last time to make sure the safety pins holding her bra were in place, draped the short black cape over one arm, then darted to look at her reflection in the full-length mirror behind the bathroom door. She smiled once again.

"Not bad," Bliss grinned when she opened the door. "Ravishing," said Reece when they found him by the elevators downstairs. Then the three of them strolled through the lobby arm in arm, past the Palm Court, where two elderly gentlemen in white tie and tails were playing "Sentimental Journey" on piano and violin, and past the entrance to the Edwardian Room, just filling now with soft chatter and the clink of glasses.

The doorman conducted them to Reece's battered Plymouth and they tumbled in. "I'm always stuck in the middle. Always!" Eleanor wailed, and they roared through the streets to the docks of the Hudson, the bright lights of the yacht and the faint sounds of a band welcoming them aboard.

Champagne in hand, the Very Terrible Three moved toward the bow of the ship, edging past men in dinner jackets and women with pearls clutching at slender throats. The pale half-moon thrust its reflection into the dark, deep waters of the river, the yacht slipped its moorings, and the purr of the engines below burst into a steady hum.

They danced, with each other and other partners, and tasted the caviar buried in the wings of swans made of ice. It was past midnight when they stepped to the rail for a last glass of champagne. A moment later a young woman emerged from the crowd.

She wore a silver satin dress that gleamed in the light and rippled into shadows as she moved. Her black hair was loosely pulled back into thick, classic curls at the nape of her long white neck. Tiny diamond earrings caught the light and flashed like her dark eyes.

Eleanor felt the sudden perspiration trickle between her breasts and was painfully aware of the safety pins holding back her bra. She wished, frantically, that they hadn't come; wished that this woman were a million miles away.

And then the woman was embracing Reece, and he was laughing and reaching down to kiss her cheek. Her brother was turning from the rail. The woman in the silver dress looked up and smiled. Bliss Houston Harlow, lean and golden-haired, bowed.

"And now you know what's happening," Eleanor said. Reece glanced up.

Eleanor was wading through the pool across from the Plaza. The skirt of her dress was gripped in one hand; the other hand batted the air for balance. She stumbled. The hem of the skirt sank dangerously close to the water, then rose again as she righted herself.

She grinned at Reece, then gave the water a vicious kick, splashing his pants leg with the spray. "She's probably got my brother on the floor of that hotel room, making mad, passionate love to him on the goddamned carpet."

15

With little thought of what they would do, only that they would do it together, Bliss Harlow and Caroline Forsythe Harrington, widow of a young American pilot and mother of an infant daughter, left the yacht hand in hand. He collected her white fox wrap, waited for the boat to complete its journey around Manhattan, and then, as the soft beat of the last waltz faded away behind them, he led her down the gangplank to the street below.

It was dark on the cobblestone streets. They walked to Eleventh Avenue where the lights were brighter and the taxis cruised, their footsteps echoing softly through the silence of the docks and blocks of warehouses. In the back seat of the cab, Bliss gazed at Caroline's fine-featured face framed in the fox as the passing lights brought her into focus for a moment, took her away, brought her back to him once again. He pulled her closer, touched his lips to her cheek, and felt desire suddenly leap through his body. She turned to him, her arms slipping underneath his coat, and offered her mouth to his. It was a long kiss, deep and open and startling, and her body was yielding, melting, to his. They pulled away from each other and sat quietly as the taxi made its way through the last of the evening traffic, east toward Fifth Avenue and then north, to the park.

Music from the Palm Court still swelled around the lobby of the Plaza, and laughter from the Edwardian Room drifted through the music. The sound of tinkling glasses, cool as spring water, embraced them, isolated them in a universe of their own.

She waited by the elevator for him to collect his key from the desk clerk, and then they rode in silence to the ninth floor and walked down the long carpeted hallways to his room. He opened the door, and Caroline stepped inside. He slipped the fox off her shoulders, dropped it across a Queen Anne chair, then walked with her through the soft dark to the tall windows and pulled back the drapes.

A half moon rode high in the black sky. Streetlamps threw pools of gold along the length of Central Park South and twinkled along the pathways of the park. To the left they could see the dark turrets and towers of the Dakota on Central Park West carved out against the moonlight. On the right lay Fifth Avenue, the occasional windows of its mansions still glowing, scattered like gems on an invisible chain. A limousine meandered past, followed by the two swaying lanterns of a horse-drawn carriage that eventually dissolved into the dark. Then it was still on the streets below, the park like a silent, private garden of their own.

He slid his arms around her shoulders and felt her heart beat hard as she leaned against his body. He let his tongue travel around the rim of her ear, feeling a shiver of ecstasy ride through her, matching his. He gazed down at the perfect face lifted to his and knew he'd never hungered for anything as he hungered for her.

"I want you," he whispered. Her arms slipped around his neck and she nestled for a moment in his arms. "Yes," she said.

He bent to kiss her tenderly, lightly, on her mouth, and then he kissed the smooth, sculptured expanse of her perfect forehead. His hands met hers and together they slipped the gown up and over her head and let it drift to the floor in a liquid pool of satin. She stood before him with slivers of lace across her breasts and pale garters traveling down slender thighs to silk hose. He freed her breasts and cupped their rich, heavy fullness in his hands. Then he traced her dark nipples until they stood ripe and erect in the moonlight. His fingers traced down her belly to caress the thighs that quivered at his touch.

She stepped back, her eyes heavy with longing, and reached up to slip the pins from her hair. It cascaded to her shoulders in a dark, thick mass. She flicked a slender finger under his tie, pulled on one end and watched it unravel. Her hand moved to the stud at his collar. He heard it pop to the floor and felt her hand move down his chest, halting at first one button, then, slowly, on to the next. When she reached his waistcoat, she stopped, and with a few quick movements, Bliss shed his clothes and caught her up in his arms. The sensation of flesh on flesh sent shock waves of desire pounding through him. He was slipping with her to the floor then, spinning in the feel of her, the smell of her, the sound of her. "Now," she was pleading, "now." Then the lace was ripping away under his fingers and he was driving into the hot, wet lushness of her. Once, twice—and he was lost, drowning in her.

He lay still between her white thighs for a moment, floating in the dark of her body and the deep soothing murmurs of her voice. He drifted, weightless, and wanted her again.

He reached down to take her into his arms, cradling her as he stood, her dark hair falling over his shoulder, his arm. He carried her to the bed and felt himself beginning to stiffen again as she lay there, glowing pale through the dark. The garters still traveled down her thighs, and the silk hose still encased her legs. But he wanted all of her, and he bent to undress her once again.

She was nude now and she reached for him. Taking his hand in hers, she guided it down her belly. Her smile was soft, her voice soft. "I will show you how," she whispered.

"No you won't," he smiled.

His mouth was on hers, hard and possessive. It roamed to her breasts, her belly, then buried itself deep between her thighs. She cried out, but his hands held her down and then her body was arching up and he was moving over her. He drove into her deep and hard until she shattered into an explosion. She sobbed in his arms, clinging to him while he held her, rocking her, needing her. Her eyes gazed into his, and their bodies began moving again, lusting for each other once more.

An hour later Bliss looked down over the rim of a champagne glass at the soft, sated body stretched out beside him in the light of the bedside lamp. "When are you going to marry me?" he asked.

"Tomorrow?" she laughed.

She sipped at her glass, and then said, "I was married once, you know, and I have a baby. A little girl named Maggie, not even a year old yet."

He pulled her closer. "I love you. I'll love your Maggie." He stopped and looked into her eyes. "I love you, Caroline."

She reached up to kiss his mouth.

"I want you," he murmured. "And I want your Maggie."

"What about your family?" she asked.

He kissed her. "They'll get used to it. In time. And yours?"

"They'll get used to it," she smiled. "In time."

And then something occurred to Bliss, and he laughed. "I'm even rich," he said, glad for the first time in his life that he was.

"Very?"

"Very."

"Good," she said. "So am I. A little anyway."

"Good. Then marry me today."

Two hours later Reece and Eleanor opened the door to Room 918 with Reece's key. The sunlight was just beginning to creep across the thick Wilton carpet. Sheets and blankets lay in a heap in the middle of the bed, and a tray sat on top with two empty glasses and an empty bottle of what had been very good champagne.

Reece switched on the light in the bathroom. Two wet towels were on the floor, two more hung haphazardly from the racks. Water still dripped in the bathtub. He reached down to turn if off, then wandered back to the bedroom.

Eleanor's face was lost-looking, wan and streaked. He shrugged. "I guess you were right, kiddo. They made mad, passionate love."

"I'm not blind, you know." She turned away and saw the note.

She snatched it up, but her hands were beginning to shake and she gave it to Reece. He unfolded it and read.

"Dear Eleanor, dear Reece," It began in Bliss's scrawl:

Dear Eleanor, dear Reece,
We're getting married. Eleanor, please tell Mother, and Reece, my excuses to Princeton and all that. Don't mind, and don't worry.

Love,
Bliss

"I'm sorry, Eleanor," and he handed her the note.

She read it twice. "Let's pack. I want to go." The note, crumpled into a ball, landed on the floor.

Bitsy's black cape dragged behind Eleanor as she walked down the corridor to her own room. She kicked off the silver shoes and slipped Bitsy's dress over her head, avoiding the mirror as she removed the safety pins from her bra.

She showered, rubbed herself dry and dressed. She pulled her damp hair back into a ponytail and put on the clothes she'd traveled in yesterday—the pink shirt with the Peter Pan collar, the schoolgirl's plaid kilt with the silver pin holding it closed at the hem, the dark-blue knee-highs and penny loafers. She slung her evening clothes into the suitcase and snapped it shut.

Reece was waiting in the lobby. He had paid for the rooms, and his single piece of luggage sat alone at the entrance. The car came around from the garage. They stepped into the street and a sudden spring drizzle. Reece wrapped his jacket around Eleanor's shoulders, and she began to cry. "Oh God," she sobbed into his shoulder. "You know what my mother is going to do? My mother is going to kill him."

Reece, touched by a pain and a loss he only half understood, held her close and then led her to the car and drove her back to Bryn Mawr.

They drove with the top down, despite the rain. Reece protested, but Eleanor was firm. "To hell with the rain." It passed by the time they were in New Jersey and they dried off with the sun and wind buffeting them along the highway.

They stopped for breakfast at a roadside cafe, and Reece ordered coffee and platters of fried eggs, bacon and pancakes.

"Where do you think they are, Reece?" she wanted to know. "What am I going to say? How am I going to tell my mother? I don't even know who she is, for God's sake."

"It'll be all right, Eleanor. Look, she's just a nice girl . . ."

"Nice *girl!* Alfred, I cannot tell my mother that that is a nice girl. She'd think I'd lost my mind."

"She is nice, Eleanor. You'll see. My father did some business with her father and we went to dancing class once or something. I mean, you know, she was just sort of around. But I always liked her, and you will too."

"Does she have any money? Is she Jewish? And how old is she, Reece? I mean, my mother *is* going to ask about that sort of thing, you know."

"She's my age, and no, she is not marrying him for

his money, and no, she's not Jewish. She's Catholic, as a matter of fact."

"Great. An older woman. She's not . . . well, sticky Catholic, is she? With the beads and the holy water? She won't make Bliss convert or anything, will she?"

Reece laughed. "Eleanor, does she really strike you as the beads and holy water type?"

Eleanor giggled, but the giggle turned into sudden tears, and when the waitress brought their order she only swirled her spoon around and around in her cup, leaving a coffee stain on her pink blouse.

They drove south along highways dotted with leisurely Sunday drivers, Eleanor wrapped in sullen silence, and Reece wrapped in the memories of a long-ago summer on a West Hampton beach.

He'd liked the bright little girl with dark curly hair who appeared on the beach one day. She escaped from her nanny to run as far and as fast as he could, to build sand castles and walk for miles collecting shells and driftwood and sea glass. There was a picture of them in a scrapbook somewhere in the West End Avenue apartment: a skinny boy in blue shorts, crooked teeth grinning from a sun-tanned face, and Caroline at ten, her wool bathing suit still wet and the lines of her face already defining the beautiful woman she would become. It was just a black-and-white snapshot, but it was a moment, pure and clear. The ocean pounding on an endless white beach, the creak of Caroline's chair, the shade of the porch, the grainy, wooden planks under his bare feet, the smell of salt, and a voice urging him to sit up straight. Then the click of a camera freezing them in a summer that went on and on, through the villages he and Eleanor drove past now as they skirted Philadelphia and sped on into the Main Line.

It was nearly one when they came into the village of Bryn Mawr. They turned onto Old Gulph Road and headed through the arch of trees toward Eleanor's dormitory at Denbigh Hall. Up ahead he could see the bell tower on Taylor Hall, and the hands of the clock pointing to the hour.

"Come to my room and visit for a while?" Eleanor asked. "Please? I don't want you to go, not yet."

"Come on, Eleanor. You have rules about men."

She shrugged. "We have rules about everything."

The campus with its eight rolling acres of green lawns and medieval buildings of gray stone was still and quiet in the Sunday afternoon. Off in the distance, two girls with shining hair strolled among the trees with their arms full of books. Reece parked the car and walked with Eleanor the few steps to the arched doors of Denbigh Hall.

It was quiet inside. The huge oak door swung closed behind them and Reece placed Eleanor's bag on the floor. The student on duty at the telephone desk waved at Eleanor and then buried herself in her book again. Reece leaned against the wall. He realized he was, in his own way, as hurt by Bliss as Eleanor, as lost somehow and unnerved. The still air of the dormitory, the dark wood of the floor, the high ceilings of the hall—they all felt safe, the college a predictable, familiar world that calmed him and soothed his tiredness and his feelings.

He glanced up when he heard the clop, clop of footsteps running down the stairs. Bitsy Wade appeared. She ignored him and went to the desk instead.

"Gloria, I can't find anyone," she wailed. "Come and help me with the john door. It's stuck and I'm *dying* to go."

Gloria looked up from her book and then stared at the telephone board at her side.

"Oh, come on," Bitsy said. "It'll only take a minute. There's absolutely *nobody* around."

Gloria put the book face down. It was Keynes's *Theory of Economics,* Reece could see now. She edged away from the desk and followed Bitsy up the stairs.

A second later Eleanor beckoned to Reece. He

picked up her bag and his walking stick and went up the stairs, past the portrait of Bryn Mawr's President McBride, down the corridor to Eleanor and Bitsy's suite of rooms.

A giggling Bitsy walked in moments later. And then, suddenly aware of their silence, she fell quiet and stared at their weary faces. "What happened, Eleanor?" she asked. "What *is* going on here?" She stood with her hands on her hips, her legs long and honey-colored in white tennis shorts.

"My stupid brother's gone off to get married," Eleanor said, and she gathered up Bitsy's book bag and tennis racket, pushed them into Bitsy's arms, and opened the door. "I'll tell you about it later. I have to talk to Reece now."

Reece stretched out in the one ancient leather arm-chair, Eleanor curled up in another and began to talk. About Bliss, and the shadowy figure of their father, about their mother and her expectations, about watching out for Bliss because their mother loved him. She talked about arguments and silences, about ponies long dead, a teddy bear once shared, and the aching sense that a part of her was gone.

She talked until the afternoon sky was dusty and gray and by then she had moved to the floor at Reece's feet and leaned back against his legs. His hand rested on her shoulder and he felt the warmth of her neck. He played with a tendril of her hair, heard her sigh, and felt her body suddenly begin to shake with sobs.

He kneeled beside her on the floor, and holding her quivering chin with one hand, he took a large white handkerchief from his pocket and gently wiped her tears away. Then he leaned forward and placed his lips on hers. She shuddered with sobs and threw her arms around him. He stood with Eleanor clinging to his neck, and they moved to her bed.

He caressed her face as they lay down, held her close and stroked her until the crying stopped. Then he reached across to turn on the bedside light and they looked at each other in the warm glow. She didn't stop him when he undid the hook of her skirt and slid it off her. One by one, her blouse, her bra, her loafers and knee socks and her white cotton panties fell to the floor. He stood and calmly, slowly slipped out of his own clothes. She held out her arms, and he eased himself down beside her. She cried out when he entered her and he tried to pull back, but she wound her arms around him, held him close, then closer.

16

The class of forty-five graduated without Eleanor. The notes of "Pomp and Circumstance" rose and fell and the confetti and the streamers wound through the air in celebration of the end of the European war that had finally come in May. But Eleanor wasn't there. She finished her exams in advanced French, advanced Latin, botany, European political history before the Renaissance, and English drama of the medieval period. She turned in a final term paper on the political structure of the trade guilds in Germany, circa 1540, and then she ordered her trunk sent up from storage and pulled her suitcases down from the top of the wardrobe. She emptied her closets of Oxford shirts and Fair Isle sweaters, silk tea dresses, and wool skirts. She folded her clothes carefully with tissue paper, polished twelve pairs of leather shoes and whitened two pairs of tennis shoes. She put six hats in six hatboxes, put eight pairs of gloves in their satin cases, and dropped her charm bracelet in a velvet drawstring bag with her strand of pearls.

She asked for a private interview with President McBride. A family emergency called her home, she said. She couldn't stay for graduation ceremonies and asked if her certificate could simply be mailed instead.

Mrs. McBride expressed dismay but didn't inquire further. She congratulated Eleanor on her grade point average of 3.4 and said she trusted that Eleanor would carry on Bryn Mawr's spirit of grace under pressure and make her contribution to the larger world to which she now belonged.

She sent her trunk and suitcases, hatboxes and tennis rackets on ahead and drove with Bitsy to the Pennsylvania Railroad station in Philadelphia. She watched Bitsy's tearful face grow smaller as the train edged its way out of the station. They waved to each other and then Bitsy, engulfed in a blast of steam, disappeared.

Eleanor called her mother from Chicago. She dreaded making the call. She'd thought about it all the way from Philadelphia, lying awake in her narrow berth. It was almost noon when they arrived in Chicago, and she wasn't due to reboard the train until three that afternoon. She took a trolley car to the Palmer House and had lunch, then returned to the station at two-thirty and placed the collect call.

"Eleanor?" she heard her mother say. Then with sudden alarm in her voice, she asked, "What's the matter, darling? Why are you calling?"

"It's nothing, Mother. Nothing really. I'm sure it'll be all right. It's just that Bliss has gotten married and gone on a little trip for a while." She chatted on through the silence that hummed along the line, coating the few details she had with bright reassurance. She gave out eventually and stopped in midsentence to wait for her mother's voice. It sounded tired when it finally came.

"And you, Eleanor? Are you going away too?"

"No—no, I canceled all that. And I'm skipping graduation, the ceremonies and stuff. I'm coming home."

"Oh, Eleanor," the relief doing battle with the sudden concern, "I thought it meant so much to you—your trip and . . ."

"I know. But it's too late. I'm in Chicago now; they're calling my train. The morning train to Dallas, day after tomorrow."

"We'll meet you, Eleanor. You'll be met," and Eleanor replaced the receiver. She sat in the phone booth, examining the numbers on the dial, and a moment later heard the muffled, distorted call for her train echoing across the station.

She pushed her way across the platform, struggling against the crowds streaming in all directions. She heard the persistent hiss of steam riding high above the harsh voice of the porter calling "All aboard. All abooa-rd" as he handed her up the steps. Then she heard his whistle, the clank of steel rods revving up, and the steel wheels on steel rails as she settled into her seat in compartment 8J.

The lights dimmed and she relaxed into the soft red leather and rested a black patent pump on the couch across from her. The phone call had been made, and she was on her way.

The train came bursting from the long tunnel with an explosion of black smoke and glowing cinders that cleared gradually to reveal endless miles of railroad track and cattle cars with "Santa Fe" and "B.B.&O." written in big white letters across their battered sides. Beyond lay the slums, and beyond them the flat fields of long grass glowing in the late afternoon sun. She stood, removed her suit jacket, and hung it behind the door. Then she stopped before the tiny mirror above the seat, smoothed back her hair, and wiped a smudge of black smoke from her cheek. She called for tea and when it came she sat with one long silk-stockinged leg across the other, cup and saucer perched in her dark lap. She watched the land unwind before her, and wondered what she was going to do next.

She knew she was as lonely as she'd ever been in her life, as lonely and hurt and lost. It wasn't only that Bliss had left behind all they ever were. It was that he had leapt, with sudden, frightening abandon, into a world outside the circle that had made them both who they were. There was betrayal in that, and it made the gnawing sense of loss worse.

She wanted to let that loss flood her. She needed this last train ride home, the train suspending her in time between what she had been and what she would be. She needed to be alone, in a way that she had never felt before, to look at herself without the paraphernalia of the past.

She sipped her tea and gazed at her reflection in windows darkened by the dusk. It was a slender face, shedding its adolescence now and just beginning to take on firmer edges and more angular planes. She touched her cheek with one long finger, then licked the tip of it and smoothed her eyebrows, and wondered if she'd ever stop looking like a vaguely female, oddly younger version of Bliss. She had the same straight nose, the straight eyebrows, and a mouth only slightly fuller than his. He'd looked like a man at eighteen. At twenty-one, she still looked like a girl, even with last year's very expensive spring suit and this year's very good silk blouse.

The girl she saw in the reflection was, she realized, essentially untouched by the weekends in New York or the years at Bryn Mawr. She was the same girl who would have said a month ago what she had been saying ever since she was ten. Don't worry about Bliss. Bliss will grow up and take his place one day. His place, they'd always known, was in Earth, at the *Bugle*. Her place was to improve her temperament, to travel, broaden herself, and then, despite her pact with Bitsy, she would find a husband. Presumably he would be suitable, preferably Texan, and preferably someone they could "talk to," her mother said. That meant someone rich, ideally someone in the newspaper business whose holdings would merge with theirs in one of those great feudal couplings of blood and power and money. They would live in Houston or Austin or Dallas. There would be elegant dinner parties and several children of course. Annual trips to Europe—if there was a Europe worth going to after the war. It had been ordained, all of it, until Bliss slipped free and was gone.

She finished her tea, rested her chin in her hand, and thought. She thought about Bliss, about German trade guilds, circa 1540, about Bitsy and the other girls she'd known at Bryn Mawr, the lives they had come from and the ones they would go on to. She thought about Reece and the moment when she lost her virginity. She hadn't thought of it then and didn't think of it now as losing anything. She remembered Reece giving her reassurance and love, caring for her tenderly, and trying to give back something of whatever it was Bliss had taken away. It occurred to her that she had plunged after Bliss, rushed to follow him out of the very last moments of childhood because she couldn't, after all, allow anybody to leave her behind. She shoved the thought away. She thought of the glow of the lamp and remembered that even their lovemaking had been a kind of goodbye.

She thought about plans and allotted places in life, expectations and ordinations. Toward six she heard the steward making his way down the length of her car. "First call for dinner. First call for dinner." Then he was knocking at her door and smiling in at her.

"You gonna eat, missy? Steak tonight, but might not last past first call."

She nodded, reached for her jacket, and then changed her mind. Nobody thought she was grown-up anyway, not even the steward. She left the jacket.

The dining car was nearly empty and the head steward led her to a table by a window. It was covered with heavy white linen that was thick and luxurious to the touch. The silver plate was solid and heavy, winking in the light of the lamp, and the bud vase held a tiny, unopened rose, a yellow rose of Texas on a Texas train sliding south.

A waiter took the white napkin, shook out its fluted folds, and placed it across her lap. She ordered the steak and turned to the window. Beyond her own reflection, beyond the reflection of the dining car marching into the thick night, the lights of a distant town were shining. She watched them sprinkle the dark, watched them fade, then cupped her chin in her hand and wondered where she was, and where she was going.

The train hurtled on for another day and another night, moving south through endless stops in endless towns—Urbana, Shelbyville, Vandalia, St. Louis, Walnut Ridge, Pine Bluff. Stations were thronged with families and the first wave of homecoming servicemen. Platforms were piled high with kit bags and footlockers. The train battled on through an endless roll call of towns, endless tunnels, bridges, rivers. It moved relentlessly across the land, its rhythms becoming Eleanor's rhythms, her thoughts rolling with the train as it went on down the tracks, taking with it a girl who abandoned herself to its pace and power and knew finally what she would do.

If there had ever been an allotted place for her, she had been released. Everything until now had been a waiting time, a prelude to the beginning of her own life. She knew that now, and knew finally that what Bliss Houston Harlow had left, she wanted. And would take.

Years later, when Bitsy Wade had finally shed her prep-school nickname and was herself president of Bryn Mawr, she invited Eleanor to travel back East once again to give the keynote address to the young women of Bryn Mawr's graduating class of 1974. Eleanor remembered her epiphany on that train, and it formed the focus of her speech about expectation and responsibility.

"We are," Eleanor said on that June day at the close of another war, "we are creatures of our own invention. Possibly we are inventions of our past, and of our times, possibly even of some mad dream in the mind of fate. But in the end, we are our own inventions. That is our tragedy, and our hardest fate."

And Honor Lee Disston Wade in her dark robes and multicolored academic hood, and Alfred Reece, standing at the back beyond the folding chairs and the oaks, knew that Eleanor was addressing, not only the young women of Bryn Mawr, but herself, and the decision she had made as a train went on turning through the night.

17

She moved back into her old yellow room beyond the nursery on the third floor and went to work at the press. "Just for a while," she told her mother, uncertain at first that she would be welcome.

"No, pet," Amelia said. "I want something different for you. There are parties in Houston—you should go. Enjoy yourself, darling."

"I did that, at school." She turned down the invitations to the parties and made sure that Rosie woke her every morning at six with a cup of Matty's coffee. By seven she was swinging through the front screen door, down the steps to Duke and the black sportscar he had waiting for her, a graduation present from Amelia. Five minutes later, she was on her way up the stairs of the *Bugle* to the old storeroom down the hall from her mother.

She had the storeroom cleaned and painted, moved a scarred wooden desk close to the window, took over a file cabinet, and had a phone installed. She had long lunches with Ernst Liepman, spent hours with the accountants, and spent days traveling through Texas with the space salesmen, learning to hustle ads. In the evenings she listened to Amelia.

Her mother was in her late forties now. She was still slender, her hair was still light, and she wore it long again, pulled back in a soft knot just visible beneath the brims of her hats. She never talked of Bliss; she talked only of the press.

She had tried to find her son. She searched methodically at first, then with anger and a rising fear. But no one knew where Bliss had gone and the woman's father no longer cared. He and his wife, he said to Amelia in their one brief telephone conversation, had washed their hands of their daughter and grandchild, and then the line went dead. She listened to the hollow echoes for a moment and then hung up herself. Later, when Bliss's checks started clearing through Texas banks, Amelia wrote. There was no reply.

She found comfort in Eleanor's presence, and more and more a kind of peace. It felt right having her there, and it was good knowing that her daughter had made her choice of her own accord. And so she talked, of the press and her work. And Eleanor listened, absorbing it all.

The press had expanded during the war. The six weeklies to the east of Dallas had become twelve and formed a solid circle around the city that people had begun to call the Big D. They went to press on Thursday nights. Sandwiches were ordered in on those nights, along with platters of catfish from the catfish parlor on Route 30. Amelia and Miss Leslie came in from their offices by the black gum tree. Ernst Liepman was there, and an editor or two from the Dallas ring. They sat at an old copy block checking first proof and clearing for the final run, then wandered the aisles talking shop with the pressmen as they adjusted the last plates and ink fonts. By seven the presses began to roll, filling the room with a rhythmic roar as the blank sheets sucked free of their pallets, whacked to the press beds, and shot out onto the stacks at the other end. By midnight a quarter-million front pages had been printed with local feature stories and the individual logos in the chain—the *Bugle-Times*, the *Fortune*, the *Busy Bee*. By two the front sections were wrapping around virtually identical inside sections that had been printed during the week. By four the trucks headed out, rolling south on Route 30, on into Dallas and the sleepy towns beyond.

Eleanor liked those evenings, liked the banter, the thrust of the machines, and the easy talk of men who laid claim to craft and taught her as they went. But as the year went on she became convinced that they were a part of the past. She'd discovered Michael Murphy by then, the number two man at KLIP. Like him, she'd become addicted to the images that flickered across a box with a seven-inch screen.

"Buy you a drink?" she'd sometimes say after work, and they'd pick up a six-pack of Pearl beer and go sit in his office talking late into the night.

He'd been born and raised in California and then shipped out to Guadalcanal and a Quonset hut where he joined the Mosquito Network, piping Frank Sinatra and "You'd Be So Nice to Come Home To" over the South Pacific. He came back in forty-four, to a job at a radio station in a town in Texas he'd never heard of before. A good many marines brought back mementos of their war: helmets, dress sabres, and Japanese machine guns. Michael brought the box with the screen.

They'd gone on the market briefly before the war, but they disappeared into the military and big-city police stations where they were used for the training of air-raid wardens. Michael thought they would come back now—big.

"Here, I'll plug it in," he said the first night Eleanor came to his office at KLIP. She sat in the dark opening a beer can while Michael fiddled with dials and a radar antenna he'd rigged up on the window. At first there was nothing except an eerie white light glowing on the screen and a distant voice that was garbled and obscure. The light buckled and blinked—and then, "Look," Michael said.

Hands appeared. They were a woman's hands, Eleanor finally saw, and there was something else. "What's that?" she whispered.

"A salad," Michael said. "We're picking up some sort of kitchen demonstration from Chicago. See, she's mixing a salad."

A face appeared, smiled broadly, then dissolved into wavy lines. The screen went blank.

The lights went on again and Michael stood above her, swigging his beer and grinning.

Eleanor went into her mother's office the next day, pulled a decade of annual reports from CBS and NBC off her shelves, and announced a month later that television was the future, theirs and everybody else's.

Will Harlow watched his daughter and didn't interfere. Her passion reminded him in some ways of Amelia. They both had the kind of energy that had been his once, energy that had been sapped out of him so long ago he didn't even yearn for it anymore. He'd made his own peace with life, tending to his patients and to a practice that had diminished over the years, as he became less interested in traveling the long distances. He left all that to the younger men who were coming home from the war.

He regretted Bliss. He sensed that he'd lost him somewhere in his childhood, but he loved the silent, earnest boy he had been, and was glad, for his sake, that he had escaped Amelia and her plans. Now Will had Eleanor, his friends and cronies, an occasional game of cards, and a little bourbon now and then. And he had Anna Janes. Every Thursday and Saturday afternoon he'd shake out his white linen suit, slip the jacket over his loose frame, and drive down to Tyler, to play poker with his old friend Bill Henry, he said. Every Sunday over breakfast Amelia asked, "And how is Bill Henry, Will? I hope you won," and that was that. He had his life and she had hers.

Then, in the spring of 1948, Ben Rawlings climbed the steps to the big white house and he and Eleanor were married the next fall. Will Harlow felt he'd done his part then and could be released from the promise he'd kept for years.

A self-made millionaire by the time he was twenty-eight, Ben Rawlings was the only child of a small-time rancher from a little spread on the scrubby dry hills outside El Paso in West Texas. There wasn't much talk at the Rawlings dinner table and there wasn't much money, and though Susan Rawlings didn't know much about books, she always said her son was smart and would make something of himself one day. She died when he was seventeen, and a year later Ben Rawlings went to the University of Texas on a scholarship he'd applied for, in memory of her in a sense. College, she'd said, would give him a leg up, a start in life.

He volunteered for the army when the war came, made captain by the time his division joined up with the invasion force that stormed the beaches at Normandy. He came home when it was over, found out his father had been dead a month, and saw that El Paso was booming. He sold the ranch, bought downtown real estate, sold it off at a profit and bought some more. He drifted into tract development with interests all over the Southwest and then decided he wanted something more.

At thirty he was just shy of six feet with dusty brown hair and brown eyes. Easy-tempered and easy-going, he spoke with a soft drawl. Banking seemed to be the right thing for him to do, and when the State Bank of

Earth went up for sale, he made the long drive to the northeast quarter of the state.

The bank had never recovered from the depression and Amelia's withdrawal. After Noah Carr finally left town in the late thirties, it became a part of the First Bank of Daingerfield, but it was too late, even then. People had already drifted away, taking their accounts down the highway to other banks in other towns, and now it was for sale again.

It took Ben two days to drive from El Paso that spring of forty-eight. He watched the countryside unwind before him, brown, dry land with an occasional mesa or mesquite blowing under the hot winds, a heathen landscape under an endless blue sky. The drive out of Dallas took him through oases of green turning into fields and finally into the rolling pine hills of East Texas. He liked the tall pines, the black soil, and the gentle lay of the land rich with crops. It was softer country than he was used to and he knew that he would buy. The place felt right to him and whatever the problems with the bank, he was confident he would swing it around.

On a Sunday a week later, with a preliminary agreement to purchase the bank in his pocket, he drove to the edge of town to meet the Harlows. It seemed to Ben as he went over the history and records of the bank that there wasn't much in Earth but the Harlows. They'd help found the town, owned land to the north and west, and owned those newspapers. That was interesting. Texas money wasn't made with newspapers; it was made with cattle like the Kings, or with oil like old man Hunt and Sid Richardson, not with newspapers. He sent a note to their home, accepted an invitation to drinks a day later, and at four that Sunday afternoon drove out to the edge of town and up the hill into the cottonwoods.

He sensed right away that he'd never met Texans like

them before. They had style and assurance, grace. It was Amelia Harlow who set the tone, something about her drawing him toward her first as he climbed the steps to the cool, green shade of the porch where she waited.

Her husband was there, lounging on a wicker chair. He rose as Ben walked up the steps and extended a thin, tanned hand in greeting. His suit hung in loose folds over his slender frame and he made a quiet backdrop to his wife.

The girl was blond, with cool gray eyes. She leaned forward, one sandal dangling from a slim foot at the end of a long, slender leg. "Welcome to town, Mr. Rawlings," she smiled, and invited him to sit beside her.

The Harlows at home, and the sense in that first instant that other people weren't as real as they were.

Ben Rawlings courted Eleanor Harlow as he'd done everything else in his life, with an easygoing smile and the sure sense that when you saw something you wanted you went out and got it.

He caught a glimpse of her turning a corner on Main Street the week after he moved to Earth. He quickened his pace to catch up. "I'll feed you dinner tonight if you promise to behave," he said, and then watched her spin around in surprise.

"Are you asking me for a date, Mr. Rawlings?"

"More or less. Probably more." He smiled when he saw her face turn pink.

He picked her up at seven and took her to a beer and steak house fifty miles out in the hills. "I'll starve before we get there," she sulked.

"Good," he said.

There was sawdust on the floors, and red-checked oil cloths lined long tables jammed with massive pitchers of beer and ranch hands in their shirt sleeves. "Very elegant," she sniffed, but he'd seen her eyes light up when they pushed through the double doors and he bent down to kiss the back of her neck.

He was the first man to ask her out in all the time she'd been back from school, a fact she announced to him over dinner. "You probably terrify them," he said.

"Really? And do I terrify you too, Mr. Rawlings?"

"Hardly. Eat your steak."

They talked about banking and television and the newspaper business over coffee, talked about growing up in small Texas towns, going away, and coming back. He ordered more coffee and then took her home, pulling up into the gravel drive just after midnight.

"Thank you," she said as she opened the door. He reached out and took her hand. They sat in his car, looking at each other in the light from the porch. "I bought a house on Willow Street the other day," he finally said. "I'd like us to go there and make love."

Eleanor looked down at the hand holding hers, a big, brown, square hand that made hers seem very small. Something was happening in her body and she nodded yes.

He drove back down Main Street, turned right on Willow, and pulled to a stop a block down from the school. They could still hear the last echoes of their shoes across the empty floors when he opened the door to the bedroom at the back. He didn't turn on the light. She was already in his arms, and their hands were traveling over each other, searching for naked skin.

She felt cool air on her breasts, on her thighs, and then she was on the bed. Her breath came in frantic little gulps until he stripped and sank into her body. They lay very still then, not moving, gazing at each other in the dark.

She realized she'd wanted him to do this all night, wanted him to claim her like this. Now his body filled hers completely, big, very warm, and she reached up to trace the line of his eyebrows and then found the almost invisible dimple in his chin. She smiled, and he smiled back, smoothing the tangle of curls away from her face and then kissing her forehead. He heard her sigh and he shifted his body, pressing deeper, then heard her whimper suddenly. He went deeper, covering her mouth with his kiss, and felt her legs come up and wrap around him in the dark.

He took her back home again two hours later. He didn't say anything, just held her against him for a moment on the porch, one hand in her hair, the other cupped around the dark fabric covering a small breast. She watched him go, and when Rosie woke her the next morning, it felt odd to reach out and not find him there.

They were married that October, and he tried to comfort her in her days following their honeymoon when Will Harlow began appearing in public with his mistress. But nothing about her had prepared him for her angry reaction and the sudden, almost hysterical sobs for the twin brother called Bliss.

Eleanor had been careful not to know that her father wasn't playing cards on Thursday and Saturday afternoons. Once, when he mentioned Tyler, she remembered and suddenly knew. And then she forgot.

Amelia kept up her façade, and Eleanor kept her illusions. Her father was made of little-girl memories of the handsome young man he'd been, a man with slender brown hands cupped under her chin or tugging gently on her braids. She loved the smell of him, the smell of hospital coats and clean, fresh laundry, of disinfectant and a faint hint of bourbon. She didn't want to know more, so she didn't.

Until she saw her father and Anna Janes in the old Ford, driving down a Daingerfield street.

She went to Ben's office at the bank at noon and he took her home to the house on Willow Street. She sobbed in his arms far into the night and finally erupted in a wail of anger at her brother that he didn't fully understand. "It's not fair," she cried. "He should be here—he's supposed to be here. God, I hate that wife of his—hate her."

Ben pulled her close and wrapped her tight in his arms. "Hush, sweetheart," he murmured, but she couldn't, and when Ben took her to bed and moved his body over hers, she was still in tears. "I want it to go away—all of it," she cried.

Two days later, Rosie and her boy George saw Dr. Will and his lady friend at the Bijou in Mount Pleasant, watching Rosalind Russell in her new picture show, *Tell It to the Judge*. Rosie told her friend Betty, who worked in the mailroom down at the press, all about it. There they were in the balcony, she and George, looking down on the white folks when they spotted them. "Eatin' popcorn and havin' a good ol' time," Rosie said with a sad shake of her head.

Matty told her to shut her mouth up, but it was too late. The secretaries at the press snapped into silence when Eleanor passed, and shopkeepers in town greeted her with a broad, sympathetic cheeriness. She felt as if she'd been wound into a betrayal with her visits to Tyler that year she was thirteen. She hated her father for that, and for the need to say to her mother, "I didn't know. I promise you I didn't know." She wondered suddenly if her mother knew about Anna Janes at all, and was surprised to find she did when the subject couldn't be ignored any longer. Eleanor was even more surprised to discover that there'd been an understanding.

"But not this public display," Amelia said. "I'm sorry you know. I know how it must hurt."

"I met her once," Eleanor said, and then she sat like a child on the couch in her mother's office, weeping uncontrollably again.

That Saturday night Amelia waited up for Will, knocked on his bedroom door, and then went in.

Will Harlow turned, startled. Then he loosened his

tie, watching her as she stood there, hissing at him across the room they'd once shared. "Did you have to flaunt it?" she whispered. "Did you have to take that child to her house? Was that necessary?"

"She didn't know, Amelia. She was—"

"She was a baby, Will. You had no right."

"I told you—she didn't know," his voice rising in sudden anger.

"And now? Now she knows. We all know now, don't we? All Texas knows about your woman."

He looked at her standing there, small and pale and hard. "Sit down, Amelia," he finally said. "We have to talk."

Even Ben Rawlings was surprised to hear that after all these years Will Harlow wanted a divorce and the freedom to marry his Anna Janes. He sat with Eleanor in Amelia's office that Sunday, watching the morning light on the stacks of papers cluttering her desk.

"So I've been told to sell the press," Amelia went on. "The press, the radio station. Sell it all. It is his, as he has reminded me, and he wants the cash."

Ben glanced at his wife sitting in the chair next to him. She looked very young with her hair pulled back into a ponytail and her breasts almost invisible in the folds of an old shirt of his she'd knotted at the waist of her jeans. "Oh," was all she said, like a kid with the wind knocked out of her.

Eleanor didn't feel young. She didn't feel anything at first. She only knew she'd done all the crying she could afford to do about handsome daddies and twin brothers who were gone. She was alone and on her own.

She sat in the Sunday quiet of the publisher's office at the press. The leaves of the black gum tree outside were once again turning wine red with the fall. She hadn't consciously thought about it, she supposed, but it had been there at the back of her head since she came home: the idea that this office would be hers one day.

She looked up at her mother's face. They had never been close like other mothers and daughters. They didn't shop or chat, but Eleanor could read that face, and she knew the pain that was there. It was her pain too, the sharp, angry hurt of having to give up what was yours.

"Mother," she finally said, "I think we have to do something, don't you?"

Later, Ben Rawlings thought that there were other things they could have done, but nothing would have been as effective as the plan his mother-in-law arrived at. It was cruel, but there was cruelty in Will Harlow's order to sell, so he opened his bank to them that Sunday morning and watched the chauffeur-driven cars pull away and head south.

Amelia and Eleanor sat behind Duke in the gray Lincoln; George followed in the black Cadillac. An hour later they rolled into a quiet street in Tyler and walked up a brick path to a white screen door.

Anna Janes's parlor was small and dark, the furniture was heavy, and the glow of the rose garden was just visible through the windowpanes. The carpet was worn, as was the fringed green cloth across the back of the upright piano, but everything was very clean and neat, as clean and neat as Eleanor remembered it.

She wondered about Miss Janes's mother, but more than ten years had passed and she would be dead by now. Her father would have gone to the funeral, she supposed, and he would have held Miss Janes close. She wondered if Miss Janes had cried or if she had held herself as she did now with her soft, big-boned body stiff and straight on the edge of her wingback chair. Her hands were folded calmly in her lap, and her eyelashes were surprisingly long and soft against her cheeks. That was something Eleanor hadn't remembered.

She looked away and instead focused on her mother, an infinitely, almost embarrassingly, more beautiful woman. Her voice was low and measured as if she were talking to a child who had behaved badly and caused them all a great deal of trouble.

"Unfortunately," she was explaining, "there is no question of divorce. I'm sorry if you've been misled, Miss Janes. But there will be no divorce. Ever."

Eleanor eyed the floor. She admired her mother, so calm and reasonable.

"The matter has gotten out of hand," Amelia went on. "We've been thinking of it for some time and we have decided, my husband and I, and our daughter." She nodded at Eleanor. "We've all decided it would be wiser if you left Texas. Found a life of your own.

"If you were to disagree, and I'm prepared to give you twenty-five thousand dollars in cash to ease your way, I will have to use my influence with the Tyler school board." She paused for a moment. Waited. "I might possibly begin a series of editorials about the declining morals among our Texas schoolteachers with you as an example, Miss Janes."

Amelia turned to Eleanor then. She handed her mother the attaché case and watched Amelia open and close it and then place the wrapped set of notes on a heavy Victorian washstand. "Needless to say, Miss Janes, we all hope that can be avoided."

Anna Janes let the weight of it sink in and then lifted her head to look at the woman across from her. She was almost sure Amelia Harlow was lying about Will and for a moment she imagined his daughter would rise to her feet and say out loud that it wasn't true. She was such a lovely girl and not so much younger than she herself had been when she took Will Harlow as her lover nearly seventeen years ago. She saw Will in his daughter, had always seen him in her, even in the gangly girl with the knock-knees and the long braids as light as wheat. She could see nothing of the mother in Will's lovely daughter. She was the daughter she'd always dreamed of, the daughter who might have been hers if Will had married her when he first promised, back at the beginning. If he'd left his wife to her newspapers and married her, given her children to hold and love.

She imagined herself rising, standing on her feet, and saying with all her force and all her strength, *Get out*. Watch me marry him. Tattle to the school board. Run your editorials. I don't care.

But she did care. She was forty-five years old and there would never be a daughter like Eleanor now. All she had in her life was the bronze plaque they'd given her once, honoring her as the best-loved teacher in Tyler, Texas. She had that, and a man she'd waited seventeen years to marry.

She glanced at Eleanor again and felt the bitter pain of hopeless longing for things to be different, to be different herself. She wished she were stronger and more daring, or young again, in love with someone else.

"Yes," she finally said. "I'll go."

"And if you would, please, a letter to the doctor. I prefer to have it in writing."

With sudden tears, Anna moved to a small desk and pulled out a pen and pad. "Do you want to write it for me, Mrs. Harlow?" she smiled. "Or may I write my own farewell?"

"Write what you like," Amelia said. "Whatever you like."

Duke stayed behind with the black Cadillac. They drove home in silence with George, focusing on his straight young back, his black jacket, and his cap.

Amelia left the letter for Will in his room that evening. She placed it on his bedside table and wondered about love; wondered, as she walked the length of the hall to her room, what kind of contempt for Will had inspired her to open low and offer half of what she carried in her attaché case.

Eleanor called her father's office the next morning to ask him to lunch. His nurse didn't answer the phone, so just after ten she decided to walk over and leave a note. She pushed her papers aside, picked up her jacket, and marched down the stairs to the street. The warm fall day gave her hope as she strode along the wooden sidewalks. It was going to be all right now. Everything was going to be all right. The Ford was outside his office, years' worth of dirt embedded in its tires, and she thumped the hood as she walked by. Her daddy loved that piece of junk. Maybe she'd suggest they clean it up and fix it like new.

The office door was slightly ajar and she peered in. The front office was dark and the shades were drawn. The reception desk sat silent; the few papers on top were stacked in a neat pile. Even the fan was off. She had turned to go when she saw his body swinging from the rope he had used to snap his neck.

She stared, at the contorted face, the tongue hanging out of the mouth, at a piece of hair caught by a streak of light struggling around the edge of a window shade. The only sound was Eleanor's moan. It began somewhere in the root of her, surged up, gathered speed and volume, and emerged finally in a shrieking wail.

Havana, Cuba

May 1945

18

Bliss and Caroline were married by a justice of the peace in Maryland. They spent their first day as a family traveling south, Caroline's nine-month-old daughter Maggie gurgling happily through it all.

For Caroline Harrington there were no problems, no doubts. It simply worked, immediately, beautifully, and irrevocably. Bliss Harlow, with his lean body, thick yellow curls, and deep gray eyes that gazed into hers, was for Caroline the culmination of all the romantic fantasies she had ever had.

As the only child of a modestly wealthy New York broker and his devoutly Catholic wife, she had learned early how to pay lip service to form and hide willful ways and secret dreams behind her beautiful smiles. The Forsythes, already settled into middle age when she was born, spoiled and indulged her. When she behaved they adored her and when she didn't they returned her to the nursery. She was a fat, pretty baby, and she flowered into a child so lush, so beautiful that Mary Margaret Forsythe thrilled to the impressiveness of her achievement. She chastised herself for the sin of pride, but because her priest was more forgiving, she began to look forward to the day when the child would grow up and accompany her on the rounds of luncheons and fund-raising teas that sustained the battery of Catholic charities to which Mary Margaret was devoted.

Caroline grew up virtually alone in the huge, dark apartment on Park Avenue. Her only companions were the young maids off the boats from Ireland, the governesses who came and went, and more often, the creations of her own romantic imagination. It was only when she went off to board at Miss Porter's in Connecticut that a larger world opened to her. All parents weren't old and all homes weren't like tombs. Despite her problems with Latin conjugations and the sheer impossibility of memorizing the lists of English kings, it began to occur to Caroline Forsythe, age thirteen, that the world was a candy box, and layer after layer was waiting for her.

Caroline wasn't quite the credit her mother thought her to be, but the only sign she gave her mother was her refusal to go on for further schooling with the nuns at Marymount. Mary Margaret saw then that the fashionable Miss Porter's had been a mistake, but the sting faded when Caroline proceeded to debut nicely at the New York cotillions and then joined her on the luncheon circuit. If her mother knew she was working a faster track in the evenings with a faster crowd that drank gin and danced in nightclubs, drove sleek cars and summered in Southampton, she ignored it.

Caroline met Tony Harrington at a bar in one of those nightclubs. He was dashing and handsome in his new-tailored air force uniform and indisputably the catch of the season. Everyone in Caroline's circle knew that, but not Mary Margaret. Tony Harrington, she said, had no background. He was not Catholic, he had no money, and he would not do.

Caroline sat in the suffocating quiet of the Park

Avenue drawing room with her hands folded in her lap. Her slender feet in their black pumps were placed one beside the other on an oriental carpet with a dreary design. She looked up at her mother through dark, thick lashes and lied. "Mama, it's too late," she whispered. "I have to marry him now." She watched her mother's face freeze. "Please don't tell Papa— please," she begged. She burst into tears. "And Mama, he'll convert. He promised."

The Forsythes blessed the marriage with a handsome dowry and a wedding at St. Patrick's Cathedral, and sent the young Harringtons off to Saratoga for a week-long honeymoon that taught Caroline the word "fucking." Tony murmured it in her ear as he slid in and out of her, and it made all her nerve ends leap. Two weeks later, he got his orders and flew off to Europe with her picture in his pocket.

He left Caroline in the dark Park Avenue apartment. Her young body hungered for what he had done to it and then it gradually began to swell with his offspring. Six months later he was dead.

She stopped wondering about her life the night she met Bliss Harlow. The moment Alfred Reece introduced them, something caged inside her was suddenly free. She felt a flutter in the pit of her stomach and a dizzy little burst of light in her head. "Earth, Texas," she said. "Now where on earth is that?"

"Nowhere," Bliss laughed, and asked for the next dance, and the next.

He called the desk from his room at the Plaza and ordered a car to drive them to Maryland. It was just daylight when they left the hotel, stepped into the black limousine, and settled low into the leather seat. They pulled out onto Central Park South and paused at the red light on Fifth Avenue. She glanced out the window and saw Reece and Eleanor splashing in the fountain under the bronze nymph with her shell shining bright in the morning sun.

"Stop," she cried. "Oh, Bliss, look. Reece will be so pleased!"

"No." She turned, and he shook his head. "I can't." The limousine shot across Fifth and in a few minutes it pulled to a stop at Park and Eighty-ninth.

Caroline raced past the startled doorman and into the elevator. She woke the old uniformed operator, who rubbed his eyes and took her up to the tenth floor. Pausing just inside the door, she listened to the early morning quiet, then took off her shoes and slipped down the carpeted corridor to her room.

The red leather suitcase she dragged from a shelf at the top of her closet thumped to the floor, and she held her breath, listening. More carefully, she opened the wardrobe doors, and stepping out of the satin dress, she blushed with the memory of sliding it off her body only hours ago. She considered the substantial display before her and then began to search for something to wear. It was her wedding day and she wanted to look beautiful. She'd be in the car for hours, so she needed something comfortable, something that didn't crease.

She finally chose a pale blue afternoon dress of light crêpe de Chine with wide shoulders and a vee neck that extended into a drape across the left hip. She reached for her jewelry box and chose a little bouquet of gold and diamonds to pin the drape in place. She shook out her hair before the dressing table mirror, brushed it back into a twist, and then perched a jaunty little skimmer to the right side of her head. It looked like a dark blue pancake with a feather, and she smiled. She put on her tiny diamond earrings and applied a lick of dark lipstick—Passion Red #17—and a flutter of powder. She stood, smoothed the dress across her hips, and admired the tilt of the hat to the right and the drape of her dress sweeping to the left.

She packed quietly, throwing underwear and stockings into the red leather suitcase, shoes, dresses, and her jewelry box. Stealthily now, she moved across the

room, through the connecting bathroom, and into the
nursery that had once been hers.

The little nursemaid was sound asleep in the narrow
bed, her round Irish face flushed, her mouth slightly
open. Maggie smiled when Caroline leaned over the
crib. Grateful for her good nature, she lifted the child
into her arms. With her free hand Caroline grabbed
clean diapers, a tiny white blanket, bottles, and baby
clothes. Her arms overflowing, she crept back to her
room.

"Hush, darling," she whispered as Maggie began to
coo. "We'll get you dry in no time." Quickly she
changed the diaper and, finally triumphing over the
resistance of the fat baby legs, she dressed Maggie in a
ruffled yellow suit. Then she flung her mink coat over
her shoulders, rested Maggie on her hip, picked up the
suddenly heavy suitcase with her free hand, and took
one last look around her room.

Starched white ruffles lined the dressing table,
matching curtains hid the broad sweep of Park Avenue,
and a pale green satin quilt was heaped with ribboned
pillows. Leather scrapbooks stuffed with letters, faded
corsages, and old secret memories sat on one shelf, and
a worn Raggedy Ann doll was propped up near the
end. Caroline put the suitcase down, darted back
across the room, and picked her up, cradling her with
Maggie. She was ready now. Off forever. Silently
she opened the door to the hall and shut it behind
her.

Gray, stern Mary Margaret Forsythe was waiting.
"What is the meaning of this, Caroline," she whispered. "Where do you think you're going?"

"To be married, Mama," she sparkled, and then she
told her mother about her wonderful fiancé from the
funny little Baptist town in Texas.

"This will kill me, do you hear? Kill me, Caroline,"
and she clutched the red-and-white striped pajamas she
wore under her red dressing gown.

"No it won't, Mama," Caroline said as she eased past her mother and down the hall.

"Caroline!" her mother begged.

Maggie began to cry, but Caroline shifted the Raggedy Ann into the baby's arms, pleased at her own cleverness when Maggie grabbed it and gurgled. "Goodbye, Mama," she said. "Kiss Papa for me. I'll write."

And she was gone—down the elevator, across the lobby, into the warmth of the waiting limousine and Bliss's arms. Three weeks later, on a white-hot day in May, they were on the tramp steamer that drifted around the high walls of the Castillo del Morro and on into the harbor of Havana.

19

The blue-green of the Gulf Stream lapped at one coast of Cuba, the blue-blue of the Caribbean lapped at the other, and in between lay an island eighty miles long—slender as a coffee bean, a gem worth the centuries of pillage by pirates, politicians, and sugar kings. War brought devastation to Europe in the forties, but to Cuba it brought, only and finally, respite. On the eastern tip of the island lay Guantanamo Bay, a strategic base for American troop ships and a source of jobs and money. The price of the sugar cane that grew in the green valleys doubled during the war, and Cuba flourished for a moment, a haven in the war-weary world and dazzling in the sun.

Nothing they had heard prepared Bliss and Caroline for the impact of the harbor. Dozens of small fishing boats bobbed around the steamer, and the voices of men and boys rang across the water as they cried up to the passengers, offering everything from fruit and fresh fish to hotel rooms and taxi service. As the ship drifted on into the long finger of the harbor, the ancient walls

of Morro Castle and La Punta disappeared behind
them, and on either side they could see white buildings
in white light on high terraced cliffs. Ahead, palatial
mansions in patches of green were slung along the sand,
and just beyond were the old city walls of Havana itself.

Gulls soared and wheeled above the three figures
pressed against the railing, and the late afternoon sun
winked silver on the dancing waves below. Bliss held
Maggie, a tiny finger in her rosebud mouth, her eyes
wide. Caroline's head was bare and she wore sunglasses
perched on the tip of her nose. Holding herself steady
against the soft roll of the boat, she slipped her free
arm through Bliss's and smiled up at him. He leaned
down to kiss her. "This is the second most beautiful
sight I've ever seen," he said, and kissed her again.

The excited chatter that had erupted as they pulled
into the harbor died down now, and the only sounds
were the hum of the engines, the waves breaking over
the hull, and the voice of the skipper calling out to the
seamen as they prepared to dock.

Porters strapped their luggage to the back of a
horse-drawn carriage, and they were taken down Malecon drive, around the yacht club and on to the Prado.
They turned left there and followed the laurel-shaded
boulevard into the heart of the city. All along the
elegant avenue, the white coral limestone of the buildings ran gold in the late afternoon light. The stores and
cafes were quiet. Ahead lay the capitol and the park,
but they turned into the Plaza de la Fraternidad, a cool
square of tall royal palms and hotels. They chose the
Grande, small and white, and dark and cool inside.
They took the large suite on the top floor overlooking a
courtyard lush with laurel and bougainvillea. From the
terrace they could hear the fountain gurgling at its
center, and Maggie crawled toward the sound, pulled
herself upright on the wrought-iron railings, and peered
down into the garden.

"Da da," she gurgled with excitement. "Da da," she crowed, and turned to Bliss.

"She called you daddy," Caroline said with delight in her voice. "Did you hear?" Bliss scooped Maggie into the air and swung her high. It was a real word, and she had called for him.

Later, as Maggie slept in the next room, Bliss and Caroline lay in each other's arms, knowing that they were a family and that they had come home. Their arms reached closer and their bodies melted into each other while the fountain splashed.

They had originally planned to stay a week, perhaps two, and then go on to Grand Cayman, Jamaica, or Pedro Cay. But the days in Havana were long and sweet, and the time passed easily. They spent lazy weeks wandering the streets or drinking coffee and aperitifs while listening to vendors hawking lottery tickets and fresh flowers, or the cacophony of a dozen languages in the noisy cafes. After an afternoon nap and the arrival of a maid to take care of Maggie, they went on to dinner at the Templete on the bay or, more often, the Floridita on the Prado where the food was French. Constantino the bartender was witty and wise and the inventor of the daiquiris frappé he always presented to Caroline with a flourish, murmuring his compliments in soft, dusty Spanish. Once they drove into the country to El Sitio for *ropa vieja* and rough red wine and a view of the screaming crowds gathered at the cockfight pits. At midnight there was a last drink at Sloppy Joe's or one of the clubs, the Sans Souci or the Tropicana with the insistent click of the croupiers and the showgirls who descended from the trees in the garden. Closer to the hotel there was the Zombie Club, where the band floated around on a turntable by the patio under the trees. The first night Bliss and Caroline dropped by, it rained a soft, lush tropical rain that sent the waiters scurrying to pull a canvas canopy up over the dance floor. It leaked, but they didn't care. They danced on, swaying to the beat of the music until the band yawned and faded away toward home. They went home too, to the white expanse of their bed.

They'd been married nearly a month and even though they made love to each other over and over, the need never dulled; it only sharpened. It seemed different to Caroline nearly every time. Sometimes it was slow and painfully sweet as their mouths moved across each other for hours until they melted, like bodies going liquid. Sometimes there was no kiss, no signal, just their bodies driving for each other, locking in pure hunger.

"Don't move," he whispered to her tonight, and she lay, open and totally available to him in the light of the Havana moon high in the sky.

They'd been at the Hotel Grande for six weeks when Caroline read about a villa for rent in the pages of the Havana *Post* one morning over coffee. Jaimanitas, the ad read. Not far away. "Let's go see it, Bliss," she said. "Just for fun. Just to look."

On a morning so windy that the sea sprayed the retaining walls of the Malecon highway, they drove the fifteen miles to the outskirts of Jaimanitas. The villa was white and surrounded by mango trees and laurel that cooled the air and dappled the light. Inside, tile floors were scattered with bright rugs, and the furniture, of rattan and heavy dark wood, was stark against the white stucco walls. The wind died down and there was a lightness to the air, the sun breaking through the clouds and streaming in through narrow windows as a maid led them to a second-story terrace, to a sudden shock of blinding light and a view of the Gulf Stream beyond.

"Oh, let's, Bliss. Let's take it," said Caroline. "Can we?"

They rented the villa, complete with the staff—

Manuel to cook, Juanita to clean, their niece Yolanda
to take care of Maggie. They bought a second-hand
Ford convertible Caroline had painted a bright, taxi-
cab yellow. They belonged, it seemed, to paradise now,
and the honeymoon in the Caribbean, designed to last a
few months, promised to drift into forever.

Days eased one into the other, languid days of love
that required few words. There were simple meals
prepared by Manuel and served on the terrace; drives
into the interior in the bright yellow convertible to see
the swampy mangrove forests, the fields of tobacco, the
plains fat with beef, the workers in the sugar cane
groves. Timeless days of bright sun and sudden tropical
showers that sent them laughing to the shelter of
mangrove trees.

They discovered a neighbor on one of their drives,
Doña Silvia Losa de Docal, who was a descendant of a
Spanish noble family that had laid claim in Cuba in the
seventeenth century. She was a widow with dark, sleek
hair, porcelain skin, and a ramrod-straight back, and
she directed the enormous sugar plantations that had
been her husband's with an efficiency that startled
Caroline. In many ways Doña Silvia reminded Bliss of
his mother, and a part of him, a part he thought he had
left behind, was vastly pleased when Doña Silvia grew
fond of Caroline and took her under her wing.

She was a member of the Biltmore Yacht and Country Club that lay on the far side of Jaimanitas. Caroline
would like it enormously, she announced one day. "She
and I shall have a *mojita* before lunch on the terrace, a
little tennis, a swim. I shall introduce her to friends and
they will find her charming."

"I'm being organized, darling," Caroline said. "Do
you mind? Will you miss me *too* much?"

"Yes," he said, "but go. And have a wonderful
time."

The club, with its terrace and lawns and thatched
cabanas, was lovely, and sweet little Incarnacion, who

showed her to the ladies' changing room, smiled and nodded as she smoothed a wrinkle from the white tennis skirt Caroline slipped over her brown legs. It was nice to meet people and to be noticed.

There was a tea and a lunch at Doña Silvia's and two months after they'd moved to Jaimanitas, there was a dinner party in their honor. The invitations, engraved on thick, creamy vellum and emblazoned with the ancient arms of the Losa family, went by hand, and that evening Doña Silvia's dining table glowed in the light of candelabra rich with drops of crystal. Blue Limoges and silver service for fifty shone below, and silver bowls of white jasmine lined yards of pristine antique Spanish lace. There was a servant to each guest, a butler to orchestrate the flow of food and wines, and a guest list that was, Doña Silvia assured them, Havana itself: President Prío Socarrás; the American ambassador, Spruille Braden; directors of Havana's banks and finance houses; the officers of Bacardi rum; and an aging European princess who wore for this special occasion every jewel of her deposed reign.

Relaxed and happy, Bliss watched Caroline across the dinner table that evening. She wore a simple white silk dress that caught the light and she shone in the sea of sequined black the other women wore. He wanted to cross the room, to kiss the hollow in her neck, taste her skin, her mouth. She smiled at him over her wineglass, her eyes sharing his secret, then turned again to her dinner partner.

"Darling," said Caroline after the men rejoined the women in Doña Silvia's drawing room, "darling, this is Fernando Machado. We've been renting his house."

Bliss turned and held out his hand. Machado's grip was firm and the smile on his well-chiseled face was broad and strong.

"I am honored such lovely people live in my little *casita*. We were there for three years." And he introduced them to his wife, a girl with dark chestnut hair and big eyes and gawky young elbows like a child's. "Portia, these are the Americans. We shall have them to lunch."

"Yes, please," she said. "Tomorrow? I see you, you know, in your pretty yellow car." Her smile was shy and her voice light, clipped with the surprising cadence of the British.

"A scandal, they tell me," Doña Silvia said later. "She is the Honorable Portia Michaels, raised in Buenos Aires, where the British and the Argentines don't marry, my dear. But you shall ask her yourself. Not about her title—that only makes her blush. But about the other—well, she is rather frank."

"Too awful," smiled Portia after lunch the next afternoon. "All Buenos Aires was riveted—for months. My poor father sent me home to England, but Fernando was so clever. He came and got me."

"How lovely," sighed Caroline. "I can't bear sad endings—can you?"

"Come," said Portia, and she stood, her hands extended to Caroline. "I think he's showing his ponies."

The *finca* spread west into the foothills of Jaimanitas, and the white walls of the terrace rambled off into lush green fields. Beyond the white fences, horses grazed. "Polo ponies," Machado said, smiling. "My second love."

He had been a breeder of Argentinian polo ponies before the war sent all the lean young men off to different battlefields. But now the young men were coming home again, and Machado was breeding ponies again, Argentinian ponies.

"Small and fast," he said, "the best," and he ran his hands down the flanks of the young stallion he had led out of a box in the stables. "He can turn on a *pesato*. Come, we show you." He called to the stablehands to saddle eight ponies and led his wife and their guests to the polo field.

It was a grueling sport—grueling on the horses and grueling on the pocketbook. A player needed at least two ponies, preferably four, and the matches were played all over the world—in Iran, where the game was invented, in England, the States, South America. "A rich man's sport," Machado said, "a very rich man's sport."

The horses that were led forward were brilliant bays and blacks, prancing and snorting in the sun. Machado and his men mounted and formed two teams of four each. Machado held his mallet at right angles to his body, saluted the opposing captain, and it began.

A smashing of mallets against the white wicker root ball, the crack of whalebone whips, the thundering feet of ponies covering the field from one lath goalpost to another. Enthralled, Bliss and Caroline watched the hard, stunning ballet ranging across the field, fierce and fast. The snorts of the horses and the grunts and cries of the men punctuated the stillness of the afternoon, each man at one with the rippling, straining, pounding muscles of his pony.

It lasted less than ten minutes and it was over. "One chukker's enough," Machado panted as he slid off the steaming, sweat-flecked back of his pony. In official games there were six, he explained as he led them back to the terrace. A houseboy wheeled a wagon of scotch and ice and chilled white wine across the flagstones. "This time next year," Machado went on, "there will be twenty, thirty ponies on the fields, and men coming from all over the world. To see them. And to buy."

Bliss sat with his Haig & Haig, thinking. By the time the sun sank, leaving the day in velvet dark, they had a deal.

Bliss put together a sale of stocks and bonds. Machado had two more brood mares shipped up from Argentina, and they formed a partnership to breed and train ponies. In the mornings, when the sun came bolting up out of the sea, you could see them in the valley west of Jaimanitas: the sleek, dark yearlings pounding down the strip; the lanky young American in his blue jeans, crouched low, riding high; the smaller Argentinian, lithe in white jodhpurs, turning, wheeling, smashing his mallet through the grass like a hammer.

Their days burst open now. Caroline buzzed in and out of the Biltmore Club and on into Havana in her bright yellow car—two mornings a week at the American Hospital and two afternoons of Spanish classes at Colégio Bolen. The dark-haired baby was thriving, blossoming in the tropical island, her Spanish as fluent as her English. In the afternoons, when the sweat-smeared man she called daddy roared up the drive in his jeep, her round, pudgy little legs carried her up from the beach or down from the terrace and into his arms.

In the evenings after the sun slipped away, the young American and his wife sat on their terrace sipping wine, cradled by the call of the crickets and the rustle of the dark, fragrant lushness around them. Their hands would link, their voices would grow soft, almost imperceptible against the distant whispers of the night ocean. Later, after they made love in the huge bed shipped from Spain a century before, the young woman would sometimes wake, watch the voluminous netting of the bed canopy swaying in the dark, and be frightened for a moment that something so perfect couldn't last. She would kiss the young man's face, his eyes, his hand, midnight kisses to keep the fears away.

20

Alfred Reece came back into their lives in the spring of 1948. They spotted him standing in the bow of the boat as it plowed toward the Havana docks. He was tall, still thin, and the red flower in his buttonhole was a daring splash of color against the gray of his suit. They waved frantically until he recognized them in the waiting crowds and raised his stick high, shouting an unintelligible greeting across the blue water. He was the first to deboard, striding down the gangplank with no suggestion of the limp that had plagued him during his last years at Princeton.

"My curiosity is cured," he grinned when he came to a halt. "You all look absolutely wonderful. I can leave now," and he turned back into the crowds.

Caroline dodged after him, laughing as he wheeled and caught her up in his arms.

Bliss leaned over and placed a loud kiss on each of Reece's cheeks. "I've missed you, old man," and then he smiled down at Maggie. "This is our daughter. Maggie, say hello to your Uncle Alfred."

With her legs wide apart in white cotton pants and her hands jammed into her pockets, Maggie was an accurate imitation of Bliss. Dark curls tumbling over her head, dark eyes curious, she stared up at the tall, thin man. Reece, grave and formal, bowed low and extended his hand. She stared at it, stared up into his smiling eyes, then finally smiled and extracted her hand from her pocket and placed it in his. *"Por qué tiene bastón?"* and pointed to the walking stick.

Caroline took Maggie's hand. "Don't be rude, darling. Uncle Alfred uses it for his bad foot."

Reece leaned forward on the stick with the silver handle. "No, no," he laughed down at Maggie. *"Es nada más que para apoyarme, querida. Es como si fuera parte de mí."*

She giggled at Uncle Alfred's careful, flat Spanish and skipped off with Bliss at her heels. Caroline slipped her hand into Reece's and led him to the car. What he had said was true. And just as the cane was part of him, he was part of them, a part she was suddenly glad to have back.

Both she and Bliss had promised to write home, but Bliss wrote only birthday notes to Eleanor, and the letters that came lay unopened on the long, dark chest in the white hall for weeks. Caroline hadn't written at all and she was startled when Bliss told her he had invited Reece down, like an invitation for the past to come into the present.

"Anything we have to know about life in the States?" Bliss asked as he headed the car toward the highway. Caroline wished he hadn't asked, and wished that the wind would take the question away. She glanced sharply at Reece in the back seat.

"Nothing," he said, and he reached forward to touch her on the cheek. "Nothing at all. Everybody's fine. Eleanor writes. I got a letter just this week. She's met some guy and they're getting married in the fall."

"Hooray!" cried Bliss, and the yellow Ford roared on, down the highway into Jaimanitas.

Reece stayed two weeks, watching a Bliss he had seen only occasionally at school. The dark urgency and the hard edge were gone. Something in him had commingled with this place and he belonged in essential ways. It occurred to Reece that he was envious, but the envy disappeared in the island world that reached out to embrace him.

They walked the streets of Havana, sometimes with Portia and Machado or Doña Silvia and sometimes alone. They ate the food, drank the wine, and lazed on the beaches at the Biltmore Club, sipping the *mojitas* that the white-jacketed waiters brought down from the bar.

"You're happy, aren't you?" Reece said to Caroline as he whirled her across the smoky dance floor of the Tropicana one starry night.

She looked up, and her answer was in her eyes.

"And Bliss has taken Maggie as his own?"

"Yes," she smiled. "There was a sweet judge who drew up the papers, and we had a little party after. Stuffed her with ice cream."

"All Harlows now."

"All Harlows," she laughed.

He maneuvered around another couple, then gazed down at her, his own eyes grave. "Well, my darling, know that if you ever need me, I'll be there," and he swirled her off the floor and back to Bliss.

They gave a farewell party for Reece the night before he left, and the staff at the Floridita remembered it for years. The chef, the waiters, and Constantino watched the daiquiris frappé rise in toast after toast to the tall, thin man with the silver-handled stick who promised he would return. They remembered that night, just as Havana would remember the horse breeder from Buenos Aires and the tall, fair-haired young American.

"The crazy American," they would say with wistful smiles when they told, as they often did, the story of the first sale of yearlings that went on the block that summer of forty-eight.

It was Doña Silvia who introduced them to Nils Lindstrom. "A Swedish count," she said. "Rather wealthy. A polo fanatic, they tell me. So dangle your ponies, Bliss. See what he does."

Lindstrom drove out to the *finca* with Bliss and Machado and made an offer of $200,000 for eight ponies. Bliss smiled, lit a long, thin cigar, then shook his head. "Sorry, Lindstrom. We're looking for serious money here."

Lindstrom turned from the fence and peered at Bliss. "You are crazy. You know that? It's a good offer, a serious offer. And a first sale to me." He shrugged. "I am famous. It will make you famous as well."

But they only laughed and drove him back to his yacht in Havana's harbor. And waited.

"So," Machado said. "You think we lost him?"

"Hell, no. He'll be back. You'll see."

Day after day, they drove by the harbor and watched Lindstrom sitting on the white deck of his yacht, sipping vodka and brooding. Then they drove on, up the drive to the Templete, ordered scotch and water, and sat on the porch overlooking the harbor, waiting. The regulars who knew everything of import in Havana gathered around and then they were joined by a larger crowd of boys and young men who came to watch the curious game the American was playing with the Swede on the yacht.

Two weeks later Lindstrom pushed through the crowd at the Templete. His voice was hard and guttural in Bliss's ear when he said, "I will offer a quarter of a million. That's my limit."

"Serious money, Lindstrom. I said serious."

"Shit," said the Swede, and stalked out.

The crowds at the Templete grew larger and stayed longer. A week later, Lindstrom was back.

"Three hundred and fifty thousand dollars," he said, and stared down at the blue water below.

Bliss glanced at Machado. The sweat was running down the Argentinian's face into the open collar of his shirt. "Make it a clean half million," Bliss said, "and we have a deal."

The bar fell silent. The minutes passed.

And then, "Right," said Lindstrom. "We have a deal."

It wasn't until Lindstrom was gone that they grabbed each other's shoulders and began to shout. Their cries of triumph rolled out, down across the docks to where the white yacht bobbed in the blue-green sea.

It was a week later, just after dawn. The sun had come up out of the east to light the fields where they rode. Machado was yards ahead of Bliss, his little filly pounding across the field, throwing damp turf into the air. She was fast and young, but she failed to make the turn, and Machado died as hard as he'd lived, with his body smashed beneath the screaming horse. Bliss shot the filly and then, Machado's limp, crushed body cradled against his own, he carried him across the suddenly quiet land to Portia's arms.

Caroline made the arrangements and held Portia through the nights. They buried him at a small village church in the mountains east of Jaimanitas, and four days later, the telegram came from the States.

"Father is dead. Please come home. Eleanor."

Bliss Harlow left Cuba and went home with his wife and child.

"Just for a while," he said.

PART THREE

Earth, Texas

April 1958

21

There was a cold snap in Texas that spring toward the end of the 1950s. Blizzards filled the East Texas oil fields with a foot of snow in mid-April, and newspapers all over the world carried photographs of the children from the border towns who trooped out to build snowmen along the banks of the Rio Grande.

It rained on and off in Dallas, and by the time Caroline drove down Merchant Street the blacktop was like a mirror reflecting the slick, lipstick-red sheen of the car as it nosed toward the freeway and Route 30 and finally shot north.

Dark was falling, and out toward the left lights glowed in the streets of a housing development. Dallas lay behind now, the skyline of the city barely visible in the rain. She could just make out the orange-red of the Shell Oil sign, a spatter of yellow from a half-dozen skyscrapers, and the blue glow of the Harlow Enterprises sign. To Caroline, the blue sign and the streets wandering off into the dark desert flats looked as if they'd always been there.

It took an hour and a half to reach the outskirts of Earth. The snow was beginning to fall again, miniature flurries that seemed to hang in the headlights.

The town hadn't changed much over the years. The roads were paved with concrete and the Model Ts and the roadsters had given way to Cadillacs and pink Thunderbird convertibles, but the feel of the place was still the same, still a small Texas town in the pine hills.

Another church had gone up in the years since Bliss had brought Caroline home. It was a red brick Methodist box that shared a tarmacked parking lot with the Harlow Medical Center Ben and Eleanor had built after Will Harlow died. On the other side of Main Street, the bank had a new façade, and Carr's Dry Goods and Drug Store had new owners, young Gary Ashmead and his wife, Loretta.

Except for a freight car every now and then, the trains didn't pass through Earth anymore. Everyone had cars and everyone drove, and down at the foot of Main Street a new gas station sat by the old railroad tracks. Out toward Sugar Hill a motel had gone up. The brochure advertised a dozen Cozy Cottages with private baths and clean linen daily. The tax assayers extended the town boundaries to incorporate the motel, and Billy celebrated by planting a new sign on the top of his Sugar Hill bar. "Billy's," it read in big white letters, and below, in green neon that went flashing on and off during the nights: "Biggest Little Dance Parlor on Earth."

In the center of what people now called "downtown," the press building had expanded, the radio tower was taller, and in the well-groomed fields beyond Amelia Harlow's house there was another house, Ben's and Eleanor's, its white adobe brick blending comfortably with the big house. And the big house was bigger, another wing built on when Bliss came home.

* * *

She could see the house now. Caroline braked as she came up into the circular drive, the gravel spun, and then she rolled around to the stables and the garages at the back. Off in the fields she heard the high, shrill voices of children playing in the snow. Caroline turned to watch and then saw the terrace door open and Amelia Harlow step into the yellow pool of the terrace light.

"Grandmelia," squealed one of the children, and they tumbled across the field in bright-colored boots that beat a path up the terrace steps. Maggie was first, thirteen now, with long black braids. Then Eleanor's son Jay, and a little girl in a blue snowsuit who kicked the snow as she ran, making it fly.

"We made angels in the snow, Grandmelia."

"Great big ones."

"Did you, darling?" Then the door slammed, the voices were still, and after a moment Caroline Harlow followed the children up the steps. She would have said she was miserable if anyone had asked, but by now even she had stopped asking questions like that.

Will Harlow had been dead two weeks when Caroline and Bliss arrived in Texas ten years ago. Bliss drove to the graveyard alone that first afternoon and was finally convinced by the fresh mound of dirt, the wilting flowers, and the row of Harlow headstones marking time. He'd already turned to leave when Eleanor found him.

He watched her, long and lanky in her blue jeans, stride across the fields. He'd missed her, he realized, missed the ease and familiarity of her. They sat under a pine tree and talked—of a public notice of a natural death, a house in Tyler with a rose garden at the back, the work at the press, a body swinging in an empty room. She asked him to stay then. "Not forever, Bliss. Just for now, a year or two?" He looked at her under the deep shade of the pine trees and saw the hurt and

need in her face. He stood and stretched, heaving his
arms to a sky that was beginning to turn all the colors of
the world. "Come on," he said. "I'll race you home."

She headed out first in her fluid-drive Chevrolet and
he followed in Ben's old blue pickup. They drove down
the hill, through town, neck and neck. She won, but he
beat her up the steps of the house, pushing through first
with a shout of laughter and a bang of the big screen
door.

"Do you mind if we stay?" Bliss asked Caroline that
evening. "Not forever. A year, maybe two."

"Stay?" Caroline asked. They were in the second-
floor guest room dressing for dinner. She heard three-
year-old Maggie gurgling at Matty in the hall and she
reached out and shut the bedroom door. He told her
about his father then, that Eleanor needed him at
home. "Stay," she said again.

It had taken three minutes flat to drive from the
courthouse to the other edge of town that morning.
Caroline had timed it herself on the dashboard clock of
the limousine that brought them in from the Dallas
airport. It took three minutes flat to drive down a
dusty, dreary main street lined with ugly little buildings
parched out by the sun. Stay. In a town that was like the
cow towns in all the grainy old Hollywood Westerns
she'd ever seen.

That morning Caroline had tried to imagine Bliss
growing up in this town, and that evening over dinner
she tried to imagine herself staying longer than what
was required of a house guest. She failed, but what she
did begin to see that evening was the bond between her
husband and his sister.

It wasn't like sex, not that demanding and urgent.
Caroline understood sex, and this was different. She
watched them take seats across from each other at the
table, and something in the way they smiled at each
other told her they were taking the places they'd taken
all their lives. They reached for their napkins at the

same time and played with the stems of their wine-glasses in the same way.

She'd never noticed that in Bliss, the way his finger circled the base of the glass, up one side of the stem, then down the other. But she noticed it now, and then there was a burst of laughter, and Caroline glanced up.

The long, high-polished dining table was heaped with steaming platters of beef. Duke was pouring wine and Matty was clearing the first course soup cups. Amelia was laughing at something Ben had said. Her face was fine-boned and fragile looking. But she wasn't fragile at all. Caroline had known that right away. What a delicious story, Amelia was saying. Daingerfield will never be the same. Caroline didn't know what Daingerfield was, and no one explained. The laughter isolated her with the image of Bliss's finger circling the crystal base of his wineglass, just like Eleanor.

Caroline suppressed the rage and jealousy, and gave up. They would stay because Bliss cared about Eleanor in ways Caroline had never counted on.

She fell asleep that night in the narrow single bed next to Bliss's in the guest room and woke the next day to watch him write out the shipping orders that would bring an Argentinian brood mare out of the port of Havana and into Galveston Bay. Three weeks later, she walked into the offices of the *Bugle-Times* to witness the signing of new corporate papers that welcomed Bliss and Eleanor to Amelia's new board of directors.

They called it Harlow Enterprises and it was Amelia's plan for the future.

She was fifty the year Will died and Bliss came home, the two events bound up in her mind. She'd tried to rationalize what Will had done, but her shame was too hot and the collision of memories was too intense for that. She thought she'd buried the old memories, but they came back now as dreams of a train wrapped in red, white and blue bunting and a girl calling out as it disappeared down the tracks. There were no words in those dreams, but Amelia woke one night to the whistle of a freight train passing through town, its long, thin cry fading off toward the south. The girl was very real that night. "I love you, Will." That's what the girl was saying. "I love you."

Amelia slept with a night-light on after that, and she kept it on until Bliss came home.

He climbed out of a limousine on a Saturday morning in October. He came across the gravel drive to where she waited, and lowered his head to kiss her cheek. Will's death was just a death then, the event that brought her son home.

She slipped a photograph of Will into a silver frame and set the silver frame among the others on the long white chest beside her bed. He was a slender man in a white suit again, lounging in a wicker chair in the dappled shade of the porch, smiling into a camera. He was the husband she wanted, a man she could mourn, a father who brought his son home.

A week later she drove to Dallas for the day.

She shrugged when Clayton Benedict told her she was crazy to expand all at once—dailies, television, tract development. She didn't want to tell him that she had to do it this way. She was making it big to intrigue her son, to hold him.

The papers Clayton Benedict drew up were waiting on Amelia's desk when Caroline walked into her office on Bliss's arm. They looked formidable to Caroline, but there was a magnum of champagne too and she relaxed. It was almost like a party, with Clayton Benedict officiating.

The legal complexities bored her and Caroline didn't pay attention to that part. The rest of it was simple. There were thirteen weekly newspapers, a radio station, and five hundred acres of land outside Dallas.

They'd passed through it on the way from the airport. It was desert really, and scrub grass.

The net worth of Harlow Enterprises was listed at six million, and operating capital was a million and a half. "And the splits in the voting stock are equal," Clayton went on. "Thirty-three percent each for Amelia, Eleanor and Bliss."

Amelia smiled. "There's one percent left, Clayton."

"That splits too. Half for Ben." He smiled then. "And the rest is yours, Caroline."

There was more legalese, but Caroline sat quietly. She was flattered and excited; she hadn't expected to be included. It was like having an allowance of her own.

"Thank you," she said when she'd signed where Clayton indicated. "Thank you very much." She kissed her mother-in-law on the cheek. "It's very kind of you." She held out her glass to toast the future of Harlow Enterprises.

"Just a year or two," Caroline wrote Portia that evening at her family's country estate in England, "then we'll sell our shares back to the corporation—and be off. New York. Paris. London, of course, and we'll be stalking the aisles at Harrods together, you and I."

"And drinking Pym's Cups here on my back lawn," wrote Portia in return. "With the local racing set. Don't worry, dear Caroline. Somehow we will survive. England will wait."

There was a party at the big house that fall to celebrate the creation of Harlow Enterprises. Maggie wanted to wear her new red cowboy boots, but Caroline tucked the boots away and left Matty to tend to her objections. She slipped into her dress and when Bliss and Maggie were ready, the three of them went downstairs together.

They made a wonderful entrance. Bliss was in black tie, Maggie was dressed in her best white organdy, and

Caroline wore a sleek, dark red dress with bare shoulders. Her matching sandals clipped down the long curve of the stairs, taking her into what she knew right away was going to be a dreadful evening.

She'd worn the wrong dress. All the other young women wore full skirts and pastel-colored silk blouses. They stared and then said in a rush of Southern-sweet voices, "How lovely you look, how nice you're here." Amelia glanced at her dress and said nothing, except to introduce her to a squat old man with a mane of white hair. "Congressman Jarvis, my daughter-in-law," she said. Then she led Bliss away.

Pappy Jarvis took her arm, chortling about Texas as he guided her through the crowd. There was no wine at the bar so she asked for bourbon on the rocks as the voices swirled around her: advertising talk and Texas politics, newspaper talk and boring chatter about the Texas weather.

Food rolled in on carts, people drifted out to the lawns, Matty came for Maggie and took her away. A man in a tuxedo and a Stetson brought her a third drink. He led her to a swing under the trees and talked about gushers and breakers in a twang that grated on her ears. Caroline smiled and listened to the creak of the swing as he strutted through stories she eventually gathered were about oil.

She laughed at his compliments, inspiring him through story after story, and when he asked if he could escort her on a little stroll through the cottonwoods she smiled and took his arm. They'd gotten as far as the gravel drive when she felt something damp on the nape of her neck and then his lips searching for hers.

"Stop it!" She reached out to slap his face.

He caught her arm in midair. "Why, you little tease. You've been asking for it all night."

Then there was a sharp expulsion of breath and the cowboy doubled over, his Stetson skidding across the gravel.

"Touch her again and I'll smash your face in, you bastard." Bliss Harlow took his wife by the arm into the house and up the stairs.

He slammed the door to the guest room and flung himself across one of the single beds. His collar was loose at the neck and his eyes were sullen.

Caroline let a bracelet clatter to the glass surface of the dressing table and watched him in the mirror. He didn't move.

"Bliss?"

She could hear the distant sounds of the party coming to an end, but their own silence went on.

She stepped out of her dress. "You saw what happened, Bliss—he tried to kiss me."

"I saw him, and I saw you." He was on his feet coming at her, his hands digging into her arms. "Don't flirt, Caroline. Ever." He started to shake her, back and forth, again and again until her terrified cries finally broke through. He stopped, staring at her with puzzled eyes.

"I'm sorry, Bliss. I didn't mean to. I didn't—but nobody else noticed me. I was so bored," and she burst into tears.

His arms went around her and pulled her close. "I know, love, I know. And I know you hate it, but I've hated it a lot longer than you. It's not forever. You'll see." He took her to bed and dissolved her sobs with kisses. She wound her arms around him in the dark and nothing else mattered. Her body was coming alive under his hands and she was searching for him, wet and panicky with emptiness, and then he was filling her, all of her. They would get through this somehow—they would. Nothing mattered but this.

She bought the lipstick-red convertible with the first check from Harlow Enterprises and filled her time designing the wing of rooms that went up at the back of the big house. It was better to tolerate Amelia's roof than build something of her own, she decided. They were here only temporarily.

Orders for furniture went out in the spring. She chose blond art deco pieces from W. & J. Sloane's in New York, Eames chairs by special order from Neiman-Marcus, and a collection of canvases from a gallery she found in the pages of one of the magazines she subscribed to now. Each evening she went down the long hall that connected the two wings of the house and joined the others for cocktails with Amelia at seven. Gradually she settled in, glad that at least Maggie was thriving.

Maggie liked living in the big white house sitting on top of Grandmelia's town, liked feeling special in this place. She was five now, with long black braids, and she was smart. Everybody said that. They said, "My, aren't you smart," and down at Carr's on Main Street Mr. Ashmead smiled and tucked candy into her hand. "Thank you, Mr. Ashmead," Maggie would say, minding her manners as Matty said.

She was very pleased when Aunt Eleanor told her she was going to have a baby, "a cousin for you, sweetie." He was born in the fall of 1949 and christened Benjamin Dallas Harlow Rawlings. Maggie helped choose his Texas name, and she thought it was interesting, the way his face grew red when he screamed, the way his hand curled around her finger. They all called him Jay and even when he was brand new, Aunt Eleanor let her sit in Uncle Ben's big chair and hold him. He was so little and so warm, like a puppy, and she was so gentle, always holding his head just as she'd been told. When he was six months old and Caroline told her there'd be another baby soon, Maggie was ecstatic.

"A sister," she said, "just for me."

"You can't be sure, darling," her mother said. "You could have a brother, you know."

"No, Mommy," Maggie said, surging with confidence. "Jay's already a boy. I'm sure I'm getting a girl."

Her sister was born in the middle of June 1950. She was a tiny, pretty baby with soft, dark curls. Kathryn was Bliss's choice, and Maggie spent the first morning on the floor of Matty's kitchen, looking through a school atlas for the Texas name to go between Kathryn and Harlow. It was harder than Jay's Texas name. Aunt Eleanor's was Austin. Daddy's was Houston, and her cousin's would be Dallas. Everybody thought of it right away.

She pushed a braid back and turned another page in the atlas.

Matty stepped over her on the way to snap her beans. "How you comin' down there?"

"Um," said Maggie, concentrating on the letters at the top of the page: "Texas Con't." Down below there were the names of more towns: Rosebud, Lovelady, Apple Springs, a town called Dew. And then she ran into the gulley between the pages again and the letters trailed off. That was the trouble with this atlas. It didn't give you Texas flat out.

Half an hour later, Maggie looked up. "Got it," she said. Her small finger obscured the small town she'd discovered at last.

"I got it, Matty," and she came to her feet. "Morning Glory," she said. "Kathryn Morning Glory Harlow."

Matty smiled. "I thought you'd choose it, just as quick as you found it."

"Nice, isn't it?"

"Just fine," Matty said. "She can be your Morning Glory and you can be her Sweet Heart Rose."

22

They called her Kate, and she and Maggie and their cousin Jay grew up in Texas in the boom years when Harlow Enterprises became one of the major conglomerates in the West.

It was Ben Rawlings who said it was time.

He'd rebuilt the State Bank of Earth, cautiously and without much fanfare making it a major financial force in the business of Texas. His investments extended beyond the narrow confines of small-town banking into oil, cattle, and construction all over the state, and he maintained a suite of offices on the twenty-fifth floor of the First National Bank Building in Dallas.

He sat on the powerful Texas Highway Commission, the boards of two other banks and belonged to the Petroleum Club, where two or three times a week he could be seen lunching with prominent politicians and fellow bankers: a big man with thinning hair and an easy smile, a wealthy man who believed in the judicious application of cash.

In the fall of 1950, over a modest lunch of strip sirloin at the Petroleum Club, he listened to an oil man with a gut-bucket Texas twang spout endless anecdotes about the bad new days. "Take Houston now," Lester Judd mourned through the smoke of his cigar. "Nice town like that filling up with fools, looking for oil under the bed sheets, and finding it. Damn well finding it."

"Won't last long," Ben said. "The big corporations will come in, clean things up."

"Too many folks coming in," Judd sighed. "Texas doesn't feel like Texas anymore. I talked to a couple of drillers to the north just this morning. Wells weren't ever much to speak of and now they're thinkin' about row houses instead. Terrible idea." The end of his cigar landed in the dregs of his glass. "Row houses are going to attract white trash. That's all. Just white trash."

Ben lit his own cigar when he was finally alone. The oil stories were old, but a development deal cooking outside Dallas, that was new.

He headed back to his office, made some calls, and two hours later he walked into Amelia Harlow's office at the *Bugle-Times*.

"That scrub lands of yours, Amelia."

She looked up, nodded.

"Things are moving in Dallas. It's time to talk real estate."

They broke ground on Harlow Acres six months later. Amelia and Eleanor drove down one afternoon and stopped to watch the bulldozers fighting the sparse land. Eleanor cut the motor and they got out to lean against the hood of the Cadillac.

It looked as it had always looked to Amelia, frozen flat. Only Dallas was different, very close now, like a toy city in the distance buckling up against her land. There would be row after row of split-level ranch-style houses out there soon, two thousand homes on five hundred acres of land. There would be lawns and saplings and new tarmacked streets. People would begin moving in, cars would sit in carports, and children's bicycles would lie at curbstones. It was satisfying to know that she'd been right.

"Who were they, Mother? Who gave this land to Daddy?"

"Corman, I think. I think that was the name on the deed."

Eleanor kicked at a rock, raising a little cloud of dust. "I wonder where they are now."

"California, I suppose."

"I suppose so." Eleanor turned to her mother with a small, wistful smile. "He'd want us to find them somehow, wouldn't he? Tell them that no doctor's bill was this big. They should take back their land."

They stood for a while longer, watching the dump arms rising and falling against the sky, then left the bulldozers to their work.

They didn't wait for the houses to go up and the cash to come in. Ben spearheaded the consortium of Texas bankers who took the development deal as collateral. He got a massive loan extended, and the expansion began.

Tender offers for two Midwest newspaper chains went out and were accepted six weeks later. Seven prime population centers were pinpointed and the Harlows began wiring the West for television.

Only a hundred stations were operating in the United States in 1950. Television made the federal government wary, and a freeze on further licenses had come down coast to coast. The FCC was preparing a major study of standards and air wave interference and the logistics of a unified system. Eleanor didn't mind. It gave her time, and while the FCC talked to the networks, she talked to her advertisers, and Pappy Jarvis, in from Washington, D.C., for the Christmas break.

"Television?" Pappy asked Eleanor when she drove out to the ranch to see him. "Not likely to last, folks say."

"It'll last, Pappy. Don't worry about that. But I'm going to need you, Pappy. Somebody has to keep an eye on the FCC."

She paced the floor of his study, her face flushed from the heat of the fire roaring in the fireplace, explaining it all to the white-haired man filling his big leather chair. The freeze could last two years, maybe longer. But it couldn't last forever. They'd know that eventually, and they'd know, months in advance, the date the new licenses would be approved. "And Pappy?"

"I'm listening, honey."

"I want my licenses right on top of that stack. Even if it costs—well, something extra."

Pappy bit off the end of a new cigar and pulled out a match. "You don't have to pussyfoot around with me, Eleanor. But I'm tellin' you, boys down at the FCC don't come cheap. Could be ten, twenty grand." He paused, raised an eyebrow, and grinned. "Your mother know you plannin' to flash that kind of cash?"

Eleanor smiled and reached down to pull on a long strand of Pappy's hair.

Six months later, the phone on her bedside table rang just before dawn.

"Eleanor? That you?"

"Pappy, God, it's the middle of the night."

"Honey, you wanted to know soon as me. It's that license application, Eleanor. You're high on the stack, right behind Lyndon Johnson. He'll be first and you're number two."

She forgot all about the hour. "What do you mean, Lyndon Johnson?"

"That's right, honey, LBJ wants a TV station too, down in Austin. Going to be in Lady Bird's name naturally, but that's all right, isn't it, honey? Lyndon's just family and second is pretty high."

"They're crazy. They don't know anything about television."

He laughed. "Well, you tell Lyndon that yourself."

The freeze lifted in 1953, and Lyndon Johnson was first and Eleanor was second. She had her television stations, all seven allowed by law, up and running in the Southwest. Amelia kept the old *Bugle-Times* building in Earth as her own and built an eight-story red-brick building out back as central headquarters. The dailies moved to St. Louis, and the television offices went to Dallas. And Eleanor was right. Everything changed.

"Dearest Portia," wrote Caroline on thick gray vellum with an H engraved at the top.

There's another party here tonight and tomorrow we go to San Antonio. Someone's air-conditioned their barn and we're all flying down to watch the cows cool off. Charming. Boring.

Bliss is always away, but things will be winding down soon and then we'll take our money. And run! You won't recognize Maggie, she's shooting up. And you'll adore Kate. Can't wait to see you. Can't wait.

23

Maggie kept a photo album in those years. She collected the photographs and snapshots in a big manilla envelope Grandmelia brought home from the office, and once a year, when summer came, she commandeered a table in the sun-room and set to work. Glue. Scissors. Boxes of little black photo tabs, and the album itself. It was a present from Grandmelia, and "Maggie Harlow" was stamped in gold on the green leather cover. "Real gold?" Maggie asked.

"Of course," said Grandmelia.

When Kate was little and nothing but trouble, Maggie worked on the album in the afternoons while Kate had her naps. Then, when Kate was older, Maggie let her sit in a chair and watch. "But don't touch, okay? I mean, I don't want ice cream and junk all over."

Jay came too, steaming up the terrace steps and down the long central hall to the sun-room.

"Don't touch," Maggie warned.

"It's my family too."

"Yeah? Well, it's my album. Here, put a little glue on this page, right there. Not a blob—mess it around. That's right."

When Maggie finished with that year's pictures, she sat with Kate and Jay in the long swing on the porch, telling them stories about the pictures in her book.

"That's me," Jay shrieked, and he kicked his legs out, making the swing creak.

"Stop slobbing up the pictures, Jay. That's really disgusting. Now . . . ," and Maggie, her voice ripe with the authority of age, began to narrate.

There were the dogs—that one was dead now, and that was the one that had the puppies. There was Grandmelia and everybody on a picnic. There was the cat with the kittens, and Jay at four with his tricycle.

"It was red. Right, Maggie?"

"That's right. Red. And there's Kate and her dumb bear."

"He's not dumb," Kate said, leaning closer to examine the studio portrait taken when she was seven. She had insisted on holding the bear called Goose Too in her lap. She'd named him in honor of the bear her father and Aunt Eleanor had when they were her age.

"Why'd they call it Goose?" she had asked her Grandmelia.

"I don't know, darling. You'll have to ask them."

But they had forgotten and Kate shrugged and said, "Never mind. I'll call mine Goose too."

The pages of Maggie's album turned. Christmas after Christmas, summer after summer. There were Kate and Maggie in matching dresses; there was Jay on his bike and Kate on her first pony.

It was summertime in that picture. She was squinting into the sun, and down at the bottom you could see the bluebonnets. Kate remembered swinging off the pony's back, slipping to the ground, and landing in the bluebonnets with bare feet.

She had wanted a pony for as long as she could remember. Maggie had a pony and she wanted a pony. He came on her birthday the year she turned five. She stood on the front porch with one hand in her father's and one in her mother's. Then Maggie came around from the stables, leading a little dapple gray with a shiny black saddle on his back.

"Oh, Daddy," she whispered. "I bet he can fly, that horse. I bet he can fly!" She ran down the steps squealing, then stopped, suddenly shy as she stood beside her first pony.

She needed the help of Maggie and a box to climb across his broad back, but her legs were too short and wouldn't sit close to his flanks.

"Wait," Maggie said, "I've got to shorten the stirrups."

"No!" I *can't* wait!"

"Well, here then. Just hold on." Maggie wrapped the reins around Kate's hands. "And don't grab his neck like that. It's not good form."

Slipping and swaying, her mouth clamped shut in supreme concentration, Kate let Maggie lead her up and down the gravel drive. "Look at me," she called to everybody when she caught her balance. "I can ride!"

Bliss taught Kate to jump the year she was six, taking her and the pony over the course he constructed in the paddocks out back. "Tight," he yelled. "Knees tight. Seat tight! Now up—*up!*" And he watched as she wheeled and turned, sailing higher and higher, lost in the slash of the mane.

It had been like that for him once, and he yearned for that now, for the days in Jaimanitas, for the sun coming up out of the water and the turf spinning away beneath pounding hooves, for the freedom of those long, simple days.

He felt bottled up in Earth, and he was frightened by the passing time. One night in March, when he and Caroline were sitting by the pool, listening to the clack of crickets, he asked her.

"Where would I like to live?" She shifted in her chair to look at him, and her voice was soft. "Why do you ask? Why now?"

"I've been thinking about it," he said. "Thinking that maybe it's time to sell out. Move on."

"Are you sure?" she said.

"Yes, I'm sure."

"Promise?"

"Yes," he smiled.

She came into his arms and he held her, burying his face in her hair. Later, curled in each other's arms, they talked until morning about possibilities: a townhouse in Manhattan, a stud farm on the North Shore of Long Island, something in Europe, the South of France.

Two weeks later, it was postponed.

Bliss resisted at first. He sat slouched in a chair in Clay Benedict's Dallas office listening to Benedict and two hotshot accountants talk federal taxes and depreciation allowances and profit and loss. They talked about delivery trucks and the rising cost of gas, the rising cost of getting newspapers into the suburbs, and finally they told him about an oil company up for sale on the Gulf Coast.

He saw his dream disappear in the massive transferal of cash their oil company was going to cost and asked Benedict to sketch a couple of alternatives. But there were no good alternatives. The oil company made sense for the future, and they needed him. They couldn't buy him out yet.

"I don't understand," Caroline said that night. "I don't understand," she said over and over again.

"It's just temporary, baby. You've got to see that." He slumped back against the headboard and tried to take Caroline in his arms. It was just a simple device for sheltering money, he explained once more, just a matter of time before the cash started flowing again.

"But we're rich now," she said. She didn't look at Bliss, didn't see his eyes asking her to understand. She stared at her own face in the dressing table mirror and understood only that they were staying.

"Baby, we won't be rich if it's not protected. If we go

now there won't be any money. They're going to buy the oil company whether I like it or not."

She shook her head and her hands went limp in her lap. He watched a tear well up in her eye, saw it roll down her cheek, and heard her whisper, "You promised, Bliss."

"I couldn't do anything else," he pleaded. "There's too much involved. It'll only be a couple of years, just . . ."

There was no change in her face, no warning movement in her body, only the tear frozen in place, and a voice he didn't recognize.

"Years?" She inched away from him, off the bed. "It's *been* years. Years and more years."

He reached for her hand and she pulled away. "We will go. I promise we will, Caroline."

She stared at him. "You're just like your father," she hissed. "They strangled him, and by God, they're strangling you too. You'll never get out. Never. You were born here, and you're going to die here." She was across the room, snatching at the door to the hallway, twisting it open, the words coming in sobbing, hysterical shrieks, ugly with panic. "Die here, Bliss Harlow. *Die* here," she wailed.

And then she was running, down the hallway, through the house, and out the screen door to the porch. Its squeaking hinge mocked her as she stopped, wrapped her arms around her shoulders, and stood, still and suddenly quiet, in the Texas night.

In a room down the hall Kate climbed out of bed. She stood very much like her mother, her arms wrapped around herself.

"Maggie?" she whispered. "What was that?" But Maggie was asleep and there was no answer. There was only the dark and a voice, frozen in Kate's mind like the photographs frozen in Maggie's album.

* * *

The days turned into long, tense days for Maggie and Kate, days of not disturbing Mommy, of hours after school whittled away with Matty and Jay, dinners alone with Grandmelia.

"Don't you worry none," Matty sometimes whispered when she bent to hug them each goodnight. "It'll blow over, you'll see." But she left a night light glowing in their room, aware that when their daddy came home, when they heard his step in the hall, Kate would climb out of her bed and creep into Maggie's, curling against her to wait for the fights to start. And they did, night after night. Miss Caroline's voice rang through doors, down corridors, right over the sound of the air conditioners, shouting that they had to get out.

Matty never heard Mr. Bliss. She sometimes thought she'd like to hear him yell too, not that she ever would. Matty knew nobody was ever going to hear Mr. Bliss yell, and she supposed Miss Caroline would come to know that too. Mr. Bliss wasn't ever going to yell.

Miss Caroline finally did figure that out. One morning she called Duke and told him to bring around her red car. Matty heard it spin off, spraying gravel all over the place, and she heard it come back that night. There wasn't any more shouting after that. There was just the red car pulling out in the morning and pulling back in at night, and the silence in between. She sometimes wondered where Miss Caroline went, and then decided she knew enough. She knew she sometimes forgot to kiss those two little girls goodbye, and that was enough for Matty.

But there wasn't anything more to know. Caroline Harlow simply drove.

She drove to Dallas, and once she went as far south as Austin, burning down the three hundred miles of the highway and back up in a day. She drove the highways and back roads that led north, passing through nondescript towns that seemed to have no past, no future, just a meager present of clapboard and brick. She drove just to drive, to move, and to keep moving.

She hated Dallas, hated the dusty little towns sagging against the old railroad tracks leading south, hated the hard immensity of a land that dwarfed everything scratched on its surface.

But she drove anyway. She drove ribbon after ribbon of highway, slashed through town after town, moved on, hour after hour. She drove the land until it numbed her and she could finally turn back, heading up into the hills and back down, into Earth.

Sometimes, coming in, she would suddenly see it all with the eye of a stranger or a traveler passing through. The rolling hills, the tall pines, the weathered clapboard houses and the newer ones of brick: they might belong anywhere, but the stranger Caroline imagined in her mind would know.

He'd see the hundred-foot-tall radio tower and the eight stories of brick with Earth *Bugle-Times* sprawled across the front. He'd see the big white house at the edge of town with its mailbox at the bottom of the hill, blank and discreet. He'd see the Harlow Medical Center, the school that bore another Harlow name, and then he'd know that this town belonged to them. They were the first family here and everybody else was only everybody else, and it was going to stay that way.

Then the stranger in Caroline's fantasy would drive on, laughing at Amelia Harlow and her dusty, dreary cow town in the middle of nowhere.

Sometimes after she'd pulled up into the gravel drive, she'd sit there at the wheel. She tried to keep her eye on the clock so she could go in before the girls went to bed, tried to let them know she loved them. She asked about their day and tried to listen when they told her stories and jokes to make her laugh. She would smile and hug them and then she would have to send them away. "Mommy's tired, darlings. Go to bed now." Sometimes Kate would cry, but Maggie understood. She would nod, take Kate's hand, and lead her away.

Caroline Harlow kept on driving. She drove through the cold snap and the snow of the April of 1958, and when it was suddenly hot again she went on driving.

They saw their father in the mornings. Kate would creep into the big bed after her mother left, and the first thing Bliss saw when he woke would be her serious eyes.

"Hi, Daddy," she said.

He grinned. "Hi."

Her night terrors would disappear then and Kate would giggle and snuggle.

"Stay with us today, Daddy?" she asked every morning. "Stay with us?"

He'd smooth back her short, thick curls, kiss her forehead, and say, "Can't today, baby. Soon."

"Daddy," Maggie said one morning, "Kate decided, and I agree. Today is soon."

"It can't be today," he yawned. "You have school."

Maggie grinned. "No we don't, Daddy. Kate made Matty call and tell them we're sick."

Bliss took them out in the jeep for the day. First they drove to Kilgore where they sat on an old beat-up couch in an office full of oil men and cigar smoke and booming voices. There were candy bars and quarters for them and compliments for their daddy on his fine-looking girls. Then they stopped for hamburgers and milk shakes in a coffee shop below rows and rows of oil derricks.

They sang songs for their father as he drove them through the development called Harlow Acres. And then they went on into Dallas and dinner at a real restaurant.

He led them through the dimly lit entrance, past big

men in dark suits and ladies in dress-up clothes. They walked right up to the head of the line, and a man with a black jacket and a white tie greeted them and smiled at their father. "Of course we have room for you and your daughters, Mr. Harlow."

The powder room was big and had pink lights and pink marble wash basins and a carpet to match. They blinked, then gazed at themselves in the long mirror.

"Wow!" Maggie said. "Matty would die. Just die."

Her jeans were ripped at the knees, and her sneakers caked with mud. Kate was wearing shorts, and the ketchup from lunch was still smeared in the folds of her grin.

There were brushes and a row of cologne bottles on the table by the basin. Maggie set to work, rebraiding her braids and brushing Kate's hair. But Kate still looked messy so Maggie sat her on the floor with a box of tissues and hairpins and twisted paper flowers into Kate's hair.

"He's going to think I'm beautiful when you're done, won't he, Maggie?"

"Who—Daddy? Yes, now sit still."

They emerged hand in hand, shy in their perfume. Kate cautiously patted the paper flowers on her dark curls. Bliss started to smile as he looked down at them, then knelt and took them in his arms. "You're beautiful. Do you know I love you? Very much?"

They nodded and then, eyes bright, they each took a hand and marched into the restaurant. It all smelled so good and their daddy was funny and patient, smiling back at all the waiters who smiled at him.

It was very late when they got home. Bliss carried a sleeping Kate to bed, pulled off her crumpled shorts, and untied her shoes. He took the last of the paper flowers away and leaned over to kiss her face.

"Kate had a good time, Daddy," Maggie whispered through the dark. "I did too."

"Me too, sweetheart." He pulled the sheet up to Maggie's chin and kissed the top of her head.

"Goodnight, Daddy."

He spent more time in Houston that spring, making the run from Earth in the Piper several days each week. He liked the trip—the roar of the jets as he brought the plane down from the clear air into the thick heat of the swampy land; the forty-mile drive to the Gulf in the cool interior of the air-conditioned Buick, and then up again in the helicopter, buzzing the rigs sitting out in the sea.

He liked the oil business after all. He could see things happen, watch the profits pump right out of the Gulf. And then, on the last Thursday in May, he didn't want to go.

He woke early that morning and felt Caroline warm and soft next to him, her arm flung across his in sleep. He eased his face into her hair. He wanted her—as suddenly, as insistently as he ever had. His hands slipped under her gown and ranged over her body, down her back, up over her breasts. He kissed her neck and felt her waken, felt the hard, urgent hunger in her as her body started moving under his, coming up to meet him.

An hour later he left her sleeping in their wide, white bed to make the ten o'clock meeting in Houston he wished he didn't have.

It was a fast flight down and he was up to the helicopter pad with time to spare. He felt whole for the first time in weeks. It was still there. They'd just forgotten for a while. And he would get her out of Texas. He'd promised, and he would, somehow.

He parked the car and stepped out to a blast of Gulf Coast heat. He kicked the blocks away and hauled himself up into the cockpit of the Bell 47G3. It was a small rig with a three-seat bench in the glass bubble.

He checked the controls, turned on the ignition, and hit the starter. The helicopter throbbed to life and three minutes later he pushed the collective and lifted off. He swung to five hundred feet and then eased the cyclic forward, moving at a steady fifty knots toward the rigs dancing on the horizon.

It was rough and noisy, not like flying a plane at all. It was more satisfying somehow to hang out over the Gulf in the bubble. He circled the main rig twice and was almost blinded for a moment by the blast of sun against steel and concrete. He pulled a pair of sunglasses from his shirt pocket, took the helicopter up to a thousand feet, leveled off the cyclic. And then the sunglasses clattered against the controls and Bliss was pulling back, pulling back.

No one knew how it happened, or why, but one of the men on the ground said it was like watching a dragonfly climb and then fall, piercing itself on the rig.

They never found Bliss Harlow's body, only the silver slivers of metal. They floated in the blue for days before they were picked up by the tides and finally carried away out to sea.

24

She knew right away that it was something awful. It was evening and Caroline was waiting for Bliss on the porch when she saw Ben's pickup coming up the long drive. She heard him cut the engine and then she stood, waiting in the sudden silence, waiting for what seemed like forever as he opened the door, climbed out, closed it behind him. She watched as he turned to face the house and suddenly saw her standing there. They stared at each other, and then Ben's arms seemed to flutter, just once, heavy and helpless. She knew then that it was something irrevocable, that something had come to an end.

She started to shake that night.

She went in to the children and told them, and then gave them to Matty and went back to the big dining room where Rosie was pouring out the tea. "Miss Caroline," she whispered. "Oh, Miss Caroline," her dark eyes wet with tears as she pressed a cup and saucer into her hands. Ben seated her and she realized that without Bliss she didn't exist here anymore.

Amelia and Eleanor made their plans and carved out the days ahead. Then they stood and walked away. "Wait," she wanted to say. "It was all right today. He loved me again today." Ben touched her shoulder as he passed, and then he was gone too.

She went to her room and undressed. She took off her silk blouse and her slacks and dropped them over the arm of a chair. She stepped out of her shoes, shed her underwear, and then she crawled into bed and started to shake.

In the old wing of the big house, Matty stood at a counter in the kitchen pouring milk. Mr. Bliss would be there when she turned to pass out the glasses. She could almost see the little boy with short blond curls and his first pair of long pants. He'd reach out a hand, take the glass, and his thanks would be in the soft smile at the corner of his mouth. Matty set the milk bottle down, let it sit. He was dead. He had grown up, and he had died today.

After a minute she picked up the milk bottle again and filled the three glasses one by one.

Jay and Maggie and Kate sat on the floor of the kitchen in their still-damp bathing suits. Matty supposed they felt safer down there now. She didn't ask them to sit at the corner table; she just bent and passed the glasses out.

Jay's face was flushed and his eyes were hot under his brown bangs. He sat pressed against the wall, his shoulders square, his brown legs out straight. "Matty?"

He took a sip of milk, and his small body seemed to relax.

"Yes, honey?" she murmured. "Something I can get for you?"

"I think Uncle Bliss will be back. Probably the day after tomorrow."

No one moved. Then Maggie's hand slipped, and her glass rolled across the floor, leaving a long dribble of white across the tile. Matty reached down to wipe it up and then glanced at Kate, at a stony-faced child staring into nothing, her eyes glazed and blank.

He wasn't coming back. Kate knew that. He was dead and he wasn't coming back ever.

Caroline shook for three weeks. She lay in her bed with her body shaking. She didn't cry. There wasn't a single tear in her; there was only the shaking. It began as soon as she lay down in the dark. Her teeth chattered, her body twitched, and when she concentrated on the shaking, trying to stop it and make herself lie still, she couldn't think of anything, not the children, not Bliss—only the shaking.

It blotted out everything. She remembered nothing about the funeral and was only vaguely aware, later that day, that Matty moved into the children's room and set up a cot between their beds. Sometimes at night she thought she heard them crying in their sleep, but she didn't want them to see her shake. She was glad that Matty was there to hold them and soothe their little faces in the yellow night-light.

And then, one night in the middle of June, the shaking stopped.

Clayton Benedict had driven up from Dallas that morning to discuss the distribution of Bliss's estate. Matty woke Caroline at noon and she went to soak in a hot tub for an hour. It wouldn't matter anymore after today—any of it. The thirty-three shares of voting stock that belonged to Bliss would be hers now, and she'd go ahead and tell Amelia today—tell her she had to buy it. For cash.

She tried to remember what the net worth of those thirty-three shares had been the last time they'd all gone over the figures. Ten million, twenty million? She didn't remember, but it didn't matter. There was lots, and if Amelia couldn't raise the money to buy it back from her, that didn't matter either. She'd sell it to someone else, gladly. Then she'd leave. She'd take the girls and leave. It would be all right then. The night shaking would stop and maybe she could afford to cry.

She applied makeup carefully around her eyes, blotted her cheeks with rouge, and hid her lifeless hair under a blue cloche that matched her dress. She was ready when Duke brought the car around at three.

She'd never liked the conference room. It took up half the top floor of the new wing at the press, a long, narrow, thick-carpeted room dominated by a heavy Spanish table that ran almost the full length. It was dark and claustrophobic, but it didn't matter today. She took a seat and a moment later nodded with easy dignity at the others who began filing in: Clayton Benedict, somber and urbane in his dark suit; Amelia, gliding pale and silent to her place at the end of the table; Ben, and finally Eleanor, looking ravaged. There was no other word for it, Caroline thought. Just ravaged.

They'd all lost weight in the weeks since Bliss's death, but Eleanor had lost more, much more. Her hair was pulled into a thin, colorless knot at the back of her head; her shoulders were bone-thin in a black dress that sagged at the neck. Caroline reached down and smoothed her blue skirt over her knees. She'd chosen the dress because it did fit—it did. She wanted to laugh now or cry or go home and change. Then there was a click of a briefcase and she turned and focused on

Clayton Benedict. And was always surprised, when she thought about it later, that she managed to go on sitting there, calmly nodding.

In accordance with the incorporation terms of Harlow Enterprises, the death of either twin bequeathed corporate stock to their children, and the right to vote the stock passed to the surviving twin. Bliss Harlow's thirty-three shares were now split equally between Maggie and Kate and all shares were to be managed and controlled by his sister Eleanor for her lifetime. Caroline retained her own half share, and it was understood that his belongings were hers, to distribute as she saw fit.

Caroline couldn't listen anymore. Bliss had a jeep, some horses, and empty clothes hanging in a closet. She felt dizzy and the room spun around her, pressing down on her that one central fact. She had her half-share allowance. That was it. There wasn't anything more.

She said nothing, but she kept her eyes lowered so no one would see and left early, with Clayton Benedict.

He took her arm, conducted her to the elevator and down to the lobby and out to the street. She stood in the sun and heat with her arm through his as her mind fought for the words she wanted to say.

"Can I help you?" he finally asked. "Something you don't understand?"

She nodded, staring at his lapel. "Can they do that to me? Give me nothing? I wasn't nothing, Clay."

He glanced around, as if she were making a scene on the street.

"You don't have nothing, Caroline. You have a piece of a very large corporation. But yes, yes they can. In Texas at least they can."

"In Texas."

"It's an old legal principle, going back to the Conquistadors and before, to Spain. I explained it to you, Caroline, when you signed. Harlow Enterprises was constructed around that principle. It sees you as a founder of the corporation. You took your percentage and gave up your legal right to Bliss's."

She traveled back in her mind to that first day she'd ever stepped foot in Amelia Harlow's office—the magnum of champagne, the papers laid out white and thick. She'd signed. She'd kissed her mother-in-law on the cheek. She'd been very gay.

She didn't say goodbye to Clayton. She got in the red car and drove home, picked up a glass and a bottle of scotch, went into her bedroom, and locked the door. She sipped steadily from a steadily filled glass until finally the tears started to come.

Long, silent tears dripped down her face, her neck, her breasts. She lay on the bed, moving only to fill her glass, letting the tears flow. Two hours later, when she was tired of herself, the taste of the scotch, and the tears streaming endlessly from her eyes, she stood, turned on a light, and looked at the figure in blue weaving across the surface of the full-length mirror.

Eleanor looked chic in comparison to what she saw there. Well, fuck Eleanor. She giggled. Fuck Amelia, and the Conquistadors too. Fuck Bliss. She marched up to the mirror and stared at the bruised-looking face with its red eyes floating in pools of mascara. "Fuck the Harlows. Every fucking one."

She stepped back, hands on her hips, and frowned. "Naughty," she giggled. "Very naughty. You know what Matty says. Matty says no," and she wagged her finger at the figure in the mirror. She pressed her face against the cool of the glass and then sank to the floor, staring at the face. She wondered how she could put it all back together again. The face. Her life. No money. No place to go. No movies even, just a dreary dump of a town that was all dark now. Even the neon lights were all shut down.

She peered closer at the face in the mirror and then leaned back, smiling at it with affection. "Come," she said, "I'm going to buy you a little drink."

She went to her bathroom and took a hot, pounding shower that made her skin tingle. An hour later, wearing a fresh yellow dress and sling-back pumps, she kissed the sleeping girls goodnight and phoned Matty to tell her she was going for a drive.

"No, nowhere special. Just come, Matty. I don't want the girls left alone."

She parked where everyone could see it—Caroline Harlow's red car, its hard-waxed surface caught in the green glare of Billy's big neon sign, blinking on and off, on and off in the warm night.

BIGGEST LITTLE DANCE HALL ON EARTH . . .
BIGGEST LITTLE DANCE HALL ON EARTH . . .

Billy's was almost empty that night. The long brass rail Will Harlow had leaned against in the spring of 1917 was still there, and the bar still had its beveled mirror. The liquor bottles that once lined it were gone; that was Billy's nod at the blue laws that theoretically allowed only beer in this town. The television set was blank tonight, and two figures at the back swayed to the juke box tune of "Blue Suede Shoes." The far wall was covered with hundreds of black-and-white photographs —pictures of cattle, horses, and wagons heading down Main Street before it was paved. There was even a picture of the old Harlow place if Caroline had known where to look.

Tommy Hardisay stood at the brass rail with three other men, young ranch hands like him from the Jarvis place. He almost choked on his bourbon when he saw her come in.

She smiled and put her purse down on the bar. "Hi, Billy."

Billy stared, his big face turning red.

"Now, now, Billy. Don't let the cat get your tongue."

He picked up a wet rag and wiped it across the bar.

"A scotch please, Billy."

"You know the rules, Miss Caroline. We serve beer, and that's all we got."

"No whiskey down there?" She stood on tiptoe, peering at the cartons stacked on the floor.

"No ma'am. We don't sell hard stuff in this town. You know that." He turned away and opened a bottle of beer. He poured a glass with a big head and chugged half of it down before he looked at her again. "Amelia know you're here?"

"You open for business or not, Billy?" Her voice was suddenly cool.

He nodded.

"Then give me a Bud."

"No Bud, Miss Caroline."

"A Coors then." She slipped a quarter across the bar.

She drank her beer and then drank another, and then accepted every bourbon Tommy Hardisay talked Billy into bringing out from the cartons stashed behind the bar. Tommy liked to have a good time when he could find it. And Caroline Harlow was ready, he could tell. She could knock that bourbon back without getting sloppy or passing out, and when they left the bar at one-thirty she enjoyed standing there in the shadows with his breath on her neck and his lips on hers. She pulled away when he let his hands roam down her front, but he knew she didn't mean it. Not really.

Caroline drove home alone and left her red car at the foot of the big white porch. She stumbled around to the back still humming a juke box tune and fell asleep that night without shaking, not even once.

Amelia asked Caroline to lunch the next day. They met in her office, took seats on either side of the table a secretary wheeled in, and shook out white linen napkins. They were cutting into cold chicken breasts when Amelia broached the subject uppermost in her mind.

"I gather you went to Billy's last night?" She raised an eyebrow, an effect that always made Caroline feel silly and stupid, as if she'd done something wrong. Well, now she had.

"Yes, I did." Caroline looked down at her napkin. "I was so lonely, and the music and other people did help. I hope I didn't offend you." She looked up with her eyes wide.

Amelia cut another slice of chicken in half and nudged it with her fork. "People in town were upset. They expect more of us, I'm afraid." She put her fork down and her eyes were surprisingly soft. "I know this is a terrible time for you. For all of us."

She stopped and Caroline let the silence fall and grow until Amelia went on.

"I must ask you not to go to Billy's again. It won't do, my dear. I think you understand."

Caroline never went to Billy's again, but she didn't have to. She called Tommy herself, right after lunch, and every night around eleven, through June and into early July, Tommy Hardisay climbed off his bar stool and hitched up his pants. He went out to his pickup and drove down Sugar Hill to the house at the edge of town.

Sissy was eighteen that summer and the only daughter of the only dance-hall owner in all of Earth, Texas. Billy's wife had gone off when Sissy was seven, and he'd raised her and two little boys alone in the frame house behind the bar. She was a pretty, slender girl with long hair that was almost blond. She hadn't gone to school beyond the tenth grade. It wasn't much use, and anyway Sissy knew by then that she was mostly good at giggling and what she called "you know."

She liked doing it with almost everybody, especially the boys who came to the bar and danced with her while the juke box played "Red Sails in the Sunset." They gave her little presents every so often, and once she bought a round-trip bus ticket to Dallas with one of those presents and spent the day walking around. She bought a pair of fancy panties at Neiman-Marcus with the rest of the money. Those black panties with a see-through heart over her left hip bone were the most elegant thing she owned.

Still, even Sissy had to say no when Tommy asked.

"Tommy Hardisay, you gotta be kidding." She pushed him away and sat in her own corner of his pickup, giggling at the very idea. She'd made love with two people at the same time just once before, but that barely counted. That was two boys and besides, she was pretty drunk.

"Honest, Sissy, I'm not. She's real friendly." He pulled her back into the crook of his arm. "Come on, Sissy. It's like a mausoleum up there. She wants a good time. She told me."

"But what about *me*, Tommy Hardisay? Maybe I won't like it." She pulled a long strand of hair into her mouth.

"Sissy, you're going to like it just fine. We'll have us our own little party first. Bottle a hooch, mess around a while, get in the mood. Hell, I can feel it comin' on right now."

She let him pull her closer, and giggled into his neck. "Yeah, I can feel it too."

Two days later, on a hot Saturday night in late July, Sissy was on her way in Tommy's truck. She had rinsed her hair blond that day, and under her sundress she was wearing her Dallas panties. She was very excited. "I never even *talked* to a Harlow before," she giggled.

Tommy parked the pickup down the hill from the Harlow place and led Sissy up through the cottonwoods to the light at the back of the house. The door was open and they were creeping down a hallway when Sissy pulled at Tommy's hand. "What about the kids, Tommy? I mean . . ."

"S'okay," he whispered. "One's away at camp, the other's down there, at the end of the hall. Sleeps like a log." He conducted her into a book-lined room with leather couches and a Mexican rug on the floor.

Caroline Harlow was wearing a dark red silk gown. Its deep vee neck was ruffled in feathers, and the sleeves were long with feathered cuffs to match the neck.

She stood and smiled. "How do you do?" and she held out her hand.

Sissy giggled, and then Caroline Harlow laughed too. She was a little nervous and a little drunk. She wasn't sure she wanted to do this, but they were here now and she would think about putting her life back together tomorrow.

Tommy slid his arm around Sissy. She could feel the sweat already seeping through his clean-for-the-occasion blue shirt, and then his hand, tugging insistently as he propelled them to the bedroom across the hall.

It was the biggest bedroom Sissy had ever seen. There was a big white bed in the middle and real paintings on the walls. There even was a long sofa, and all the colors were soft in the candlelight. Sissy stepped onto a thick carpet, and felt just like Lana Turner walking into a movie set. When Tommy nodded, it was easy to step out of her dress and stand there on the thick rug in her black lace panties.

Caroline Harlow swayed across the room, almost stumbled, then turned and sank to the bed. Tommy's hand ran up and down Sissy's back, gently sending her across to the bed. She sat down, and then Tommy was kissing her, pressing her back. His mouth was slipping down her body, around her nipples, into her navel. He stripped off her panties and nudged her legs wide.

Another hand was on her breast now; another mouth kissed Sissy's. It was the weirdest feeling, and just for a second she wanted to giggle. And then the mouth went away and a breast tumbled from the red gown. Sissy heard herself moan. The nipple was large and ripe. It came closer, and Sissy flicked out her tongue and touched.

Sissy was having a wonderful time when, nearly an hour later, she glanced up from Caroline Harlow's breasts and saw Amelia Harlow staring at her. She sounded, Sissy declared later, just like God.

"Get out," Amelia said. "Get out of my son's room. Get out of this house."

Caroline called Alfred Reece. It was August and the New York streets were hot and steamy. She and Maggie were back in the East and somehow Kate wasn't, wouldn't ever be, according to Amelia Harlow. Caroline needed Reece, and he said he would try, but none of it, custody law, estate law, none of it was his kind of law.

But he put the phone down with promises and found himself remembering a yacht suspended in the Hudson, the lights spangling the dark, and the perfect, perfectly unattainable creature who emerged from the crowd and the music that spring night. He wished he could reach down into time now, take the girl with the dark hair and dark dreaming eyes, and spin her back, let her dissolve into the crowd, let her dance on.

25

"GREETINGS," began the court order, like a cheerful holiday card.

GREETINGS:

The Honorable District Court, Fifth Judicial District, Titus County, Texas, requests your presence on or before 10 o'clock A.M., Monday, September 10, 1959, then and there to answer the petition of Caroline Forsythe Harrington Harlow and entitled:

In the interest of Kathryn Morning Glory Harlow, a child.

Sincerely . . .

Signed with the illegible spidery scrawl of the Titus County Clerk, stamped with the round seal of Texas, it arrived in Amelia Harlow's office the first week in June: a single 8½ by 11 sheet of mimeograph paper that finally brought to an end the ten months of hysteria and long-distance phone calls.

Caroline Harlow, in the elaborately shrouded language constructed by the New York law firm she'd first engaged, had called her mother-in-law a manipulative, dynastic, interfering bitch. Clayton Benedict, in language slightly less shrouded, responded that his client's daughter-in-law was a slut, incompetent to raise a cur dog.

Amelia had prevailed. Caroline had signed a custody agreement and nine-year-old Kate Harlow hadn't stepped foot beyond the 4,137-mile-long border of Texas since her mother's exit.

Technically, Round Two was to begin in the courthouse in Earth, but it began in London a day after the court order was issued. "I want my child," Caroline Harlow announced to the reporters she called to the suite she'd taken in the Connaught Hotel in Mayfair. "I want her and I mean to have her." Hours later, when the afternoon papers hit the London streets, there it was on page three: *"I WANT MY CHILD."*

The next day it moved up to the front pages and rolled out over the Atlantic. "I WANT MY CHILD," cried the headline in a Chicago tabloid, and below: *Widowed Mother Seeks Custody.*

Amelia Harlow saw that tabloid and knew that the other papers would follow. The phones would start ringing and the story would start breaking in every newspaper and magazine in America. They wouldn't, she supposed, ask her for personal interviews. They would respect her privacy that far, but no further. There would be no special courtesy to a fellow publisher, no gracefully discreet headlines set in conservative fourteen-point type and quietly buried in a page-four news hole. The big-city editors would be meticulous about libel, but within the broad confines of those ambiguous laws, they would let the gossip columnists and the photographers run riot in Harlow territory. They would have to. If the situation had been reversed, she would have done the same.

"I WANT MY CHILD." The Chicago tabloid was still on Amelia's desk two days later when Clayton Benedict drove in from Dallas. He picked it up, shaking his big head in disbelief.

"She's crazy, pushing it like this. Put Sissy on the stand and we'll nail her to the courtroom floor. Texas judge hears what we got and Caroline won't get within ten feet of that child."

"No."

It was a whisper, but he heard it, and he glanced up. The desk was cluttered with books and newspapers, paperweights and pencil holders handcrafted by two generations of children. The woman seated behind it stared blindly at the tabloid before her. He went to the bar and poured bourbon over ice. "Something wrong, Amelia? Looks to me like an absolute equation. They testify. She loses. Period."

"Find another equation, Clayton."

It began to dawn on Clayton Benedict then that Amelia Harlow had no intention of letting Sissy testify, and then he had the first of the visions that would plague him for weeks to come. It was a vision of himself in a courtroom rising to plead her case and having nothing to say. He downed the bourbon and let his anger propel him across the room. "What the hell's the matter with you? You know they have to testify."

She stared back at him, her eyes hard with her own anger. "I won't have dirty laundry dragged out and aired in every newspaper and magazine in this country."

"It's a judge, Amelia. Not a jury. Just a judge. You want to throw the public out? The press? Throw them out. You want the records sealed? So seal the damn records for a hundred years. But she has to testify."

She reached to snap on the desk lamp and then changed her mind. "No." She was a small, hard figure in the gloom, and her face was hollow in the late afternoon light.

He poured himself another bourbon, then wandered to the long set of windows looking west at a big red sky. He loosened his tie, ambled to the dark couch, and sank back into the plush velvet. He raised one leg to the low coffee table, then the other, gazing into his glass of bourbon. "We never talked much, you and I, but I guess you ought to know that I look back over the years every now and then. Always remember the early days and the first time you came into my old man's store-front office. You were just a girl in a summer dress, and me, I watched you walk in from the street and wished you'd go away.

"I'm glad you didn't, Amelia. I've always been glad about that. You got rich, I got rich." He sipped his bourbon. "Damndest thing ever happened to me."

He sank deeper into the sofa, his voice soft and dreamy in the dusk. "I never did figure out how you got so smart. How long we been at it now? Thirty-five, forty years? And in all that time I never did figure that out. No schooling to speak of. No daddy to fix it all for you and tell you what it was all about. People used to say it was Will calling all the shots. Then when he was gone, you'd hear it was Bliss, or Ben, or me. I don't know if you ever knew that—about people thinking it was me put it all together.

"I never quite know what to say to folks like that, but I'll tell you one thing. I look back over all those years we've been doing business, all the way back to the girl in her white summer dress standing there in that office. You weren't like other people, Amelia. Even then. You knew exactly what you wanted. And never—never in all those years did you want something you didn't have the nerve to go out and get. Except now."

He swallowed the last of the bourbon. "First time

I've ever known you to sit around wasting time, wanting something you don't have the guts to get."

The bourbon was gone. The light was gone. He examined an empty glass.

"I loved my son," she finally said. "I've begun to think that I didn't love him enough. If I'd loved him enough perhaps I would have let him . . . let him simply be. It's a terrible thing—that. To know you didn't love enough."

He glanced away, afraid for a moment of the grief stamped on her face. Stop, he wanted to say. Stop. But her words kept coming, dredged up from some dark agony inside her.

"And now it's too late. He's dead and all I have left is his little girl.

"You speak about nerve?" Her voice was low and her gaze was directed beyond him to a place in the dusk he couldn't quite see. "And you're right, Clayton. I don't have the nerve to do as you ask. You want me to display her in public as the child of a woman with the morals of a cat? I can't do that. Even if I lose her, I won't do that."

"Nobody would blame her, Amelia. Not a little girl."

"Wouldn't they, Clayton?" Her voice was tired and old. "Wouldn't they?" she said again. "You don't know how wrong you are, Clayton. How very, very wrong."

The room was silent for a moment and then, from deep below them, he heard the slow, muffled roar of the presses beginning to roll. He put his feet on the floor, eased out of the couch, then slipped into his jacket and straightened his tie. "It doesn't have to be a public hearing, Amelia. I told you that."

"You told me that, Clayton."

He searched for her face in the shadows beyond the desk, but there was only the dark. "I'll try to find another way, Amelia. I don't . . ."

He wanted to say he didn't think he could stand to

fail her now, but he left it unsaid. He was certain he would fail. She'd trapped herself, protecting Caroline to save Kate, and the trap would shut in court.

He stood in the shadows for a moment, then finally left, closing the door softly behind him.

"It's the trial of the century," the item began, "down Texas way." Amelia found it on her desk the next morning. It had been clipped from a gossip column in the New York *Daily News* and Sarah Leslie's note was attached. "They sent this up from downstairs. Terribly sorry.—SL"

It's the trial of the century, down Texas way. With any luck, darlings, we're going to hear how the daughter-in-law of the media got caught with her panties around her knees. . . .

Amelia picked up the phone. Ten minutes later, she was on her way up Sugar Hill.

It was eleven when she pulled into the clearing in front of Billy's bar. He was already there, turning his Stetson in his big red hands. She cut the motor.

"Sissy's talking. I can't have that, Billy."

"I know she is, Amelia. And I told her to stop her mouth. Told her that twice now, but you know what kids are these days. No manners."

"It has to stop, Billy."

He looked at her for a while and finally nodded. "Pappy Jarvis around?"

"He's in Washington. He'll be in next week."

"Well, you talk to Jarvis. You tell him to tell that Hardisay boy to marry my Sissy. Jarvis has connections, let him find a nice place for them somewhere else for a while. California, maybe. Sissy would like California, Amelia."

Amelia took Billy's hand. "Thank you, Billy."

"No thanks necessary, Amelia. They'll like California. They'll be happy as pigs in corn."

HEIRESS SHOPS AT NEIMAN'S

The headline ran big and black across the front page of the Monday edition of the Dallas *Morning News*. Just below there was a picture of a girl in a plaid sundress with black Mary Janes and white ankle socks. At first Kate didn't even recognize the face with the white eyes all flattened out on the gray, grimy page she held in her hands. The photograph had been taken just before Grandmelia pulled her back into the limousine, away from Neiman's and the hands pushing, touching. She didn't have a chance to read the article. Matty took one look, then picked the paper right out of her hand. But Kate didn't really want to read the story. It was the picture that held her attention. The rest of it was still quite vivid in her mind.

She and Grandmelia and Duke had driven down to Dallas the day before yesterday to go shopping for all the stuff you had to have for camp—regulation blue shorts and regulation white sneakers and regulation riding boots and riding pants. The only good thing was you got to buy it all at Neiman-Marcus.

Neiman's was beautiful. You got to go in through the big glass front doors and walk very, very slowly down the main aisle. The big sparkling glass display cases were full of whole rainbows of stuff, china and silver and leather and silk stuff with funny names like Goochey Poochie. The elevator operators always shook your hand and said, "Welcome back, Miss Kate," and upstairs there were little secret rooms with soft wall-to-wall carpets and flowers in little vases and curvy satin sofas you couldn't put your feet on. Ladies with scrawny necks went slinking up and down in different outfits while a short gray-haired lady with a funny

accent stood around talking about cut and fabric and
workmanship, about lee-tle cottons and am-por-tant
furs and special lee-tle sporty costumes Neiman's had
acquired with Madame Harlow in mind. Didn't Madame think it was perfect?

Madame didn't, and Kate was more interested in the
code language of *haute couture*. "Grandmelia," she
whispered the first time her grandmother took her up to
one of the special rooms. "Grandmelia, what does she
mean—'little'? I mean the dress isn't little at all. It's got
this huge skirt and . . ."

"The prices, pet," her grandmother whispered back.
"She means the prices. 'Little' is expensive and 'important' is outrageous." Kate giggled.

"Shh now," her grandmother said, and nudged
Kate's shoe off the sofa. "We have to be serious or we'll
hurt their feelings."

Afterward, they'd go down the street to the offices of
Harlow Enterprises. It took two elevators to get you to
the top floor, one to fifteen, one to thirty-two. Once
you were there, there were people walking fast down a
lot of halls, nodding at Grandmelia as they passed and
stopping her every now and then to talk about news.
People called her plain Kate here, and they let her sit in
the big chairs lined up along a table in one of the rooms
that were always half dark. You could swirl around in
those chairs and see lots and lots of TV sets flickering
through the dark with different pictures on all the
screens.

She'd gone there lots with Grandmelia this year, but
that Saturday in June there was no visit to the Dallas
office, no Neiman's even.

Duke pulled up in front of the store and two men
emerged from nowhere just as Kate darted from the
car. They pushed through the crowds and trapped her
there on the hot, muggy street. She'd stopped, curious
and a little confused, and then something had flashed in

her face and she was alone in a throbbing circle of hard, hot, white light. There was a voice she didn't recognize —"Turn this way, Kate"—and then a hand, touching.

She screamed. She screamed and screamed, groped blindly for her grandmother, felt herself lifted into the cool of the back seat, and heard the door slam as the car jerked away from the curb. Then her grandmother was pressing her forehead with a handkerchief soaked in something tart-smelling and murmuring over and over, "There now . . . there now . . . Shh now, shh now, pet."

By the time they were halfway home, she understood. She was famous. She was nine years old. She didn't sing or dance or act. She wasn't smart, at least not like the kids on the TV quiz shows. But she was famous anyway.

She was famous because they were rich, and when you were rich and something happened to you, all the newspapers had to write about it. The thing that had happened to her was that her father had died and her mother had gone away and nobody knew now where Kate would live.

"Remember, Kate?" her grandmother asked as they skidded through the Dallas streets. "We've talked about that, and about the judge, just last week."

Kate nodded and stared out the window as the last bits and pieces of the city flashed by. Grandmelia had explained it all, time and time again, after Mommy and Maggie left. Grandmelia had explained everything.

Mommy and Maggie had left Texas. Mommy and Maggie weren't Texas people, not really family, like Kate was. Everybody liked them of course, and Kate should write them and maybe she would visit them. One day. Except now Mommy didn't want Kate to be a Texas person anymore, and that was a decision that everybody would talk about with a judge.

Kate understood that, but she didn't like to think about it. Not now, not when Grandmelia told her that

Maggie and her mother were gone. "Gone?" she'd asked. "Maggie's gone?" She'd felt something begin to happen in her stomach and then she shut the door on it and didn't think about it.

Except she had to think about it now. Her head hurt from the white lights and she had to think.

"Daddy was a Texas person, wasn't he?" she finally said.

Amelia didn't consider her answer before she gave it; she simply gave it. It was an answer that came from all she had ever hoped Bliss would be, and it came automatically.

"Of course, pet," she said. "Of course he was a Texas person. And you were his Morning Glory. His special Texas child."

The car shot onto the highway, rolled toward home.

July came and Amelia Harlow's granddaughter went away to camp again in the granite hills of Central Texas. The regulation uniforms finally came by courier from Neiman's. They did look dumb, but she didn't care anymore. The sun came up and went down over the high bare hills, the wind sighed through the thickets of oak along the creek, and Kate was grateful just to be anonymous.

Dear Matty,
I am now at Camp. You should see the food they give us. You could throw up. Please remember to feed the dogs and cats for me. Thank you.

Love,
Kate

Dear Jay Jay,
Here I am again. You can stand on top of this mountain here and see the whole world. The food stinks.

xx from Camp Weeny Roast Ha

Dear Grandmelia,
Please send sox. I lost mine in the wash.

                                        Love

To fulfill her grandmother's instructions that she
write her mother at least once a month, Kate started
three letters, ripped them up, and completed the fourth
at the end of July. Finally she stuffed it into one of the
preaddressed, pre-stamped envelopes Grandmelia's
Miss Leslie had provided her.

Mrs. Caroline Harlow
C/O Alfred Reece, Esq.
523 Park Avenue
New York City, New York

Dear Mother,
Thank you for your letters. They came to me at
Camp. Camp is fine.
                                        Love,
                                        Kate
                                        P.S. Tell Maggie hi.

She sat on her cot thinking about that last line.
"P.S. Tell Maggie hi." She thought about it for
almost an hour and then she copied the letter over
again, word by word, and signed only her name.
There was no P.S. now, and she threw the original
away.

The afternoon call to tack up came and she got in
line, pushing and shoving with the other girls. When
the sun set that night and it was dark, she lay in her cot
with her arms around Goose Too and thought.

She thought about her father for the first time in the
year he had been dead. She thought about him very
slowly, drop by drop, careful not to let the memories
flood over her.

* * *

The August first issue of *Life* magazine hit the newsstands with a black-and-white photograph of a little girl and a teddy bear on the cover.

Kathryn Morning Glory Harlow sat on a bench with one leg tucked under her and the other swinging free. She wore a simple dress with a round collar and looked straight ahead through large eyes, a serious expression on her face. One hand rested on the bench beside her leg, and the other held the teddy bear with his ribbon, carefully, so the camera would be sure to capture his likeness too.

Inside, there was another picture of Kate and a series of aerial views: a housing development, offshore oil wells, a small town split by railway tracks.

Eleanor turned the page.

And there they were—dozens of photographs were from Maggie's family album, another of Caroline's dramatic gestures to let the world in on her widow's plight. Eleanor wondered how much *Life* had forked over for the exclusive and then she turned back to the beginning.

The aerial view of Earth was old, one of Bliss's she supposed, taken from his plane. There was the big house; her and Ben's; the cottages for Matty and Duke, Rosie and George; the stables and garages. A white brick wall had gone up since that picture was taken. They had contracted Brown & Root of Houston, and within three weeks a ten-foot white brick wall with barbed wire on top surrounded five acres of land.

Eleanor turned the pages of *Life* and looked again at the familiar old pictures. There were Jay and Maggie and Kate in front of a Christmas tree wearing the sweaters she'd given them that year. They were all alike, with snowflake designs and silver buttons at the neck. She looked for other pictures of Jay, but there weren't any. Only Kate.

She stuffed the magazine in a drawer, pushed the

odd, uncomfortable resentments out of the way, and went to find her son.

It was very bright and quiet outside. She could hear Matty clattering a pan in her kitchen and Duke's thin, toneless whistle drifting around the side of the garage where he was polishing the Cadillac. Jay was under the porch of the big house, his white T-shirt just visible through the slots. He spent a lot of time under that porch now, more and more secretive as the hearing approached.

"Jay," she called, her voice echoing across the yard. "Come on, let's go to Carr's for ice cream." She watched him scramble farther under the porch. She couldn't see the white of his shirt now, but she called again. "Come on, Jay." He didn't stir and she walked down the steps and across the yard to fetch him.

26

HARLOW VS. HARLOW TODAY

In New York, at the downtown plant of William Randolph Hearst's *Journal-American*, they put the September 10 edition to bed with the headline in big forty-eight-point type, a couple of teaser lines, and three photographs on the front page.

A carefully staged formal shot of Amelia Bliss Harlow took up the left-hand side. The photograph had been taken at the *Bugle-Times* and it showed a slight woman wearing a fixed smile of assurance, her elegant face carefully framed by the dip of a hat.

On the right-hand side of the page a younger woman laughed into a camera. A white sundress left her shoulders bare and her slender arms reached back, resting against white railings. There was something utterly carefree about Caroline in that photograph.

And between them, the by-now famous photograph of a little girl clutching a teddy bear. It had been cropped for the cover of *Life* a month before, but they ran it whole in the *Journal-American,* the pastoral shadows of the photographer's backdrop intact.

The story started with the teaser lines on page one, then ran over and filled up the whole of page four. Only the *New York Times* gave the front page to other stories—the *Times* and the twenty dailies in the Harlow chain. Robert F. Kennedy had been appointed Chief Counsel of the Select Senate Committee on Improper Labor Management Activities. Eisenhower was golfing in Florida and the Yankees were leading the race for the pennant. The *Times* ran the Harlow case big on page five. In the Harlow dailies it got buried, at the bottom of page three.

BATTLE FOR MORNING GLORY BEGINS

AMELIA HARLOW CONFRONTS DAUGHTER-IN-LAW
HONORABLE BEAUREGARD DARBY
PRESIDES IN TITUS COUNTY TODAY

It was nearly dawn when Caroline heard the plop of the Dallas *Morning News* outside her door. Alone in her room at the Cozy Cottages Motel, she climbed out of the sweat-stained sheets and wrapped a robe around her. She hadn't made the front page. Amelia was there, and Kate. They'd written about her of course, as the outsider who had come to take from Texas what was theirs.

Caroline let the paper drop back to the stoop and stood leaning against the doorjamb, waiting for the day. Out on Route 30 a caravan of cars passed, the headlights shining through the early morning fog and the stands of pampas grass. She could see a station wagon, two pickups, and an old two-door with a big bruised-looking trailer hooked up behind it. A radio in

one of the vans played a Country-Western song that
flared up, then melted away.

Caroline closed the door and went back to bed. She
knew she still wouldn't sleep. She would lie in bed
thinking and they would call her at seven. She'd get up
then, order coffee, and run a hot tub. She would dress
carefully, and go.

Ten miles down the road, the vans from the television
networks sat in a silent ring around Court House
Square, and their transmission cables snaked their way
around the roots of the live oaks. The sleeping bags
littering the lawns had gone for fifteen dollars apiece to
the people who'd arrived on Saturday morning to find
the motels and rooming houses filled with working
press. Those who came later paid triple the price.
"Supply and demand," the Ashmeads explained patiently to the crowds jamming the aisles of Carr's.

Up at the other end of town, the wall with the barbed
wire looped its way around the five acres of Harlow
property, its whitewashed brick glowing through the
half light. At the back of the big house, in the wing
once occupied by Bliss and Caroline and two little girls,
doors and walls had disappeared. The rooms had been
slashed into one open space, and Caroline's furniture
was gone. A piano filled one corner now, and comfortable sofas and chairs covered in chintz were arranged in
groups.

Amelia Harlow sat alone in one of those chairs
and watched the dawn slide her into another Texas
day.

Upstairs in the old nursery, yellow flowers on a field
of blue papered the walls, a pattern not unlike the one
Evangeline Harlow had chosen for her daughter-in-law
years before. A single child slept there now. She turned
over, and her thumb curled into her mouth. Then, as if
she remembered she was too old for that, she let the
hand hang free.

Outside, double gates of iron grill stood planted in

the cottonwoods, staring blindly down Main Street where life was just beginning to stir.

Out on Route 30 the caravan turned into Main Street. There was a "No Parking" sign in front of the press building, but they pulled in anyway and began to set up.

Red-and-white striped awnings appeared, balloons, cases of soda, and finally the display racks for the teddy bear souvenirs marked "GOOSE TOO OFFICIAL REPLICA MADE IN USA."

Shops opened and Main Street filled with cars. The courthouse doors opened at nine, then closed again fifteen minutes later. Main Street still swarmed with people pushing for a place up front.

27

"Oyez. Oyez."

It was ten sharp when the bailiff came striding into the courtroom with the age-old cry. And again: "Oyez!" At the back of the room the sheriff moved to close the big double doors. Upstairs a deputy nudged shut the door to the press gallery. It was quieter then, the voices from the street reduced to a distant murmur. When the bailiff called out again, there was the faint sound of the court reporter's machine running a pace behind his voice. "Fifth District Court of the Sovereign State of Texas now in session. Judge Beauregard Jackson Darby presiding. All rise."

Two hundred bodies came to their feet as he entered in a billow of black robes. He was a massive man with a white head of hair and bright eyes behind half-moon glasses. He gathered his black robe up in a thick hand and climbed the two steps to the dais where the flags of the United States and Texas fell in neat ripples. He settled into the high-backed leather chair and swiveled to face the people.

He was an East Texas man, born and bred. Elected to the circuit bench of the district court in the middle of the depression, he had served with distinction for a quarter of a century, waving away, year after year, the offers of loftier jurisdictions and higher courts. Beau Darby was, as he always used to say to his long-dead wife, a country judge, used to country ways. He looked out at the faces before him keenly aware that this was the last moment when the scales of justice lay level. The stories would begin, events would unfold, and people would come to the stand to prevaricate, lie, and announce truth as they saw it or wished it could be. Slowly, bit by bit, the scales would begin to move.

He'd been in this courtroom many times and liked it. The benches before him, the gallery above, were all of solid golden oak. It was a simple room, lit by natural light streaming through windows set high in the white-washed walls.

He glanced down at the contestants in this case. There was the petitioner in black linen with her dark head high and her eyes hidden behind dark glasses. At the other table Amelia Bliss Harlow gazed up at him from the shade of a dove-gray straw hat. He knew all about Amelia Harlow, acknowledged her now with a slight nod, and saw her nod in reply.

Judge Darby had played poker a couple of times with Will Harlow and had liked the man well enough. That must be his daughter, Eleanor, in the row behind her mother. The man with her, with his arm protectively across her shoulders, had to be Ben Rawlings, a decent, fair-minded businessman, so he'd heard.

He glanced up to the back wall and caught the hand of the big clock shifting to 10:03.

"Custody hearing today," he began. "Matter of Kathryn Morning Glory Harlow, a lawful minor. We have Clayton Benedict over here for Amelia Harlow, and that's John Henry Mack. He's representing the petitioner, Caroline . . ." He thumbed quickly through the file before him. "Caroline Harrington Harlow."

He looked up now, peered over the top of his half-moon glasses. "Now, nobody here wanted to get involved in a jury trial. That right, Mr. Mack? Mr. Benedict? Everybody understands that that was possible and everybody waived that right, and I want that clear for the record." He looked from one to the other, waited for their nods.

"Another small point, gentlemen. We all know you've been to fine law schools. Mr. Benedict's a graduate of our own University of Texas down in Austin, and Mr. Mack went to Columbia University Law School, up in New York City. We know everybody's passed their bar exams and everybody's chock full of the knowledge of the law, ripe and ready to show off to members of the fourth estate who've honored us with their presence here today."

There was a giggle from the press. He peered into the gallery and silenced it with a frown. "But the fact of the matter is, in a petition of this nature, the law in her majesty is not interested in procedural chess games and a lot of fancy rules of evidence. Mostly, she's going to be interested in everybody getting up here and saying their piece, so I don't want a lot of objections raised or a lot of arguments on the fine points of law. Fact is, gentlemen, I went to law school too, and on that note we'll begin. Maybe Mr. Mack would be kind enough to start us off. You prepared to do that, sir."

It wasn't a question, and Henry Mack suppressed the urge to shoot to his feet like the military cadet he'd once been.

It wasn't much of a military school, and his B.A. degree wasn't much either, but he'd graduated from Columbia law with honors. He was a freckle-faced young man from Galveston and he'd been lonely in the

North, but when he went back home he discovered he
didn't belong there either anymore.

Dallas felt better—"Yankeetown," the diehards of
Galveston called it. He took the classic route: a stint in
the public prosecutor's office, then on to one of the big
firms in town.

He was out on his own by the time Caroline Harlow
came into his life as a referral from a Wall Street firm.
He wasn't the first Texas attorney they'd tried, but he
needed the business and accepted the case. He flew to
London and met her and the older daughter in their
suite of rooms at a hotel: a skinny kid who disappeared
with a nursemaid, and a faintly disheveled young
woman who begged him to help her somehow.

It wasn't until the end of August that he began to
sense she might win. The preliminary witness lists were
exchanged that week. Benedict got his and he got
Benedict's. He saw then that there was no Hardisay on
Benedict's list, not much of anybody from what Henry
Mack could see.

His opening statement was brief; Benedict's was
briefer: card players, playing close to the chest. He
called his first witness to the stand.

The bailiff's voice twanged and there was a stir as
people craned their necks for a better look. "State your
full name."

"Caroline Forsythe Harrington Harlow."

"Your place of residence."

"Suffolk, England."

The bailiff held out a black Bible that was well used
and frayed at the edges. "Do you swear to tell the
truth, the whole truth . . ."

A moment later Mack walked to the stand.

"Maybe you can begin by telling the court more
about where you currently reside, Mrs. Harlow."

She had a nice voice, Darby thought. She sat on the
edge of the hard, upright chair with her hands in her lap

and spoke of a house outside London called Chatham Manor.

"My elder daughter and I are there as house guests," she went on.

"Guests of whose, please?"

"Of an old and dear friend of mine. Of my husband's and mine, actually. Portia Michaels Machado. It's been her family's home—well, for some time."

"And the accommodations? How many rooms, the grounds, its relative position to the nearest town and so forth?"

"It's a very large house, with stables. They ride, you see, both my children. It's just a minute or two from the village. And there's a day school there, a very good day school really."

"So we can say, can't we, that you've made appropriate arrangements for your children?" Mack leaned against the dais. "Attractive arrangements, would you say?"

"I hope so, Mr. Mack. Maggie . . . well, I think any child would be very happy there."

"Maggie is your child by your first marriage, is that correct?"

"Yes. I was widowed during the war. When she was just a baby, not quite one."

"And you were subsequently remarried to Bliss Harlow, by whom you bore a second child five years after your first?"

"Yes, that's correct."

"Kathryn Morning Glory Harlow, in fact. The subject of this case."

"Kate," she nodded. "My little girl Kate."

"The children were raised together, here in Texas . . ."

"Yes."

"Grew up together for some eight years?"

"Yes."

"But Kate now resides in Texas? And you and Maggie abroad?" There was disbelief in his voice and he began to pace the courtroom floor with his head tipped to the press gallery. Darby tapped a pencil on the dais and then stopped. There was no point in pushing. He was going to play to the gallery no matter what. He'd milk them for every headline he could get.

"Is that by your choice?" Mack was still pacing with his face pulled into the same worried frown.

"No."

"I see." He stopped then and sat on the corner of the petitioner's table. "Tell us about your children," he asked. "Were they close?"

"They adored each other, Mr. Mack."

"They shared a room, I understand?"

"Yes."

"They got up together in the mornings."

"Yes."

"Dressed together?"

"Yes."

"Went to school together every day?"

"Yes."

"And loved each other, very much."

She nodded, and held her head high.

"I see. Perhaps you can tell the Court the circumstances under which these two children were separated?"

"Yes," she said. "If . . . Please, if I just might have a glass of water?"

The water was poured, and Caroline took her time sipping it. She handed the glass back with a nod of thanks.

"And now," Mack said, "in your own words, please."

Darby very much doubted that the words would be her own. The Texas press had never reported the real reason for Caroline Harlow's sudden departure from town. Still, the word had spread, bringing out-of-state reporters knocking on people's doors. At first Darby supposed that one of them would find the story, verify it, and print it. But the summer wore on and nothing happened.

He was fully prepared for the story to blow in court. He'd combed the statute books lining his library and had his clerk prepare a précis of precedents from cases involving similar ugly stories. But one thing was sure. Caroline Harlow wouldn't tell her story. She sat carefully in her seat, reciting repackaged facts.

It was a tale of sudden widowhood, deepening depression, and the decision to take her daughter Maggie on a holiday back East.

"Maggie," Mack prompted. "But not Kate."

No. The child his client had come to refer to as "my little girl," a slight, almost imperceptible emphasis on the word "little," had been at riding camp. It was an event she'd looked forward to and her mother didn't have the heart to disrupt her stay there.

"And did you subsequently discover," Mack asked, "that someone else did have the heart?"

"Yes." There was hopelessness now in her voice. It was the weary, beaten hopelessness of a woman who had lost a game she didn't know was being played. "When I arrived in New York, I phoned the camp to make arrangements for them to send my little girl East at the end of the session. They said she was no longer registered. They said that Mrs. Harlow had flown down that morning to take her home. I asked if my little girl was all right, if something had gone wrong. No, they said. Amelia Harlow had just taken her away."

"And did you then call Amelia Harlow?"

"Yes." A bitter smile played briefly at her mouth. "They said she was 'engaged.' I asked if I might hold or call back at some convenient time. Her secretary came on the line then. She said Mr. Benedict would be in touch and then she hung up. I waited all afternoon, and finally he called."

"His exact words please. To the best of your recollection."

She nodded. "He said he was sorry but my little girl would not be coming to New York. I said I would return to Texas, but he said he couldn't advise that. He said it would be a waste of a plane ticket, that my money would be better spent on an attorney so visitation rights could be arranged."

"And were such arrangements made?"

She nodded again, misery in the curve of her neck.

Beau Darby had seen the depositions. There were sheafs of them from the firm of Wall Street attorneys she'd first engaged. He knew the firm by reputation; he knew that pinstriped Yankee style and the arrogance with which they would approach a small firm of rednecks in the West. The rednecks, Clayton Benedict and Associates, had responded true to form. They'd slapped their terms on the table. Kate Harlow would spend the school year in Texas. She could spend a week in the winter with her mother and a week in the summer, both weeks in the company of adults to be designated by her guardian and grandmother, and if the gentlemen from New York didn't like it they could blow it out their collective ass.

And Caroline Harlow had signed. She left New York and went to England, and there she canceled the plans for her daughter, the housekeeper and the chauffeur to join her in St. Moritz. Instead, on thick white bond edged in blue and engraved with the seal of a Suffolk manor house, Caroline Harlow had given the order to sue.

She was describing that decision now, and Beau Darby, waving away Clay Benedict's objection, cupped his chin in his hand to listen.

"I was frightened when I signed," she was saying. "Amelia Harlow is a very powerful woman. I didn't even know she wanted my little girl, and then suddenly she had her. I was frightened, and so I signed."

She glanced down at the hands clasped together in her dark lap, and when she raised her head again she was crying. The tears throbbed in her voice, slipped down her face, and dampened the neck of her dress. "Then I changed my mind," she said. "She's my little girl, you see? Not hers. Mine."

Henry Mack concluded his questions and left Beau Darby to remember those words during the noon recess. She's my little girl, you see? Mine.

Clayton Benedict's cross-examination of Caroline Harlow began after lunch. He gave Caroline a formal nod of his head and started with caution and concern in his voice. If she didn't want to sign the custody papers, why had she done so? There was no answer, other than fear. But fear of what, he wanted to know as he paced the courtroom floor. He stopped, astonishment stamped on his face, when the one-word answer came.

"Her."

Had his client threatened the witness in any way?

She shook her head, and spoke an almost inaudible "No."

Had any member or representative of the family threatened her, directly or indirectly? In print or by any other means?

Again, "No."

Caroline Harlow's sexual exploits hung over the courtroom as Darby sensed they must have hung over her the day she signed. Benedict frowned, seemingly helpless in the face of her apparent lack of sense. "I can find no clue, none at all," he shrugged, "that would suggest my client has custody of her son's only child by anything but your consent, freely given, and with proper legal advice. Can you?"

But the witness only stared at him, numb and blank. "Can you?"

The question came again, and then again. "No," she finally said.

Clayton Benedict nodded and meandered back to the table where Amelia Harlow sat. He extracted a single sheet from his briefcase files and when he spoke again, his voice was harder and more Texan.

"Let's see. You've been married twice?"

"Yes."

"Your first husband left you a widow as well?"

"Yes."

"But not for long. That right?"

"I beg your pardon?"

"How long were you a widow? The first time around."

"I'm afraid I can't recall exactly. It was wartime and he . . ."

"Says here Anthony Harrington died in November 1944. That's U.S. military record. Sound familiar?"

"I believe that date's correct. Yes."

"And you remarried when?"

"April 1945."

"Let's see now. That's December, January . . ." He counted the months on his fingers, held up one hand, and waved it like a flag. "I count five." He reached over to the pitcher of water, poured a glass, then let it sit. "Did your parents introduce you to Bliss Harlow?"

"We were formally introduced by a mutual friend."

"And where was that?"

"At a gathering . . . of friends."

"Big yacht party, was it?"

Caroline glanced up and found Eleanor's face among the spectators. Their eyes met, held, and then Eleanor glanced away. Caroline turned to Clayton Benedict. "You might call it big. I wouldn't."

"Two hundred or so, would you say?"

"I didn't count."

He was pacing again, with his hands in his pockets. "Lots of drinking? Champagne and all?"

"There may have been. I don't recall."

"Don't recall? Really?"

"Really, Mr. Benedict."

He gazed up at the press gallery and then turned to her with a grin. "Thought all you ladies remembered each and every detail of that sort of thing. Right down to the color of the ties all of us poor slobs forgot we wore. Well, never mind." There was a snicker, a clap of the gavel, and he began to pace again.

"Let's see now. Woman widowed five months . . . gets together with a few friends. About two hundred or so. Has a little champagne . . . well, maybe. She doesn't really recall. She meets a man. Imagine that. Now remind me. What year was that?"

"Nineteen forty-five."

He repeated the date. And then he said, "But Bliss Harlow was only a schoolboy in 1945. A *wealthy* schoolboy, but a boy nonetheless. Maybe we better amend that. Recently widowed woman on the party circuit meets wealthy schoolboy . . ."

But Henry Mack was on his feet. "This has gone far enough. If Mr. Benedict is trying to establish that my client actually met her husband, I'm glad to grant him that. And if he wants us to grant an age difference, we're happy to. About a year, year and a half if I remember correctly."

Benedict turned. "Well here now, I must apologize to my young colleague." Then he turned to the witness again. "You wearing black?"

"As you can see, Mr. Benedict, I am."

"You in mourning?"

"For my husband? Of course. Not officially but . . ."

He cut her short. "Yes or no?"

"Yes. Yes, I am."

He nodded, then shoved his briefcase aside and revealed a stack of magazines. He picked one up. "Recognize this?"

"Yes, of course. It's the London edition of *Vogue*."

"And this?"

"Town and Country."

"And this?"

"*Harper's Bazaar,* the French edition."

The magazines lay fanned out on the table. He gathered them up and came to the stand. He flipped a magazine open and held it high. "Mind reading this caption for us?"

Caroline looked.

She'd felt well that day. She remembered that. It was a black-and-white photograph, but her suit had been beige. She read the caption. "'The enclosure at New Market, Caroline Harlow in attendance with Peter Post.'"

"And again?" He held another glossy page up for display, and then another, and another. She read, on and on.

Colin Roberts had escorted Caroline Harlow onto the downs for the annual Roberts shoot. Hugo Morris had joined her in cheering the Americans on at Wimbledon. The gala opening of London's newest glamour casino had been graced by Louis Negin and Caroline Harlow, recently of New York. The cameras had been there, snapping away.

"Is the merry little widow on the prowl again?" Benedict drawled. "I'm surprised you have time for one daughter, much less two, aren't you?"

Henry Mack objected loudly. The question was withdrawn, but it was too late. His client's cheeks were turning hot, and laughter was skittering up over the sound of the gavel.

Clayton Benedict was back in his seat, tipping it to a comfortable angle. The sweat was running in his hands as his voice broke hard across the room. "And tell us—what day school does your daughter attend, Mrs. Harlow. State its name."

Caroline closed her eyes. Henry Mack had drilled her time and again, told her over and over to expect a question like this. She knew Maggie's birthdate, Kate's, the names of ponies, dogs. She could see the school. It was a brick building at the end of High Street in the village with a wrought iron fence, an entrance for girls and one for boys. The sign above spelled the name in script. She fought to read it, but there was nothing there. "I'm sorry," she said, "I can't seem to remember just now."

28

LADY PORTIA MICHAELS MASHADO
TESTIFIES IN TEXAS COURT

BRITISH ROYALTY DEFENDS AMERICAN CAROLINE

They got her title wrong in the Chicago *Sun*, spelled her name wrong, and mistakenly made her royal. The *New York Times* was one of the few papers in the States to get it right: The Honorable Portia Michaels Machado of Chatham Manor, Chevely, Suffolk, England.

She came and went quickly that second morning of the trial, and what the *Sun* did capture was the impression she made with her thick chestnut hair high off her slender face and her high, elegant cheekbones. If she had been shy once and unsure, there was no trace of that in Portia now. She was as they discribed her in the *Sun*: regal, and every inch a lady.

She knew Caroline had been stupid, but it didn't matter. She opened her house to her and sent the maids to plump the eiderdowns and turn up the heat. She fed Maggie chocolates, poured Caroline tea, and listened to her until the tears ran down her own face. Caroline had been good to her once, and Portia was good to her now. One stood by one's friends, and Portia wasn't naïve. She'd heard of far worse sexual exercises among the British upper classes—particularly among the upper classes. You didn't lose your children over that sort of thing. Portia had everyone she knew over to dinner, a gesture that said, "This is my friend from America. Please be good to her as you are to me."

She loathed the idea of appearing in a public court, but Caroline had no family and no real Texas friends. There was no one else. So Portia left her manor house and made the drive to London. She flew to New York, on to Dallas, and waited that morning in an antechamber in the courthouse in Earth until a guard came to say it was time to testify.

It went as they'd discussed. Was Caroline Harlow a good mother? Quite sweet, we all thought. Portia had been told she would have to be descriptive and she was, and then there was a series of questions they hadn't discussed. Did Caroline make friends in England; was she entertained? Was that considered seemly?

"Seemly, Mr. Mack?" And then she saw what he must mean. "Of course. It is not the custom in England for widows to throw themselves on burning biers. Do you still do that in America? I thought not."

The press gallery thinned out when Portia made her exit, and few papers reported on the second witness that day. She was a black woman who refused to state her name until Amelia Harlow nodded her head.

Matty took her seat in the witness stand with a sniff, gripped her white handkerchief tight, and eyed the young man before her with disdain.

"Good morning, Miss Matty."

She replied with a crisp thrust of her chin.

Henry Mack stepped closer to the witness box and began to establish, with excruciating patience, her long and faithful service in the house at the edge of town. "And would you say," he asked, "that Mrs. Harlow was a kind and loving mother?"

"Miss Caroline? Well . . ." She stopped dead.

Henry Mack sighed. When he spoke again, his tone was sterner, less deferential. "Have we spoken before, Miss Matty?"

"Yes sir, we have."

"Did I come to visit you, here in town?"

"Long about last month, I expect. Mrs. Harlow said I had to see you, long as you asked. So I did."

"And did you tell me that Miss Caroline loved her girls?"

Clay Benedict rose to object. "He's leading the witness, your honor."

"Not having an easy time of it, is he, Counselor? Mr. Mack . . ."

Henry Mack shifted his position, obstructing Matty's view of her employer. He smiled his cherubic smile. "Miss Matty? Let's try one more time. Did Miss Caroline love her girls?"

"Well." She slumped in her seat, twisting the white handkerchief into small knots. "I guess so. She played with them some, read them stories. They seemed to like it well enough."

"Did you ever hear Miss Caroline shout at the girls?"

"Once in a while maybe."

"Oh? Like when?"

"Well, when they played up too much."

"Did you ever see Miss Caroline hit the girls?"

"No sir, I didn't."

"Thank you, Miss Matty," genuine gratitude in his voice. "Your witness, Counselor."

"Just a couple of questions, Matty." Clay Benedict strolled toward the stand with his hands in his pockets, then rested back on his heels. "Remember back, can you, to that last spring before Mr. Bliss passed away?"

"Yes sir, Mr. Clay."

"Now, did anything change in the family at that time?"

"Yes sir. It did."

"Tell us what happened, Matty, what changed that last year."

"Well," she leaned forward. "Mr. Bliss, he was in Houston a lot, and Miss Caroline, she was always off in

that red convertible of hers. And things got real quiet
and then real loud."

There was laughter and Matty sat back hard in the
chair. Darby banged the gavel.

"What do you mean, Matty? Things got real quiet
and then real loud?"

"Well, Mr. Bliss and Miss Caroline, they didn't
speak to each other, 'cept to yell. They'd both go off in
the morning and then when they got home you'd hear
Miss Caroline yell. Nights I'd find them two girls all
curled up together in one bed, Miss Kate frightened
half to death."

"All right, Matty. Now, where did Miss Caroline go
every day?"

"I don't know, Mr. Clay. But she'd get in that car of
hers and head on out about nine. Wouldn't come back
till dark."

"Did that happen often, Matty?"

"Yes sir. Least three or four times a week for a long
time. And if she wasn't out she was locked in her room.
Might just as well have been out."

"Ignored her own children, Matty?"

"Yes sir. Yes, she did," said Matty, and then she left
the stand and the courtroom and went back home,
pleased that Mr. Clay had finally asked the only
question she thought mattered.

The witness Henry Mack called after the lunch recess
was a woman by the name of Potter. The name hadn't
appeared on Mack's final witness list and it was two
o'clock by the time the appropriate motions had been
heard and approved and the double doors at the back
of the room opened to admit her to court.

She hesitated as she entered, then seemed to startle
at the sound of the doors closing behind her. She
composed herself and walked down the aisle. She was a
large, soft-bodied woman with a sweet face, wearing a

simple cotton dress and sturdy shoes that sounded on the floor boards. She'd come as far as the half gate when Beau Darby saw Will Harlow's daughter jerk to her feet.

A hum went through the courtroom, but the sound didn't drown out Eleanor's choked sob as she gripped the rail separating her from her mother. It had been years since Eleanor walked into that woman's front parlor and caught the reflection of the rose garden at the back. Her name had changed, but her face was very much the same.

The clock stood at three-thirty when order was finally established and Anna Janes settled into the stand. At the request of Clayton Benedict the courtroom had been cleared. When she began her testimony there was only the judge and the attorneys, the court reporter, the petitioner, and Amelia Harlow in a dove-gray hat.

It was nearly five when Judge Darby climbed into the car waiting out back. He let the driver work his way as best he could up the hill and into the line of cars jamming Route 30. Then he leaned forward and tapped on the glass, instructing him to take the side roads home.

It was a seventy-mile drive and dark by the time he arrived. He sat alone over dinner, his housekeeper serving and then clearing in a silence that respected his.

He was more certain now about the woman Amelia Harlow was. And he had an image, one that a black housekeeper had forever fixed in his mind, of two sisters huddled together in the dark, taking courage from each other in their fears.

The gossip and the innuendo could have no place in his decision. And the mother—well, she was a gadfly, but what harm. At this trial's conclusion, she would have her daughter back.

He slept that night wrapped in the comfort of the straightforward simplicities of law and the next morning woke to a phone call that sent warning signals ringing in his head.

29

It was going to take forever to get down Main Street. Kate could see that now. No time at all for Duke to slide the Cadillac out the gates and down their hill, but it would take forever to push through that crush of cars and people ahead. She settled back into the seat and watched the faces floating in the green-tinted glass of the Cadillac. There was no sound except for the air conditioner and Duke, sitting straight and tall up in the front seat, whistling tonelessly through his teeth.

Matty said that ever since he was a little boy, Duke whistled like that when he was mad. Kate was pleased Duke was mad, and she was glad he carried a gun. The gun was the best idea he'd ever had. It meant the photographers with the cameras would keep their distance this time and she would be safe.

She pulled Goose Too into her lap and reached out for the stack of playing cards on the serving table that flipped down from the front seat. She dealt the cards for solitaire, and they made little snapping sounds against the veneer.

They'd gotten as far as Carr's when the car suddenly rocked and the cards started to slide. She started to scream, but the sound was silenced by the bigger scream of Duke's horn, and then the car stopped rocking and she could see the faces scattering and those bears waving in their hands. She went back to her cards.

She heard about those bears yesterday after Matty came back from court. At first Kate wanted to kick Goose Too hard, stuff him into a bottom drawer, and close him up in the dark. But that had been impossible. It wasn't Goose Too's fault. It was hers.

Mostly hers. She supposed she'd known that all along.

It had taken a long time to think it out, and it hurt. It hurt with an ache that sometimes made her get up from her bunk at camp, and afterward, when she came home, it sometimes made her leave the blue window-seat in her room and go downstairs and outside to think about other things. It had taken a long time to sort out the pieces, but she finally had, and finally told Grandmelia last night that she needed to speak to the judge herself.

She could see the trees around the courthouse when she glanced out the window again. She hadn't quite finished her game, but she put the cards back in their box, then pulled Goose Too closer and buried her face in the worn plush of his brown fur. She took a deep breath, and when Duke opened the door, she climbed out.

There were people, and cameras flashing, two long rows of police stretching all the way up the courthouse steps. She began to walk.

A moment later, Judge Beau Darby rose from his desk to answer the knock on his door.

The hallway was empty except for a black chauffeur down at the far end and the little girl who had something she wanted to say. He recognized her features from the photographs: the tight cap of dark, short-cropped curls; the perfectly oval face; the heavy-lashed eyes. Not brown, as he had expected, but steel blue, startling and wide. The ruffle of her blue-and-white plaid dress grazed her knees, and squares of light played on the round toes of her shoes. She stood looking up at him with the bear in her arms.

"Come in, Kathryn."

She stepped forward and he closed the door.

"Kate, sir. Please call—" The voice, firm and husky

for a child, suddenly gave way as she became aware of
the court reporter and the sound of his machine.

"Hello," she said. The reporter nodded and she
turned back and looked up at Judge Darby.

He smiled. "You'll get used to that in a minute or
two."

"I will?" She tipped her head to one side. "Are you
sure?"

He considered carefully before he spoke. It was clear
she wasn't an easy child. "Not positive, no ma'am, but
pretty sure." The answer seemed to please her. They
both smiled.

"Well, Kate. I'm Judge Darby, and I'm handling this
case that's got everybody all stirred up around there."

"Yes, sir. They told me."

"They? Who's they, Kate?"

"The lawyers." She glanced down. "Excuse me, the
attorneys. My grandmother said 'attorney' is the polite
form. Is that really true?"

"Well, I was an attorney once, but people called me a
lot of things."

"It's not rude?"

"No, child, no. You come on over and sit."

"Thank you." She moved to the leather wing-back
beside his desk, perched on the seat, and wiggled back
into its arms. One shoe curled under her, and the bear
sat on her lap.

Beau Darby creaked back in his chair. "So, I expect
the lawyers have been telling you a lot of things to say.
Lawyers are like that. They talk a lot. But I suppose
you know all about that."

"Well, no, sir. You see, I've been thinking." She
gazed directly at him.

"Have you, Kate? Why don't you tell me all about
yourself—how old you are and how you like school. All
about yourself."

"Well, a lot of it's just boring. Like I'm nine and I'll

be in the fourth grade, and there must be millions of
nine-year-old girls doing the same old thing." Her voice
took on a kind of sing-song and both legs curled up
onto the chair. She sat Indian-style with her elbows on
her knees. "Maybe I should tell you just the interesting
parts instead?"

He smiled. "Tell me the most important thing about
yourself, Kate."

"The most important thing?" She thought for a
moment. "I'll tell you what I came to say, all right?"

"What's that?"

Her gaze, very blue, very direct, met his. Her
answer, and the formal, measured language she framed
it in, very nearly had the effect of physical assault.
"What I came to say, sir, is that I wish never to see my
mother again."

They sat in absolute stillness, the little girl looking up
with wide, trusting eyes at the elderly, heavyset man
looking back at her.

It had been a long time ago, another century, when
he'd been a nine-year-old boy, but now, watching those
wide eyes, he had a vivid impression of himself as a
skinny boy in overalls. He was standing in a field staring
up at a man. The sun was hot on his neck, and he could
feel the overalls scraping across his bare chest, the
sweat gathering under his arms, and the sudden desire
to scratch.

He was staring at his father, whose hand was raised,
ready to fall across the face of his son. No, the boy said.
They stared at each other for another instant, the arm
still in the air. The itch became unbearable, but the boy
knew he couldn't move. Then he watched the arm fall
and the man turn and walk away. The boy picked up
the scythe and began slicing across an endless field of
hay hot in the sun.

Almost seventy years later, with decades of love and
pain and experience in between, and he couldn't re-

member anymore why that boy said no. But he was back in that field again, in that moment of absolute certainty and rightness.

Judge Darby spoke with Kate Harlow for nearly an hour more. Nothing changed, and nothing of substance was amplified. They spoke of her father, his family, and her sister. "My half-sister," she corrected him. "Well, that's all right," he said. "You love her very much, don't you?" She examined the buckle of a shoe. "I haven't seen her for a long time. She lives in England now. Did you know that?"

They spoke of England. It would be an interesting place for a girl from Texas like herself. "No," she said.

She refused to talk about her mother and there was never any answer to the question why. Only "No." And two days later, when the public was allowed back into the courtroom and the press back into the gallery, Judge Beauregard Darby's decision was based on that no.

He glanced at the child's mother as he settled in his chair. He wondered again what had happened, what she'd done, what she hadn't done, and then he lowered his eyes to the single piece of paper before him and began to read.

Kathryn Morning Glory Harlow would remain in the custody of her paternal grandmother. Visitation, subject to court review, would be arranged by respective attorneys. At the request of Amelia Harlow, records of this hearing were declared sealed for the one hundred years allowed by Texas law.

The sound of the gavel was loud in the silence and Judge Darby left the bench.

Darby never spoke of the Harlow case after he issued his decision. He turned away the reporters and television people with their requests for interviews, and he turned away the editors of a university law review who asked for an article on the legal points involved. He didn't answer their letter. There were no answers and there were no legal points. There was only a child whose persistent certainties had finally become his own.

He half expected his decision to be contested in a higher court, but fall came and a winter that was hard and dry. The decision stood.

Earth, Texas

September 1960

30

The scream started near three in the morning and then erupted into a single, piercing shriek of "No." It was always the same—the same word at roughly the same, silent hour of the morning, and Amelia Harlow did as she had been doing for a year. She put aside the work she'd brought with her, crossed the few steps to Kate's bed, and took her in her arms.

Kate sat bolt upright under the canopy. Her face was flushed with sleep, and the pupils of her eyes were huge and black, unresponsive to light. Amelia held the small, rigid body against hers until she felt it soften and finally go limp. Then she laid Kate back against the pillow and brushed her forehead with a kiss. She left, turning the light out as she passed, leaving the old third-floor nursery folded in the dark.

Amelia went down to her own room, one hand gripping her file of work and the other around the bannister so that she would not stumble on the steep steps. A small carafe of red wine was waiting on the white chest beside Amelia's bed. She poured a half glass and sipped. Then she too finally slept.

The screams came once and sometimes twice a week. Amelia was always there. The screams had become a part of her life in the twelve months since the trial, an unwanted presence in the white-walled compound at the edge of town. It was a delayed reaction to death and change, the doctors told her. It will pass.

Up in the old third-floor nursery, Kate slept, oblivious to her own screams, and woke each morning glad she was who she was. She was Kate Harlow, age ten, and once she had done something she'd had to do. She had walked into the courthouse at the other end of town and said what she had to say. She'd said it firmly and nicely, like Grandmelia said things, and she'd got what she wanted, like Grandmelia did.

She hadn't said it all. She hadn't told the judge that she'd thought back, way back, and knew her mother was a witch. It would have been complicated to explain it all. It would have taken a long time to say how she'd thought and looked, and finally found that nearly forgotten night when she heard her mother screaming. "Die here," her mother had screamed. "Die here."

It would have been complicated to explain that then her father did die and that her mother had gone away, and that witches did things exactly that way. They cursed their curses, and then disappeared down long halls.

The most complicated part of all would have taken . . . but Kate didn't know. Hours maybe, maybe more. It would have taken a long time to explain about the day she'd worked her own magic and made her father stay home with her where he was safe. That had been a very nice day. They'd gone to look at oil derricks and somebody had given her a quarter. Her daddy didn't fly his plane that day. He didn't die that day, but Kate had picked the wrong day.

Kate said none of that and, once it was over, she put it all away.

She forgot about the witch, forgot about the magic, forgot it all until Caroline came back.

"I won't go. I won't," she screamed when Grand-melia told her she must. Caroline was in a hotel room in Dallas, waiting to see her, and she had to go. "I won't," Kate screamed.

"You have to, darling," Grandmelia said, and pulled her into her lap. Kate knew she was too big really, but it felt good. She held Grandmelia's hand the whole way in. "We'll go to Neiman's afterwards, pet, and have ice cream," Amelia promised as Kate stepped out of the car. Duke took her across the lobby and handed her to a bell captain. The bell captain pushed an elevator button, and Kate took a deep breath and switched into a different gear.

The elevator doors opened and closed. The hallways stretched out before her. Another door opened and closed, and she was in a room with a big bed. Kate, darling. How sweet you look. The voice was high and shrill, just like she remembered it. Die here.

Kate didn't look up, but she could tell that her mother had a new hair style that was smoother and longer and she wore a shiny new pin. Kate concentrated on other things, the pattern in the rug, the wallpaper, her shoes. She did what she was told, and nothing more. A box wrapped in bright paper and a red bow was placed in her lap. Open it, darling. She pulled the ribbon free, took the paper off the box, and stopped.

"How can you be so slow, darling? I always tear the paper off presents. Can't wait."

Kate had a sudden unbidden memory of her mother tearing polka dot paper off a box from Carr's and laughing wih pleasure over the perfume she and Maggie had saved up their allowance to buy. Her mother liked presents, but she didn't. She wouldn't like this one. She would unwrap it, but she wouldn't even look.

"Kate," her mother said. It was just that, just her name, but there was something old and familiar in the voice, and Kate glanced up and caught the look in her mother's eyes. She couldn't bear that look. The eyes asked for too much and Kate had nothing to give. "I'd like to go home now," she said. She stood up, looking away from her mother.

The door opened and the hallway stretched out before her. The elevator doors opened and closed. She hated the funny feeling inside that something terrible had happened, but she didn't know what it was.

And Kate dreamed. "Die here," the witch said. No, Kate said.

She dreamed about a day somebody gave her a quarter. Daddy, don't go today. They went to look at oil derricks and somebody gave her a quarter. He didn't fly his plane that day, but it wasn't the right day. No, she said, in her dreams. No. It's not the right day.

And then, when the filly was older, Kate rode, making up for not choosing the right day.

"Daddy was born right here, wasn't he, Grandmelia?"

It was a raw Saturday afternoon during the fall Kate was ten and she was taking Grandmelia out to the stables for a surprise.

"Yes pet, he was. Right here."

"Didn't he go away for a while, when he was older?"

"He went to school back East. Yes."

"And then he came home?"

"No, not right away. You remember, darling. He went to the island called Cuba for a while."

"Why?" Kate stopped to rub the mud off the toe of her new riding boots.

Amelia pulled the collar of her coat up around her neck. Kate's questions always bothered her. "It was after the war. He was young and wanted to travel." She walked on and Kate came running behind her and slipped her hand again into Amelia's.

"And that's where my horse came from. Daddy liked his horses, didn't he?"

Amelia nodded and then watched as Kate saddled the bay, a last filly bred from the Argentinian brood mare Bliss had shipped home from Havana.

She sat her horses the way her father had taught her, light and tight and jockey-high for the jump. She rode seriously now and had switched to an English saddle. Kate was good and Amelia admired that.

"Did you see that?" Kate called out to her from the paddock.

"I did," Amelia called back.

"You know how high those fences are, Grandmelia?"

"Very high, pet."

"Five feet, Grandmelia. She's ready now," she said, and she swung off. "I thought at first I'd quit school and take her into Dallas, to one of those trainers they have there. But I guess a trainer can come here, to our house. Okay?" She tugged at her grandmother's hand, winding Amelia into participating in what became an unnerving rite of exorcism.

The trainer came, an old Texas cavalry man by the name of Alec Riddle who'd been training Texas high-jumpers for generations.

Kate rode in the mornings, the afternoons, and on into the evenings under the lights that now lit the paddock out back. She rode her guilt and she rode her father's bay horse. She concentrated on riding higher, smoother, cleaner, on the fences looming up.

They started traveling six months later. They entered Texas shows first, and then went on into the national circuits that qualified Kate for the ring at Madison Square Garden the November she was twelve. "It's the only show that matters," she said when Grandmelia objected. "The only one."

Mr. Riddle took the bay into New York by train and Kate flew in a day later with Amelia and Eleanor. "I wouldn't miss it for the world," Aunt Eleanor said. She took care of the hotel reservations, booking them all into suites at the Plaza on Fifth Avenue.

"Fifth Avenue?" Kate wailed. "The Garden's not on Fifth Avenue. I want another hotel."

"There isn't one," Eleanor said. "Not one we'd want."

Kate sulked about that all the way into New York with her nose pressed against the window of the plane. And then, one hand in Eleanor's, one in Amelia's, she pushed through the photographers at Idlewild Airport and climbed into the waiting limousine. She was grateful her aunt was smart. The doormen at the Plaza would keep cameras away.

The National Horse Show began on Tuesday, and they sat in the first tier for the International Jumping event that night.

Everybody had told her it wouldn't be like other shows—and they were right. The Garden was enormous, the crowds were huge, and there were thousands of people in dress-up clothes. The Meyer Davis Orchestra played between events, and popcorn and cokes came by on trays. The lights dimmed for each class, and when the ribbons were awarded they came back up and the music played. Kate ate the popcorn and waited for Saturday.

Eleanor took the trip to New York, not for Kate, but for herself. She was thirty-six and she felt as though everything in her had come to a halt. As memories of the trial ended and the chaos it brought to their lives disappeared, she realized that she would always feel as though part of herself was missing. Bliss was dead and a part of her life was cut off. But sometimes she felt as if she had just stopped.

She and Ben had argued only once in their years of marriage. He'd liked Caroline, he said. She was a pretty thing, open to liking and being liked, and he'd raised hell after the trial.

"Stay out of it," Eleanor said. "Just stay out of it, Ben."

"I'm damned if I'll stay out of it," he shouted, and he kicked the bedroom door closed.

Eleanor flung herself in a chair. "She's white trash. She's not fit to raise my brother's child."

"She's the kid's mother, for Christ's sake. You think about that, Eleanor. You want someone to snatch Jay?"

"Stop it," she screamed.

But he hadn't stopped. There was a kind of violence running through their lives—she had to see that.

"You're ridiculous, Ben," and she stood, started across the room.

He came after her, blocking the door. "Was Anna Janes ridiculous? Or Will? And now she's hustled Caroline out of here and convinced the child to stay. She won't let go, of anything, anybody she considers hers."

She reached up to slap his face, but he caught her hand, then held it as he glared at her. "Bliss was an aimless sucker. You have more in your little finger than he had in his whole vacant life. But there's arrogance in you too, Eleanor. You won't let go either."

"Get out." She wrenched her arm free. He yanked open the bedroom door and made sure it slammed behind him.

He came home before dawn and climbed into bed with her, held her in his arms and made love to her as he always had. Maybe there was something special about being a twin, he said, something he didn't understand. But he loved her and he'd let it alone.

She forgot about the fight in the years after the trial, but the feeling went on, the sense that she'd stopped.

That November she flew to New York with Amelia and Kate.

She called Alfred Reece their second day in town. "Come fetch me, Alfred? At five or so?" She waited for him by the entrance to the Palm Court.

He arrived just after the hour. The silver stick was in his hand, the flower was in his lapel, and he still had the same elegant lurch to his long stride. It seemed to Eleanor, just for a moment, as if nothing had changed. But everything had changed. She reached up and kissed his cheek. "Can we go someplace else? I can't stand this place anymore."

They walked out to Central Park South and turned toward Fifth. The fountain across from the hotel was empty and the nude statue above was iced from the last frost. She tried to smile and they walked on east.

A row of horse-drawn carriages lined the street, the heavy breath of the horses visible in the cold. "Come on," Alfred said, "let's take a ride."

They went into the park and left the city behind. There were just the horse's hooves, the occasional grunts of the driver, the far sounds of the traffic to remind them the city was still there.

He took her hand in his, held it beneath the blanket covering their legs, and they talked of their lives now. They talked of their sons, of Ben, and of Alfred's wife, Jenny. And then Eleanor asked, "Why didn't you stay after Bliss died, Alfred? I thought you would." She looked up at him. "I remember being glad you were at the funeral. And then you were gone. I needed you then."

The wind was coming up stronger through the park, and as Alfred turned to her, the weight of the past was in their hands. "We'll go back now," he called to the driver.

She didn't touch him as they walked through the lobby of the Plaza, into the elevator, and down the long carpeted corridors to her room. She closed and locked the door behind him, moved to the bed, and folded the sheets down. She took off her coat, dropped it on a chair and turned to watch him. He undressed, then she undressed and stood, immensely vulnerable, waiting for him in her half slip. He walked across the room and held her against his bare body, and then laid her back and took off her slip. He pulled a blanket over them and pulled her close. He felt her arms reach around him, and then her body began moving under his, the need building, not quiet and gentle as it had been before, but relentless and demanding and angry. He thrust into her and they watched each other through wide eyes in the half light of a New York afternoon and finally slept.

When they woke it was dark, the lights strung out over Central Park the only reminder of the world. She reached over to turn on the bedside lamp. "Thank you," she said, and started to cry.

The tears came from some part of herself Eleanor had never been able to touch, tears for herself and Alfred, for Bliss, for everything that was past. He reached for her, wrapping her in his arms and stroking her hair until the tears were gone. "Better?" he finally asked.

"Alfred, am I ever going to be happy again?"

He tipped her chin in his hand. "You will be. Not today, or tomorrow. But it'll settle."

"We made him stay, my mother and I."

"I knew Bliss too, Eleanor. He stayed because he couldn't find anything better to do. That's the way he was."

"And now he's dead."

"And everybody's lives are torn apart, but it'll settle." He held her, and then her body eased over his and he was inside, rocking them both to a peace, and an end.

They ordered eggs and toast and coffee from room

service, then showered and dressed. "You're happy, Alfred, aren't you?" she said.

"Yes, I am."

"I'm glad." He left then, her kiss still warm in the palm of his hand.

31

Kate waited through the Fine Harness Championship, the Black Watch Marching Band, Working Hunter Under Saddle, and the New York City Mounted Police's demonstration drills. She got up early on Saturday morning and dressed in the hotel. Everything was new: black leather boots, tan breeches, white shirt, white cravat, black hacking jacket, black hunt cap.

She and Alec Riddle curried the horse until all fifteen hands of her shone. Kate combed her mane out long and flat against her neck, and they waited together for the event that would begin at eleven.

The call came at quarter of and Kate moved into line. She was third. A girl was first, then a boy, their big long-legged hunters standing sixteen, seventeen hands high. Kate heard the announcer's voice, and then from the ring came the cry of a long brass hunting horn.

The girl's time was good, and the boy's wasn't bad either. Then Mr. Riddle cupped his hand, lifted her up, and the white light of a camera flashed in her eyes. She waited, stone-faced, for the crazy red dots to go away. Grandmelia was right. She should probably never have come to this place. She nudged the bay into the arena and appreciative applause ruffled the Garden.

She felt the difference right away. It smelled different, the sound was different, the audience stretching from the ring right up to the ceiling. And then it was all right, like it always had been. Just them. No audience, no lights, just the pounding of the canter on the packed surface and Mr. Riddle's voice in her head, "Keep her loose, keep her loose." And the more distant sound of another voice, "Seat tight. Knees tight." Around once, and then back.

"Ladies and gentlemen," a voice sparked across the loudspeaker.

Kate didn't even hear it. She was up high on her neck, and then she let her out.

She let her out fast. Form didn't count, a couple of knocks didn't count. The poles had to stay up, the cardboard bricks had to stay up, and then all that counted was the clock.

Six jumps. High jumps and higher. Broad jumps and short turns. She took them all at an angle, aiming her in the direction they'd have to go next. Left, right, straight ahead, cutting down the dead time between the jumps, riding hard against the clock.

Seven down. Eight down. Nine down.

And then she was skidding across the last turn in a blast of sawdust and ten thousand people jerked to their feet. But all there was in the world for Kate was her father's bay horse and a five-foot ten-inch white fence. She was high and hard on her neck, raking tight across the turn, and she was out. They were pounding, pounding down the strip, gathering for the jump. Sweat and leather whined, and they were up.

They were up, uncoiling forever over the last high white barrier in Madison Square Garden, the small rider lost in the lash of the mane and the shatter of lights.

Amelia and Eleanor found her as a groom led her and the bay out of the arena. She sagged against the side of the enclosure with the blue ribbon tight in her hand. "I did it, Grandmelia. I did it. It's over."

They took her to Reuben's that afternoon for sandwiches and New York egg creams. She ordered chocolate, as the waiter suggested. "That's the best we got in New York," he smiled. "Chocolate egg creams."

They went next door to F.A.O. Schwarz afterward, winding in and out of the early Christmas crowds, choosing books and games in the largest toy store in the world. Nice, Kate said. Almost as nice as Neiman-Marcus.

32

For Maggie Harrington, life was divided into a Before and an After.

There had been a real mother once, a family, and a place for her in a white house at the edge of town. And then there was the slap. A hand shaking her awake in the night and the command to pack. Everything. Now. She balked and then came the slap. And after that, the nights in New York and London, Paris and Rome and Mykonos, her mother in the next room with a lover, and an *au pair* girl down the hall. Maggie would wake up sweating from nightmares of that house and the laughter. She hated Them. They'd sent her away. They kept Kate and sent her away.

Sometimes, lying on a dormitory bed watching the snow fall in Paris, she had daydreams of going back home again, without her mother. She'd arrive in Dallas on a plane and be met by a car and a black chauffeur who would drive her through the summer night to the house in Earth. But even in her daydreams the house was dark, the doors and windows were shut, and she'd sit up with a jerk, sweating.

And that's how they left—right after the slap, in the middle of the night, in the car Duke pulled out to drive them to the airport. They didn't speak to each other and didn't touch. Her mother was worn and silent. Her dark hair was disheveled, her eyes were dark behind dark glasses, and a mink coat was thrown over her shoulders. Maggie, a thirteen-year-old in blue jeans and a T-shirt, followed her through the Dallas airport, up the steps of the plane, and into the last row of the first-class department.

There were no explanations. Caroline's explanations came later, after the court case was over and lost.

Maggie was sitting by herself in the drawing room of Portia's manor house the afternoon her mother came back from the trial. She heard a car door slam and heard the car drive away. There were voices in the hall and then the drawing room opened and her mother came in.

"Maggie?"

There were tears in her mother's voice, and Maggie, her eyes fixed on the book in her lap, knew that what the newspapers had said was true. She hadn't believed it, not really, but she believed the feeling in the pit of her stomach, the sensation of something giving way.

"I lost Maggie. They told Kate lies about me. They must have. She didn't want to come."

Maggie looked up and watched her mother head for the cabinet where Portia kept the scotch.

"Lies?" she said. "They didn't have to lie to Kate. All they had to do was tell her the truth."

Caroline stopped with her hand on the latch of the cabinet.

Maggie settled deeper into the arms of her chair. Her voice was quiet and even. "All they had to do was tell her about that man. The one who came to visit you every night after Daddy died. I saw him come to the house, so I knew. And I saw the girl. I knew about that too."

Maggie pulled herself out of her chair and walked to the drawing-room door. "Are we leaving here soon?"

Caroline looked at her, numb. She hadn't thought about it. They had no place to go.

"I want to go," Maggie said. "And I want to change

my name. Back to Harrington. I hate it, Caroline.
Everyone knowing I have a mother who's been declared legally unfit." She shrugged and then went
upstairs to her room.

Caroline pulled her hand off the cabinet latch. Both
her children hated her, and she did remember the name
of Maggie's school now. It was the Rookery School,
High Street, Chevely. The letters were embroidered on
the pocket of the blue jacket lying on the arm of the
chair a foot from where she stood.

It felt as though a lifetime had passed when Caroline
finally reached into the cabinet and poured a scotch.
She would call the solicitors in the morning and arrange
to have Maggie's name changed. It might help, and
they could travel and forget. She would be very gay for
Maggie, very good, and then maybe Maggie would
forget.

Maggie was a tall, thin, sullen fourteen-year-old
when they left Portia's manor house that winter. Maggie never asked where they were going and she didn't
care. Years later she would say that all she knew of
Europe was the location of the better johns. Up the
marble stairs of the Georges Cinq, bear left. Down the
stairs at the Hassler in Rome, turn right. Beyond the
reception desk at the Quisisana on Capri, turn right at
the newsstand, past the bar.

Tutors came and went; Caroline's lovers came and
went. Maggie sat in hotel rooms filled with the hollow
sounds of foreign towns. She never stopped waiting for
Kate to walk in the door and never stopped writing
postcards in her head. Dear Kate. Here I am at the
Parthenon. Wish you were here. Dear Kate. I wish you
were here.

They both traveled under the Harrington name that
year. They took trains for the most part, private cars,
and once they took a boat, a small passenger ship that
slipped free of its moorings in the Sicilian harbor of

Syracuse and steamed out into the choppy surface of the Mediterranean at dusk, bound for the English island of Malta fifty miles south.

It was just after dawn the next day when Maggie woke in her stateroom. The motors had been cut. She wrapped herself in a trench coat and went down the passage and up the steps to the top deck.

Ahead lay the island of Malta, like a tall, fragile-looking wedding cake on the blue plate of the Mediterranean. The ship wheezed and steamed on. They'd come opposite the harbor, like a slice cut out of the wedding cake, when Maggie noticed someone else standing by the rail, a small, square man in English tweeds, tears streaming down his leathery, middle-aged face. He smiled sheepishly, then took a large handkerchief from his coat pocket and blew his nose.

"I fought here during the last war," he said. "A very great battle it was, and we held the island of Malta. Yes, we did. I fought in a good many battles in the last war, but that was the hardest and the bravest and now I'm coming back. A little holiday, just on my own. I must say, you know, I'm rather touched. Rather like coming home."

Maggie nodded and felt the tears gathering in her stomach. He had homes. One was probably in the country, a cottage maybe. And he had this one to come back to on Malta. She had nothing. She leaned harder against the rail, trying to stop the tears.

"And you, young lady? Are you on holiday too?"

"No," she said. "Well, yes, in a way. I don't know anymore. I travel."

"Ah," he finally said. "I see."

The ship steamed on, toward the high, white-walled harbor of Valletta, an American girl and a retired officer of the British army in tears on the deck.

She took her first lover in Mykonos, borrowing him from her mother's bedroom for a day on the beach.

Stilianos was nineteen, a bronzed, broad-shouldered Greek who fished off his father's boat, and Maggie saw right away, that second night in Mykonos, that Caroline had snapped him up.

She and her mother had gone to dinner at a small cafe on the docks. They were sitting outside drinking retsina when Maggie saw the change on Caroline's face. Someone was coming through the crowd. Maggie was sure it would be the fisherman, and it was.

Maggie reached for the bottle of retsina and glanced at Caroline to see if she noticed. She didn't. But Stilianos did. His sudden, small smile leapt across the table at her.

"No more wine, darling." Caroline moved the bottle away. "One glass before dinner is enough."

Maggie shrugged. She was very aware now of Stilianos, and very aware of the way her body was coming alive. It was hard not to stare back, and later that night, the image of Stilianos moved through the dark house with her, across the hall and up the stairs to the second floor.

She stripped out of her jeans and T-shirt, felt the smooth, freshly laundered sheets under her back, and smelled the smell of salt and sunshine as her face turned into the pillow.

It was natural for her hands to move across her body, for one to stop at a breast and feel the nipple swell under her fingers. Little shivers, and then the other hand followed, moved to between her legs. It was wet, and her body moved easily against her hand. Slowly, and then faster until there was a totally new feeling washing through her body.

The next afternoon, she found Stilianos on the beach, dozing off in a corner by the rocks. He blinked awake and pulled himself to his feet. And then, his English awkward and inadequate, he pointed to his crotch. "You want?"

Maggie had thought about this moment last night,

but she didn't feel anything now. She wasn't even sure she could move.

Stilianos's smile was white against his tan, and his hands began working at his black trunks. He pulled them down his hips, down his brown thighs, and off his body. He was pale where the sun hadn't been, and his penis was pink. Suddenly Maggie wanted to giggle. It looked almost like a large pink shrimp. She watched him touch it, watched it move, stand erect, and then he was lowering her to the sand. His eyes were very serious as they gazed into hers. He slipped off her bikini bottom, and then his hands were working down her belly, between her legs, and the sun was blotted out.

It was all very fast and very easy and very nothing. Then it was over.

He was lying beside her, playing with her hair and cooing something Greek; then he stopped. Maggie sat up. A figure in a caftan was coming down the beach. Maggie groped for her bikini bottom and snapped it up over her thighs. And then Caroline was there, clawing and sobbing and screaming at Stilianos as he struggled to stand up, batting at her arms while he tried to get his bathing suit back on. He gave up and disappeared down the beach as Caroline, her face broken and contorted, knelt in the sand.

A month later, Maggie stood in the marble entry hall of a building on the outskirts of Paris. Her hair had been trimmed to just below her ears and she wore the gray gabardine uniform of a school known to accept spirited girls.

"I'll run away."

Caroline fought back her tears. "Don't be ridiculous, darling." She hugged her daughter. "I'm sure you'll like it here."

"I'm running away."

Caroline turned and gave a little wave. Panic bubbled in Maggie's stomach. "I will!" she called after her mother as Caroline stepped through the doors into the snow falling in the courtyard.

It snowed on and off all that winter in Paris. But it had stopped when the new girl arrived from America. Maggie remembered that. The snow had stopped.

Her name was Peggy and she was from Chicago. "Once. But not anymore," she told the old girls who came to look her over toward midnight of the day she arrived. "Now it's Geneva. That's where my father is. And Venice. My mother lives there. They're divorced."

She ran through it again in French, then she looked up and gazed directly at Maggie. "You're from Texas, aren't you? You're the other Harlow girl."

One of the Italians focused her flashlight on Maggie. "This is Harrington. Maggie Harrington. From New York."

"No, she's not." The new girl shook her head. "I saw you in *Life* magazine. That was terrible, what happened to you and your sister."

Maggie backed out of the yellow circle of flashlights. "My name is Harrington. I don't have a sister. I never did."

"Yes you do."

There was silence in the room, and then the voice followed Maggie down the empty corridor. "Her name's Kate. I remember it all."

33

Spring came to the pine hills of East Texas, and long summers that were hot and still. Amelia Harlow never had occasion to leave the West after she brought Kate back home from New York. Harlow Enterprises was Texan and Western, and Amelia never left again.

She looked back occasionally to the first summer

she'd been in Texas. She'd been a girl then, so over-whelmed by the heat that she'd kept smelling salts in her hand out of fear of fainting. Texas didn't feel hot to her anymore, and August, when the pine hills seemed to dance in the glare, felt only warm.

But it was hot that Sunday morning in August when Amelia stood on the porch and watched Eleanor drive the Lincoln away from the big white house. She watched her fade into the cottonwoods and disappear through the iron grill gates as she headed for the highway that would lead to her father's grave. Minutes later, Eleanor was dead.

It rained that night. Amelia stood at her window watching the red lights of the radio tower blink through the dark and the drizzle. Her anger emerged then, the old familiar instinct to protect and attack.

PART FOUR

New York

The First Monday in August 1975

34

Alfred Reece sat alone in the back seat of a gray
Mercedes winding its way through Central Park. The
headline was on the bottom right-hand corner of the
New York Times. "President of Harlow Enterprises
Dies." Her picture was in a section at the back. It
wasn't the usual stock photograph. Eleanor was smiling
at someone off camera and her hair was caught back in
the wind. Reece stared at the photograph, waiting for
the waves of feeling to ease.

He'd seen her last in New York, a handsome woman
of fifty in a blue sweater and tweed skirt who stood in a
group of people at a conference where she'd given a
speech. They were planning to leave and get a drink
when somebody had taken her arm. "I won't be long,"
she'd said. "Can you wait, Alfred?"

"I'm late already," he'd said and leaned over and
kissed her cheek.

The Mercedes was at the foot of the park drive now,
caught in the bottleneck at the Fifty-ninth Street exit.
The only sound was the distant noise of a Monday
morning rush hour in New York.

He supposed a part of him had always been in love with Bliss Harlow's sister. He'd carried his memory of her for years, to law school and on into the early years of his marriage, the memory of a girl in a room at Bryn Mawr, the light from the lamp falling across her face. With the memories, he carried the regret, that something in him told him not to pursue her, that his life was someplace else.

He was twenty-five by the time he graduated from Harvard law and his first client was a man who'd been a friend of his father's.

He called him Uncle Eddie back in those days, the short man with the big belly who came panting up the beach at West Hampton waving petitions in his hand: money to be raised for the war in Spain or the orphans of Europe, millions to be raised for Palestine. Nobody knew where Eddie got his money, but he had it. When Alfred saw him last, he was on his way to Hollywood. A chorus girl wanted to be a star, and Eddie was going to write the scripts and produce the movies that would make it come true.

Eddie was willing to admit he'd gone to a couple of Communist cell meetings, but he wouldn't name the names of people he'd met there. "They were nice people, Alfred. It doesn't feel right."

Eddie went to jail for a year in the fifties and came out blacklisted. It was a bitter man who sat in Reece's small New York office with a script every producer in Hollywood had rejected. "It's the best thing I ever wrote, Alfred. They were my friends once. Now they don't talk to me on the phone."

Reece sent the next script out under a pseudonym he cooked up for Eddie, and four years later, it won an Academy Award for the best original screenplay of the year. In the packed theater in Hollywood where the awards were presented that night, the producer of the film stood and handed a note to the usher who came up the aisle. A moment later, the master of ceremonies was raising his hand for silence.

He unfolded the note, stepped to the microphone, and then read out loud to a nationwide television audience the unknown screenwriter's acceptance speech. "My regards to Hollywood," Eddie had written. "I reserve my thanks for my attorney and agent, Alfred Reece."

Eddie died a few years later, an old man who had made his young attorney and agent a celebrity in the entertainment business. Reece and his partners moved out of their offices in the backwaters of New York, and he and his wife bought a house on Riverside Drive.

They'd met at the opera his last year at Harvard. Callas was opening in *Butterfly* and he went with a party of his parents' friends and found himself seated next to a young woman with a cloud of dark hair.

"My real name's Genèvieve," she told him during intermission. And then she added a little wistfully, "But nobody calls me that."

He smiled down at her. "Then I'll call you Genevieve," he said.

"No you won't." She was very sure. "Jenny's so much easier and, sadly"—she smiled then—"I seem to be a Jenny, not a Genevieve at all."

He did call her Jenny, and that's what Jenny Kass was—small and warm, bright like her name. Their first and only child, Nicholas, was born the year after they married. He was a boy of thirteen by the time Eleanor called from the Plaza that day in November. "Come fetch me, Alfred," she asked, and Alfred left his Park Avenue office and went to meet her.

Eleanor went home to Ben after that night in the Plaza, and Alfred went home to Jenny. An unfinished piece of business from the past had been folded away and put to rest. As he sat in the back seat of the Mercedes winding out of Central Park and down into the city, Alfred Reece began to measure the future.

35

Maggie Harrington was at Philip Shaw's house in the Hamptons when Alfred Reece called on Monday morning. She spent that afternoon on the beach with the New York newspapers in a straw bag at her side.

The sun was hot, and the sky was a clear, bright blue rolling up from the ocean and across the dunes. The South Shore of Long Island was lined with twenty-room mansions, and the beach around her was dotted with summer residents who were in the Hamptons to be seen, like Maggie was.

She stretched and turned to get the sun on her back and buried her face in her arms. Summer by the ocean—and the sense, hard and sharp now in the hour after Alfred's call, that this kind of summer wasn't real. Summer was Before, when it seemed the sun would never go down on the huge, heathen spaces of Texas.

Even in the pine hills, the green always dried out in summer and there was a lot of dust to kick around. There was a quality in the air then that Maggie called slow and quiet, but thought of now as empty and waiting.

Summer then had an openness of faraway sounds of air conditioners churning through ice-cold rooms and crickets she thought would drive her mad but lulled her to sleep at night instead. Echoes of a black woman's voice calling her in out of the heat for lemonade and ice, and a dog panting at her side as she lay in the tall reeds where they said snakes lived, wishing she could see just one of them so she could get it with her BB gun.

There'd been a family, a sister, friends at school to play with, her own horse, and a pattern to her days that held her life together. There'd been a man that she'd called daddy, tall and blond, like the woman who died yesterday.

Maggie was thirty now. She'd been back in the United States for twelve years. Alfred met her flight from Paris the September she was eighteen. He was waiting at customs, looking for the girl whose school graduation portrait he had been sent, when he heard a cry of "Uncle Alfred!" A girl with long black hair pulled up on her head leaned over the customs barrier and kissed the air on both sides of his face. She wore jeans and a T-shirt and she'd abandoned bras.

He'd planned to take her directly to the Sarah Lawrence campus north of New York. But he thought better of it and directed the driver to the house on Riverside Drive.

Jenny didn't let him down. She greeted Maggie as if she was expected, and later, in the privacy of their bedroom, she sat calmly filing her nails while Alfred blew.

"I'm damned if I'm going to unleash that—" and he jerked a thumb in the direction of Maggie's room. "Not without taking some precautions, I'm not." He was pacing, long legs scissoring back and forth. "You'll just have to see to it. God knows I can't." He collapsed on the edge of the bed. "I mean, Jesus, Jenny. Did you *look* at her!"

Jenny had.

"Maggie dear," she said over breakfast the next morning. She poured another cup of coffee. "I've made an appointment for you with my gynecologist."

Maggie broke open a brioche. "How come?"

"To fit you with a diaphragm, dear."

"I haven't even met anybody yet."

"No, but you will. Believe me."

"You get into all that stuff, you sort of lose the spontaneity, don't you?"

Jenny sipped her coffee. "There is the pill of course."

"No. That really fucks up the hormones and I'm sure that's not the kind of fucking we mean. Is it?" Maggie smiled.

"One o'clock, dear. We'll take a cab."

Maggie tolerated Sarah Lawrence and loved New York. She worked her way through three semesters of debutante parties, two semesters of probation, and a half-dozen assorted beds. Then she found a friend and a pattern to pin her life together again.

Philip Shaw was assistant instructor of her play production course. They were going to mount a production of *A Midsummer Night's Dream* and when he said, "Okay, ladies. We need a stage manager," Maggie raised her hand and said "Me?"

He yelled at her at every rehearsal for a week, bolting up out of his chair with what Maggie thought was astonishing speed for a fat man. She was surprised when he spoke quietly one day and asked if he could have a minute of her time.

"I understand your French is good?"

She nodded.

"What's the word for shit?"

"*Merde.*"

She pronounced it exquisitely.

He patted her on the head. "Then let's cut the *merde,* Miss Harrington."

He was in his late twenties and he'd grown up in a small town in the Midwest. "I thought I was the only homosexual the world ever produced," he told her one night over coffee. "Me and Oscar Wilde."

"Until you came to New York," she smiled, and was glad when she heard him laugh. She liked him, and it felt good to have a friend who'd grown up alone as she had.

He'd tried it as an actor for a while, finally gave up to write plays that no one ever read, and then gave that up too. "I'd like to read them sometime," she said.

He shrugged. "Sure. I got drawers full."

In February of her junior year, Maggie walked into Alfred Reece's office with a script of Philip's. "I'm going to produce it," she grinned. "On Broadway." She laid the binder on his desk.

"You've got to be out of your mind." He didn't even pick it up.

"No. I mean it. If you won't help me, someone else will. It's a very good play. It's very funny and everybody's going to love it. Now, I need money and advice and well—you know."

"Put it on at school, Maggie. I'll come. I promise."

"I can't. I quit."

Two hours later she had a sheaf of notes and the legal vocabulary for what she wanted to do, and a promise from Alfred Reece that if it wasn't preliterate, he'd try to dig up some backers somewhere.

Payoff was a warm, funny play about an out-of-work actor who couldn't function in a world that wasn't like the movies. It wasn't bad. Alfred read it again that weekend and made a couple of calls. The backers auditions began the following week, and six months later they opened at the Wonderhorse Theater on East Fourth Street to a heavily papered house: actors' friends, Philip's friends, and Alfred's entire client list.

Maggie stood beside Philip at the back of the theater that night and watched the lights black out. She'd been living on cigarettes for days, but she didn't care. There wasn't a curtain, but she didn't care. The light man took his cue, the red gel came up on a boardinghouse in the Midwest, and a few minutes later, the sound of laughter began running through the house. She reached over to Philip, took his hand, and then wrapped him in a hug. On the marquee out front, black letters spelled out his name, actors' names, and her name. Maggie Harrington, Producer. People would read that name and know she'd done something. She wasn't just the other Harlow girl. They'd know that now. Even in Earth, Texas, they'd know.

Payoff ran for six months and went on to become a stock production in the regionals. It was easy for Maggie to raise money now. She bought American rights to a London hit and produced a comedy that finished its Broadway run and went on tour.

She opened an office in the theater district and hired a high school dropout to log in the scripts that the postman dumped in bags at the door. She bought the two top floors of a brownstone a block away from Lutèce. Liz Smith wrote about it, and *Women's Wear Daily* photographed it.

Then Philip finished a new play, and Maggie forwarded it to a film producer who was in the audience on opening night. He liked it, and she and Philip flew to Hollywood to close the deal for a motion picture Maggie would co-produce. Reece negotiated the final points of the Paramount contract by phone from New York, and that night Maggie and Philip left their rooms at the Beverly Hills Hotel and headed downstairs to the Polo Lounge to celebrate.

And for Maggie it was a celebration, not just of the film deal but of her life. She hadn't had the nightmare about the big white house for over a year. The Beverly Hills Hotel was better than a house in a small Texas town. Being here meant something, not just to her, but to everybody. There was a telephone in the bathroom of her suite and when she picked up the phone the operator said, "Yes, Miss Harrington. Who would you like to speak to?" Not, what number, but who.

"Mr. Mull at Paramount."

"I'm sorry, Miss Harrington, Mr. Skolnik's on that line. I'll get back to you."

Maggie liked the sense it gave you of belonging in this town.

A round table in the corner of the Polo Lounge had

been reserved for her and Philip that evening. Maggie reached over to toast Philip.

"To us, Philip. Can there be more?"

"To you, Maggie," and he raised his glass.

Outside, a dark red Ford Mustang pulled up the circular drive, passing through tall palms standing against a starless sky. A red-coated valet came down the ramp and opened the door for the girl and then for the boy. The boy was blond and tan from surfing, and there was a proprietary air about him as he took the girl's elbow and led her up the steps.

She was eighteen and new to the University of California. She wore a white cotton sundress scalloped at the neck and hem. She'd bought it right after she'd registered. She'd never been out of Texas before, not really, and it looked like a California dress, looked the way she wanted to feel. She tucked her arm through the boy's, and they walked across the carpeted lobby and into the Polo Lounge.

She blinked. It was dark and noisy. There was a sudden burst of laughter from a table in the corner. Then her eyes adjusted to the light and focused on a face she knew.

"I want to go home. Now." She turned and pushed past the young man. He grabbed her arm.

"Hey. We just got here. They'll have a table in a minute."

"No. I have to go. Right now." Her hands were sweaty, and she could suddenly feel her feet going clammy against the leather soles of her sandals.

He looked at her, puzzled. "What *is* this? What's going on?"

"Nothing. I have to go, that's all." Then her young voice rose and broke through the clatter of glasses and laughter. "Now. Right now."

The voices in the room dropped to a buzz. There was a giggle from somewhere in the banquettes, and then

the girl and her date pushed their way out and were
gone.

At the table in the corner, Philip edged over to take
Maggie's arm, and his face bent to hers. "Maggie?
What is it—Maggie?"

She sat with her glass still raised to Philip and
remembered: a house where she had once lived, and a
sister she'd named Morning Glory and taught to ride.
A girl with paper flowers in her hair.

And now Maggie sat alone on a beach in the
Hamptons. The sun was setting at her back, and ahead,
low on the water, there was a full moon. The sand was
cool and gray under her feet, the beach empty except
for a lone fisherman casting off from the shore in the
distance.

What she wanted to do was dive naked into the calm
beyond the surf. But she heard a sound over the pound
of the waves, and a jeep came bouncing up the beach, a
white Renegade that passed with a splash of sand. She
reached into her straw bag, pulled out a sweater, and
knotted the arms against the wind. She stood and began
to walk the line of the dunes toward Philip's house.

It seemed to her that it had all gone bad again after
that night in the Polo Lounge. She'd taken her co-producer's word for it that the budget for the film was
good, and then they went over by half a million and the
head of business affairs at the studio basically said
tough. He went around and around, but that was what
he was saying. They were to bring it in, on budget, or
Paramount would be forced to close the film down.
That was when Maggie dipped into her own corporation and took the money invested in her next Broadway
musical.

No one knew. Her co-producer came up with two
hundred and fifty thousand. She came up with two
hundred and fifty. She didn't ask where he got his; he
didn't ask about hers. They went into the editing room

at the studio, came back out to collect another big fat check from the studio, and then she paid the money back and it was fine. It was just fine. She'd known that it would work out in the end.

She went back to Broadway after that. There were more plays, another musical, and then another film. This time she turned down the offers from the studios and put her own package together.

She went over budget by a million this time. She did call the studios then, but it was a bad year in Hollywood and Maggie Harrington was disposable.

She sat alone in her office in New York and thought about that night in the Polo Lounge. Kate would never fail. Kate had everything. She had nothing. She was Maggie, always the disposable one.

This time there was no up-front fund waiting to go. Maggie fired the accounting firm that handled office cash flow and dispersed the backers' profits from the shows that were on the road. She gave her office manager a month off and wrote out rent checks and salary checks herself. Then she drew a bank draft for a million dollars and finished shooting.

"It's just temporary, Uncle Alfred," she pleaded when Reece hauled her into his office a week later.

A backer, a long-time acquaintance of Alfred's, had phoned to complain. He didn't like to say anything, but Miss Harrington's office said she was away and where was the check? There were often delays, what with one out-of-town bank and another, but she was usually not this late. He was terribly sorry, but he did need the cash.

When Maggie finally finished her story, Reece buzzed for his secretary. He asked her to issue a check to the gentleman who'd called, then he started to yell.

Embezzlement was still a crime and if she damn well didn't get the cash flowing, everybody was going to get nervous. Somebody would put it together and a subpoena was going to walk in the door with her name written on it. "And let me tell you what *Variety* will do with that story," he bellowed. His hands were flat on the desk, and his face was lined with rage. "Front page. You know what that means, don't you?" he snarled.

She nodded. It would mean she was through. She'd never be able to raise another dime.

He packed her off to Philip Shaw's house in the Hamptons. When he figured out where the fuck you raised a fast million, he'd said he would call. He didn't even look at her when she said goodbye.

That was Friday. Then three days later, on the first Monday in August, he called.

They talked for a long time. Then she hung up and went to find Philip on the deck.

"I think it'll be all right. I'm about to inherit—I don't even know yet. Sixty million dollars or something."

"Are you serious?" She nodded, and he pulled himself out of his chair and gave her a hug. "I would have visited you in jail. Swear to God I would have." He grinned and held her at arm's length. She raised her eyes, catching her reflection in his sunglasses. "My Aunt Eleanor's dead," she said.

It was almost dark now, and the sky behind Maggie was a silvery blue. The ocean was calm under the moon, and the surf was breaking in running pools. She lit a cigarette, stubbed it out, and finally went down to the water. She stripped quickly and went in. There was a shock of cold and another when she came out, but it didn't help. Nothing felt right, nothing at all.

36

Kate never saw the boy who took her to the Polo Lounge again. He drove her back to the dormitory and tried to take her hand as she opened the car door. "Hey, wait," he said. "What the hell happened?"

"Leave me alone," she screamed. "Just leave me alone." She slammed the door behind her and ran up the path.

She packed that night, shaking as she tried not to think of Maggie. It was Maggie—she'd seen her right there. She looked so glamorous and grown-up, and then there'd been that funny moment of recognition that seemed to go on and on. Until now she'd blocked that face out, just as she'd blocked her mother's out, but there she was again. She wasn't supposed to be there; she wasn't supposed to be anywhere near.

Later she lay in bed to wait for daylight and finally fell into an uneasy sleep full of half dreams. She walked into the Polo Lounge and Maggie was there. Kate crossed the room looking glamorous and grown-up too. "Hi, Maggie. Remember me?" And then she woke up.

She left Los Angeles on the first plane to Dallas the next morning. It was early afternoon when she got home, and the house was still and quiet except for Matty who fussed then finally left her alone. She sat by the window in the big room at the back of the house and watched the sun move across the sky toward California. Pale curtains drifted at windows; hard-polished floors stretched out, reflecting the carved legs of the piano and the etched curves of chests, their surfaces filled with silver-framed snapshots and formal photographs of a Kate growing up.

They were pictures full of activities: ballet class with eleven other girls in tutus, swimming at a lake with friends, water skiing behind a speedboat with a boy named Danny. She'd had a crush on Danny the summer she was sixteen. There she was in the dress she wore to her first piano recital. The piece she'd played, a Rachmaninoff prelude, had been received with a rush of applause from Grandmelia, Uncle Ben, and Aunt Eleanor in the high school auditorium.

There was a portrait of her in the black riding jacket that hung upstairs in a closet collecting dust. There were photographs of holidays with Amelia and travels with Ben and Eleanor and Jay. They'd never gone to Europe. No one ever suggested it, everyone silently understanding that Europe was Caroline's. They'd divided the world up, everyone staying on their own side of the line. It had all been perfectly all right until Maggie broke the rules and stepped over the line.

She was prepared for Grandmelia by the time she heard Matty's voice announcing her return from the *Bugle* offices. "That child's waiting for you, Mrs. Harlow. Back from California, lock, stock, and barrel."

"Kate?" Amelia hurried into the room. Matty closed the door behind her and Kate stood to hug her Grandmelia.

"What happened! Did something happen?"

"Nope. Promise." Kate sat down and swung her leg up over the arm of a chair. There weren't any feelings now except for her stubborn loyalty and refusal to let Grandmelia know that Maggie had mattered. "I didn't like California." She went fishing for an invisible piece of lint on her jeans.

That was all that Amelia Harlow got from Kate. She began making her own inquiries the following morning and knew before noon that Maggie Harrington was in Hollywood now. She didn't know the details of their encounter and she didn't ask. But she knew her instincts were right. When Kate said she'd try Mexico

City for a while, Amelia didn't argue. She only wished Maggie Harrington could be erased.

In January, Kate left Texas for Mexico City. Two weeks later she met David Frank, a thirty-year-old British anthropologist who'd taken a temporary post at the university for the spring.

She'd spent that Saturday at the National Museum taking notes for an exam. She'd gone through the Olmecs and the young gods of the Uastecs, the fire gods and the pyramid builders of Veracruz, and was standing before a glass case of surgical instruments when a soft voice said, "The Aztecs were a bloody bunch."

She looked up.

He smiled. "The gods need to be fed."

He was short and shaggy-haired and wore a wide hat pushed back on his head.

"The Aztecs believed that it was the human heart that made the sun rise every day." He grinned then. "That's what I think too. It's the human heart that makes the sun rise every day."

She liked his quizzical grin, the Englishness of his voice, and his face, which was fine-boned with blue eyes. He introduced himself and she walked with him through the halls, listening to him talk about dead civilizations. They passed under the stone mushroom cap that sheltered part of the patio, and then they were outside, under the trees of Chapultepec Park. "I don't know your name," he said.

"You haven't stopped talking long enough for me to tell you," she said, and walked on, sure that he would follow.

The next afternoon they joined the crowd of thousands waiting for the arrival of the pilgrims who'd walked two days from Toluca to Mexico City to pay homage to the Virgin of Guadalupe. The Paseo de las Palmas filled with old men resting under wide palms.

Women set up taco stands, and young girls dressed as flamenco dancers passed by with boys in white shirts and black trousers. A sigh ran through the crowd and the pilgrims came, chanting songs, their arms full of wreaths and flowers for the shrine.

They took her car to the pyramids at the edge of Lake Texcoco next day, spent an afternoon shopping at the National Pawn Shop, and drank tequila under the lavish stained-glass canopy in the foyer of the Gran Hotel Ciudad. There were bullfights at the Plaza and dinners in out-of-the-way restaurants on small quiet streets. When he said, "Kate, come to bed with me," she nodded.

His rooms were small and spare, and the white-washed walls were lined with books.

"There's a toothbrush in the bathroom," he said as he took the jacket from around her shoulders.

"Did you expect me, David?"

"Yes." He kissed her neck. "I love you and I want to marry you and I bought you a toothbrush."

She unwrapped the fresh, blue toothbrush, brushed her teeth, and splashed cold water on her face. It was very cold and it made her shake, but her hands had started to tremble anyway.

The room was dark when she came back, and he was waiting on the bed. His chest was bare and he held a cigarette in one hand. He stubbed it out as she sat beside him and came up to kiss her cold mouth. "Is this the first time for you?" he asked.

"Yes," she said.

"Then we'll make it very special."

His fingers trailed the lines and curves of her thighs, then traced down her neck to her breasts. He held them for a long moment in his hands before slowly lowering his mouth to her nipples. He tasted one, then the other, circling them endlessly with his tongue until her whole body began to throb. "Don't stop," she whispered. "Please don't stop." Then his mouth was traveling

down her body and along her thighs, nudging them
wide, then wider. A hand was on a breast again, harder
now, and his mouth was between her thighs.

"Please, David," she whispered. Sweat broke out in
the palms of her hands as her hips began to undulate
under his mouth, wanting more, wanting deeper.
"Please," she begged. Then his body was on hers and
they were coming together, sharp and hard and deep.
She cried out, just once, as every nerve in her seemed
to turn to liquid and then she was sobbing with the
relief.

They stopped sightseeing after that night and she
stopped going to classes. All that spring she lay in his
bed, waiting for him as he shed his clothes, his body
like a shadow in the nighttime room lit by a candle. She
longed for his skin against hers, the length of his body
in hers, and his voice whispering, "I love you, Kate."

She moved into his rooms and left only rarely. They
went out for dinner together and came back together.
When he left for classes, she waited for him to come
back to her. In May she knew that she was pregnant.

They went to dinner that night at the Cazuelas, a
room in an eighteenth-century building on a rundown
street northwest of Zocalo. "Marry me," he said over
cocktails.

"That's four times in the last two months. Ask me
again, David. Just for luck," she said, and she reached
for his hand.

David didn't ask again. But it wasn't, she thought
later, it wasn't that. It was something in his smile and
the quick, perfunctory way his hand avoided hers and
reached up to ruffle her curls. Suddenly Kate understood.

He called for the waiter and ordered snapper broiled
on open charcoal. When it was served and the fresh
pepper was ground, when the wine glasses were refilled
and the dark-jacketed waiters faded discreetly away,
Kate asked.

"How many children do you and your wife have, David?"

The wineglass paused halfway to his mouth. Then he took a sip and replied. "Two."

Kate dug her hands into the napkin in her lap. "That must be very nice. Little boys?"

"Kate . . ."

"Or girls?"

"No. Sons."

"Give them my regards." Kate stood and placed her napkin carefully over the fish, covering the plate.

She had no friends at the university, but she found one later that night. She was a Mexican cleaning lady who shuffled into the dormitories to begin her morning rounds and found Kate sitting on the floor behind a sofa in one of the common rooms.

She peered down at the girl curled there, and when she bent over to touch her hand, she unleashed the tears.

She never understood completely, through the sobs and the faulty Spanish, the story of what had happened or the girl's remorse about her mother. But she held her anyway. She knew all about wanting dead mothers back, about men and women and misery, and she knew a doctor who was, she said, simpatico.

Kate Harlow left Mexico City a week later. It took ten hours to get to the border and she drove it flat out. She was in Texas now. The land and the roads were familiar, the pine hills of home eight hundred miles to the northeast. Her foot pushed the accelerator down flat on the floor.

It was dark when she pulled up in front of the *Bugle-Times,* but she'd seen the light at the windows and the night guard let her in. When she pushed through the door of Amelia's office, Eleanor was sitting on the couch and Amelia was at her desk.

They glanced up, and Kate came across the suddenly

quiet room. "Please hire me. I'll work hard, I'll do anything. I need to go to work."

She was twenty-five now and she'd learned the business the way Eleanor had, from the ground up. She forgot about Maggie and her mother again in the years since Mexico City. It seemed to take more energy this time but she'd succeeded finally, driving their faces away in long, exhausting hours at the press.

She spent that Monday morning at home with Amelia and came up the steps to the *Bugle-Times* at noon. She nodded at staff members as she passed, grateful no one pressed her with condolences and sympathy. She went into her own office, picked up the phone messages lying on the desk, and flipped through the slips.

Technically, Grandmelia had said, Maggie should have half of the share of private stock Kate had been voting for two years. But it had belonged to her father and it was Kate's proudest possession. It would go on belonging to her, Grandmelia had said. Trust me.

37

Clint Dossey left Dallas Monday afternoon. He flew to New York, checked into the Pierre, and Tuesday morning he took a cab to the Seagram Building on Park. It was nine o'clock when he walked into the law office of Cave, Brown, Cave & Reece to deliver the envelope Clayton Benedict had entrusted to his care.

The receptionist, a trim middle-aged woman with blue-rinsed hair, looked up. Her voice was crisp. "No, Mr. Reece is not available without appointment."

"I'll wait," he said. He handed her his card. "Won't take long. Tell Mr. Reece that it concerns a client of his. Margaret Harrington."

He watched her glide down a gray-carpeted corridor.

She passed by several closed doors and then stopped at one. She tapped lightly, waited, then stepped inside.

The reception area, unlike so many spaces he'd been asked to wait in, was large and airy with a view of the Empire State Building to the right and the Chrysler Building to the left. Construction work was going on full blast down below, just as it was all over this town, and he suspected that before long the view would disappear behind another office tower. He wondered again how anyone could live in New York City, and then he turned from the window and eyed the magazines on the reception room table.

They weren't the usual law reviews and J.D.s. There were issues of *Variety*, the *New York Times*, *Hollywood Reporter*, and *Women's Wear Daily*. The walls were covered with glassed posters of films and plays, and one was devoted to what he knew were storyboards, drawings of scenes from the movies. He looked closer, recognized Jimmy Stewart in front of the Lincoln Memorial, and thought it might be *Mr. Smith Goes to Washington*. He toyed with the idea of having something like that in his own law office, but this wasn't a social call and he doubted that he'd have the opportunity to ask Mr. Alfred Reece where he too could find storyboards. In any case, they wouldn't look right in his office. He wasn't in the entertainment side of law.

The receptionist returned to her desk, glanced briefly in his direction, and rolled a piece of office stationery into an IBM electric.

A door down the corridor opened and a young man, in his mid-twenties, Dossey guessed, came down the hall. He was just under six feet, with dark hair, and he wore chinos, a blue open-necked Oxford shirt, and a dark blue blazer. He walked into the reception room and held out his hand. "Mr. Dossey? I'm Nicholas Reece."

The son. Yale '71, Harvard Law '74, and still wet behind the ears.

Clint Dossey took the hand. "It's your father I'm here to see."

He saw a question in the kid's eyes, got ready for an argument, and saw the moment pass.

"He won't be here until around ten. He has a heavy day and I can't guarantee he'll see you."

At least Reece had weighed the situation right, knew he wasn't about to be fobbed off.

"I'll take my chances if you don't mind."

Nicholas nodded and disappeared down the hallway. Dossey sat. He'd wait all day if he had to, but he didn't think that would be necessary. His guess was that he'd be in Alfred Reece's office about ten minutes after he arrived. Reece would be expecting him, expecting someone by now.

It was just after ten when the front door opened again. Dossey kept on looking at the headline in *Variety*, "Boffo Bucks Nixed," and watched from the corner of his eye as a tall middle-aged man with a silver-headed stick and a red carnation walked in.

Reece nodded at the receptionist and then continued down the long corridor and into the southern suite of offices. He placed his briefcase on the far corner of his desk and pressed an intercom button. A moment later his son appeared. A grin was working at the corner of his mouth.

"See the smart pair of boots in the reception room?"

Reece nodded and pressed the intercom again. A few moments later the receptionist ushered Clint Dossey into his office and closed the door.

He moved across the room with surprising grace, the boots silent on the carpet. Reece nodded at a wing-back chair across from Nicholas and watched as Dossey sat and placed a briefcase on the floor beside him.

"You represent a young woman, Mr. Reece. Name of Maggie Harrington."

"That's correct." He opened the briefcase and placed a plain white envelope squarely on the surface of

Reece's desk. "I'm here on behalf of Clayton Benedict, ultimately on behalf of a client of his, Amelia Harlow."

His voice was soft and the Texas country drawl was unmistakable. "I'm a messenger, Mr. Reece; I can't negotiate. I can't engage in discussion. I can return to Texas with a simple answer. Yes or no."

Reece nodded and Dossey eased a boot over his knee.

"Mrs. Harlow set up a family corporation a while back, Mr. Reece. But a lot of water's gone under a lot of bridges since then, and Mrs. Harlow feels it's time to remind Miss Harrington she's not family anymore. When she dropped the Harlow name and took back her own—well, Mrs. Harlow thought that was a wise thing to do. She thinks it's best if Miss Harrington keeps it that way."

He spoke rapidly and comfortably. Reece listened, waiting for him to come to the Harlow Enterprises stock that had brought him here.

"Miss Harrington might want to entertain some second thoughts about who she is now," Dossey went on. "But Mrs. Harlow doesn't advise that at this point. She'd be forced to contest Miss Harrington's adoption papers in the international courts, and Mrs. Harlow wouldn't want to do that, Mr. Reece. Wastes a lot of cash and a lot of people's time."

"She has something in mind, I assume." Reece was carefully polite. "Something to save my time."

Clint Dossey clicked his briefcase shut, stood, and nodded at the waiting envelope.

Reece stood too, with his hands in his pockets.

Clint Dossey hesitated for the first time and thought better of offering his hand.

"I suggest you discuss the matter with your client, Mr. Reece. I'd appreciate hearing from you within forty-eight hours. I'm staying up the way, at the Pierre." He moved to the door. "Gentlemen." Then he headed down the hall.

Nicholas reached for the envelope and slit it open. He glanced at the contents and then passed the check and the waiver agreement to his father. The check, payable to Maggie Harrington, was for two million dollars. The waiver agreement would forfeit her share of Harlow Enterprises.

"Not bad," Nicholas said. "At least the cash will come in handy." He headed for the door. "Want me to call her?"

"Let me think about it for a while." Reece swung around in his chair.

He thought about Eleanor, and he thought about Bliss. It occurred to him that he'd always mourned Bliss Harlow as he mourned Eleanor now, in silence.

He wondered about that for a while. Then he finally turned and pressed the intercom.

Maggie sat on the steps of Philip's house, shaking. The sun was warm on the beach below, but she wasn't cold. She was angry—the image of a big white house very sharp and very clear, the doors and windows shutting on her again.

Alfred was right. She should go. She should fly to Dallas, just like the dream she'd had all those years, and drive through the night to that house. But they wouldn't lock her out, not this time, and she wouldn't go alone.

She scaled the steps and went across the deck. "Philip," she called into the kitchen. "Philip, I'm going."

She called Alfred and then half an hour later she dialed the international operator and asked for Rome. Static came over the line, followed by the faint echo of an Italian voice. Maggie repeated Caroline's number and waited for the connection to clear.

She'd seen her mother last at a restaurant in Rome. She'd been in Italy for the Italian premiere of her first film and they'd met for lunch at Tre Scalini. Caroline had talked of her baron, Maggie of her plans for the next Broadway play. They'd been carefully polite, and Maggie, relieved that it was over, had flown back to the States the next day.

"You need her now," Alfred insisted. "Believe me—you need all the help you can get. Call her," he said. "If you don't, I will." And now the static was clearing and Maggie heard her mother's voice on the phone.

"Pronto . . . pronto."

She sounded very distant, very far away, and then suddenly very near.

"Chi parla?"

Maggie's eyes filled with tears. It was all so stupid—she never cried, except at old movies.

38

It was noon on Wednesday when the Baroness von Buehler removed her sleeping mask. She opened her eyes to another cloudless, perfect day. Light was streaming through tall jalousies at tall windows. A breeze was drifting in from the city. Somewhere in the street outside, a workman was whistling with what Caroline had come to think of as a purely Italian ecstasy. And then the thought was there, clear and sharp on the edge of the day, with all its anxiety and anger and relief. They were going back.

She slipped free of the white sheets, let her white silk gown fall to the floor, and moved gracefully to the white tiled bath.

She bent to turn on the lion's-head faucet in the huge sunken tub, then picked up the house phone and heard the ripple of an Italian voice. *"Un quarto d'ora,"* she replied, and replaced the receiver in its hook. Coffee with steamed milk and a dusting of chocolate, one perfect hard roll, and a pot of marmalade would be waiting for her on the terrace in fifteen minutes. She stepped into the hot tub and toyed with the images in her mind.

White, all white. But her white was not like Amelia Harlow's white. It was soft and sensuous and full of energy, a color that blended with all the other colors in the room in a voluptuous play of light. Red velvet stripes ran through the pale fabric on the Empire chair. There was a mauve throw at the foot of the bed, and silver ran through the white silk on the walls. Prints and flowers were everywhere. It was a gay room for all the white.

Caroline soaped her body and thought again of Eleanor. She tried to find some triumph, some small taste of revenge in that death. There was nothing to feel anymore. She stepped from the tub and took a thick white towel from a chest piled high with white towels.

She moved to her dressing room, sat at the glass table, and ran a brush through her slightly damp, still-dark hair. Her finger touched each of the bottles stationed there, and then she glanced into the mirror and let the face register.

She was fifty-four years old, and it had been fifteen years since she'd seen Kate. She'd been a little girl then, standing rigid and silent at the door of a hotel room in Dallas just after the trial.

It hurt to see her. Caroline hadn't expected that, but it did. It hurt with an intensity that almost took her breath away, and then she was chattering to fill the silence up.

"Come in, sweetheart. It's so nice to see you," she said, and she led Kate to a chair by the window. "You look so sweet, darling. So pretty."

But that wasn't quite true. The face was blank; the eyes were blank. Kate's hands were rigid in her lap, and her red sandals sat flat on the floor. Like a cardboard child someone had put in the chair.

Caroline went to the chest of drawers. "I brought this

for you—all the way from London, darling." She
handed her the big gaudy box with bright striped paper
and a huge red bow.

"Open it, darling. I can't wait to see what you
think."

Kate pulled the red bow open and untied the knot.
She rolled the ribbon around her hand, smoothed it
out, made it neat, and then placed it beside her.

Caroline watched. "How can you be so slow, darling? I always tear the paper off presents. Can't wait,"
and she laughed and heard her voice break, high and
shrill.

Kate looked up, then bent again to her task. She
lifted the scotch tape from each end, folded the paper
back and opened the lid.

She opened them all, one after another, twenty-five
beautifully crafted miniatures for the doll house Caroline had shipped ahead to Texas.

Caroline chatted on. "See, darling? Chairs and
chests, a little footstool even. And you'll love the doll
house. It's red and white, and the nicest one at
Harrods, I thought. Red . . ." But she'd said that. She
stopped.

The miniatures were lined up on the floor. There was
no more tissue now and no more miniatures to unwrap.

Caroline fought the silence with a smile. "Shall we
play with them?" she asked. "Or maybe we should
order lunch and then play—what do you think?"

There was silence. "Kate?" Caroline said.

Kate looked up, and then spoke for the first time. "I
would like to go home now."

It took a moment for Caroline to realize what she'd
said and then, blinking back the sudden tears, she
called the lobby. She didn't trust her voice anymore
and she silently kissed Kate goodbye and watched her
walk down the hall to the elevator doors. It was only
when she returned to the empty room that she saw the

miniatures. They lay untouched, lined up neatly along-side the tissue and the ribbon.

Caroline never went back to visit Kate after that. She'd poured all the courage she had into those hotel rooms in Dallas. She had nothing left.

There was only Maggie then. Maggie, the quarterly check from Harlow Enterprises, and the shopkeepers she visited every year at the beginning of June.

Un petit cadeau, s'il vous plaît. Pour ma fille.

Cerco un regalo, per mia bambina.

A birthday gift for my little girl, please. Something pretty.

Dark-suited gentlemen nodded at her from behind the counters at Aspreys on Bond Street. Young women with white cuffs showed her through the boutiques on the Faubourg Saint-Honoré. And finally, after she settled in Rome, a round little gentleman toured the floor of Buccellati with her and came to greet her with hands spread wide.

She looked less beautiful in some years, a little pasty in the face or drawn around the eyes. But he greeted her each year with a greeting that told her in subtle ways that only she truly graced the premises of Buccellati on the Condotti in Rome. "And your daugh-ter, *signora*," he always asked when it was time to get down to the business at hand. "She is fine?"

Her Italian was not good, but he was kind, like all his countrymen when it came to matters like that. He spoke slowly and chose simple phrases, as you would for a child. He kept a card in his files listing the items she had purchased each year, and he let that, and the little information he had, guide him in the choices he helped her make. The girl was dark like the mother, with blue eyes. He suggested gold, not silver, for he himself preferred silver on blondes. Occasionally he pointed out a little sapphire, to set off the eyes.

As the gift was wrapped, they would chat of Rome and the ceaseless strikes, of the June weather that was always so fine. Her own name changed over the years. It was French when he knew her first, then Russian, and finally German. But the name on the mailing slip was always the same. He wrote it out himself in his elaborate European hand: To Signorina Kathryn Harlow, Earth, Texas, USA.

Each year he slipped in the little card she handed him, gave the package to the girl to post, and showed the *signora* to the door. *"Buon giorno, signora."* Then, very slowly so she would understand, "I will see you again next year."

Each year it was the same. Caroline stepped out to the narrow street, stood for a moment in the warm afternoon, then rummaged through her bag for her dark glasses. There was always the unbearable emptiness, the anger, then the slow walk to the glitter and life on the Via Veneto, where she could find a nameless young man to kill the bitterness of the afternoon.

She chose a cafe, a table, and an aperitif, her eyes behind her sunglasses, scanning the scene. Finally, a young man approaching, waiting for the nod that said he could sit with her. She'd buy another aperitif for the young man and make polite conversation. *"Andiamo,"* she'd say as she downed her drink and stood and dropped the charge on the table. He would follow. They always did, the young men understanding that she didn't want the polite amenities of conversation anymore. She wanted them naked and young and hard, thrusting into her, making her forget.

The young men went, and like the gifts, were forgotten until next year.

The house in Rome was a marriage settlement, and Caroline first saw it on the tour she took with the real estate appraiser she hired to sell it. She forgot why she married, or even divorced. Maggie was in school by

then and without Maggie she'd begun to drink heavily
and tended to forget a great deal.

But she liked the house. Its massive carved wooden
doors opened off the street to a courtyard with a pool in
the middle. A cherub, streaked green with age, was
spitting water, and one of his hands was long gone.
Their footsteps echoed as they passed through the
musty hall and mounted the winding marble staircase to
the baroque space of a gallery at the top.

It was a perfect house for parties, she thought as they
walked on. She'd been to hundreds of parties, but
never in a house quite like this. Perhaps she ought to
stay and give parties in this house in Rome.

She decided when she saw the terrace. It was a
perfect house, and Portia would help. Portia had
remarried recently, a Ponsonby with a French embassy
post. She would begin with Portia's diplomats and go
on from there.

There was another marriage to forget in the years
ahead, and June always came. But Caroline had become what she'd always wanted to be, a hostess on the
Continent, and she was almost disappointed to look
back and realize that she became a baroness because of
someone else's party.

"Come, sweet. You must," Portia called from Paris
to say. "We celebrate the queen's official birthday at
the embassy next week and we're longing to see you.
We are."

Caroline went to Paris and there he was. She'd
always liked tall men, and he had good-looking lines in
his face.

"Which country do you represent?" she asked when
they'd been introduced.

"None of them, thank God. And I'm afraid I find
these functions a bore." He smiled. "Don't you?"

"I've been bored for years."

"Come." He led her through the crowded rooms, out
to Avenue Foch and a clear, sweet Paris night.

The Baron Wolfgang von Buehler was quiet, silver-haired, and Caroline's senior by several years. As they toasted Queen Elizabeth II over dinner at the Ritz, he fell in love.

He courted her with flowers and amusing lunches at the Cafe Lipe, afternoons at Longchamps for the races, and dinners at Maxim's. He was romantic in his court-ship and he proposed on the lawns of the Luxembourg Gardens, over a picnic of smoked trout and baguettes from Fauchon. "Will you marry me, Caroline? Will you do me that honor?"

Carefully she closed the hamper. The bottle of wine was empty. There were children's voices in the distance and mobs of red geraniums at the borders of the park. Her heart was pounding and she felt, just for a second, like a girl. "Yes," she said. "I would like that very much."

They split their time between Munich and Rome. The young men were forgotten and Caroline was happy. Not like she'd been with Bliss, but she had been young then. The whole world had been young then, a very long time ago.

Her coffee was cold when she came to the terrace. She rang for another and sat beside Wolfgang, his presence quiet and comforting. She loved this view from her terrace: tile roofs the color of pumpkin, the gray arch of a church against the sky, a white fountain in the piazza below, just visible down a street of water-stained walls.

The coffee came, hot and steaming with milk. Wolf-gang looked over the top of the newspaper. "You don't look well, my love. Beautiful, but not well."

She smiled and sipped her coffee.

"You don't have to go, Caroline. What's past is past."

"It's not really the past, you see."

"Yes. Well." He paused and then folded the paper. "Shall I go too? Would that make it easier?"

He was very kind, and very good, but Caroline would go alone. That afternoon she ordered the bags brought up and spent the evening doing something she did very well. She packed.

Three days later, on the first Saturday in August, Alfred Reece met the Braniff flight that deposited the Baroness von Buehler in Texas once again. "We're meeting on Monday morning," he said. "It's all arranged." Then he collected her luggage and led her out to the rented car where Maggie and Nicholas were waiting. She kissed the air at Maggie's cheeks, shook Nicholas's hand, and settled into the front seat.

39

Earth, Texas, didn't look like much of a town to Nicholas Reece after all.

They checked into the Cozy Cottages Motel that Saturday and he went to find Maggie. "Come on," he said. "Show me your home town."

"You saw it, Nicholas. Main Street—that's the beginning and the end."

There wasn't much else to see. He'd known about this town and the Harlows for as long as he could remember. It was just a small Texas town—he'd heard that too, all his life. But it had grown in his head, and it was hard to reconcile himself to the reality of the low-slung clapboard buildings and quiet, dusty streets baking in the heat.

He parked on Main Street and stepped up into the shade of a covered sidewalk. The shops that lined it were small and nearly empty. He strolled past Bill Ray's Hardware, Trixie's Beauty Shoppe, and a larger store next door with dry goods displayed in the window. A hand-lettered sign under a photograph bordered in black was propped against the green glass, and he stopped to read it. Eleanor Austin Harlow Rawlings, 1924–1975.

Nicholas looked up. "Carr's Dry Goods and Drug Store" was painted on the glass, and he pushed through the door and went in.

He passed through dry goods and toiletries, stopped to look at the magazine rack, and then walked on over to take a seat at the soda fountain counter.

It was an old mahogany counter, polished by thousands of elbows and soft damp cloths. Eight stools lined the front, and plates and glasses on glass shelves were reflected in a long mirror. There were cake and pie stands, three huge coffee urns, a glass jar of iced tea, and a smaller one for straws.

The man behind the counter set an ice cream sundae in front of his only other customer. "There you go, Miss Kate," and then he moved down the counter, wiping the clean surface cleaner with his soft cloth.

Nicholas ordered a cup of coffee and sat watching the young woman reflected in the mirror. She ate her sundae slowly, bite by bite, flipping through the pages of her magazine.

She was downing the cherry she'd saved for last when Nicholas moved his coffee cup down and took the stool next to her. "Miss Harlow, I presume. Miss Kathryn Morning Glory Harlow." He held out his hand. "Nicholas Reece."

She glanced up, then looked down at the magazine and turned a page. "I think you should leave."

"I haven't finished my coffee yet," he said, and he rattled the cup in its saucer.

"Well, I've finished my sundae." She closed the magazine, spun away from the counter, and slid to the floor.

Nicholas shook his head. "No you haven't."

The man behind the counter set another sundae in front of her with a sheepish smile. "He ordered it, Miss Kate."

She glared at Nicholas.

"Betcha a buck you can't eat two."

She shrugged and sat down.

She ate faster this time, ignoring him when he said, "It's not anything like I'd imagined." But she watched him in the mirror as he stirred his coffee, and finally gave in.

"What isn't?"

"This town. It's tiny. But you look about right, pretty much as I'd imagined."

"Talk about something else if you want to talk."

"Tell me something, then. You've been in New York. Did you like it?"

"I don't remember." She pushed the sundae dish aside. "Thank you, Mr. Reece. I gather I'll see you on Monday." He watched her wind through the aisles to the door.

"It's Nicholas," he called out. "And I owe you a dollar."

Kate let the door shut and headed for the car. She would have liked to call him Nicholas if things had been different. She pushed the thought away and turned the key in the ignition.

Nicholas watched the Porsche reverse into Main Street and then swung back to the counter and ordered another cup of coffee.

The funny thing was she didn't look anything like he'd imagined her. He supposed he'd always thought of her as the kid on the cover of *Life,* and of Caroline as the woman in the Harlow case.

He'd met Caroline once when he was a boy. She was sitting in a chair in their living room in the house on Riverside Drive when he came home from school. His mother had smoothed back his hair and taken him in to introduce him to the woman sitting by the window. She'd looked up and said, "How do you do, Nicholas?" He'd said how do you do, and then he'd been excused and gone to his room, almost overwhelmed by the sadness in her face. Caroline went back to Europe; he went on to prep school and college, taking with him a boy's impression of a town in Texas so big, so overwhelming, that it could make a woman that sad.

He smiled at the reflection of himself in the mirror. It was just a little town, nothing going on but the occasional rattle of his cup in the saucer and the drone of the air conditioner.

He paid for his coffee, then walked back down the aisle and opened the door. He stepped out into the heat and glanced up Main Street. It was empty and nothing moved.

Earth, Texas
The Second Monday in August 1975

40

They were scheduled to meet in the conference room at the *Bugle-Times* that Monday at ten. Jay Rawlings left San Antonio at seven. It was just after nine when he landed the Piper at the back of the compound in Earth. He shoved the controls back and felt the vibrations rolling up through his hands, into his shoulders and down his back as he bumped to a halt at the hangar.

The green Mercedes coupe was waiting. He turned on the ignition and headed toward the white glare of the compound walls. He turned right, taking the side road down into Main Street.

Somewhere inside he was angry, but he couldn't pinpoint it, and didn't really want to, not yet.

He remembered that period in their lives vividly, the crowds converging on Earth, the photographers' flashbulbs, the high white wall springing up in the cottonwoods. He knew it was safer to pretend with Kate that none of it was happening, but it was happening, and it was frightening. First Uncle Bliss, then Maggie and her mother—all of them, gone.

It took a long time for the tension to lift but it did,

revealing a new fact of life to twelve-year-old Jay. "If we'd just known," his mother took to saying, "we'd have named you Bliss." That was when Jay knew that Bliss's place would be his.

And now his mother was dead and they were back. "We can't wait," his grandmother had said. "We have to act." Well, she'd made her offer and they were back anyway.

He'd received the call from Alfred Reece himself. Jay stared at the yellow flashing button on his Dallas office phone and finally picked up. "I think you want to speak to my grandmother, don't you, Mr. Reece?"

There was a slight pause. "I really don't think it matters, Mr. Rawlings. We're arriving Saturday. I suggest the *Bugle-Times* offices at ten on Monday." Then his voice changed, became softer, and Jay heard a kindness he didn't want to hear. "I'm sorry about your mother, Jay. Really sorry."

Jay hung up and then called his grandmother.

He was twenty-six now. Ben would have been content for him to go to the University of Texas, as he had. But Jay's Uncle Bliss had gone to Princeton, so Jay went to Princeton, and then on to Philadelphia and the Wharton School of Finance. He came back to the executive vice-presidency of Harlow Enterprises and an office on the top floor in downtown Dallas. Nothing much had changed, and it pleased him that Harlow Enterprises had waited for him.

He took the corporation public that year. He invited his mother and his grandmother to his Dallas office, sat them down, and went through it all, point by point. The inheritance tax structure was changing and if they didn't go public now there wouldn't be anything left. The IRS would siphon off eighty percent of their net worth, and they'd go bust by the end of the century. He stuck a foot on his desk and waited for Grandmelia's applause.

And waited.

It was his mother who finally got Grandmelia to see it his way. Then Jay put it together and flew to New York to watch it break out on the floor of the stock exchange. It wasn't news to anybody by then. Jay made sure of that. The package he put together was the best conceived offering of glamour industry stock anyone had seen in years. He saw the proof when he stood in the gallery of the Exchange watching the frenzied trading on the floor. Harlow Enterprises didn't stop until it went off the map.

He gave a party for his New York people that night. Kate, his mother, and most of the Dallas heavyweights were there. Everyone was there but Amelia. He was winding through the crowd when his mother took him by the arm and led him to a long bank of windows overlooking Wall Street. "I know you mind her not being here. But it's hard for her, Jay. She's old, and she has a hard time giving anything up."

He nodded and took a sip of his drink. "Bliss Harlow would have done it. He would have taken the fucking thing public. Doesn't she see that?"

He was never quite sure when he stopped trying to measure up to Bliss. But a year later, when he was in San Antonio on business for a day, he drove out to the condominium where Nina Benaros lived.

He'd known Nina for almost as long as he could remember. She was a little girl of five when she first visited Rosie and her boy George for a couple of weeks one summer. He was eleven then and he and Kate taught her to swim. She was cute, splashing around in the pool like a brown butterball in her white bathing suit.

She reappeared in his life the summer he graduated from Princeton. The young woman who came to visit Rosie this time was very slender and wore her dark hair pulled back off her face. No one saw him meet her by the pool one night, take her hand in his, and lead her into the cottonwoods. He undressed her there, silently taking the pins from her hair and letting it fall to her waist. He ran his hands over her, then knelt before her in the dark.

He didn't see her again after that. It wouldn't do for an heir to Harlow Enterprises to be seeing a girl with Mexican blood. But that afternoon in San Antonio he pulled the Mercedes up in front of her condominium and sat waiting in the heat until he saw her coming down the bare, blank-looking street.

And a year later, standing in a San Antonio hospital with his forehead pressed against the glass of the nursery window, Jay watched his son and smiled. He was small, not even six pounds, but those fists were waving hard. He was one quarter Harlow, one quarter Rawlings, and half Tex-Mex mongrel. But he was a son. His son.

"Bliss Houston Harlow Benaros. That's his name," said Jay, and he spelled it out to the registrar. It took up too much space on the birth certificate, but he made them do it over again until it finally fit.

It was quarter to ten by the time Jay pulled up in front of the bank. He waited for a teller to admit him, then went across to his father's office. He knocked and went on in.

Ben had spent most of his time since the funeral sitting where he was now, at his desk. He felt more at home there now that Eleanor was dead. It was quiet and he could drink a little in peace.

There was a line of windows overlooking the parking lot and the hills out back, but the curtains were drawn. The only light was from the lamp with the green shade sitting beside the bourbon bottle on the desk. There were a couple of Remingtons on the walls, and a Russell sculpture of a cowboy on a bucking horse on the table behind the long couch. Eleanor had contributed the longhorns hanging on the back wall. Each

morning for a dozen years Ben had skimmed his
Stetson over his shoulder, aiming perfectly for its
accustomed place.

"Pop?"

Ben looked up and finally nodded. Jay watched him
come to his feet. The bourbon didn't work well for his
father and Jay was sorry that he stayed as sober as he
did. They walked out of the bank and down the street
toward the *Bugle-Times*.

41

The conference room on the top floor of the press
building was somber looking that morning, the windows shuttered against the light bouncing up from the
streets. The long oak table was newly polished. Pencils
and a fresh yellow pad sat at each of the nine places.
Glass ashtrays formed a row down the center.

Amelia arrived first. She'd discussed the seating plan
with Clayton earlier that morning, but she changed it
now. She put Kate on her left next to Ben. Clayton
would be on her right, and then Jay. They were
officially here to discuss legal points and financial
statements, Clayton said, but Amelia knew better. She
would sit at the head of the table where she belonged.

She made a mistake in trying to buy Maggie off and
she didn't intend to make another. Alfred Reece's call
announcing this meeting had enraged her, but she
would go through with this charade, and when all the
cards were on the table, she'd call their hand.

She dressed carefully for the occasion in a dark dress
with a high neck. Her pale hair, streaked with paler,
lighter colors, was pulled into a knot under the dark
brim of her hat. Nothing in her appearance or her
steady eyes revealed the brittle, hollow feeling inside.
She'd made sure of that.

When Kate and Clayton arrived, when Jay and Ben

were in their places, they would turn as one to watch the door. When the others walked into the room they would see her strong.

Clayton ambled in. He shook his big head when he saw her at the head of the table. "Some things don't change, do they, Amelia?"

"No, Clayton. Some things don't." She nodded at the place on her right.

Ben and Jay arrived. They leaned in turn to kiss Amelia's cheek and then shook Clay Benedict's hand. Kate walked in at ten sharp. She wore a summer suit, high-heeled sandals with open toes, and her long legs were bare. She took her place at her grandmother's left, then looked around the table and smiled. "Well," she said. "Bring on the Christians."

They'd been shown into an anteroom when they arrived and been asked to wait until they were called. They waited, the silence buzzing in Maggie's ears. She examined the lithographs on the wall, then rearranged herself for the third time in a leather chair. A leg encased in white cotton duck pants crossed over the other and went swinging up and down. A white sandal dangled from her bare toes. Maggie stared at the bare arch of her foot. "Maybe we should try the door," she yawned. "Maybe the old lady locked us in and buried the key." No one smiled, not even Nicholas. In his gray suit and dark tie he looked as grim as a schoolboy waiting for exams.

He'd been moody and irritable since his tour of town on Saturday, very unlike Nicholas. Maggie had watched him go, then pulled herself out of the motel swimming pool, stalked off to her room, and flung herself across the impossible orange bedspread. She finally changed and went through the connecting door to her mother's room. They sipped at Caroline's scotch until Uncle Alfred knocked.

"Dinner," he said, and stood grinning in the doorway with a tray in his hands.

Maggie groaned. "Remember the food in this town? You could *die.*"

"You have to eat, darling."

"Caroline, don't be motherly, do you mind?" She swung off the bed and smiled up at Alfred. "Pâté and champagne, right?"

"Wrong. Catfish and cole slaw."

"Oh, Christ," Maggie said when she lifted the cover. "It really is."

She ate like a horse and then lay awake all night, her nerves stretched so tight that every joint in her body seemed to itch.

On Sunday she swam fifty laps and slept around the clock, waking on Monday to a day so hot and blue that she felt, for one mindless instant, as if she were twelve again. When they drove to the *Bugle* offices, she refused to look at the town or the streets. She felt the cool shade of a tree when she got out of the car and memories threatened again. She stuffed them away, strode through the lobby and into the elevator, and finally entered the air-conditioned anteroom where she sat now, examining the arch of her foot.

It felt chilly, now that she thought about it. She concentrated on the chilly arch of her foot and willed her whole body to cool. She was still concentrating when the door opened and a voice said, "Please step this way."

She got up and followed Uncle Alfred, thinking about ice.

Amelia Harlow stood when the knock came, vaguely conscious of four other bodies stirring to their feet. She watched the door and measured them as they entered, two by two: a tall man in his fifties with Maggie at his side: a young man in gray with Caroline.

She had thought about this moment on and off. She'd grown almost curious to see how Maggie had turned out and how well Caroline might have aged. She glanced at the two of them and clinically noted the familiar flash of Maggie's black eyes and the money that coated Caroline, like cream warding off age. There was money in her dark hair, her black glasses, her gold jewelry, and the linen fabric of her dress cut in classic lines.

She noted it all but focused on none of it. She saw only Alfred Reece, and her children.

They'd spoken of—Reece, they'd called him. They'd spoken of him often back in that summer during the war. And now, at the far end of her conference room, he stood, a long, hard, elegant man with a walking stick and a red carnation in the dark lapel of his suit. He was an aging man with an aging face, but her children would never grow older or go on aging like their Reece. It made her want to smile, and weep. Then the doors swung shut and he stepped forward.

"My regrets on the death of your daughter, Mrs. Harlow. My regrets to you all."

Amelia nodded and managed to say, "Thank you. Won't you have a seat?"

Caroline's hands dropped into her lap and lay there quiet and relaxed, compliments of a Valium tablet. She sat alone on her side of the table with four empty chairs separating her from the Harlows at the far end. She glanced at Nicholas and Maggie across from her and Alfred sitting alone in the chair at the end. Then, with her eyes safely hidden behind her darkest glasses, she fixed her gaze on an invisible point over Maggie's head.

She'd avoided looking at all the faces waiting for them when they came in, knowing that if she allowed herself the luxury of one, she would be drawn to Kate's. Sensing that she sat cater-corner from her,

Caroline stared at the spot on the wall and listened to the hum of attorney voices grinding up.

She'd been to so many meetings like this over the years. There had been separations to be arranged, divorces and alimonies, and once the distribution of an estate in the room where they now sat. Meetings in English, French, Italian, and always that hum of the attorneys. She could hear it now, the careful droning, steady, careful, rising, falling. It would change eventually. It always did. Something would be said or suggested, and then something would happen. Something always happened.

The spot she stared at on the wall grew bigger and blacker and she found herself thinking of snow, and Stockholm. No, not Stockholm, a little town somewhere outside Stockholm. She couldn't remember the names of the country house or her hosts or the lover she'd traveled with that winter. She just remembered the sauna and running out into the snowy night, rolling in all that white.

She frowned at her spot and wondered why she'd thought of that. Then realized she was about to look at Kate.

She focused harder on her spot. Then gave up and took the plunge as she'd taken the plunge into the Stockholm snow, quickly, with a little intake of breath. And found herself staring at steel-blue eyes that stared at her.

She turned away, glad she'd taken the Valium. She could feel it working, like cotton, cushioning the rush of love and regret and recognition.

She would have recognized that face anywhere. The eyes were the wrong color, the skin was wrong, the hair was wrong. Caroline had never worn her hair cut short. But everything else was the same. Kate had left her child face behind and become a near replica of Caroline by the time she was seventeen. She could still remember that year and the daily examinations in the mirror, each more intense than the last, before she finally knew that the face in the mirror had changed, that it was beautiful, and that it was hers.

Caroline smiled. Hers, and now Kate's.

Her face changed again after that. She went to Havana with it, and when she came back to the States it was different somehow, sleeker, simpler. The eyes were not so big and lush. She felt an ugly little taste of jealousy that her daughter had managed to save that face longer than she. And then Caroline didn't care. It was still her face. She reached into her bag, extracted a cigarette, and celebrated her genetic coup with a puff of smoke.

The attorney voices droned on. Clayton Benedict's was rumbling harder, but Alfred's was still on a pleasant course, a deep, slightly scratchy voice saying no. The words were "disinclined" and "unalterably," but they meant no, didn't they? Nobody wanted Amelia's cash; they wanted more. He didn't say that, but that was the point. Caroline smiled again and then realized, through the cushion of Valium, that something was beginning to happen.

"I don't believe I understand, Mr. Reece."

It was Amelia Harlow's voice that was slicing down the length of the conference table. "Perhaps you would be good enough to explain." The voice lifted, and then fell again.

"Isn't two million dollars enough to keep Miss Harrington out of jail?"

Caroline's left hand twitched. Just once. And then it lay still. They knew after all. How very like them it was, to dig out the dirt on Maggie. And it was so like herself to see that, too late.

Kate Harlow smiled, and then she gripped her pencil harder and forced the smile away.

She'd constructed a labyrinth on the yellow legal pad lying at her place. The pencil point sat frozen at the lower left-hand corner of the sheet. She raised her eyes and saw Jay looking at his father with a quizzical little frown. Only the two of them—the children—had been kept out of it. Kate didn't care. Whatever it was, it was going to work. She could feel it in the sudden silence at the other end of the table. Maggie was in trouble. She would take the two million and get out of town and nothing would change. Nothing at all.

Kate smiled again, and missed the exchange between Nicholas and Alfred Reece. There was a slight widening of Nicholas's eyes and an almost imperceptible nod of Alfred's head.

"Well, it's a beginning, Mrs. Harlow."

Kate glanced up and watched Nicholas Reece come to his feet.

"I congratulate you, by the way, on the accuracy of your information. Care to reveal your sources?"

Grandmelia's voice was almost amused. "No, Mr. Reece, I don't."

"But I think you already have, Mrs. Harlow." His voice was not amused. It was hard and flat, and that was when Kate Harlow knew something was wrong.

The silence that had settled at the far end of the table seemed to tip and slide down to hers. Kate made her body stay still and forced herself to go on watching as Nicholas Reece reached up and loosened the knot of his tie. He glanced at her, and Kate looked away and began pushing her pencil across the yellow sheet. His voice went on.

"Tell us about your messenger boy with the big black boots, Mrs. Harlow. Did you send him up and down the theater district of New York, looking for something? Anything? Did you tell him to talk to the box office people, hang around backstage, find something? Is that what you told him?"

He paused, let his voice sink into the silence. "What did you tell him when he came up dry, Mrs. Harlow? Try Alfred Reece's office. Is that what you told him?"

Kate glanced up at Amelia. She could almost hear her grandmother's voice in her head. She would call him "young man" and tell him he was wrong. "You are in error, Mr. Reece. We aren't like that. We don't behave in that manner." But the only voice she heard was Nicholas Reece's.

"In the end that's what Dossey had to do, didn't he, Mrs. Harlow? He hiked into my office in the middle of the night and found a file in the safe marked financial, confidential. You know that, and now we know that."

Clayton Benedict's chair tipped away from the table. "You can't prove that, boy."

Nicholas smiled. "Sir, I'd put money on it."

They stared at each other for a minute and then Clayton Benedict's chair tipped back to the table.

He doubted, he said, that such an act had been committed, but the counselors Reece would do well to keep in mind that the gentleman in question was in his employ, not Amelia Harlow's. "My client would have no knowledge," he went on. "She would not tolerate anything of that kind."

There was a snicker from the other end of the table. Caroline staggered up out of her chair. The sudden movement sent it reeling to the floor, and then a stunned silence filled the room.

"Come now, Clayton," she said with a small, savage smile on her lips. "Do you call it breaking and entering? That's what they call it—isn't it, Alfred?" She glanced at the woman sitting at the far end of the table. "That's what they call it, isn't it, and that's just the least of it. Isn't it, Amelia?"

Caroline reached for the back of the empty chair next to her. She needed to hold onto something. She felt airy and light, and it wasn't just the effects of the Valium. It was something else. She smiled. Amelia

Harlow was sitting down and she was standing up. That was it. She gripped the chair tighter with suddenly sweaty hands. "Do you remember Will, Amelia? Do you remember Anna Janes?" Her voice was too small and she said it again. Louder. There. They heard it this time.

"Caroline—" Clayton's voice cracked down the table, hard with warning.

"You remember them too, don't you, Clayton? That was worse than breaking and entering, wasn't it?"

She glanced at Kate again. She looked like a small animal caught in a headlight, afraid of hearing something she didn't want to hear. But there was curiosity— Caroline saw that too. She turned again to Amelia sitting calm and unruffled at the head of the table. She hated that look. She always had.

"I think we all remember Anna Janes, don't we, Amelia? All of us except Kate. And Jay." She tipped her head and smiled at Eleanor's son. "No, Jay doesn't know either, does he? Poor Jay."

"That's enough, Caroline." It was Ben, and his voice was tired and old. "Can we just get on with our business, gentlemen?"

"This is our business." Caroline's voice was suddenly full of tears, and she forced it under control. "It's your business, Ben. My business. Everyone's. Amelia strangled Will Harlow. You and I both know that, Ben. And then she strangled Bliss and took his daughter away from me. But we had two daughters, Ben. Two—that's why she set up Harlow Enterprises the way she did. Bliss would never have allowed her to cut Maggie out. Never. And now he's dead and Eleanor's dead, and Maggie's right here, Ben." She stopped. Ben wasn't looking at her anymore. He'd turned away. Caroline's voice rose again. "Eleanor's dead, Ben."

Amelia turned to Clayton with a small nod of her head. "Get her out of here, Clayton."

Caroline felt the stunned silence dissolving around

her. Men's throats cleared and a chair moved. Amelia had said that to her once before—get out—and she had. Caroline's shoulders heaved and her voice skittered up and down the scale. "She's dead, Ben. Eleanor's dead," and then Kate Harlow stood up.

"I'm leaving."

Her face was white and her hands were trembling. She couldn't stand it anymore. She couldn't bear that voice shrieking and screaming. She pushed her chair back and made it down the length of the conference room. She was pushing at the doors when Caroline caught her hand. "I'm sorry, Kate—sorry for everything."

"Don't touch her." Amelia came to her feet and her voice lashed out. "Don't dare touch her. You've done enough damage here. Leave her alone. Get out."

Caroline dropped Kate's hand and turned again to Amelia. "No, I'm going to finish, Amelia.

"Your son loved me. The day he died he wanted me." Her voice faltered and she closed her eyes and went on. "He made love to me again and that was when I knew you'd lost, Amelia. We were leaving. Bliss was going. We were all going, the four of us." She struggled to keep her voice steady, very aware of Maggie and Kate listening to her. "But he died and you kept him just the way you wanted. I always wondered if Kate knew her father wanted to go, knew who she chose when she chose you."

"Stop it."

Amelia's voice sounded very close. But Caroline shook her head. "Don't tell me to stop, Amelia. I think Kate should know who she chose." She blinked and looked directly at Amelia. "I think she should read the court transcript, Amelia."

"That's enough."

Her eyes held Amelia's and followed them as they glanced at Kate. But Caroline saw it too, the simple, pure curiosity in the face of the young woman standing

at the conference room door. Caroline's arms relaxed
at her sides. "I dare you, Amelia," she challenged. "I
dare you," she said again. She felt suddenly tired. Her
courage was running out; the Valium was running out.
But she knew she had won. She waited patiently for
Amelia's reply, and nodded quietly when it came.

"All right, Clayton. Do what you can."

42

It was nearly five when the courier left the courthouse
with his package, and it was six when Kate sent word by
Matty that she would not be joining her grandmother
for dinner. The Harlow women ate separately that
evening: Amelia in silence at the long dining room
table, and Kate in her room, curled up in the blue
window seat in the late evening light. She was oblivious
to the taste of the food on the tray Matty had prepared,
and finally oblivious to everything but the pages on her
lap.

The binder stamped "In the Matter of Kathryn
Morning Glory Harlow, a child," was clumsy and a
little unwieldy. She read her own testimony first,
entered as a deposition in the appendix at the back. She
read it through twice and finally was able to recall the
room, its furniture, and its occupants. There'd been a
judge, a court reporter, and a toy bear whose presence
she sensed rather than recalled. Nothing in the deposition struck her as familiar. No word or phrase—except
for that one: "I wish never to see my mother again."
She remembered that.

She turned back to the beginning, to the cry that had
called the Fifth District Court into session fifteen years
before, and began to read.

It took a minute to get used to the format, like an
abbreviated playscript that left her to fill in the pacing
of the attorneys, the occasional crack of the gavel, and

the presence of people gathered. She read slowly, wondering now and again if someone had shouted or started up out of a chair. She read slowly and deliberately, and then the steady pace of the testimony suddenly changed, erupting into spastic seizures of objections and denials. The courtroom was cleared, the doors were ordered locked, and the windows were shuttered against prying eyes. Kate flipped the pages, lit now by a reading lamp, and scanned the sheets thick with argument and counterargument, searching through the long paragraphs for the continuation of the testimony. Finally she began reading again, vaguely surprised that it seemed so innocuous at first.

She'd never heard of Anna Janes before today, but she was there: a woman from Tyler, Texas, living with her husband in Arizona; a stranger with something to say. She imagined Anna Janes Potter as a shy woman, speaking cautiously as she responded to the attorney's questions.

"Well yes, sir, yes. Amelia Harlow is familiar to me."

MACK: Maybe you can tell us how you knew her first.

WITNESS: As a newspaperwoman. She was famous in Texas for that, written up in magazines and interviewed on the radio and such. An example of the new woman, they called her then. Later I knew her as the wife of the man who was my lover and fiancé.

Kate stopped. She traced back up the page, and read that paragraph again. She'd seen a picture of her grandfather once, a man with tender eyes and a wisp of a smile. He was a kind man, Aunt Eleanor had said, and a good doctor. Everyone loved him, she'd said. But no one had ever mentioned Anna Janes.

Kate found her place again, found Clayton Benedict's objection, the Court's denial, and then went on reading.

"When did you meet Dr. Harlow, Mrs. Potter?"

"It was a September in the 1930's, and Dr. Harlow had been suggested as the best supervising physician for my mother. He paid a house call and then after that he came every Thursday and Saturday for seventeen years, Mr. Mack."

"As personal physician to your mother?"

"And as my lover and fiancé. My mother died in 1940, nearly ten years after Dr. Harlow first saw her, and by then we had been planning to marry for some time. Ever since the Christmas of 1933."

"But Dr. Harlow did not seek a divorce at that time and you were not married? Why is that, Mrs. Potter?"

"Because he was afraid."

"Of . . ."

"Of his wife."

"Objection, Your Honor. That's conjecture and we object absolutely to . . ."

"Afraid, I say. Afraid he'd never see his children again . . ."

"Objection, Your Honor. Again and again," and Kate could hear the gavel rapping sharply in her head.

"Order in the court. Order, I say. I'm telling you all under pain of penalty that I won't have it. Mr. Mack, instruct your witness to restrain yourself and while you do that I'm going to instruct Mr. Benedict that his objection is denied. I'm accepting . . ."

There were further arguments, and Kate skipped again down the page.

MACK: Thank you, sir. Mrs. Potter, tell us now why he was afraid.

"I'd like to give an example if I may. It was wartime and Dr. Harlow's son wanted to go. He talked with his father and went back East to enlist. She stopped him; she reached right out and stopped him."

There were more paragraphs of objections and arguments and a final court order that the objection to hearsay was sustained. But something had fallen into place for Kate. She remembered old questions and old memories of a young man who had wanted to travel. She turned the page.

"But circumstances changed one day and Dr. Harlow made plans to leave his wife?"

"Yes."

"Describe for us, please, the events that led to that."

"His son eloped and ran off to Cuba. Dr. Harlow said his mother couldn't reach out to Cuba and would let him be. His daughter married soon after that, and we were free to make our own plans, plans for our own wedding."

"But it never took place?"

"No, Mr. Mack. It didn't. It was 1948, a Sunday in October of that year. The doorbell rang and Amelia Harlow was standing there. Her daughter, Eleanor, was with her. There were two cars parked out front, and two chauffeurs, and the girl carried a briefcase. Amelia Harlow came inside and spoke for some time, Mr. Mack. Her threats were quite explicit and graphic."

"Threats, Mrs. Potter?"

"She told me she would humiliate me publicly if I didn't leave town and Texas immediately. She said divorce was out of the question and that I would be better off starting over somewhere else. She took the briefcase from her daughter, and handed me twenty-five thousand dollars. In cash. She said that if I didn't leave she would write about my morals in all her newspapers and see me fired. Then she left. But the second chauffeur didn't. He said he would be glad to help me pack and then assist me with my bags and tickets at the train station. I didn't know what else to do, so that night I left."

"Did you ever hear from Dr. Harlow again, Mrs. Potter?"

"Yes. She insisted that I write a letter and she took it

with her. A month later it came to my forwarding address with some old circulars and bills."

"Is this the letter?"

"Yes."

"Would you like me to read it to the court?"

"Please read it, Mr. Mack."

" 'Dear Will, Something has come up and I have decided I must leave. Please do not attempt to find me. Love, Anna.' "

"There's more, Mrs. Potter, at the bottom of the letter. In a different hand."

"Yes, in a different hand. That's Dr. Harlow's hand, and I can tell you what it says. It says, 'She won after all, didn't she, Annie? Somehow she won.' "

"Dr. Harlow wrote that?"

"Yes. He wrote it and mailed it and then he killed himself. The newspapers said it was natural causes, but people knew he'd hung himself. Eventually, I knew too."

"Mrs. Potter, I know—I think I know how difficult this has been for you. I have only one more question. I'd like you to tell the Court if you can why you came here today."

"Caroline Harlow called me. She said she needed proof that there were threats, that other people had signed papers they didn't mean to. I'm not a brave woman, Mr. Mack. I said no at first, but I thought about Dr. Harlow. There was nothing I could do for him anymore, except say for him what he would have wanted to say. Dr. Harlow's son wanted out of this town; he wanted to live his life in a different place. It was sad that he came back to die here, Mr. Mack. He died here after all that, and now she won't let the little girl go either. And the little girl isn't Amelia Harlow's, Mr. Mack. She's not."

Kate Harlow turned off her reading lamp and sat staring into the dark. There was more testimony, but she didn't want to read it. She only wanted to do what she was doing now, stare into the dark. She wished that it were a blacker dark, black enough to blot out the images in her head.

She saw herself as a child, a child very far away, very isolated. The little girl she saw was dipping into her feelings, bringing them out to examine, one by one by one. She chose a feeling and put the rest away—shoved them back, way back, slammed a lid on them and stamped on it hard. She walked into a courthouse and held out the feeling she had chosen, offering it for examination. She was a very sure-sounding little girl.

The girl came closer. She was growing bigger, older. She was twenty-five, and still a little girl, still chasing the daddy that had been dreamed up for her by a Grandmelia who had lied.

Amelia found her nearly an hour later. She climbed the narrow steps to the attic, pushed open the door, and felt the onslaught of dust and heat and the faintly musty odor of the discarded past. Kate was sitting in the far corner in a pool of yellow light cast by a bare bulb.

"I saw the light from the terrace," Amelia said. "There's a fan. Shall I turn it on?"

"Yes, all right."

It was cooler after a moment and Amelia made her way across the bare floor and stepped into the sea of wrapping paper and ribbon and twine. She bent to take a seat on a wooden crate.

"Do you mind?" Kate said. "There's a chair just over there. I want to open that box next."

Amelia stood and found a chair in the shadows. It was an old wicker rocker from the porch and its arms were worn and cracked. She pulled it into the light and settled into its familiar shape.

Kate sat Indian-style on the floor in front of her. Her bare legs were almost invisible in the mounds of tissue and faded ribbon and boxes and toys. There was a paint set, a stack of picture books, and a doll in fancy dress. She wore a long rope of pearls and a shorter chain with a gold heart. A diamond bracelet encircled one wrist; a sapphire ring encircled a finger.

"I never opened any of them," she said.

"You didn't want to."

Kate glanced up, her eyes cool and direct. "No, I didn't. I had to make a choice, and I did. You told me I was his Morning Glory, his Texas child, and that's what I chose to be. He was a Texan, so I would be too. He was a part of Harlow Enterprises and I would take his place. He rode. I rode. He belonged here and I never wanted to leave."

"Kate . . ."

"Don't. I've listened to you long enough."

"Then listen to me once more. Your father married a woman who didn't belong here, because he didn't belong here, Kate. He didn't belong anywhere and that was the tragedy of his life."

"But they belonged to each other, Grandmelia, and I belonged to them. Nobody belonged to you."

Amelia reached down to touch the young woman at her feet. "We all need to belong somewhere, Kate. Your father never found his place. When would you have liked for me to tell you that? When you were nine? Or ten? Fifteen?"

"It was my right to know." She looked at her grandmother, then reached into the pocket of her shirtwaist.

"Here are some of the cards she wrote, Grandmelia. Listen." The envelopes were small; the cards were plain white.

" 'Dear Kate, You are sixteen, a wonderful age to be. Happy Birthday. I will think of you all day.'

" 'Dear Kate, I had pearls like this when I was twenty. I was always very proud of them. I hope you will be too.' "

She slipped the cards back into the envelopes and looked up. "Would you like to hear more, Grandmelia?"

There was no answer. She stuffed them into her pocket, bent over the crate, and began ripping at it with her bare hands. It was old now, and as rusty nail after rusty nail gave way, the squeaks echoed in the silent attic space. The sides fell away, and then she went to work on the cardboard case inside, ripping and tearing, until the doll house emerged. A two-story red doll house with bright white shutters and a black roof.

She stood and rummaged through the boxes until she found one marked with the return address of a Dallas hotel. The miniatures spilled into her lap, the chairs and tables, a couch upholstered in dark velvet, a tiny footstool. She chose a miniature painting of a field of white flowers, then reached into the doll house to prop it against the mantle of the fireplace.

"It's very sweet, don't you think, Grandmelia?"

Amelia closed her eyes, rested her head on the back of the rocker for a moment, then gazed down at the face tipped up to hers.

"They're all very beautiful, all the gifts. She was trying to win you back, Kate. Of course the gifts would be beautiful. But you didn't want the gifts. And you didn't want to go."

"No, I didn't want to go. I made my choice. I chose the father you made up for me."

She moved to her knees and then to her feet. Her skirt was dusty and she reached down to shake it clean. Then she waded through the mounds of tissue and ribbon and began stuffing the waste into a carton. "Did you know I thought she killed him?" she asked.

Amelia stared up at her. "No," she said. "Of course I didn't know that."

Kate shrugged and went on jabbing the paper into the carton. "I think there must have been, even then, some corner of my mind, like a secret room somewhere. If I opened the door and went in, I would know that it wasn't true, that he'd only died. I suppose it was easier to blame—someone. And I wanted to blame her. I wanted to hate her so I could stay and grow up here. Just like Daddy. And join Harlow Enterprises, just like Daddy."

She gave a hard little laugh that tripped over itself, rippling into sarcasm.

"Harlow Enterprises, where Sundays are our favorite days, aren't they, Grandmelia?" She turned on Amelia and her voice rose. "Sundays we drive down to Tyler with the black cars and the black chauffeurs and the attaché cases stuffed with cash. Sundays we terrorize old maid schoolteachers with the god-almighty power of the press. And where did he hang himself, Grandmelia, which room?"

Amelia wasn't aware that she'd moved or that her hand had lashed out. But she left a white welt on her granddaughter's cheek. The only sound was the rocking chair still rocking on the bare floor.

They stood for what seemed a long time before Kate spoke again.

"Where did he hang himself? I'd like to know."

Amelia turned and sank back into the chair. She nudged the floor and let the chair rock. "In his office." And then she said, "I was twenty when I took over the *Bugle*. All the Harlows were dead." She stopped, and after a moment she went on. "I thought my husband was dead too. I had nothing so I took the *Bugle* and I worked. I brought a newspaper alive and it saved me. And then my husband came home and called the paper my plaything.

"It didn't matter until he wanted to marry Anna Janes. And then he wanted to sell it all, take the profits and go. So no, I didn't let Will Harlow and his woman take my life away from me."

She stopped for a moment, gazing off into the shadows. Her voice was softer when she went on.

"People were hurt, Kate, and I can regret that. But people will always get hurt. That's the way things are, that's the way they will always be. You'll have to learn to live with that, Kate."

She glanced at her granddaughter then. Kate's face was pale and her eyes were wide. "Grandmelia, you can't think what you're saying is right."

"Right?" Amelia nudged the floor again and made the rocker rock. "Power and money—great power, Kate, and enormous wealth, have been handed to you. They didn't come to me. I've made my own rules. You'll find that's necessary a great deal of the time."

"Who are we to make our own rules? Who are you, Grandmelia?"

There was no reply. "I think I'd like to finish here alone," Kate said. She stared at Grandmelia, watching the emotions cross her face—arguments and counter-arguments, anger, frustration, appeal. Finally Amelia stood. She shrugged, and then, steadying herself against the still-rocking chair, she put a hand on Kate's shoulder and waited. Kate didn't look up but she heard the silence as Amelia left and the door closed behind her.

43

They'd come back to the motel at noon. Caroline hit the scotch and Maggie hit the pool, grinding out fifty laps, churning the water, making it boil.

Alfred spent the afternoon on the phone with Clayton Benedict, negotiating what he called Maggie's stay of execution. By the time she had stripped out of her suit and changed, he was at her door, waiting.

"Okay, kiddo. Let's go see Texas."

"There's nothing to see."

"Yes there is. Let's go."

She drove down Main Street first, the white walls rising like a fortress at the far end, and then turned up into the pine hills.

They drove for an hour or so. The land was dry and the roads were dusty, and by the time she pulled into the graveyard overlooking town, the sun was beginning to set. It was an August sunset, like the ones she remembered, the bottom of the sky rippling with color and the top still blue. But there wasn't a top to the sky in Texas; it just went on and on. You could see stars sometimes at sunset when the light was right, and you could see them now, way out there. She cut the motor and they sat for a moment in the heat. Then they got out and walked across the stubble into the shade.

Their markers lay side by side: Bliss Houston Harlow and his sister, Eleanor Austin, the flowers banking her headstone were wilting in the heat.

"Do you think I'll ever stop caring?" she finally asked.

"That he died, you mean?"

"And that I had to leave."

"You're over it, Maggie; you just don't know it yet. This is a small town. The world's a big place."

The two of them had dinner at a steak house down on Route 30 that night. The waiter smiled and nodded when he brought their drinks. "It's Miss Maggie, isn't it?" he said. "Thought I recognized you."

She looked up into an unfamiliar black face.

"You wouldn't remember me," he said grinning. "But I remember you. I watched you grow up in this town. I heard you were back."

"Yes," she said. "Just a visit."

By midnight she was back at the motel, trying to sleep, her head swimming with the old childhood images of this town. The images were distant now, like faded, static images taken from someone else's life.

Only Caroline was clear, all the Carolines: a young Caroline in a bright yellow car under a bright Cuban sky; an older Caroline, her face gray and her eyes puzzled as she formed the words that said Bliss Harlow was dead; Caroline rising to her defense against Amelia. Maggie fell asleep that night, grateful for the first time in her life that Caroline had, in her own way, always been there. An hour later she woke to a knock on her motel room door.

She stuffed the pillows around her ears, but the knocking went on. "Shit," and she turned on the bedside light and padded across to open the door.

It felt odd at first, finding her there. And then it didn't. "Hi," Maggie said.

"Hi," said Kate.

They stood for a moment looking at each other in the heat of an August night and the glare of a neon sign, and then Maggie opened the door wider and Kate stepped inside. "I have to talk," she said.

Maggie closed the door and went to sit on her bed. Kate took the chair. She wore jewelry she hadn't worn this morning and she was playing with the car keys she held in her lap.

"I'm sorry about this mess."

"It's a little late for that, isn't it?"

Kate nodded and glanced down at the keys. "I would like to make it all right." She took a deep breath and looked up. Her voice was steady. "Grandmelia can stop you, but she can't stop me. You have as much right to the share as I do. I'd like you to have your half."

"That's nice." Maggie lit a cigarette and sent a little curl of smoke spinning up toward the light. "How long has it been? Fifteen, sixteen years, and someone finally remembers that I was Bliss Harlow's daughter too." She leaned back against the pillows of her bed. "Not that your giving it up makes much difference. I'd get it anyway."

"I'd rather have it this way."

"Me too," and Maggie smiled.

There didn't seem to be any more to say. Kate stood and headed for the door. Then she stopped and turned back. "I saw you once."

"I know."

"You make movies, don't you?"

"Yes, that's what I do now."

Kate nodded, then opened the door. There was a glare of neon again, and the distant sound of laughter in the motel courtyard. The sound died out. "Maggie. I want you to know I missed you."

"Did you?" Maggie asked. "Then why did you do it, Kate? Why did you stay?"

Kate didn't answer right away. Her voice was flat when she finally did. "I thought she killed him." She gave a helpless shrug. "I was little. I hurt."

Maggie stubbed out her cigarette and watched the smoke fade away. Kate was halfway out the door before she called out to her. "Wait," she said. "Your mother's next door. I think you should say hello."

"Maybe another time."

"I'll call her. I think you owe her that." She picked up the phone.

A moment later, Kate watched Caroline come through the door.

She wore a blue silk wrap with a pale stripe and she looked tired to Kate, the sheen of this morning's meeting wiped away with tissues and anxiety. And vulnerable, as vulnerable as Kate felt.

This was her mother. Other women talked of their mothers, but she never did. The woman standing in front of her looked out of place in this room with the orange plaid bedspread, the pale green stucco walls, and the burnt-orange carpet strewn with Maggie's clothes. She didn't think of the fact that she came from that body and had nursed at those breasts. She kept those thoughts far away and out of reach. She thought only that Caroline was a stranger here, and the gap was enormous.

"Hello, Kate."

"Hello," Kate said.

They waited, not knowing what to say.

Caroline looked at the face that was so like hers. She hadn't been able to watch Kate's face change over the years. She knew the child's face, and now she knew the adult's. There were no years in between, no memories, only space. She was a stranger to her daughter. Suddenly she was painfully conscious that her hair was a mess, that she wasn't wearing any makeup, that she wasn't ready and didn't know what to say.

"I don't know what to call you," Kate said.

"Call me Caroline if you like. Maggie does."

Kate reached up to touch the pearls she wore around her neck. "I never said thank you, Caroline. I would like to say that now."

Caroline glanced at the pearls, the gold heart, the sapphire ring. It was worth it, she thought, worth it to have said I love you through it all, said it year after year, never knowing that she would be in the same room with her again, never knowing she would be able to say it now, aloud to Kate.

Then she remembered the shopkeeper, the cafes, the young men. Tears slid down her face. "I suppose she told you that I was a whore."

Kate stared at her, startled and uncertain. "No, she never said that. We never spoke of you at all." Kate paused, and then, "Why would she have called you a whore?"

Maggie smiled and brushed back her hair. "Mummy was very naughty," she said. "There was a cozy little *menage à trois,* right here in Earth. Except Mummy got caught.

"It was after your father died, Kate. I . . . I was very lonely here." Caroline reached for one of Maggie's cigarettes with shaking hands. "There is no excuse. I was very stupid and very spoiled." She sat on the side of Maggie's bed. "I loved you and Maggie, Kate. You were my children and I lost you."

Maggie put an awkward hand on Caroline's shoulder and took the unlit cigarette out of her hand.

"I don't know what I'd have done without Maggie. I don't know how I've lived without you, Kate." She rummaged in her pocket for a handkerchief. There wasn't one, and finally Maggie handed her a tissue.

Kate crossed the room to Caroline. "It's not your fault. It's my fault, I know that. I . . .

"I have to go now," she said. "I'll make things right, I'll make up to you somehow." She desperately wanted to know about their lives, but she wanted more to be very alone.

She asked for their addresses. They found paper and pencil, wrote them down, and then watched her go.

Maggie climbed off the bed after a moment and crossed the room to shut the door Kate had left ajar. She lit a cigarette for herself and one for her mother. They sat for a while in the quiet with their cigarettes, and then Caroline leaned over to kiss Maggie goodnight. She went through the connecting door to her own room and finally slept.

Kate left her mother and sister and stepped into the hot August night. There had been no promises. She made none to them, they made none to her, but she would see them again. They would have lunch or dinner and perhaps one day they could be friends. She had their addresses, but they wouldn't be able to find her. She didn't live here anymore; she didn't know where she lived.

She walked toward her car, faster and faster until she was almost running. She stopped by the Porsche, taking in gulps of clean air.

"It's early to be out."

She turned and saw Nicholas Reece walking across the parking lot.

"Or late," he said, digging into the pocket of his jeans. "Here's the dollar I owe you." He handed it to her and she started to cry.

I haven't cried, she thought, not once—not today, not in years. I won't cry now. I'm going to stop. But she couldn't stop, not the tears sliding down her cheeks or the sudden feeling of relief as his arms went around her. He held her, soothed her, stroked her hair, and whispered comforting words.

"Come on," he finally said. "You need a drink." He led her to his room and pushed her gently into a chair. He gave her a small glass with a shot of scotch in it. "You need that. Go on, drink. It'll help."

Its warmth slid through her body, and the tears began to stop. She caught her breath. "Thank you," she said, and held out her glass for more.

The hand holding the bottle was slender, fine-boned, and covered with a light, dark down. She sipped again and Nicholas sat on the floor at her feet. He took the glass from her, and put his hand over hers. "You don't have to tell me anything, Kate, but it might help. I'm not your enemy. I don't want to be."

"I know you're not," she said. Then she began sobbing again and his arms went around her. He held her for a long time while she sobbed and talked. None of it made much sense to him. He knew only that she was hurt and lost, that her Grandmelia had betrayed her, and that her father was dead. He held her until the torrent of words and tears stopped, stroking her hair and then her body with his kind, strong hands. Then his mouth was on hers, very gentle and infinitely tender.

He lay back on the floor, pulled her down with him, and they undressed each other. She reached for him and felt the dark hairs on his smooth chest. She knew she was exhausted and drained, but her body didn't care. It was alive and she wanted this man. She reached closer and he was inside. She felt him filling her, moving inside her, wanting her. And then on wave after wave, they were riding toward each other.

When she woke, Nicholas was leaning on one arm, watching her. He smiled. "What are we going to do now, Morning Glory?"

"No one calls me that." She smiled. "Ever."

"Well, I do." He nodded toward the window. "It's almost morning." He touched her face. "And you're very beautiful."

"I don't know what I'm going to do," she said.

"Then come with me, Kate. Come to New York. Marry me."

She stared at him. "Marry you?"

"Marry me, Kate." He leaned over, put his warm, moist mouth on hers, and she dissolved into his kiss.

44

Matty didn't know how many morning cups of coffee she'd made for Amelia Harlow, day after day, for more than fifty years. It was the one duty she refused to relinquish when the new staff came in and she'd retired to her rocker on the porch of the house the Harlows built for her and Duke when they first came. At seven-thirty each morning she was in the kitchen of the big house measuring out four cups of coffee into the electric percolator. She drank one cup before going on upstairs, there were two for Mrs. Harlow, and one was left in the percolator for herself when she came back down.

This morning was different. For the first time in all those years and all those thousand cups of coffee, Matty didn't relish the task before her.

She took the silver tray from the pantry and placed a

linen napkin across its surface. She took a bud vase
from the cupboard, clipped a rose down to size, put it in
the vase, and placed the vase on the tray. She poured
the coffee three quarters of the way up the bone china
pot. She walked the long hallway to the foot of the
stairs, and then went up to Mrs. Harlow's room.

It was dark. Matty put the tray down on the table by
the door and walked across the room and pulled back
the shutters. Sun flooded the room, and by the time
Matty picked up the tray and put it down on the bedside
table, Mrs. Harlow was awake.

"Good morning, Matty."

"She's gone," Matty said, her voice full of sudden
indignation and anger.

"What do you mean?" Amelia struggled to sit up.
Her face was drained by the light.

"Miss Kate. She's gone. Packed up a couple of hours
ago and drove off. Just like that, with young Mr.
Reece."

Matty waited with her hands folded across her stomach, and watched Amelia Harlow take in the news. She
wanted to say something more to her or reach out, but
she kept her lips tight and her hands clasped one across
the other, only her heart going out to the woman, the
suddenly old woman, she watched.

"That will be all, Matty." Amelia picked up the
coffee pot and poured.

She poured her first cup of coffee and sipped it black.
She poured her second cup of coffee. She filled the tub
and bathed. She dressed in a dark linen suit and a pale
lavender blouse, set a brimmed straw hat on her head,
and went downstairs.

George drove her through the cottonwoods and the
iron-grill gates and on to her office at the press. It was
just after nine and she worked steadily through the day:
calls to St. Louis and Austin; dictation and a contract
from New York; a luncheon meeting that Kate had

arranged with a Chicago publisher. The pile of papers and questions on her desk gradually disappeared. By four o'clock that afternoon her desk was clean except for the pink telephone messages that had come in during the day: Clayton Benedict, Ben, Benedict again, Jay.

She supposed they wanted to comfort her, or say, "It's a mistake. She'll come back. Let it settle and she'll see. She can't give all this up, her work, her place here." But they would be wrong, Amelia knew that. Kate had created a life for herself once before and she was capable of doing it again. She tossed the messages into the waste basket under her desk.

It was seven when Jay knocked at the door of her office. "You didn't answer your calls, Grandmelia."

She pushed away from her desk, and swung her chair around to face the window. "I don't want to talk about it today."

"I have something to tell you, Grandmelia." He stood waiting for her to turn around or nod. When the nod came, he began.

"I have a son."

The words came as if he'd rehearsed them a million times, as if nothing would stop them now. He talked for a long time, defensive in his pride, and when he'd finished she still didn't say anything. She'd only heard the names. Bliss. And Benaros. She wasn't surprised, only a little sad about the love and the hate and the little piece of revenge that lay in Jay's words.

His hands were in his pockets, and his eyes were on the floor. "I suppose you know Kate is giving Maggie her half share. I think Maggie would sell it, and I'd like to buy it for the boy. I'd like to do that for my son." He looked up. "If you don't mind."

"No, I don't mind. And I'd like to meet your boy sometime, Jay."

Then he left and she was alone in the room that was

growing dark around her. She turned to the windows again.

"Who are you, Grandmelia? Who are you?" Kate had asked last night. It startled her, that question skidding out of the shadows like that. She thought of that now as she stared out at the red lights of the radio tower blinking on and off, on and off.

Captain Jack was in his room, putting on his tiny shirt and tails. The girls were tripping down the central stairs, their red-and-white striped dancing stockings bright in the shatter of lights from the big chandelier. It was dark outside on Bienville Street, and the Professor was swinging down the walk—down the walk and up the steps and on into the parlor where the piano sat. His suit was dove gray and he wore a bowler to match. The diamonds flashed in his teeth and he was playing now, his big black head thrown back, his eyes gay. His hands were going up and down the keyboard, pounding out a dizzy ragtime beat. "Baby, baby," he was calling. "Come sit with me. Come hit that big old high C. Baby, baby," and then it all began to fade, until there was only the echo of a ragtime melody in her head.

She thought then that if she had told Kate, she would have understood. If she'd said to her, this is how it was, this is what I came from, this is who I am. A trick baby from nowhere who found my place. There was war. Plague. I didn't die because I wanted to live. But the streets of a place called Storyville, and the man called Carter Harlow, Publisher, were her secrets. It was senseless, she supposed, to have kept them all these years.

She gazed into the dark, the melody just an echo. "Baby, baby . . ." fainter, until it was gone.

She reached through the silence after a moment and picked up the telephone, then called for the car to take her back to the house.

It was almost dark as George eased the car down

Main Street. At the gas station at the corner, the old man tipped his hat, then melted back into the shadows. The car bumped across the railroad tracks, picked up speed as moved up the hill, and then disappeared through iron gates standing open under the big hollow cup of the big Texas sky.